The
Blue
Period

Praise for *The Blue Period*

"Luke Jerod Kummer's tenderly crafted portrait of Picasso as a young artist, just starting out in a foreign country and grieving a great loss, cuts through the stereotypical bravado so often associated with the artist to add richly shaded layers of emotion, insight, and smartly noticed detail."

—Rachel Corbett, author of *You Must Change Your Life: The Story of Rainer Maria Rilke and Auguste Rodin*

"Lusciously written and deeply imaginative, Kummer's debut is an edgy, elegant reimagining of a period in Picasso's life that forever changed the art world. It takes readers from the heat of Spain to the underbelly of Paris, as we follow the artist through friendship, dizzying infatuation, sex, and tragedy as he tries to claw his way to success. A book that feels as passionate and bold as Picasso himself."

—Karin Tanabe, author of *The Gilded Years*

"Luke Jerod Kummer's *The Blue Period* is a vivid, well-researched re-creation of the world from which a great artist emerged and a richly imagined meditation on the relationships and tragedies that shaped both his life and his art."

—John Biguenet, author of *Oyster* and *The Torturer's Apprentice*

"Like the subject of this eloquent and incisive novel, Kummer proves himself a true artist with a top-rate imagination and a special gift for dialogue and description. An historian with artistic sensibilities, he paints a complete and colorful picture of Picasso during this period, ensuring a deeper understanding of him for future generations. This important debut novel shows that Kummer may have immortality in him as well."

—Eddie Chuculate, author of *Cheyenne Madonna*

The Blue Period

A NOVEL

LUKE JEROD KUMMER

Little
a

Text copyright © 2019 Luke Jerod Kummer
All rights reserved.

Published by Little A, New York

www.apub.com

Amazon, the Amazon logo, and Little A are trademarks of Amazon.com, Inc., or its affiliates.

ISBN-13: 9781542049979 (hardcover)
ISBN-10: 1542049970 (hardcover)
ISBN-13: 9781542049962 (paperback)
ISBN-10: 1542049962 (paperback)

Cover design by Isaac Tobin

Printed in the United States of America

First edition

Lydia Csató Gasman—I feared I'd found you too late
but then discovered you were already here.

There in the distance we behold a black cloud of swirling sands, gyrating in the wind. Terrified, you cling to me, watching death approach.

I fear not death. When it comes it shall find us standing firm, welcoming; our embrace rendering us one, arms entangled like feverish snakes . . .

C. Casagemas, Barcelona, ca. 1900

PART ONE

CHAPTER 1

Madrid, February 1901

When you wake from siesta in winter with shadows long and the sun groomed to set, the days can seem to end almost before they've begun. A chill cakes the air. Squares empty. Soon, all that is left are vagrants, crazies, drunks, and the sorts of lovers who can't go home, these bodies immune to the cold.

Ever since arriving to Madrid from the south more than a month ago, Pablo has carried an easel during these in-between hours to the magnificent Plaza de la Constitución. He is no stalker of fleeting, roaring light—no impressionist. Nor is he a Romantic slave to some idealized sky. Instead, he is captivated by the plaza's ancient redbrick walls and rows of ironwork balconies stretching above imposing granite columns and arches. This is a place for pondering what's gone and what's next. And despite the promises he made to his family, Pablo has no idea what lies ahead. Just the other afternoon, he had an inkling to paint the outcasts, those who linger in the barren twilight.

But today, the nineteen-year-old artist sets up near a desolate café to paint a different image, one that's been haunting him.

Pablo's big dark eyes fix ahead as he shivers beneath a floppy hat pulled over his ears. His delicate hand—its fingertips escaping through cutoff knit gloves—continuously moves a thin round brush across the canvas's gray background. He remembers how he and Carles fled Paris under the cover of night like assassins, not two weeks before Pablo wound up here. His poet friend's ringing voice still follows him as he renders in dusky contours the woman he's also left behind—hair of lampblack, gaze like lightning, canny smile of the Sphinx.

A storm of pigeons has gathered by the café to peck at the crusts of *bomba* rice that a pudgy restaurant worker scraped from a casserole and flung onto the ground. Pitched coos and the noise of their claws scratching against cobblestone echo within the plaza's four walls. Searing red eyes bob up in the corner of Pablo's vision.

How, he wonders, could a dishwasher have known such a cruel way to taunt me?

Pablo's father painted pigeons—that's the only goddamned thing the old man ever could paint—and Pablo despises them. He's grown sicker of his homeland by the day. He longs for France and all the wonder it has left to reveal.

Above the din of the birds, Pablo hears racing footsteps just as the flock explodes into flight. A crop of hair, eyebrows, glasses, then a whole face appear over the top of the easel. Pablo looks up. It's Cinto, the boyishly handsome medical student with lips that curve like Cupid's bow. Pablo knows him from Barcelona. He's soft with his words, cautious, sweet. Like Pablo, Cinto arrived in the capital around New Year's. But he looks panicked, sweating with his jacket open and holding a crumpled letter. His short, exasperated breaths are white bursts in the February air.

"Carles," he puffs. "Dead. In Paris. A pistol."

Years later, Pablo will recall the inexplicable sensation when his life was ripped into two: the age when Carles was alive and another after he was gone.

"Pajaresco, he was with him," says Cinto. "And that girl, the half Spanish. It's what you said, Pablo! She made Carles crazy—killed him!"

Pablo looks down at the centuries-old pavement. It has heard inquisitors' verdicts and bears the stains of heretics' ashes. But in this moment, the stones remind Pablo of when he was small and his father showed him how to grind rock and make pigment. Nearby, a low pitiful sound comes from a lame pigeon left behind by the flock.

"No, Cinto," Pablo replies, his paintbrush touching the supple neck of the woman who has emerged onto the canvas as if from a whorl of smoke. "I did."

PART TWO

CHAPTER 2

Málaga, December 1884

It was the earthquake when Pablo was three that first married life with calamity.

Pablo's mother had draped herself across a window seat in the salon ever since coming home from Midnight Mass with spasms the night before. He sat with his tiny feet swinging from a chair's edge on the other side of the room, contemplating the way Doña María's round cheeks grew taut each time a creature writhed beneath the plump midsection of her maroon gitana dress. The pouf of hair resting on a pillow behind her head quivered as she chomped her lip.

Don José poured his laboring wife a thimbleful of sherry and stood close to let her squeeze his willowy arm. He was her opposite. Where she was short, plump, and radiating Mediterranean warmth, he was tall and long faced, his blanched patrician cheekbones beset by a neat reddish beard. She sipped the syrupy liquid, and they watched the clock hands for two and a half hours until Don José decided his wife needed stronger medicine. Perhaps his physician brother, Salvador, could convince the pharmacy to open on Christmas. He told Pablo to keep an eye on his mother as he threw a silk cape around his frock coat and ventured into the darkness.

Don José was gone for a long time. Pablo snuggled up below where his mother was sprawled out. He rubbed her swollen calves. He retrieved his *lápiz* to amuse her with the lifelike pictures she always praised him for. Doña María looked down at him and mouthed thanks to the Lord for what she'd already received. Her precocious black-haired son, with dark eyes large as a baby orangutan's, was pondering the most agonized smile he'd ever seen when the paper beneath his pencil began to vibrate and his studied lines grew into wild scribbles. Then, suddenly, it was as if Judgment itself were at hand.

Plaster from the ceiling of the third-floor apartment on Calle Merced began to fall around them in giant flakes, and Don José's spooked pet pigeons bounced off the walls. Doña María, still moaning in pain, snatched Pablo by the scruff of his neck and crawled them through the blizzard of down and debris. They cowered in the pantry, foodstuffs tumbling onto their heads. Doña María whispered the rosary and pressed her son's cheek to the belly of her dress. When Don José finally came bolting upstairs, she was too scared to speak.

"Hurry," Don José ordered when he found them in the pantry, covered with ghostly white flour. "The next quake is coming!"

Small as he was, Pablo detected the Brandy de Jerez and pipe smoke hovering like the devil's cologne and knew what Doña María was thinking: his father had returned carrying with him no tablets, no tonic, no tincture, and no wafer cachets because, in all those hours, he never did make it to the drugstore.

Don José pulled his wife to her feet and swaddled Pablo in his cape, slinging him over the shoulder like an onion sack. The Ruiz Picasso family fled through the fiery streets to a thick-walled one-story home standing directly on bedrock that belonged to Papa's art museum colleague who was away visiting Rome.

The rumbling carried on the next afternoon, each episode an anxious eternity. Everyone in the province would run outside and find the horizon shaking like a branch in the wind. They'd scour the firmament for sun or stars—something fixed to know everything was not being torn asunder. Sacked by Moors, reclaimed in the Reconquista, now rattling off the ledge of the Iberian Peninsula, Málaga prayed six hundred more would not die as had happened on Christmas.

Three days after the first quake, Pablo's sister was born between tremors. The family had huddled themselves inside two adjoining chambers in the center of the house, so Pablo heard the shrieking and believed his mother doomed. He saw the newborn when it was still glazed with blood and waxy white film, the head stretched and purple like an eggplant. It looked dead, and Pablo waited for someone to blow cigar smoke into the nostrils, which is how he'd heard Uncle Salvador had resurrected him from stillbirth. But then she moved, the way a beetle floating in bathwater does when prodded, flailing her limbs, pausing, flailing some more.

Before this, Pablo had not known such destructive or formative powers as evidenced by the earthquake or this momentous creation. Now acquainted, he understood that they would never be strangers to him again.

Home, even after the apartment was repaired and expanded with an additional room, seemed much smaller. Spinster aunts on both Don José's and Doña María's sides became full-time boarders, ostensibly to help with chores and childcare. At first, Pablo enjoyed having more people to entertain with his growing arsenal of charms. He was also initially inquisitive about the tiny being with a chubby face and wrinkled flesh. But their living quarters soon felt cramped, and he became fearful of her, too. What would she do to his household position as top-billed performer? After all, owning handsomeness, poise, and talent, he'd staked his claim. She had no right to try to nudge in.

But Lola fell harder for Pablo than anyone. He soon regained center ring and came to appreciate showing off for his new devotee, captivating the girl with savage faces, high-wire acts on the camelback sofa, and the same miraculous drawings that first elicited adoration from his mother and aunts.

As Doña María told everyone, her son's first words had not been "Mama" or "Papa," but *"Piz! Piz!"* as he screamed for his pencil every moment one wasn't squeezed into his little fist.

Pablo always began his pictures by placing the graphite at a seemingly random point. Then, he would not pick it up until the image was complete. His audience never knew what would leap from mind to page. The game repeated endlessly. The family spent equally on rag paper and potatoes.

When Doña María needed to free herself for housework, she'd challenge her son with ever more complicated feats.

"Make for me a jack donkey with a limp," Pablo's mother cried. "Now I want a blind rooster searching for the start of day."

Pablo also received religious commissions from Aunt Pepa, a dark and ancient woman possessing a mystical aura that she earned by spending each day kneeling in a broom closet she'd converted into a shrine. She wrapped herself in gauzy black garments and headdresses. Her fragrance was of rodent dander and incense. When she spoke, which was seldom, it was in verse and rhyme, reciting to Pablo tales of prophets and miracles, saints and martyrdoms. He became close to her in a way no one else was.

And with Aunt Pepa's ancient Egypt spinning in his head, Pablo's treasured lápiz became his very own staff of Moses, granting him power to conjure whatever he could conceive. He practiced fixing his vision to dissect an object's every detail, reconstituting it in his mind and then on paper, magically.

"He was born with my big black eyes," Doña María would say. "But they see the world like his father, the painter."

Don José was, after all, the house's famous artist, a commanding presence who would sit for long sessions in thrall to the easel before him. All his life, he'd emulated the old masters. He was a drawing instructor at the local Escuela de Artes y Oficios and worked as a curator and resident painter at the municipal museum of fine arts.

After noticing Pablo's undeniable knack with a pencil, however, Don José started to see his son—the first male heir on either side of the family—as validation, proof he'd handed down the prodigious creativity coursing through his veins. And so, at age five, Pablo began formal instruction in the arts under his father's expert and unceasing tutelage.

"First, the child must learn fundamentals," Don José expounded to Doña María. "Here's where many an artist fails." But he was speechless as Pablo produced not only realistic images but also granted them life, as might a young Michelangelo or Carducho, that Italian who carried the Renaissance to Spain, just like Prometheus brought fire.

Many of Pablo's earliest days were spent drafting figures alongside his father, but later that year, the family had no choice but to deposit their child each morning in a room that smelled of mold, where terrifying grown-ups scolded him and frequently sequestered him from the other kids, who mocked him for the pigeon feathers stuck to his uniform.

Pablo hated school. Why, he thought, learn letters and numbers when there aren't any in my pictures? Who are these foolish boys and girls who can't draw a line, even with a ruler?

Before noon, he would inevitably escape and scurry to Don José's studio, and his father would have to drag him back screaming. Pablo fretted that his family might abandon him to this claustrophobic prison for good. As insurance, he began to take to class something his father loved—a paintbrush or a palette or one of Don José's precious baby pigeons—believing the man would return for it, if not to his only son.

~

At breakfast one morning, Don José surprised Pablo with a set of watercolors. The boy was fascinated by the bright squares arranged like fantastically gaudy tiles in the japanned tin. But the paints on the page proved messy and difficult to manipulate. The colors, Pablo thought, got in the way of the lines. He felt no romance for them. As a result, when Pablo was nearing six, his father decided to push up introducing oil paints, which belong not only to art but also science. If he wasn't learning in the classroom, at least he would at home.

On a brisk evening in early autumn, Don José untied a leather pouch at his workbench and dumped a few yellowish lumps onto a glass tray.

"We're going to make pictures with rocks?" Pablo asked.

Out of his pocket, Don José took the pencil he'd confiscated from Pablo earlier that day after discovering that he'd refused lunch at school. "What's this?" he asked Pablo.

"My lápiz!"

"That little silver rod inside the wood is stone. When you rub against paper, this makes lines and shadings."

"Where does it come from?"

"The ground. *Everything* is from the ground," Don José said. He pointed to the crumbles of yellow ochre, which looked faintly moist, and promised someday they would journey to a place outside Málaga where Pablo could dig them up himself. "Just like playing in mud."

Don José then unlatched a maple box full of tin paint tubes and placed one on the workbench. It oozed yellow also. He told Pablo it was the same as those rocks. All you had to do was add a bit of linseed. Don José said when he was young, there were no tubes. "We mulled stones till the grains turned thin as snow and mixed it with the oil. Carried our paints in pig sacks, just like the old masters."

Pablo asked, "Who are the old masters?"

"The ones who gave us eyes."

"God gave us eyes."

"They're like little gods. His helpers, you might say. Before the Italians, we could barely see."

Pablo pointed to a high shelf where stood a lone phial of blue that shone even in the dim lamplight. "What's that?" Pablo asked.

"Only the most beautiful pigment ever found," Don José said, uncorking the bottle with great care and tapping out the cool, deep-blue powder onto the table. "Ul-tra-ma-rine," Don José said, one syllable at a time. "From beyond the sea! The land of Babur and the shahs!"

Pablo told his father it looked like the gown Mother Mary wore in the picture in Aunt Pepa's room.

"Yes, that's right, Pablito! Mary always wears blue."

"How come?"

"It's the color of heaven."

"I thought blue is sad."

"Blue is many things," the man said to his son. "I'll tell you, when a little boy is very sick, his mama and papa pray to the Virgin and promise to dress him in this color. They ask her help because Mary knows what it is to lose a child."

Don José sprinkled the blue dust onto Pablo's palm and poured three drops of linseed into it. His father touched a thumb against his son's hand and made little circles, pressing into the young flesh and massaging oil into the particles. "Go ahead, Pablo. It's paint, like in the tubes."

Pablo rolled the pigment and the medium together with his fingertips until they melded to become a slick liquid brilliant as the air above the ocean at dawn.

The man pried open the clamp of a tall jar, and the pong of mothballs filled the air. He removed a paintbrush and told Pablo the bristles were made from Siberian sable, "an animal more ferocious and fine than any of the little girls in your classroom, Pablito." He tickled the boy's nose with the tip, which was soft as silk.

Don José dipped the brush into the pool of blue in Pablo's hand and slathered a streak of heaven onto the canvas that had been waiting blankly at his easel.

So it was that Pablo came to appreciate paint and learned to love color almost as much as he loved lines. For his sixth birthday, he received a set of hog-hair brushes. He cherished them like he did his beloved lápiz.

Over the following years, Don José taught Pablo all his secrets, just as he himself had learned them: how bleaching linseed oil in the Málaga sun each July produces the best paint for the whole year, how to size canvas with glue made from boiling rabbit skin, how to scrape palettes with a dull blade and mix the chips with solvent and marble dust. The only imprimatura worth the effort is lead white, he would say—creamy and long, smooth and sweet—blended with homemade bone black, two-to-one.

Young Pablo took these lessons and admonitions as sacrosanct because they were spoken by Papa, the great artist. He hung on every word, swelling with pride from such attention and encouragement. At Don José's side, Pablo learned to imitate the immortals so that one day he might join them.

CHAPTER 3

I

La Coruña, November 1891

Outside his home, Don José had earned a somewhat different reputation. Locals called him "the Englishman" because of his attachment to imported attire. Without ever having traveled far beyond their poor province, Pablo's father perpetually strode its dusty streets with a top hat and cane, as if he'd just been hobnobbing with the queen. He showed up at barrooms, bullfights, the theater, and a humble music conservatory, offering opinions on art and aesthetics that recalled certain sherries: strong, cloying, and best taken in short doses. So, while famous, he wasn't a celebrity—no cause for celebration, anyway. Rather, to nearly everyone in this small hard-luck city, Don José was that notorious fop on continuous parade and also the finest painter of pigeons around.

Of course, the man could render other subjects. Different birds, for example. Rarely, he did a human that had some appeal. His museum colleagues would note how he endowed even these men and women with certain avian features—darting eyes, a puffed breast, heads prone to wobbling.

The pictures would always be done in Don José's best—that is, suf-ficient—imitation of the courtly style of portraiture that had dominated Spanish art for centuries and showed no signs of abating at the academy, where Goya, dead for more than sixty years, was still controversial. That fad called impressionism, which had ruffled Paris two decades ago, was gaining ground in Spain more slowly than Protestantism. Don José held it to be a worse sacrilege.

But somehow, when Don José painted pigeons without affectation but only pure admiration, they appeared ready to flutter off the canvas. He was like a violinist who has perfected a single sonata that he plays ad nauseam. The origins of this obsession were unknown to even Don José, as if owing from some Vedic past life.

As far back as anyone could remember, though, Don José main-tained a dovecote on the roof, and pigeons flew freely in the Ruiz Picasso house. Aunt Pepa tolerated them in honor of Saint Francis so long as they did not alight on her statues. No creature should shit on the head of Christ.

Don José, who was not very religious and preferred a brothel bed to a church pew, waxed mystical only when he spoke of paint, the old masters, and pigeons. With an olive branch in its beak, the gall-less pigeon is a sign of life, he would tell Pablo. It can also be an omen of misfortune to come.

Cover its eyes, and the pigeon will flap to the sun till falling like Daedalus. They carry messages from star-crossed lovers, fly between detached battalions, navigate peril without fear.

If the bird perches on your table, there will be sickness in the home.

A pigeon can mean hope or signal death—it takes a diviner or a painter to know which, Don José observed.

No soothsaying was needed, however, to see that Don José's own station in life was tenuous. Even Pablo sensed it, noticing the tense conversations between his parents over his puny salary and considerable expenses. After school, Pablo would come home and hear his mother turning away tailors, tobacconists, or the owner of the late-night *tasca*, each inquiring about unpaid bills. In the evenings, his family ate gazpacho and fried whitebait, *jamón* and oxtail now tastes of the past.

Worse, the rest of Málaga's fortunes were sinking, too. Everyone spoke of troubles. Winemakers gave up more of their vineyards to aphids each year. The cotton, iron, and sugar trades had soured. Cholera took its toll. Money to maintain the museum where Don José worked was scarce. When his curator's salary was revoked, he managed to stay on by restoring paintings damaged in the earthquake for a modest fee. There was such a backlog that the family scraped by, even if keeping up appearances became tight. While Doña María descended from a lesser-caste family, Don José—though cash poor—boasted of distant noble blood and was dedicated to impressing the public with refinement befitting a baron-grandee.

Until a new cost arrived.

They christened the unexpected child Concepción, to be affectionately called Conchita. She was long and fair, like her father, and born with ringlets that Pablo delighted in gently stretching so they bounced back like springs. There was no denying she was the prettiest of the three children. But having already established himself as the household's irreplaceable talent, Pablo was confident Conchita posed no threat and instantly adored her. He devised a game where he'd bring embroidery scissors to a newspaper's edge and fervently slice toward the middle, twisting and wending the blades across the page as the paper took the form of a kitten, a bullock, or anything he imagined, all to be unfurled for Conchita's applause.

But Don José was struggling to keep the growing family afloat.

When the museum closed a few years after Conchita's birth, Don José had no choice but to beg the family patriarch, his well-connected brother, Salvador, to help him secure another job. Pablo's father languished, growing deeper in debt. When the only position to be found was at an art school in La Coruña, a seaside redoubt in the distant province of Galicia and as far as one can travel in Spain before drowning in the freezing northern Atlantic, Uncle Salvador put in a good word. Don José grudgingly accepted.

So, as his tenth birthday approached, Pablo watched him bid goodbye to his friends, family, and Andalusian home. He caught the man crying while packing up the glass jars of colored pigments in his studio. At first, Pablo's impulse was to rush over and gather himself around his father's waist. But in the next instant, he felt anger swallow his empathy the way a fierce, opaque Indian red will overcome a translucent green on a canvas. For his father, he saw in that moment, had failed them.

Pablo boarded a cargo ship with his parents, sisters, and a flight of pigeons stuffed into a crate. He'd never been at sea before. They steamed away from all they knew, straight into a gale. Each day felt like riding out a nonstop earthquake. The sickness lodged itself just below Pablo's sternum. It slept and woke on its own schedule. When it roused, he was left sweating, gagging, and panting in horror.

After more than a week of rocking to and fro, they pleaded to disembark at the port of Vigo and began the journey's final leg overland. Just as Pablo had known instantly he hated school—even now he could be undone by simple arithmetic—Don José detested La Coruña as soon as they'd pulled up in a crammed carriage under a dismal drizzle.

The family had few acquaintances in this new place. Don José was informed at the art school that his methods and style were passé. His colleagues there treated him as an outcast. Beyond their apartment window stood a great, foreboding lighthouse, where storm clouds always appeared to gather. Don José spent whole afternoons staring at it through the dripping panes.

In cold and wet La Coruña, Pablo saw the man he looked up to become something other than the towering artist he'd believed in. Pablo watched as children pointed and giggled at his caped outfits and harsh dialect from the south. He overheard people on the street dismissing him as a featherbrain who tried to pass himself off as a leading artist and aristocrat. In Málaga, Don José may not have been revered, but he wasn't jeered at. Here, in this northern exile, Pablo's father was reduced to a backwater buffoon.

~

Pablo, meanwhile, found a kind of freedom in La Coruña. Don José's energy for instructing him had diminished, and Doña María was busy chasing his little sisters. Nor were aunts around to mind his every move. For the first time, Pablo roamed with the street kids, shot cork guns, corralled calves into mock bullrings, and traded Buffalo Bill comics. He learned that the charisma he'd cultivated and used to great effect inside his home worked just as well outside of it.

Come summer, though, Pablo retreated to the Playa de Riazor to bask in the fleeting Galician sun before it disappeared for another year. The solitude of these excursions pleased him. The beach's shoreline was strewn with short and squat wooden cabanas painted in pastels and mounted on wagon wheels. Beachgoers would pay to enter these contraptions, and their owners would whip up draft horses to pull the rickety shacks into the sea. Now deposited on a sandbar far from the public's gaze, the occupants luxuriated privately in the briny water, which was said to smooth bathers' skin.

Pablo would settle on an outcrop of rocks, the huts coming in and out of the ocean marking the passage of a day. He'd make drawings of gulls fighting the breeze, cormorants diving to pluck an eel, fishermen in oilskins hauling rafts of octopus. Or sometimes, while staring into the distance, Pablo would become lost in his thoughts as he watched waves seek land, noticing how their excitement increases as they approach shore—the way children run, laughing, into parents' arms. That age seemed remote to Pablo now. No longer could he speed toward his mother and father as Lola and Conchita did, bright-eyed, baring teeth and love.

One blinding white afternoon, Pablo left his perch for the chilly, thigh-deep surf. As he was wading along, holding his totable sketchbook in the air above him, he felt something slick and almost wetter than water move against his knee. He looked down and found nothing.

But a few feet away, just beneath the waves, he saw a group of them—narrow, silver-blue fish, motionless and sparkling in the sun.

Pablo rushed forward and plunked his hand in, but the school dispersed. They reassembled, and he charged again, missing once more. He became obsessed with catching just one. Each time, they edged deeper, now almost to where the rolling waves might swell over his head. He'd never learned to swim. When he leapt and finally felt a tailfin wriggle in his fist, a shiver ran down his spine, right before the fish splashed away.

But as Pablo stood up, he sensed an absence of weight. Then he remembered how, when he pounced, he'd heard a small plunk. He turned around, and there it was, open at the hinge—his sketchbook was being carried away by the current. A gift from his father, it contained every drawing Pablo had made in the months since he'd arrived in La Coruña, starting from when Pablo could barely render two-point perspective convincingly and spanning to now, when he could draw a tall ship, each mast and sail perfectly foreshortened. He longed to show Don José how he'd advanced—and the thought of losing his artwork terrified him.

The buckram binding floated for a moment on the surface amid rafts of foam, but then the pages absorbed the water, and the book began going under, swaying side to side as it sank to the seafloor.

Pablo scurried over and tried to pick up the book with his toes, but he couldn't touch the murky bottom. He scrunched his face and dived, pulling himself lower with cupped hands. The water stung his eyes and tasted like oyster broth. The object slid away from him, and he came up for air. He was a little closer to shore and could almost stand. He looked toward shallower water, where the cabanas had dragged bathers into the sea, the waves coming right up to the stairs. Pablo spotted the book wedged underneath one of the hut's wheels, making it easy prey.

With a deep inhale, Pablo took another plunge. When he emerged with the waterlogged sketchbook in hand, his bangs curtained his brow and dripped saltwater onto his lips. His eyes were tearing up, but he swelled with the pride of a victorious matador.

Pablo's sight cleared slowly. When it returned, a strange, transfixing creature was just a few feet away. His spine shivered again. There before him was a mass of tangled orange burning like fire. Galicians, who carry the blood of the Celts, are among the few peoples in Spain who have inherited this hair color. In fact, the wet, curly growth reminded Pablo of his father's beard after he would wash away the pipe tobacco scent from his chin. This, however, was much more compelling and forbidden even to see. But he was frozen in awe.

Finally, Pablo's stare ascended to meet a young woman's gray-green eyes set in salt-edged, freckled cheeks. She wore a light chemise on top, and her arms prickled in the breeze. In her hands were the wet candy-striped bloomers she was washing the sand from when she'd indiscreetly opened the cabana door and squatted on the steps, sure no one was around. Her small nose twitched, and Pablo could feel her surveying his tan frame, his wide black eyes, the dripping book.

Pablo was ashamed at how excitement had stretched the sheer fabric of his shorts. But he detected on her face the flash of a smile right before she scampered up the plank stairs, the cabana door shutting behind her. He felt pregnant with new desire, euphoric, scared, and more awake than ever. Somehow, he was also sad, as though he knew he were close to the end of a dream.

∽

In fall, Pablo attended the art school where Don José taught, though not often his father's courses. He had difficulty concentrating or pretending to, having learned all these lessons before. Pablo's paintings of the plaster casts of limbs his teachers brought in were done in half the time and were always finer than the rest. In Málaga or La Coruña or anywhere, Pablo decided, nothing was more boring than a classroom. He entertained himself by ignoring instruction and sketching whatever was in his mind. A bloody bullfight. The locusts he imagined Aunt Pepa eating, like John the Baptist in the wilderness. Or the girl who sat in the front of class, Angeles. Countless pages he filled with her reclining on blankets of cloud, surrounded by lyre-plucking cherubs. In Angeles, Pablo finally found something at school that captivated him.

The other students—who regarded the laconic son of the too-tall, red-bearded Englishman with eerie reverence—snickered when they caught Pablo trying to figure out how to draw the intricate braid of her hairdo with a Conté crayon. And Angeles became aware she'd hooked an admirer.

~

When it wasn't raining or foggy (in La Coruña, it was almost always one or the other), the instructors let the students work *en plein air*.

The class strolled outside to the tip of a peninsula to render the rocky shoreline and the Tower of Hercules, a giant rectangular lighthouse that had been built by Romans atop a ridge. As Pablo was setting up one day, he spotted a familiar figure in a yellow dress slip past the teacher to the stairway leading to the tower's lantern. With the instructor distracted by another student, Pablo quickly followed, spiraling to the top, where he opened a heavy door. A dole of doves circled beyond the catwalk's railing, flapping in the boundless gray. Angeles stood in the middle of the platform, the wind whipping the lemony pleats of her skirt against the outline of her slight frame.

"If you're going to draw me," she said, her voice almost yelling to be heard above the forceful air, "you should get the eyes right." They were, of course, what had attracted Pablo to Angeles initially, their intense light and heat. He had studied them for weeks now, hoping he might capture that supernal spark.

"What happened to your eyes?" she said. "They're funny."

All his life, Pablo's aunts said so many complimentary things about his big dark eyes that consumed half his face. *"Guapísimo!"* they'd cried. Never had these been mocked.

The girl noticed Pablo's mouth stiffen.

"Oh, not so funny? You take yourself pretty seriously, don't you?"

Pablo wasn't going to admit it if he did.

Angeles turned away from him and peered down over the railing toward the expanse of Costa da Morte. She asked Pablo if he would plummet from the edge of the lighthouse's crown for her.

He replied, "Would you kiss me before I do?"

"After."

"Are you crazy? Kiss a bloody pancake?"

"It's the only way to know you'd really leap," she said. "What if the kiss were for nothing, nothing at all?"

"How am I to know I've been kissed by a pretty girl if I'm dead?"

"Faith."

A shrill pea whistle cut through the wind.

"You'd better take the stairs," Angeles said, making for the door.

But then she clattered back and placed her lips on his cheek, making a little suctioning sound.

Pablo's heart thumped in his chest as he watched her disappear down the lighthouse's stairway like jewelry swallowed by a drain. He felt graced to receive even briefly such a gem, apprehensive of what Providence might seek in return.

~

It was the dreariest winter anyone could remember—wet and cold, cold and wet. Pablo was barely thirteen.

Over supper, Don José recounted to his family how he'd carried a box easel to the rooftop and painted a bird whose ankle was tethered by a cuff connected to a tiny copper chain. He'd shivered so much that the picture's lines resembled those blurry dancers of Degas that he despised. So he packed up his brushes and surrendered, unclasping the pigeon. When she flew off, a toe was left frozen to the ledge.

Not long after, Conchita, now seven, woke with a cough that sounded like the bark of a gaffed seal. Then, a few days later, a brush-stroke of red appeared in the handkerchief after Doña María wiped Conchita's nose. The girl's complexion grew ashen, and she drenched the bedding with sweat on Little Christmas. She was kept alone, forbidden anything save porridge, warm milk, aromatic tea, and drops of a belladonna decoction.

In the middle of the night, Pablo would visit his sister, lighting the candelabra on the sconce with a long match. In bed, she lay swaddled in a wool blanket of powder blue. Bargains had already been made between Doña María and the Mother of God. Conchita would wear this color for the next seven years, just as Don José told of long ago.

Pablo took her fingers into his own. In his other hand, he clutched the scapular dangling from his neck. He called upon an even higher power, God Himself, a backup if his parents' accord with Mary failed.

"It is Don José's son," Pablo said aloud, unsure whether or not heaven hears prayers uttered only in our heads. "Papa says I'll be the greatest painter in Spain, better even than Goya."

Pablo paused, in case confirmation might be forthcoming.

He offered to let his Maker take it all back and vowed never again to create art. No oils, no watercolor, no charcoal, nothing, so Conchita might live. Pablo kissed her burning forehead. Later, he confirmed the pact by snapping his pencil like a pagan sacrifice.

The following morning, Pablo awoke to a hushed conversation in the parlor, the word *diphtheria* drifting down the hall. He'd heard of the disease before; it had ravaged dwellings nearer to the sea. The surgeon-and-tallow-chandler across the street, who somehow knew Uncle Salvador, had ordered from France a new elixir, an antiserum extracted from horse's blood that might cure her. Pablo kneeled and made the sign of the cross, thanking the Lord for answering his call.

Upon returning to class, Pablo told the instructors his hand had been injured doing chores, leaving him neither able to paint or draw. When he admitted he was strong enough to write, they allowed him to read of the Renaissance and record notes instead.

Sitting at his school desk, gazing at a plate of Titian's *Venus*, Pablo daydreamed of Angeles's lips. He pictured her striking the same pose as in the folio, naked save the ring on her finger, sprawled over white sheets during the lighter side of twilight, a spaniel sleeping at her feet, one hand lazily clutching a spray of roses while the other rested indecently at her groin. His pencil moved across the paper, almost of its own accord. When Pablo looked down at the page, he choked on his saliva and gasped before slamming the notebook shut. He'd made a portrait of Angeles.

Could this crude sketch be considered art? Surely not. No. It wasn't a real drawing but merely a trifle, a vulgar joke, like a comic in a smutty magazine. The All-Knowing has got to realize this.

Carefully opening the notebook's cover just an inch, Pablo peeled back the first pages. His excitement returned. The picture really looked like the girl he'd yearned for. The reproduction of her delicate cheeks had been executed shrewdly enough. And those eyes—celestial and sultry— yes, they *were* flawless!

Yet Pablo knew this phenomenon was only possible because of his gift from God.

He tried to convince himself that he'd neared the line but not quite crossed it. Had not broken his vow. Not intentionally.

Pablo raced home after school, bursting through the door and running to Conchita. She was curled up, resting quietly. Pallid still but her chest was rising and lowering. He sighed with relief.

A telegram arrived announcing the serum had passed through the Pyrenees, Doña María told him. It could be in La Coruña any hour. "Your sister is going to be OK, thanks be to the Virgin."

Forty times at the side of his bed, Pablo praised God. He dug his fingernails into his forearm, the first of many acts of penance, he told himself. He might not have crossed the line, but he knew he had done something wrong. He would devise novel offerings tomorrow. Maybe he needed to break his fingers.

Eventually, he drifted to sleep.

Awaking to an insistent banging, he found Don José hovering by the front door, barefoot and gape mouthed in the morning light. Gold-plated instruments and the serum poked out from the satchel of the physician standing near him. But before the sky had finished changing from black to indigo to purple to red to orange to blue, Conchita was long dead.

Days later, the family trudged behind a mule dragging the cart that carried Conchita's matte coffin. As they walked, another procession passed with glistening, taffy-colored horses and carriages with shiny spokes. Pablo was envious before he was ashamed. Without a wake or even a marker, Pablo's sister was laid into the grassless January sod.

Pablo knew the catastrophe that travels with creation had finally arrived to claim her, its way cleared by his broken vow.

But the indignity of the funeral and all of La Coruña, these were Don José's fault alone.

II

For months, the family sagged under the weight of a leaden sky. Pablo's father stared at incomplete canvases, his brush vibrating inches from the stretchers. He watched the window, waiting for the rain to end, the fog to burn away. It seemed to emanate from that wretched Tower of Hercules in the distance, a lighthouse not projecting a ray to lost ships but dispensing evil.

After one such spell, Don José removed a pair of shears from a kitchen drawer and wrenched open the trapdoor in the ceiling above, as if still deciding whether to slice his wrists or plummet from the rooftop. Instead, Pablo's father returned a few moments later from the dovecote and hung a pigeon's snipped-off feet—limp and red, like a pinch of whole saffron—from a nail on the wall in his alcoved study.

"Paint the outlines, claws, and scales. I'll do the rest when I'm back," Don José told Pablo before exiting the apartment.

This assignment was an exercise Pablo had occasionally undertaken, now that his father's eyesight had begun to fade.

"That's what separates artists from arses, the hands—and the feet, too," Don José would say. "Draw a thousand, no, no . . . a million pigeon feet, and one day, you might render a human hand correctly—might!"

Pablo remembered how, years before in Málaga, he sometimes found his small clenched fists enclosed inside the grasp of Don José's long fingers. Father and son would peer together as they opened their hands, analyzing each digit, each joint.

"Look how your second finger begins to point even when you don't command it. Try. Squeeze tight. Tighter! Now release them all at once. See there—see how it's out of the gate before the rest? It wants to show what's ahead. Remember this when you draw. Let the fingers move on the canvas as they wish, just as yours do."

Back then, Pablo revered this instruction. But even before Conchita's death, the luster of those lessons had dimmed. Don José heaped praise on Pablo but also endlessly chastised him—dressing down his uninspired works as mockeries of nature, reminding him that only imbeciles ignore shadows—all to prod his son toward painting the masterpiece that he could not manage himself.

By Pablo's teens, though, he estimated his work equal to Don José's and, in some cases, superior. The implications troubled Pablo. What business, then, did his father have correcting him, doling out advice? Pablo had grown tired of this apprenticeship and was bored with painting pigeons. Seeing Don José so emptied now tore down the last regards Pablo had for the man.

And the family was sinking closer to privation. Lola, Pablo's eldest sister, turned to mending the neighbors' clothes to augment the pittance the art school paid Don José. At night, she stayed up late darning instead of doing homework.

His father had uprooted the whole family, brought them to this awful place, because of his chosen profession—or his lack of talent within it. Either way, Don José had failed to keep his home warm with a stoked fire, his children healthy, his wife loved. Pablo wondered: Was his own artistic ability really a gift from God, or had Don José merely handed down a jinx, then? If the latter, should Pablo be made to suffer all his life pursuing what had so bedeviled his father?

Pablo was back lying in bed and paging through cowboy comic books with the room's door parted when he heard the man fumbling up the stairway leading to the top floor. Doña María rustled in bed. The lamplight extinguished with a sigh.

Don José pushed through the apartment's entrance and collapsed loosely onto his studio chair in the alcove where he painted. Pablo quietly watched through the open doorway as his father grabbed at his pipe and sniffed the air upon finding the clay still warm. The man turned to the brandy cask, which was filled lower than when he left, and Pablo regretted not thinking to add water to bring the level to what it was before. But Pablo's confidence rose when Don José glanced over to the easel, where the painting was now complete—no denying the pigeon's feet Pablo had rendered on the canvas weren't nearly identical to the ones dangling from the wall.

"That's that," the man announced before sucking his teeth. "I couldn't do a goddamn pigeon finer myself, nor could Michelangelo. 'Spose you've not much to learn here, anymore. Ignored by so many would-be Manets, at least pigeon painting is a discipline that will serve you many years," Don José let loose with a groan. "Even after your masterpiece."

Pablo continued turning the pages of his book.

"Hear me, boy?" Don José burst into a loud laugh that segued into a sputtering cough. "I might never paint again!"

Pablo got up and walked to the studio to see if he could quiet his father before Lola awoke, at least.

"Your landscapes instructor says you're quite the prodigy," Don José said, wiping his nose with his palm and then flipping open a newspaper on the table so he could glance down at the headlines. "You'll pay the bills, eh, with me retired? Why, I won't lift a brush!"

"Don't say that," Pablo replied. "It's a promise we never keep."

The graying man's eyes narrowed. Don José almost spoke but stopped short, instead mouthing the word *we*. He tapped the ash out of his pipe and set it down before leaning forward in his chair. "And you should know how?"

Pablo raised a finger, but only the first syllables exited his lips before Don José's open hand struck him below the cheekbone.

He smothered a whimper.

"Speak up, boy. I'm long in the tooth, short on eyesight, and having the damnedest time hearing you. You were about to expound on some insight you had, no?"

Don José removed tobacco from his pocket and told Pablo to compose his thoughts, returning to reading the paper unfolded across the table. "Of all the vileness Paris permits," he said of the astonishing report that France had banned bullfights, "to think it would make illegal such a noble pastime. It's all right. One might say, 'The French don't know how to kill a bull any more than they make real art.'"

Pablo shook as Don José growled, "Only a Spaniard understands the chief component to painting is pain! Not that which they call in France—what's it? *Ennui?*" The man cleared the table with a forearm as he rose, shattering bottles of pigment and varnish.

"Yes, I'll give you Delacroix," Don José said, drunkenly. "A porpoise caught in the tuna net. The rest, they're too busy sodomizing one another to paint anything worth hanging in a pissoir. That's the only hurt they comprehend. But not us—we understand what it is to be knifed in the heart and live! Study that yet, did you?"

Pablo felt his eyes welling with tears. "What should I learn from you, if not to paint? Can you teach me to make a fortune? How about just enough to put a stone on Conchita's grave?"

The blow that came next sent Pablo to the ground. The man knelt to meet him there, stabbing the air with his long finger an inch from Pablo's nose. "Art emanates from suffering, bitterness, and hard, crystallized loathing buried in the soul. A paintbrush is a pickax! Mine your misery!"

The bite of turpentine filled the room. Don José reached for his pipe, stood, and lit it. "You'll be sorry and so will everyone you meet, boy, but you'll be good," he said. "That is my gift. I've granted more than you know."

CHAPTER 4

Barcelona, September 1895

After almost four years in cold, wind-lashed Galicia, Pablo longed to return south to the simple comforts of Málaga, where lizards ducked behind window shutters and the Mediterranean rays had first awakened his skin's Moorish tones. Instead, he and the rest of the family followed Don José to Spain's northeast, where a teaching position waited for him at an art school in Barcelona. The job at L'Escola de la Llotja—which was situated on the second floor of the city's old stock exchange, the landmark for which it was named—turned out to offer neither prestige nor prospect. But at least it provided a means to flee. In the family's new home, however, they found a city that was big, proud, dark, and in the worst of moods.

The Catalans, whose claim to this area as an independent region extends a thousand years, were the most unwelcoming people Doña María said she'd ever encountered. Their language sounded to the newcomers like stuffy-nosed gibberish punctuated by guttural consonants. Their culture, conspiratorial and heedful of outsiders, was as impenetrable.

The family took an apartment in the Barri Gòtic, a seamy quarter of ancient, soot-covered buildings. Dank alleys wended through it like the slithering paths of a worm-eaten gourd, narrow enough to inspire bouts of claustrophobia and perfect, Don José warned, for thieves. The balconies dangling from the walls on either side of the passageways faced so near to one another that neighbors heard every illicit lover and broken dish. Pablo was wonderstruck by how commotion and desolation came together in Barcelona the way an aroma of hazelnuts toasting or pimientos frying was always laced with fetor.

While the rest of Spain persisted in being practically medieval, Barcelona had hurtled itself into the bounty and indignities of the Industrial Revolution. Its textile factories turned out the Jacquard fabrics that adorned gentlemen's waistcoats and draped over ladies' shoulders across the continent. The city's streets were bustling with migrants, mill laborers, and opportunists. The ports teemed with dockworkers and saw footloose sailors coming and going from Marseille to Manila, the Caribbean to the Barbary Coast. After Saturday night, taverns were dirty with sweat, swill, stink, and blood. Every type of contraband was found in Barcelona, especially in Barri Xinès, the red-light district. Vice, locals said, lacked only a trade union.

As the turn of the century approached—the whole world full of anxiety and hope for a brighter, less cruel future—Barcelona was then both a harbinger of change and a tinderbox.

The Ruiz Picasso clan quickly learned the city was haunted by ghosts left behind by a spirits-smuggler fond of anarchist literature who'd lobbed Orsini bombs—explosive-packed prickly pears of death—into the Gran Teatre del Liceu a couple years before they arrived, murdering twenty-two operagoers during the "William Tell Overture." Not long after the family was to mark its first year in Barcelona, dozens more would be mauled by blasts at the Corpus Christi parade. Afterward, hundreds of men, women, and children were rounded up in a dragnet and locked in a castle on Montjuïc hill, side by side with prisoners from the restive colonies. They were beaten, boiled, and stung with knitting needles. Their sides were slit open before being set upon by rats. Six were executed.

Another mustachioed Italian anarchist soon arrived from Paris, locating the Spanish prime minister near the Roman baths of Santa

Agueda and shooting him dead, appealing to his shrieking widow, "Pardon, madam. I respect you as a lady, but I regret that you were the wife of that man."

Working-class angst was the radicals' lifeblood; the intelligentsia channeled it to feed their own ire. More curiously, anarchists often shared common cause against the Madrid government with Catalan nationalists—odd bedfellows since that movement included Barcelona's conservative upper crust. Both Catalanistes and *anarquistes* yearned for the region to escape the Spanish crown's weight, each promising to emerge triumphant the way a magnificent, shiny beetle crawls out of dried-up dung.

Long ago, the city had become the most sophisticated perch on the Peninsula. As the rest of Spain withered, upright Catalans were busy seeking to rebirth their beloved capital, looking to fair-faced Paris rather than Madrid as a surrogate. Using money pouring in from textiles, the wealthy erected grand churches and theaters in the nouveau style embodying belle epoque ideals of fluid form and grace in nature. Barcelona, then, was beautiful when it was not ugly.

This was the place Pablo's family arrived in the years before the war—that great moody metropolis of the Mediterranean that attracts as it repulses, charms as it forebodes, caresses as it cuts.

～

At fourteen, Pablo once again found himself plunked into someplace strange. This time, he couldn't even understand what the damn people were saying. As stimulating as Barcelona was, he was eager to make his displeasure known and acted indifferent about this move, a smug convict transferring jails.

Don José, born middle-class and sunk now to just scraping by, was hard on Pablo so his son wouldn't go bust as he had. Besides relentlessly pressuring the boy to perfect technique, he also decided they must pursue a new tack. To win favor and increase the value of his output,

Don José concluded a painter must carefully select his subjects. No one before him in all of Europe accomplished what he had with the pigeon. But Don José admitted it had brought him no money and no good. So he pushed Pablo to sow his reputation and land profitable commissions through large religious compositions. After all, anyone in Spain knows churches have more gold and silver than banks.

Soon after arriving in Barcelona, this plan was validated when Don José charmed a convent of Vincentian nuns into letting Pablo paint a mural behind their altar. Don José entered Pablo's work into every show, talking up the prodigy he'd sired as though he were a prize horse.

All the while, Pablo bit his tongue and tried to remain obedient, always remembering that awful night in La Coruña, of which neither father nor son spoke. But relations between them were perpetually on the verge of erupting again. Many evenings, Pablo escaped their apartment via the roof and drifted through the Barri Gòtic's shadow-drenched labyrinth like a tadpole floating through reed grass, meandering in and out of crocodile jaws.

During the daylight, however, Pablo attended La Llotja. He was among the class's youngest, but he painted more skillfully than his professors and gained instant notoriety. Arrogant and aloof, when he couldn't follow what the teachers were telling him in Catalan, Pablo simply cocked those endless eyes and wagged a hollow grin, his brush continuing to twirl and caper, dapple and fandango. This certainly aroused his classmates' curiosity, but such a demeanor deterred introductions, even invited scorn. He was careful not to show how their teasing bothered him. Luckily, he often didn't comprehend the words anyway.

A few months after starting classes, Pablo was sitting on the school's front steps when another student walked up to him. Flaxen-haired and well-built, he looked several years older. Pablo recognized him as a decent painter, although only of country scenes. Pablo didn't see why people confined their art like this, forever repeating themselves.

"Back home, people call me Pajaresco," said the young man, hold-ing out a thick, blistered hand to Pablo. "You can call me that, too."

It turned out he was from up in the mountains in a remote farm-ing settlement nestled not far from the river, a place called La Horta de Ebro. Pajaresco reminded Pablo of the American cowboys he'd read of in pulp paperbacks—few words, a square jaw stippled with auburn, and a cigarette between his teeth. It was obvious enough to Pablo this farmhand didn't belong in the stodgy school where Barcelona's best families sent their sons to be painters. Pablo liked him for that.

And as he himself was from a dusty province at the bottom of Spain—hardly different to *Barcelonès* than the outlaw Texas of his comic books—Pablo might even borrow something of the older boy's des-perado swagger.

"All them other kids, they're too squirmy and dumb to paint noth-ing good. The teachers won't let them near the ledge," Pajaresco said to Pablo. "But it's like you was hatched full-grown, a painter right outta the shell."

Soon, the two of them could be found strutting in big, bowlegged strides down La Rambla, the leafy promenade running from Plaça de Catalunya to the seaport. Burnt caramel and the calls of newspaper vendors reciting bloody headlines wafted through the air. The pavement was lined with flower-sellers and stacked cedarwood cages filled with canaries, parakeets, finches, and a macaque monkey clenching the bars. Pajaresco showed Pablo how to whistle "all aboard" to shopgirls. He treated Pablo to strong tobacco and booze at the seedy joints of Barri Xinès with the cash he'd saved from odd jobs.

From Pablo, Pajaresco learned to fix the perspective in his bucolic paintings. And when Doña María saw that the boy was living away from his family, she invited him to Sunday suppers for home-cooked meals.

"Don't try too hard fitting in here," Pajaresco comforted Pablo after dinner one day. "These city people might kick a dog if they thought nobody was looking. They call themselves Catalan, but the true *Catalunya* is up there." He pointed through the windowpane to the escarpment beyond the rooftops. He promised someday he'd show Pablo real living, back home in Horta.

Hardly after Pajaresco had spoken, his parents fetched him to come work the land and avoid the military draft. Anybody could see that war with America was approaching.

Around the same time, Don José heard from his fellow teachers there was nothing left for his son to learn at La Llotja. Just before Pablo turned sixteen, Don José borrowed money from Uncle Salvador and shipped him away.

～

Pablo became withdrawn in Madrid, the sprawling capital where his father enrolled him in the country's finest art institute. He didn't write his parents, made few friends, and grew disinterested in anything but his artwork. He also noticed how easily incensed he could become, just like Don José. The mindless jabbering of his classmates and instructors drove him mad. But he seldom spoke up himself because he didn't want to engage with anyone. He couldn't determine who he was anymore. As a child, he'd been the entertainer. Then he was the talent. Now, at the San Fernando Royal Academy, all the students and teachers were technically adept, but no one's work stood out. Yet they each harbored an opinion about how Pablo should paint, the same way his father had. They seemed determined that art be concerned with mechanical sophistication and completely without novelty, human emotion, or depth. Here, Pablo felt without contour or form, like he might have picked the wrong vocation—or, rather, that it had been unjustly chosen for him.

After eight months, Pablo's tongue became coarse and swollen like a starfish arm. He was diagnosed with scarlet fever. Doña María was terrified. Despite Lola barely being a teenager, the family sent her to nurse Pablo and bring home its prodigal son.

CHAPTER 5

La Horta de Ebro, June 1898

Pajaresco got to make good on his promise much sooner than either one of the young men anticipated.

Pablo arrived in Horta in a battered donkey-led wagon after his mother deemed Barcelona no place for someone in his condition. Instead, she arranged for him to recuperate amid the fresh highlands air. He relished learning from his friend the farm's routine. Pablo and Pajaresco fed the soil around the family's olive trees with bonemeal, cleaned pomace from the press, plowed fields, chopped firewood, and held hot barbs to each other's skin to remove ticks.

And they painted.

They'd wander off with their canvases, brushes, tubes of color, and easels tied in burlap bundles, eating fig cakes, drinking handfuls of cool water from streams and purple liquid from a smelly goat-bladder wineskin, finding ridges that in the sunset became ribbons of gold. After exhausting every subject close by, one morning they packed their bags onto a dun-colored mule and marched into the mountains, where the landscape was still wild. Brown finches skimmed through the trees, and Pajaresco moved in great strides, a gundog panting beside him in the heat of the sun. When the animals tired, they tied them up by a river, left food, and carried on.

Pablo, still convalescing, could barely keep pace himself as they bouldered up hillsides, leaping from one rock face to another. On a steep incline, a sapling he'd grabbed on to broke in half, sending him sliding toward the canyon far below, his arms and legs kicking up dust.

Pajaresco scrambled down the scarp, catching Pablo's wrist just as he was going over the ledge. "You saved my life," Pablo exclaimed with heavy breath as his friend's powerful arm hoisted him up.

"So we live to paint another Virgin," Pajaresco replied.

The two climbed higher and made a camp in a limestone cave. A spring nearby nursed the river. They washed their clothes and let a narrow waterfall drench their heads and roll off their backs. Pablo was warmed by Pajaresco's friendship, but the fear he'd felt while tumbling—the sensation the earth was opening up to an infinite void beneath him—lingered.

~

Pablo and Pajaresco did not put on clothes even after their skin had dried in the sun, going instead like Pacific tribesmen. They maimed a hare with buckshot from a Holland & Holland and killed it, skewering the animal longwise on a beech branch. The meat was unrelenting and spare, but it was free and it was theirs, and they were free and they were alive. When the sun went down, they guzzled wine, and Pablo laid the ends of sticks in the fire until their tips glowed. The night's blackness became an edgeless canvas on which to render that most pagan rite, the Spanish bullring. In the air, he drew the thick-muscled outlines of bulls, horsemen, and toreros with the orange embers and watched them disappear.

When Pablo awoke the next morning, there was someone standing before him, a shadow encircled in early light. Pablo looked around and saw Pajaresco had taken the shotgun hunting. But he was not frightened. The figure was lean faced, with a sharp-edged nose and hair like gall ink. His skin was the color of baked terra-cotta, with a white patina of ash at the elbows. He must have been about Pablo's age, perhaps slightly younger—or was he older? The boy talked with a strange accent—not Catalan, not Aragonese, not Basque—and said he was with his flock, passing through. But Pablo saw no one with him, creature or man. His calves were round, like pomegranates, and his stomach bare, a vest covering his ribs. Slung over his neck was a jute sack. A mandolin poked out.

Pablo walked with the boy through the tall sedge past a growth of blue borage by a hornet's nest. They followed the river, carrying Pablo's brushes and rolled-up canvases.

"Further up, you can catch sturgeon," the boy said. "Long and black, with little whiskers, mothers full of eggs." Had Pablo seen the boar, he asked. The falcons? The lynx?

"There's no lynx here," Pablo said.

"She's hiding," the boy said. "Townspeople try to kill her, but she's too smart. Hear her, if you know what you're listening for."

Pablo asked the boy if you could really make paint from the river, and he told him it was true. Alongside them, the water grew wider, then narrow again.

The boy called out the names of trees and plants as they walked, telling Pablo the properties of each. Tea of valerian for catarrh. Climbing bindweed berries for cancer. Gentian to regain strength after a sickness. "Syrup from cooked mulberry seeds together with honey makes you feel desire," he said.

"Aunt Pepa uses a special thyme."

"For desire?"

"For her appetite."

"No," he said. "For mating."

The boy announced there was no paint in the river here, though, so they sat down on a rock cluster that shimmered with quartz and took out their easels and bundles of brushes and tubes. On the horizon was the faint movement of a distant storm. Pablo watched the traveler's graceful handwork and saw how effortlessly the poppy bulbs against a cerulean sky came to life on his canvas. The boy swore no one had taught him even to hold a brush. It reminded Pablo of his father's stories of the boys from the barren scrubland: too poor to have a proper matador's suit, but they could plant a sword between the bravest bull's shoulder blades as if their hands were guided by angels.

When they returned to the cave, Pajaresco was waiting. He'd tracked a boar nine miles but made a dangerous error after getting the bastard in range. "You can't graze a boar," he said.

The three hunted quail—killing, plucking, gutting, and stuffing a half dozen of them with chanterelles. The boy removed from his sack sausages wrapped in rough paper and cooked them with thistles and wild leeks. They huddled in the night like ferrets to keep warm.

In the small of the morning, before even Pajaresco rose, the boy led Pablo along the stream in the other direction, its pebbly shores colonized by foxtails and nightshade. Fish gathered in eddies and leapt out and in. The two foragers batted away black flies. Their footsteps sunk into the moist earth. A twig snapped. The boy grabbed Pablo's collar.

"Is it the lynx?" Pablo asked. "I forgot the gun."

"No," the boy replied, swiveling his gaze through the air, searching. "We're all right here." He pointed at their feet.

Pablo saw the muck they had been walking through was soft and ruddy, with bright yellow running through it like gold veins. It was the ochre deposits Don José had told Pablo of long ago, when he was tiny.

"Paint!" Pablo screamed.

"Nature," the boy said, "hides herself." He fetched a handful of the moist clay and held it out. Pablo dipped his forefinger into the outstretched palm, and rust-smell filtered through the air, mixing with sticky rockrose.

Without knowing why, Pablo dragged the yellow tip of his finger up the boy's forearm, leaving a wet ochre stripe. The boy's grip closed around Pablo's wrist, and their eyes met. He pulled Pablo slowly, hand-over-hand, and Pablo let himself be hauled closer. Their feet and ankles sank into the wet ground as they began to explore one another. Nearby, the cool water kept running away.

That night, after the faint orange turned to silver cinders, the boy woke Pablo once more to say his people were leaving. "Give me your hand," he whispered. With the tip of his knife, the boy cut a curve from thumb to little finger on their palms. They pressed the oozing surfaces together, smearing the blood between them like warm paint.

"Brothers," they said. Then Pablo watched him go, listening as his departing footfalls grew softer until there was no trace.

When the sun rose, Pablo spread out the iron-rich clay as instructed, cut it into pieces with his knife, and ground it with the bottom of a tin cup. He stirred the fine powder with linseed oil and painted the hillsides. The picture was better than what he had done in Madrid, or Barcelona, or anywhere before. Pablo thought he might never leave here.

Then the rain came. Pajaresco had intended for them to depart that day, but they were forced to shelter beneath the limestone slab, watching the water drape down. There was no dry wood and no place to build a fire. They tried burning their easels. They shivered through the night.

After two days in which they ate or drank nothing besides handfuls of flour mixed with rainwater, Pajaresco said they must go. He feared the cave would flood while they slept. They fretted how the river already must have overrun the easiest paths to the farm.

On the journey back to Horta, Pablo began to feel his fever return. When they arrived at the tree where they'd tied up the dun-colored mule, they found it weak and dripping wet but still alive. The dog had chewed through the rope long ago.

Near nightfall, just as it stopped raining on Horta's outskirts, a carriage full of men wearing threadbare pantsuits and crumpled hats of straw and banana leaf crossed their path. Their arms and legs were wraith-thin, their eyes pale-yellow harvest moons. One rested his chin weakly on the guard of a saber, and Pablo recognized the returning soldiers. He knew then that Spain would lose to America.

For the rest of the summer in Horta, and then after it became cold again, Pablo dreamed of the stranger and the hidden place where he had taken him. In his sleep, the colors of the landscape kept changing, tones coming and going, even the boy shifted. But the pigment would always be buried there in the mud.

CHAPTER 6

I

Barcelona, March 1899

With a stroke of ink from the queen regent's pen, the war—the one Yanks called a "splendid little war"—was over, just as Spain was being invaded by its own defeated recruits.

Platoons of riflemen waded to Barcelona's shores from the maimed boats that carried them. Gaunt and gnarled, they languished from fever, dysentery, typhoid, and the mal air of tropic ports. Their wounds had slow-dried into stucco. The health board feared the whole population would be infected as more soldiers hobbled along La Rambla on peg legs, begging for alms, loose tobacco, and rum. But no one could stop this lost regiment from cursing the Crown it had defended, insulting the cowards who'd bought draft exemptions, or beating cheating wives.

The bawdy houses in the Barri Xinès were packed. Madams scribbled numbers on strips of paper, handing them out to the lines like delicatessen tickets. Riots nearly broke out when the women barred the doors.

The mothers who'd prayed to a panoply of saints for their sons to return now swore off the faith. In bars and at bullfights, over the dinner table, and kneeling in church pews, the city boiled with hate for the

country claiming it. Barcelona, always grumbling, was now fully apo-
plectic. Why ever should it be forced to belong to this deflated nation?

Just beyond living memory, Spain presided over a conquest greater
than Rome's or the caliph's. It sprawled, bronze and fit as a satyr, across
the globe. But the empire on which the sun never sets was gone now.
Cuba, Puerto Rico, Guam, the Philippines—the territories providing
the last of its foreign cash—vanished overnight. All became shiny new
baubles belonging to America. Having spent the New World's riches
like roulette winnings, Spain's coffers were empty. The military had
been crippled, and the nation's standing was in tatters. Barcelona and
the Catalans wanted out.

This was the melee Pablo returned to after nine months in Horta.
There, Pablo resided among old men spewing stories of when they had
taken up arms with militias against Spanish royal troops during the First
Carlist War. Pablo had formed his own opinions now, grown bolder.

But Don José vehemently opposed the arrogant ingratitude of the
separatists, just as he mocked the impressionists whom he said rejected
tradition because they weren't up to the task of maintaining it.

When Pablo uttered *Catalanisme* sentiments after coming home, it
made the two of them fight so sharply, it was impossible to say if Pablo
stormed out before he was banished or if it was the other way around.
Pablo had become too accustomed to no yoke, no family, no Don José
to mold his ideas by brute force. He wasn't prepared to adopt again
the humility of living at home, to feign being a son who only silently
wished his father dead.

With Pajaresco kept behind in Horta to tend next year's wine buds
and no other friends in the city, Pablo found refuge at the brothel where
he'd gotten to know a coat check girl. The subterrestrial feel of these
places was more satisfying than the sex, although Pablo couldn't deny
he desired that, too. On Pablo's first excursion with Pajaresco, he'd been
eager to lose his virginity—cast it off like wet shirtsleeves—and bask
in the overwhelming contentedness he imagined awaiting on the other

side of this rite. But the act disappointed him and wasn't what he'd been dreaming of since his lust was first awakened in the waters off La Coruña. He'd kept going back to Barri Xinès's brothels with Pajaresco, though, always hoping the next time he would find what was missing from the last.

Now, though, Pablo couldn't afford sex, and he was happy to hover instead around the coat check girl who called herself Rosita. Despite customers' petitions and her revealingly high hemlines and low necklines, she rendered no services besides, for a couple pesetas, safeguarding jackets and valuables. Sometimes she even held the customers' revolvers. Once, she told Pablo, she'd discovered in a satchel a crude device grafted onto a piece of leftover ordnance from the war. She'd prayed the man would finish his business before the bomb went off.

Pablo would sketch Rosita late into the night. She watched as he did so, and they chatted about longing to travel, the peacock boa she fancied, and how she'd give anything to attend the theater. She was pretty, more every time Pablo looked at her, with an explosion of crinkled brown hair and an intelligent smile. He'd never talked so freely or so long with a girl who was unrelated to him before. She was sophisticated and outgoing, unusually so, he thought. Maybe they both didn't belong here—not in this brothel, not in Spain. Pablo made sure his pictures were as beautiful as Rosita hoped to be. She told him he was not a bad flirt, even if he lacked experience, called him cute with his big eyes. And having worked the whole summer, he was no longer scrawny, either.

This is how Pablo came to live for a while in the closet that was the overflow of a coatroom. Rosita brought him fish-maw soup in the evenings and coffee or chocolate to start the day. But he reckoned the situation wouldn't last, one way or another. He not only had no money but also was running out of paint.

Guilt nibbled at Pablo when he was forced to peddle the pictures of Rosita on La Rambla, displaying the girl in ways that would have shocked her parents, who thought she was a concierge at an inn. But it was with those pesetas stuffed into his pocket that Pablo stumbled into Els Quatre Gats, a place Rosita said he ought to visit, him being an artist and all. She did warn that he wouldn't find any women to paint there. Kindred spirits, possibly.

Pablo had heard of this tavern before. It had been carving out a niche new to Barcelona and unique on all the Peninsula—bohemian chic, laced with political, philosophical, and stylistic ideals both homegrown and imported. Founded by Catalans who'd lived in Paris a decade earlier and drunk at Le Chat Noir, Els Gats had become Barcelona's indispensable watering hole for artists and intellectuals. It established a whole manner of talking, dressing, and carrying on. The *modernista* or *decadente* mode synonymous with this particular bar was becoming easy to spot on the streets now. Trappings included sharp-tailored clothes that plucked and chose flares from yesteryear, mismatching in the same outfit some exotic item from the Orient, maybe, or a pair of pointy French shoes.

Among the tavern's regulars was a not-too-subtle sympathy for anarchism. There was ardor for everything subversive, really, anything to fit this end of an age.

Wagner? All right.

De Sade? Definitely.

Verne? Has a way of making even illiterates give a good think.

Verlaine and Rimbaud? Divine!

Were there real anarchists at Els Gats? Like the one who'd stabbed the long-locked Empress Elisabeth of Austria through her corset with a machinist's file straight into the right chamber of her heart just that year? These new Goths who would sack not Rome but all the Industrial Age? Who'd made every theatergoer in Europe wonder if a bomb were not ticking beneath the seat? Perhaps. Or maybe only poseurs came to Els Gats. You never knew. It was part of the mystique.

~

Down a narrow lane Pablo found the ornate art nouveau town house where Els Gats resided on the first floor. Curving consoles and lushly decorative metalwork balconies emerged from the building's sides. A pointed archway leading into the tavern was festooned with a tangle of vine. He paced fitfully up and down the sidewalk for a few minutes before gathering the nerve to step through the grate door.

The air inside smelled of grease fires and was woven with rills of tobacco smoke. Bright ceramics from the south decorated the walls interspersed with portraits of self-possessed, raffish men, their expressions droll and side-glancing. Pablo nabbed a seat at an empty table near the high oak bar in the rear.

As Pablo's eyes roved the room, he noticed that some of the faces surrounding him matched those on the wall. In the center of the tavern, a dozen consorts had perched around a refectory table, their fists filled with wines, brandies, and *carajillos*—the latest rage, made from coffee and Cuban rum. These were the Barcelonan artists his father always disparaged and silently envied—beloved by critics and lauded in the magazines. Pablo began sketching the scene while listening to their rapid-fire banter about philosophy, poets, and assassins. They never stayed on any topic for long and savaged one another with as many barbs per measure as they could manage, almost like they were trying to notch points in a game.

Someone with cable-wire spectacles and the bloodless face of an Eastern mystic had been busy claiming God's own son was an anarchist and bellowed, "In Zeno's *Republic*, which historical Jesus would have read—"

"Right, so what?" interrupted a round-faced good-timer with a fixed grin. "We know the guy had an itch for whores and wine."

"Hush, Nonell, or you'll bring the wrath of God down upon our tapas," said a man picking at a plate of grilled octopus. Gold cuff links the shape of elephants gleamed at his wrists, and Pablo sensed he was more important than the rest. So, too, did Pablo see something familiar in him. Was it the nose, lengthy and fine? Or perhaps that haughtiness in his voice, like the screech of a door hinge. Whatever it might be, Pablo swore he knew this man.

"God's dead. Haven't you heard?" cried the one called Nonell.

"Hegel wrote that first, you know, long before Nietzsche," replied the Eastern mystic.

"What's he say killed Him?" asked a little man with deep-set eyes.

Nonell shouted back, "Probably came to Els Gats and had the shrimp!"

"Drown out the disease, why don't you?" barked the weather-beaten bartender dangling a long clay pipe from thick, puffed lips. "The more expensive the wine, the better it disinfects."

"That's right," Nonell said. "Touch of cholera hearties the constitution."

But then, at once, everyone remembered aloud the soldiers coming home from Cuba with ruined guts and agreed it was nothing to laugh at.

The man in cuff links changed the subject to tout how he'd just got back from France and was painting up a storm.

"Is everyone off to Paris?" said a curly-haired beanpole with crooked teeth and a look of introspection. "You'd think we were laying groundwork for an invasion."

"Say, there's an idea—secede from Spain and join the French!" Nonell said, thumping his empty goblet against the wood. "The food's all right, and how 'bout those fancy broads on the postcards? *Ma belle!*"

"Painters can live like royalty in Paris," said that important-sounding man who couldn't quite be placed and whose sleeves sported tiny pachyderms with real-ivory tusks. "In Barcelona, your pictures are sold for less than sin."

"A painter king? Oh, I likes it. How about you, Casas?" Nonell posed roguishly. "You already act like the big grandee of this tavern— hear ye, King of the Gats!"

The lot of them pounded the table and howled as Casas leaned back in satisfaction, exhaling a wheezy guffaw.

And Pablo finally remembered exactly who this character was.

Shortly after Pablo's family moved to Barcelona, Don José had staged a First Communion scene with Lola as model to shop around his boy-genius's technical prowess. He entered the painting into a show at the city's Palace of Fine Arts, and the family made a pilgrimage there. But Pablo was mortified when he overheard a gaggle of older artists mocking his work. One of them called it "very cute" and let out that repugnant guffaw Pablo would never forget. Casas was older now, with gray flecking his beard, but he still had that laugh.

Those men, Pablo learned then, composed Barcelona's so-called avant-garde, a phrase Don José said as if crinkling it up to throw in the trash. Their work was raw and gutty, their images painted in a simple style Pablo had never before seen. Such a far cry it was from anything in the Prado or what his teachers and father offered. And the artists were not dressed like academics or corpses. They were wing-collared playboys, dashing adventurers. The people mulling in the exposition hall that day were raving about works made by these real, live artists, who were now sitting in a circle at the table before him. He looked up to the very idea that painters like this could exist, while hating them for having dismissed him.

"And there is the Louvre. Don't forget about that," the mystic pointed out, returning to the inventory of Paris's attractions. "Pity we must go all the way to France for a museum, though. Why is it that Barcelona hasn't a single one?"

"What, hang the walls with paintings from the likes of you hacks?" a tipsy voice called out from somewhere outside the circle. Pablo turned and saw a young man sitting alone on the other side of the room. He was scribbling in a notebook.

The table booed.

"Do tell, young Carles," said Casas, "how a wit like yours might keep the gaslights burning by writing poetry and not selling it anywhere?"

The fellow, tall and spruce like a teenage Chopin, stood up, and said in English verse:

> And Wit, was his vain, frivolous pretence,
> Of pleasing others, at his own expense.
> For Wits are treated just like common Whores,
> First they're enjoy'd, and then kickt out of Doores.

The man named Carles doffed his hat and returned to his notebook as if he'd never bothered looking up.

"Poets do, after all, specialize in gibberish," Casas dismissed him to the crowd.

"And what's a blowhard specialize in?" Carles fired back, nonchalant. Furious laughter erupted until Casas scowled, his easy demeanor vanishing.

Pablo couldn't believe it. This upstart hardly looked a year older than him. Yet he'd challenged the elephant bull? And no doubt won!

After some grumbling, the banter resumed, and Pablo took his pocketful of coins to the bartender and ordered leg of roast chicken and a cup of coffee, which tasted like laundry water. When he returned to his chair, the wisecrack who'd hollered across the room was standing over Pablo's open sketchbook, staring at the picture Pablo had made of him battling Casas.

"Say, that ain't half bad," he said and offered his hand. "Carles Casagemas. I stopped adding 'extraordinaire.' It's too much, don't you think? What's you, an art student or something?"

"Art school dropout, actually."

"La Llotja?"

"For a while. Then the Royal Academy."

"Oooh, Madrid. Fancy stuff. Why'd you quit?"

"I told my family I was sick. That much is true. I was—scarlet fever. But I couldn't take all the nonsense, either. How many times can you hear instructors who paint like cows swear you're doing something the wrong way when you're doing it right?"

"Tell me about it. Cows. That's probably being kind."

"It was an education, just not the one it was meant to be. And you, why are you stranded by yourself instead of sitting with the bunch?"

"What, them? Oh, they were going on about nihilism one day, and I stopped caring."

Pablo feigned understanding.

"Anyway, those guys are idiots. I mean, I must love 'em—I keep coming here, right? But they're fucking idiots."

"They dress nice."

"Yeah, I guess. In fairness, a few are all right. Like Pere, the glum fellow behind the bar. You met him yet?" Carles fired a wink to the pipe-smoking man wearing a Brittany sweater before turning back toward Pablo and noticing his drab dish of meat smeared with gravy. "Know the first thing you did wrong?" Carles asked.

Pablo looked at him blankly.

"Don't ever order the food here. It's rubbish." He pointed to the plate. "I bet you think that's chicken?"

"That's what the menu led me to believe."

"Well, I tell you, I was kicking around at the wharf one day, when all the sudden, I spotted Pere in a rowboat casting about, tossing bread crusts into the water, waiting to catch the seagulls with a net!"

Pablo felt the corners of his lips plunge as he nearly gagged.

"I know! If you're desperate, you might survive the omelet. But I wouldn't risk it. What's that you're drinking? Coffee? You from some kind of religious order?"

"It's cheap."

"Now this is the sort of injustice I can't stand," said Carles. "I've had seven—no, eight?—beers and a liter of cava already. And you've had but one cup of that piss Els Gats calls coffee."

"It tastes like soap."

"Hey, that's a good sign. Pere never used to wash the dishes before. Isn't that right, ol' man?" Carles tapped his beer glass with a fingernail, and Pere noticed him and smirked. The bartender hauled over two great big steins overflowing with Estrella Damm to Pablo's table. "One for my Cervantes; one for the little Goya he found," he said. Carles sat down across from Pablo.

While chatting, Carles mentioned something in passing about his father being a diplomat. Pablo had deduced he came from a well-to-do family, given his dress and erudition. As an aspiring poet, it seemed he was the black sheep. From Pere's comment, though, Pablo figured Carles must be pretty talented at least. He sure talked smart—and fast, wasting no time filling Pablo in about Els Gats.

"See that jackass over there?" Carles said, aiming a finger at Casas. "Thinks he's hot shit. Is, I suppose. All depends on who you ask."

"Yes, we've had a run-in before," Pablo replied. "Doubt he remembers."

"What? Owe you money? I heard he owes half the city money. Pere was born broke, and running this bar is making him poorer. But Casas squanders more than most will ever know."

"It's not like that."

"Every critic in the city licks Casas's balls. Had an exhibition at some gallery in Paris almost ten years ago. When he came back to Barcelona, they anointed him God."

"I think he's an ass."

"Good. You're learning quick. Now, that tall guy, with the curly hair and mangled chompers? That's Pichot. He's all right. Smart as fuck. Went to Paris but somehow managed to not come back arrogant. Damn good painter, too. Same with Nonell, the one who'll still be grinning at his own funeral. Scratch that. Nonell is sort of an asshole, on second thought. Paints miserable stuff, too. Not miserable paintings. I mean paintings of miserable things—sick, dying, degenerates, cretins. While I'm feeling generous, don't get me wrong about Casas. He can paint. But if you ask me, it's nothing special. All he's famous for is style. Style is everything with him—no substance at all."

Pablo studied each face carefully.

"And if you can't decide if Manolo is a crackpot or a hustler, either way you'll be right," Carles kept on, describing the small man with sunken eyes. "I already told you about Pere. Real heart and soul of the joint. Been all over the world. Paris, yeah, but also Mexico, Chicago, maybe even the Far East." His voice bubbled with admiration. "Oh yeah, the scary guy with specs is Miquel Utrillo. Once a week he puts on performances—hosts them. Maniac piano music, Chinese puppet shows, weird choreography, poetry readings, shadow plays, that kind of arty thing. Some's good. Rest is boring as shit. I come and watch, though. What else have I got to do, right?"

Carles and Pablo—mostly Carles—went on and on that night till last call. After two weeks of being gone, Pablo walked back to his parents' apartment in the small, silent hours, tiptoeing inside. Somehow, he no longer needed to flee his stifling home life in search of a precious breath of air; he'd found one. In the morning, his mother's intercession permitted him to remain and helped patch up things between Pablo and Don José.

~

As Carles predicted, Els Gats became Pablo's regular escape. He would sit at the bar, sketching, observing the two distinct types of patrons sharing the space.

First, there were the older, established artists and intellectuals—the known names who swirled snifters and smoked cigars and pipes, their snuffboxes laid before them on the big table like blazoned heraldry. They used the coarse language of the wage slaves from the political theory books they read, but Pablo never saw dirt on their shoes. Always high-shine. Glistening.

Then there were the misfits—the young fellows who found spots in twos or threes on the room's margins. Most were in their teens, like Pablo. No one knew their names. These ones drank beer, not brandy, and smoked cigarettes—occasionally gold-tipped, in gross imitation of Oscar Wilde. They talked foreign writers, class struggle, and art, but just as much recounted exploits with girls, defacement of property, petty crime, and other hijinks. A few were real guttersnipes.

Carles didn't fit into either camp. He was friendly—and equally unfriendly—with both. In age, he straddled the sets, being just on the cusp of twenty. And he was a mercurial sort. Most often he'd enter the tavern and find a table to sit at alone, writing verse in his leather-bound journal, drinking alcohol in quantities hardly tolerated by those twice his weight. It was a public performance of solitude, Pablo thought. By the end of Carles's evenings, though, he'd always become a different man, gregarious and hurling clever insults, mostly at Casas's band.

Pablo's contempt for Casas quickly grew. Carles had gotten him right—a stylist, not an artist. His works were attractive, but nothing an average student at La Llotja, if coached, couldn't produce. Yet he had the ego of an Olympian, engorged by so much flattering press and the sycophants who picked up his tab. While Pablo did feel affinity for the modernistas—so different than the starchy classicists his father revered—he also could see how he'd inherited no small dose of Don José's taste and temperament, skeptical as he was that these new aesthetics gave no-talent imposters like Casas too much leeway.

Each time Pablo returned to Els Gats, he looked forward to conversing with Carles, but instead the poet acted like a stranger to him, as if that first night had never happened. Was this Carles when he's merely drunk, as opposed to very drunk? Had he simply decided Pablo was a bore? Or, somehow, was Carles testing out Pablo's fitness as a comrade? He felt out of place and alone at Els Gats, as he had at every school ever attended. And yet, for once, Pablo wanted to belong. He sat there by himself one evening after another, wearing the floppy hat Pajaresco gave him in Horta, drinking the awful coffee or sometimes a beer, wondering how he might make Carles notice him again.

~

One Friday night, Pablo arrived at Els Gats to find a makeshift stage set up at the back of the tavern. All the windows were blacked out, and a sheet of pale cambric veiled the rear wall. The tables were arranged in rows with scores of visitors huddled in the chairs. Pablo grabbed the last open seat in front and settled in.

The gaslights dimmed. The room turned black. A lantern illuminated the cloth, and it glowed hazy yellow, like a dust-laden sunset. The crouched puppeteers were nearly invisible as they manipulated sugar-paper cutouts mounted to doll rods. The shapes traveled across the scrim, dark horsemen undulating as a phonograph played Wagner's *Twilight of the Gods*. At first, the effect was mesmerizing, helped along by the strong anise-flavored spirit Pere was handing out. Pablo imagined that it was almost like being at one of the shadow-puppet plays at Paris's famed Le Chat Noir.

But, after a time, the spectacle tired. There was no narrative. The loud music prevented anyone from talking. Yet it seemed rude to leave. Pablo tightened his jaw to contain a yawn. His thoughts wandered. He remembered how in Málaga, he'd entertained Conchita by bringing embroidery scissors to a newspaper's edge. Even then, his work had more artistry than this show, more life and imagination than these arrogant clowns and what they called avant-garde.

Pablo's muscles felt loose, the drink working like ether.

From his coat pocket, Pablo removed a tobacco pouch he'd begun carrying. He was determined to become a diehard smoker. Pablo rolled a squat cigarette and struck a match. But since he wasn't used to punishing his lungs, he coughed. It got worse, drier and drier, louder and louder. He doubled over and grasped the table.

The audience shushed him.

When Pablo unclenched his eyes, his still-lit cigarette had nearly rolled onto the paper menu. He snatched it away. Christ, he'd almost started a blaze—what a way to make an impression, burning the place down. Pablo drained his glass, willing his embarrassment to fade.

Pere handed Pablo another. After a deep drink of it, he reasoned, why the hell not? He studied the shapes of the puppets galloping across the backdrop, and got to work, furtively and furiously.

～

Just as in the Liceu, with the music's crescendo came a surprise. In the upper corner of the screen, a terrifying creature appeared before the audience, gliding above the horses with a heraldic eagle's sinister-facing sharp bill peering above spread wings—and the gigantic bust of a nightclub dancer.

Murmurs erupted across the room as the audience awakened, and then the crowd grew noisier. Amid an aura of light emanating from the front row was Pablo, holding a menu—perfectly formed into this bird-woman's shape that he'd projected—in front of an ashtray filled with a burning box of matches.

There was applause.

"*Venga!*" yelled someone in the back, bringing his palm down hard on the tabletop. It was Carles, in a high, starched collar.

Pablo made the Valkyrie swoop at the horsemen, burying the riders' heads in its shadowy bosom. Laughter broke out, and his eyes met

Carles's. He flashed a smile at Pablo and clacked a fork against the table, sounding like the clattering of castanets. *"Así se baila!"*

A pair of teenagers who'd been brooding at the room's edge stomped out the rhythm. Carles shouted and trilled like a flamenco caller swept up in song and enticed the winged woman to shimmy and shake on the screen. Through Pablo surged a joy he'd not felt since he was a boy in Málaga when his mother, aunts, Lola, and Conchita swooned over his ingenious creations.

One of the hangers-on from Casas's clique, drunk since afternoon, leapt onto a table to dance. The pounding, laughing, whelping, and banging of glasses drowned out poor Wagner.

"Disgraceful," Pablo saw Casas mouth.

The impromptu dancer and Carles joined Pablo in front to take a bow. The cheering was only overcome when a decrepit man roared at the top of his asthmatic lungs the banned Catalanisme anthem, and the motley crowd belted it out, defying the streets to silence them.

Young and old rapped Pablo on the shoulders. "Where did you get the idea?" They asked. *"Bravissimo!"*

Pablo overheard Casas ordering Pere to call the cops. The bartender reminded him the tavern was teeming with anarchists and rascals. They'd lock up half his customers, he said. "Why, Carles was nearly arrested last year when he blindsided a police officer abusing a youth with a blackjack during a street protest—gave 'im a solid hook," Pere recounted. "Besides, I thought those little shits were pretty funny."

～

Pablo didn't see Carles again at Els Gats for days, until one evening he spotted a skinny figure leaning against the plaster wall outside the archway, a cigarette blooming in his hand. The young man started off and tilted his head for Pablo to follow.

Forty-five minutes later, they were padding together up the beach, still having not exchanged a word. The air smelled of kelp and then burnt rubber. The sun was setting, a fog rolling in as if a blanket were being laid over the churning sea. In the distance, Pablo noticed bituminous streaks of cloud slicing up the magenta sky. As they walked north, he could see these trails came from smokestacks. Carles routed them away from the water, and they climbed a knoll strewn with discarded mussel shells. Past a cluster of date palms stood a row of depressing apartment buildings belonging to the working poor who resided in this industrial zone and filled the factories during the day. Carles turned northward again, and Pablo was surprised to be confronted by a pair of obelisks flanking tall iron gates. Beyond them was a cemetery.

"If you see dogs, don't run," Carles said, throwing his coat over the sharp points and then shinnying to the top just as night was falling. Pablo followed behind him, jumping down into the fog creeping beyond the fence.

They navigated the labyrinthine graveyard by matchlight. Instead of plots, the dead rested in chambers along honeycomb-like aisles two dozen feet high. Families erected marble statues nearby rather than use hedge markers. The very wealthiest residents had private mausoleums done up like pharaohs' lairs. In front of one of these, Carles stopped.

"Who's here?" Pablo asked.

"I had a sister," Carles said. The smell of wet leaves and decaying duff hovered at their noses.

This news conjured in Pablo's brain the image of Conchita, a perfect lithograph. He wanted to tell Carles he knew how it felt, to recount everything. And he had questions, so many questions. To start, did Catalans practice the same custom of dressing the sick in blue? But he couldn't bring himself to confess his guilt or probe Carles, so he simply said, "I'm sorry."

"No. I'm the one who should be apologetic," Carles lamented, pausing as if he also had more to say. "A fever took her, when she was younger than I am today," he explained. "She was a new wife, new mother. I was a boy. I don't even remember what my own sister looked like. Her face is a blur, except sometimes I can see a pair of heart-shaped lips. Or maybe I've imagined that, too."

Was Carles also consumed by remorse for his sister's death? Pablo felt so drawn to him now, as if brought together by fate.

"Why did you take me here?"

"I didn't want to be alone."

"But how come you came?"

"To ask forgiveness," Carles said.

"For what?"

"I've dishonored her, I'm afraid. But how am I to be blamed when love cannot be bridled? And mercy what I endure," Carles replied, adding a series of stanzas in French.

Pablo did not speak the language, and his friend was becoming too cryptic. He sighed in frustration.

"A poem by the late Charles Baudelaire," Carles revealed.

"About what?"

"A guy who walks into a bar."

"You must be joking."

"The contrary," said Carles, his face newly pained.

Pablo was torn between wanting to know more and desiring to return to that interlude of levity a moment ago when he thought Carles was kidding. "What's it like, this bar?"

"Fabulous in every way. All the people are dressed lavishly. Choice cigars, sublime liqueurs, roulette where you always win."

Pablo tried to lighten the mood again. "Better chow than Els Gats?"

"Best."

"Where's this?"

"Paris," Carles said.

"Figures," Pablo said. "How'd he find such a place, then?"

"Devil brought him, of course. The two of them drink awhile, make chitchat, and gamble. Before long, Scratch wins the man's soul."

"There's no suspense in that."

"Well, turns out Satan's an all right fellow. Not an asshole, you know? He's at peace, see, because he doesn't have to work anymore. Each aspect of progress—science, philosophy, rhetoric, art—he's insinuated himself in them. Modernity does his mischief now. In fact, he's feeling so generous that even though he's bagged another soul, the devil decides to give the bastard whatever he wants—fame, fortune, women. Plus, he'll throw in one more thing, the grandest gift of 'em all."

"What's that?"

"He says he can rid the man of ennui."

Pablo furrowed his brow. He'd only heard the word before uttered in contempt by Don José.

"You know, that touch of sadness that never leaves you, won't let you be free? Makes you always feel a little bit like . . ." Carles went silent again. He brought a match to the cigarette in his mouth. "So the devil says to Charlie he'd be willing to give him the possibility—think of that, just the possibility!" Carles's wild yell echoed among the graves. "It's the chance to end once and for all this bizarre affliction, the source of misery."

Pablo looked at his new friend and felt in his diaphragm like he'd swallowed a bumblebee. "That's what's got you, isn't it?"

The match was extinguished with a sudden breath in the dark air; Pablo knew it was because Carles didn't want him to see his eyes. "Every goddamned moment, long as I can remember," he said. "I keep hoping there's someone who can make it disappear. But every time I think I've found her, she turns me away. My poetry, that's my only balm."

Pablo desired to unravel Carles, wanted to know what tormented him. Was there anything he could do to relieve his suffering, this ennui? And then, Pablo thought, might Carles understand his own burden? Was their sadness and guilt the same?

They left the graveyard and trekked back to Pablo's street. He started to say that there was a bottle of Jerez in his father's cabinet that they could drink from. But before the words came out, Carles had vanished.

~

By autumn, Don José was busily plotting Pablo's next painting, a production of grand scale, maturity, and poignancy, something to electrify every last critic and judge—a masterpiece to deliver his son bona fide prestige. It should be an oil in somber tones of a priest administering the final Eucharist to a dying woman, on the largest canvas Pablo'd ever painted. Everyone would see it was only suitable for a museum or a very wealthy patron's wall. He'd already arranged for Angel Soto, the teenage son of a family friend, to model as the novice priest. He'd even fed a beggar to pose as the old woman and finagled for Pablo to gain use of the storeroom in a garment factory to accommodate the oversized canvas.

Pablo hated everything about this idea. But so long as he lived under Don José's roof, he was forced to relent.

For many weeks during that fall, Pablo labored over the damn thing, with his father regularly checking in. Just as he was pulling on his smock one morning, the doorbell rang at his parents' apartment. It was Carles, the brim of a tweed cap pulled jauntily over one eye. He had the come-out-and-play expression of a six-year-old. Pablo had barely seen Carles in a month. He'd missed him. This was the perfect excuse to escape for the afternoon.

The two shuffled outside onto the bustling street. It was an unseasonably warm day, and traces of rosemary roamed the air. They smiled as they walked and talked and flung spent cigarettes into the wind. Carles jabbed a rolled-up art magazine into Pablo's stomach and filled him in on the latest from Els Gats, which Pablo hadn't been to since he'd started the dreaded painting. Casas's one-man exposition at the

Sala Parés, Barcelona's most coveted gallery, had gone swimmingly and gotten rave reviews, apparently. "Even the fucking bishop came," Carles said. The tavern was changing, he asserted. "Bunch of fakes. No clue about anything. I tell you, I don't even know if I'll go back."

They reached a dilapidated, soot-stained building on Carrer de la Riera de Sant Joan, in between the noisy market and cathedral. "There's something I want to show you," Carles said, opening the gate and leading Pablo up an uneven stairway. At the last landing, he kicked open a flimsy door and light flooded into the new studio he'd found.

"In Andalusia, this is big enough to sleep a family of six," Pablo said, "plus pigeons."

"Want to share it with me?"

"I have a little spot, Carles. Above the corset-makers."

"Sure you do. But that's for totally different work, paintings for your father. Don't get me wrong. I like tradition. I'm very traditional, really. But here, you can paint in the new styles—Lautrec, Mucha, all that's the rage in Paris. You'll be brilliant at it! And Don José won't be breathing down your neck, telling you it's all degenerate, wishy-washy stuff."

Their voices bounced around the high-ceilinged loft's bare walls. There was no furniture save for a rickety table, a few folding chairs, and a davenport made of satinwood. A single unframed, finished canvas was leaned in the corner, bearing the image of a very young woman in a boatneck black evening gown, her extended gloves shielding china-cup arms. Her eyes were closed, as if she were daydreaming. On the table, Pablo found a charcoal-and-pastel study for the picture.

"Carles, you didn't tell me you paint. You're a poet. And an artist, too?"

"Your words, not mine. I daub for fun. You know, when verse and getting varnished are too much bother."

"It's good," Pablo told him. "You ever displayed anywhere before?"

"Yes, right here. You sound like you'd buy it. Tell ya what, how about I rent it to you? Come view it every day while you work, and when you're done, pay me back with something you make. Whatever you want. I don't care. I know it'll be phenomenal," Carles said. "Just keep me company."

Pablo's friend couldn't possibly know what this offer meant—to not have to go home to his parents' or to that unventilated storeroom. He must find some other way to compensate him.

"You want to see something else?" Carles asked.

"Have you got another studio hiding?"

"No, but it's a thing of real beauty," Carles said. He lifted the davenport's hinged top and carefully removed a box of solid Gabon ebony with opal inlay and purple velvet lining. Inside was a pistol, just small enough to fit into a vest pocket, with an ivory grip and finely engraved silver barrels.

"Belonged to a Swedish esquire," Carles said, explaining his father got it as a gift when assigned to the diplomatic legation in Stockholm. "He doesn't even know it's gone."

Pablo couldn't deny how pretty the object was or how much it reminded him of the stories set in the Old West that he'd read. In them, boastful cardsharps and ladies' men always kept a spare derringer tucked away. And yet he was apprehensive, knowing how bloody were these tales.

"Careful, friend," Pablo warned. "A gun's like a penis. You never know what somebody might do with one, especially when they're drunk or in love."

II

Pablo was finishing the last touches on a braid of garland when he heard the studio's door handle turn behind him.

"What in Christ's name have you done?" Carles said as he stepped inside.

While Pablo's friend had been gone for the holidays in Sitges, where Carles's mother's family was from, he'd transformed every inch of the loft into a palace scene befitting a sultan: walls painted over with marble columns and scrolls, floors bearing flattened furniture laden with tropical fruits, a medieval harp glistering in the corner where it was superimposed, exotic flowers blooming everywhere, and gold ducats piled into two-dimensional heaps. He even stocked mock bookshelves with Cervantes to Shikibu, de Castro to Thoreau.

"You haven't read these, Pablo, have you? You couldn't have known!"

"Good guesses."

"I'd say, my friend. I'd say."

The only thing Pablo hadn't painted over was the davenport, which looked expensive.

"How in hell did you do this? I said you could repay me with *a* painting—not painting the whole damn studio! It's so marvelous!"

"I wanted to give us all we deserve," Pablo said, nodding toward the tantalizing harem posing on a far wall with fistfuls of grapes.

"Say, I think I've seen that redhead somewhere," Carles said coyly.

"Then tonight, we'll look for her," Pablo proclaimed, letting his palette and brush fall by his feet, "or her sister anyway—in Barri Xinès."

But he saw his words had wiped Carles's face blank. "I can't, Pablo. Please don't ask me to go, not tonight. I've suffered a long train ride. I really won't be any good."

"Nonsense," Pablo said, as he marched Carles down the stairs. "We've got something very important to discuss."

Later, in the brothel's salon, Pablo discovered that Carles truly had been sapped, though. The girls paraded by in lace undergarments, advertising their *especialidades de amor*. But Carles was in a daze. Pablo left him on a ragged velveteen sofa with a luscious blonde. When he returned, Carles was asleep, the woman gone.

"Wake up." Pablo shook Carles. "How much have you had to drink?"

"Not enough," he said drowsily, his eyes still closed. "Glass of Burgundy. A mild digestif."

"Carles, there's a poster contest for the new year—the new century, that is. I read about it in the magazine you gave me. Don't you even want to hear?" Pablo slapped his cheeks to rouse him, and Carles's eyes opened for a moment, but his pupils looked like the heads of nails.

"Take me home, Pablo."

"Are you sure you're OK?"

"Yes. Please, I can't stand it here. These places depress me."

Pablo threw Carles's arm around his shoulder and helped him do a scissors step back to the loft. Soon as they were inside, Carles folded onto the floor. Pablo lay down beside him, draping an unstretched canvas over them for warmth.

In the middle of the night, Pablo turned onto his stomach and roused in discomfort. He felt around beneath him and removed an object, smooth and cold. By the rays of the moon coming through the skylight, he could see in his hand a small amber bottle. It must have fallen from Carles's pocket. Pablo unscrewed the stopper. It smelled of strong vapors and cinnamon. He placed it on the davenport so neither of them would roll over again and break it.

In the morning, Pablo awoke to an empty studio. Carles was nowhere to be found.

He filled his hands with water from the sink and washed himself, pressing each nostril shut with a knuckle as he blew through the other. He glanced over at the davenport: the amber bottle had disappeared with Carles. Pablo curled up the canvas and pulled on his shoes, thinking to himself that poetry was hardly Carles's only balm.

∼

By the time Pablo arrived, past noon, Els Gats was already abuzz. A boyish, pretty-lipped young man he'd seen before accosted him.

"What mischief have you planned for us?"

"Oh, the shadow puppets. That was nothing. Too much *anís* that night."

"Nothing?" said the kid with spectacles. "Only the highlight of my life, next to getting accepted into medical school, which I'm not proud of. Just that I dread the other option my father gave me—accounting. No, it actually tops that. You know, we've all been talking about you. Not only because you saved us from certain death by boredom. I heard what you did with Carles's studio. Transformed that dumpy loft into an oriental idyll, like water into wine."

"Let's not get carried away," Pablo said. He looked past the young man and around the tavern but didn't see Carles.

"How did you learn to paint like that?"

"Well, when I was small, my mother told me to draw a blind rooster searching for the start of day. The rest is history, I guess."

"I have no clue what you're saying. But call me Cinto. Did you know that is how they make goldfinches sing better, poke out their eyes? It's physiological. When the brain is no longer burdened with sight, it reallots itself for other tasks."

"You're a medical student?"

"Third year. I give myself a fifty percent chance of survival."

Pablo said he'd attended too many drawing classes where instructors claim to be anatomy experts. "Names for everything. Lateral, medial . . ."

"Proximal and distal! That's pretty good. Don't forget the posterior."

"That's the one thing I did pay attention to," Pablo assured him.

"It's amazing, female anatomy," Cinto said. "Almost like a woman has an invisible brush, using it to paint a canvas inside her, bringing it to life. You and I will never do that."

"Placenta the greatest palette?"

"You could say."

Pablo, worrying where Carles might have gone and being distracted, hastened to change the conversation to the poster competition.

"I figured that's why you might have come," Cinto said. "Where's your entry?"

"Haven't done one yet. Do you know who's the judge?"

"Come on, Pablo. You can't guess?"

"Why am I even surprised," Pablo groaned, realizing at once there was no way he could win.

"In the land of the blind, the one-eyed man is king," said Cinto.

"Yeah, and someone should poke out Casas's other eye," Pablo said. "What made him so goddamned precious anyway?"

"His chest is full of confidence because everyone in Paris knows his name. If you matter in Paris, you matter everywhere."

Paris was all the young men at Els Gats talked about now, like it was the Promised Land. Puccini's *La Bohème* had swept across Europe, leaving behind a wake of romantics. Carles had taken Pablo to see it at the Liceu. The girls in the audience swooned for Rodolfo. The poet's struggle for transcendence captivated Carles, too. Pablo's only observation was that Marcello, the opera's painter, had bungled the canvas on stage. "Hideous," he'd said. "Better to quit and paint gutters."

But Pablo was as fascinated by Paris as the rest, and Cinto's diagnosis confirmed what he'd already concluded—Paris was the only place to become the artist he wanted to be.

"Listen, I've got a date with an anatomy diagram," Cinto said, excusing himself but inviting Pablo to his parents' apartment anytime. "They're usually away. And bring Carles with you."

Pablo took a seat at the bar after Cinto left. Pere was smoking his clay pipe and polishing stemware, which, even when he was done, looked like it had been washed with wheel grease.

"Seen you sketching here. Makes me think of someone I knew once," Pere said gruffly, without looking from the tulip-shaped *copita* in his hand.

The man had never spoken to Pablo before, and he didn't know how to respond.

"Have you heard of Lautrec?" Pere asked, looking up.

"Of course," Pablo replied.

"A funny little man. Hear his ways are catching up with him. Cupid's plague," Pere said in his low voice. "Should you ever make it to Paris, though, you must eat at Lautrec's house. I know what they say about my cooking. It's poppycock, I tell you. But Henri is not like me. Pours his soul into the pot. Always, with everything. That's his way. Barely five feet. Bones brittle as marzipan. Looks like his bottom half was driven over by a horse carriage. But I've seen him wrestle a brute to within an inch of his life. Paints, prints, draws, and assembles glass every conceivable hour."

Pere told of how Lautrec was a terrible drunk, "but in such a wonderful way. Reminds me of Carles in that." He glanced away before returning his gaze to Pablo. "Together, you two have got something—talent, soul. Most people, this is what they lack, even if they've found fame. Now it's a matter of desire. I don't mean longing for success. Everyone wants that. I'm talking about climbing down and surveying the depths of what it is to be mortal. That's the ticket to the divine." As the weathered man said this, he extended his yellowed thumb and forefinger in front of Pablo's eye and rocked them back and forth as if tuning a dial, a gesture that asked Pablo if he understood.

From reproductions in magazines, Pablo had noticed the skill of Lautrec's brushwork, which was superior in his estimation to Renoir and Monet. And he saw the expression and tenderness the painter gave to the prostitutes and every other inhabitant of the Paris demimonde—how he breathed into them life.

Pere stretched to place the glass he had been polishing onto a high shelf but then turned around, as if he weren't quite done with the moment. "Do you really want to know something?" he asked.

Pablo nodded.

"Then you will."

~

When Pablo returned to the studio, he found on the floor a pearly-papered invitation to the Three Kings Ball later that night. Carles must have left it for him, not understanding Pablo's family was much humbler than that of a diplomat—the only formal wear he owned was from his Catholic confirmation years ago. Pablo ran to his parents' and dredged up a box stuffed with costumes Don José had procured over the years for painting different scenes, mostly religious. It might have been a long shot, but when the guard at the chancery that night saw the friar's frock, he waved the holy man inside. Pablo blessed him.

This was the grandest *feria* in the most opulent ballroom Pablo had ever laid eyes on, with furniture encrusted with geometric patterns of iridescent abalone shell, brilliant chandeliers, and edgeless art nouveau motifs wreathing easily through the baroque. Revelers mingled in the corridors and dipped crispy *neules* into cava, their teeth gleaming beneath masks.

From the courtyard, where a commedia dell'arte troupe was doing acrobatics and pantomiming, he spotted Carles up in a balcony, all alone, his hands covering his face. Pablo quickly pushed upstairs.

"She's gone," his friend stammered when Pablo got to him. "Announced to be married."

The bleary poet reached into his vest pocket and retrieved the amber bottle, pouring a few drops onto his tongue.

Never had Pablo witnessed anyone so shattered since his father in La Coruña the morning after Conchita died. "Where are your parents?" he asked.

"What do I want them for? I should have sailed to Havana," Carles bayed, dribbling on about how he was in the naval academy before his family withdrew him when war against America appeared on the horizon. "But you can't get shot at by the nation your father serves, right? A diplomatic incident is what that's called. Now she's to wed some wretched military officer instead of her uncle, the vagabond."

"You're related?" Pablo said, seeing the pupils of Carles's eyes were nailheads again.

"Yes, you fool. You viewed her mother's grave—my sister's—remember? It's sickening—how my deranged desire has smeared the memory of her! So you know now what everyone else can plainly see. That there's always been something amiss about me, a piece out of place," Carles moaned. "I'm a moon ejected from its orbit, wandering the solar system. Who can blame me for trying to cling to someone so precious who was also so near?"

Pablo began, "You're a magnificent poet, and any number of women would . . ." But Carles was already slumped against the balustrade, his face blue veined, his chest barely moving. "Carles, what the fuck have you done?"

Pablo hoisted Carles over his shoulders and raced three blocks away to the only place he could think of for help. When Cinto responded to the pounding on the door to his parents' apartment, Pablo handed him the amber bottle. The medical student rushed Carles to the sofa and returned with a jar of charcoal powder, water, and two sugar cubes. He mixed them into a black, swirling cloud.

"Hold his nose," Cinto told Pablo before pouring the concoction down Carles's throat. He coughed the fluid up, and they dosed him with more.

"You're drowning me," Carles warbled.

Pablo thought it ironic how much his friend was fighting back; a moment ago, he'd seemed intent on dying.

Finally, his breathing returned to normal. Carles remained in a stupor, though. They walked him around the drawing room in circles for hours.

"What's that stuff in the amber vial?" Pablo asked.

"Laudanum. We give it for everything from consumption to menstrual colic," Cinto explained. "People find out they enjoy it, though. In small quantities, it's no worse than a few cordials. But Carles ingested enough to tranquilize a moose."

$\sim$

Cinto kept Carles stashed away there, since his parents were out of town, as Pablo sat watch. Carles roused the following afternoon, and Pablo gave him water. The day after that, he asked for something to read, and Pablo retrieved from the studio the book he'd seen him working his way through, a red leather one thick as a slice of layer cake—*Anna Karenina*. He also grabbed oil painting paper and supplies. Pablo was mixing his colors beside where Carles lay on the sofa with the book in his hands when he finally asked, "What's it about?"

"Passion, I suppose," said Carles, looking up from the heavy volume. "And death. Or jealousy. The peasants, too. Also, religion. And even art."

"Well, which is it?"

"All of them. It's a long work."

"Oh yeah? And what's Anna got to say about art?"

"She's quite fond of it, for sure—as is her lover. Although, the author seems to take a rather skeptical view."

"How can an artist not like art?"

"Interesting. You mean to say because Tolstoy is someone who makes art, he should have affinity for his own lot, right? But don't you see a sort of parallel in how so many humans—responsible, after all, for begetting each successive generation—seem to act as if they hate humanity itself?" Carles let his reply linger for a moment before gluing his eyes again to the page. Pablo was still silently mulling the question when, a while later, Carles added, "What a shame—she's just died."

"Anna?"

"Yes. Suicide."

"At the end?"

"Not quite."

"How can that be? It's her story."

"Actually, this is many people's story, or rather one story told from multiple perspectives, seen through different eyes, as it were. That's one of a novel's main pleasures—briefly you get to inhabit the vantage of the divine."

"You mean each and every view at once? Well, that's certainly something you can't do in painting," Pablo said with finality, adding detail to the picture he was working on of three dancers flittering by a french window.

"How can you say?" asked Carles. "Ever tried unfixing the perspective in your work, making impressions seen from a variety of points?

Who knows? It might end up being more realistic in the end—or more egalitarian, anyway."

"An image painted from all different angles? Impossible."

"Think about it. In a novel, the author doesn't even have to abide by laws of time. Might someone so free up painting someday as to compose pictures where the present, past, and premonitions are all shown at once? Just the way we experience real life? Or, maybe you're right—it is a bit far-fetched."

"Guess we'll never know," Pablo said, having difficulty following Carles's fanciful flight. "You look better at least. All done vomiting guts and glory?"

Carles laughed a little. "Yes, and you know what? I believe I've fallen out of love with my dear niece, besides a typical filial affection. I even offer benedictions to the bride and groom."

"Good of you," Pablo said cautiously. "Perhaps I ought to try reading one of these big, fat books. Seems to work wonders."

"I'd rather you kept painting."

~

In the days after, not only did Carles cease pining for his niece, his habit with the amber bottle made a retreat, too. Pablo and Carles, meanwhile, became closer than ever. There were few absences between them now. People joked they were two churros stuck together. Evenings, one painted and the other wrote by the light of a hurricane lamp fueled with kerosene pilfered from the chancery. And they talked and talked. They even started to sound the same. And yet, together at the studio, in the crisp of the night, they each felt more fully, distinctly themselves.

They found novel ways to entertain one another, too.

Since Barcelona's critics fawned in particular over Casas's likenesses of the city's moneyed elites, done in bold black lines on top of soft watercolor, Pablo decided to poke fun by making similar portraits with inexpensive Conté crayons and a wash of diluted palette scrapings. Except Pablo drew the scrappy young people who came to Els Gats: aspiring artists and artistes, poets and playboys, ragamuffins and radicals, bookworms and bandits, drifters and decadente dandies. The works soon filled up the loft, more than a hundred of them piled on easels and stacked on the floor.

"The studio looks like the lair of a spree murderer," Carles said.

In fact, though, when Pablo wasn't jesting, he did feel a twinge of patricidal guilt. For the past year, he'd been signing his work only with his mother's Italianesque name, Picasso, dropping his father's Ruiz, which sounded too common, like the hiss of one of the neighborhood dogs. Each time, he did so with contempt for Don José. Then he would stare afterward at the signature, seized by guilt, anxiety, and nostalgia. He'd not been home now for a month. Mostly, he did not miss it, but sometimes, he felt abrupt urges to eat supper at his mother's table, which was laden with the sultry flavors of *Andalucía*, the orange eddies of fat stirring with ñora peppers, blood sausage, saffron, and laurel. To look at his father once more, no matter how he sometimes hated the man.

After word got out about the portraits cluttering the studio, Carles cracked one night that Pablo ought to stage the most scandalous show Barcelona had ever seen. Then, they decided that maybe this was a brilliant idea. One February morning, everyone woke at dawn and met in front of the tavern. Pere let them in, and they set to work using carpet tacks to hang Pablo's portraits in every corner of Els Gats.

The pictures had soul, Pere proclaimed. Even Utrillo, master of the puppets, couldn't argue. Carles knew acquaintances who were cub reporters at the newspapers, and he managed to have them write a few lines about Pablo's debut. Some viewers didn't realize these works were *not* rendered by Casas until noticing that the subjects weren't high muckety-mucks but just the tavern's surly squirts. Others even quietly compared Pablo's unframed images favorably to those in the Sala Parés.

Don José came when he read the papers. As soon as Pablo saw him walk in, he felt uneasy, certain his old man would scoff at these pictures so unlike anything that would ever elicit his father's praise. But instead, Don José stroked his beard without comment and ordered beer for Pablo's friends. He then spent hours regaling them with stories about his son, the prodigy painter. It was a triumph Pablo couldn't have imagined a year ago, before Carles.

Slowly, the gang's activities began moving away from Els Gats to the studio covered in the grandeur of Pablo's trompe l'oeil. The place belonged to all of them now. It was a refuge where the new generation could meet to drink spirits, cava, and coffee. They smoked cigarettes for whole afternoons there, and—when they could find it—bits of Moroccan hashish that looked like rat droppings and made them feel they'd entered the gilt frame of a Delacroix, a world of intoxicating cadmium yellow and feverish reds, of turbans, tigers, ecstatics, and odalisques.

III

It was during a rare occasion when Pablo returned to his parents' apartment for dinner that the letter arrived.

Carles had dutifully accompanied him, although Pablo knew his mother was wary of anyone who didn't wolf down her food. Doña María had spoken badly of Carles once before when he declined a lumpy, heme-colored stew—quartered sheep's liver in curdled blood. As Don José fetched wine from the cupboard and Doña María headed downstairs to receive the postman, Carles hurriedly spooned much of his lukewarm, mayonnaise-based potato soup—a *Malagueña* specialty—into Pablo's bowl.

"You're getting mail here again?" Doña María asked Pablo, handing him the red envelope she'd brought up. "Does that mean we might see you more than once in a blue moon?"

"I'll always come for your cooking, Mama. Can Carles have more soup?"

Carles kicked him under the table.

"Well, are you going to open it?" she asked. "You have a sweetheart, don't you? Maybe she wants to give me grandchildren? Go ahead. Read me her name."

Doña María ladled the creamy broth, thick as hide glue, into Carles's bowl. In the middle, a slice of hard-boiled egg, which Carles despised even more than mayonnaise, floated like a lily pad.

"No, no, Mama. This looks official."

Don José sat down and uncorked the fat bottle of deep-red wine resting at his feet.

"What if it's the draft?" Carles reminded him.

"No. Don't open it," Doña María said sharply. "My son isn't going to be a soldier. I've seen what happens." She crossed herself. "I can't think of it."

"Nonsense, Mother," said Don José, whom he addressed this way whenever he wanted to speak definitively as Father, arbiter of disputes. "If Pablo is called up, we'll buy him out of service."

"With what money? Your salary for six months won't cover the cost," she said.

"Why, we'd send him home to Málaga. My brother, Salvador, would help in our time of need. It's not a question."

"Uncle Salvador? Again? He is a kind Christian, but we are always 'in our time of need,' like a dog forever in heat."

"That's enough! We have company," Don José said, bringing the goblet to his lips and taking a sip. "Point is, Pablo has a promising career as a painter. Doesn't make sense getting his fingers blown off."

"Well, at least the war is over," said Carles, although Pablo could still be shipped off to Morocco for service.

"That's right," said Don José. "Your old man, he has a position with the Americans, no?"

"At the consulate, sir."

"Something lofty, eh?"

"I don't think we have to worry about the draft," interrupted Pablo, who hoped to not discuss politics or status. He pointed to the return address on the envelope: Paris.

"My word," said Don José. "Open it up. Go on."

Pablo used a butter knife to slice open the envelope. The stationery was heavy, with lustrous marbling; the type was a delicate sloping font. It was written in French. "I'm an art school dropout," he said, passing the letter to Carles. "You handle foreign correspondences."

"I'll read it while you draw a picture of me."

"If you would be so kind, Don Carles," said Don José. "We're anxious."

"Of course, sir."

So Carles began. *"Merci, M. Ruiz y Picasso pour votre soumission L'Onction des Malades.'"* He paused. "Did you submit that oil painting you'd been working on to somewhere, the one of the priest?" he asked Pablo. *"Last Rite*, was it?"

"Last Moments."

"Yes. We submitted it together," Don José said.

"We did?" asked Pablo.

"You were very busy," Don José said. "Hardly around. I couldn't find you."

Carles continued. *"'Vous êtes accepté comme l'un des représentants de l'illustre nation d'Espagne lors de l'Exposition Universelle . . .'* Pablo, your painting, it's going to be in the fucking World's Fair!"

Pablo kicked Carles under the table for cursing in front of his mother.

Doña María screeched, "The World's Fucking Fair?"

"No, darling. The fucking World's Fair!" Don José corrected her. Before the last word left his lips, he and Doña María had both leapt from their seats and thrown their arms around one another, Pablo sandwiched between them. He was confused, but smiling.

～

Even before everyone got drunk on the strong Monastrell wine at the dinner table that night, it was decided Carles must travel with Pablo to

Paris. Don José explained that his boy didn't even speak French. It also couldn't hurt, he confided after Carles left, for someone with diplomatic connections to accompany Pablo in a strange land.

The next morning, Don José set about to raise funds for his star pupil's journey. When he couldn't sell his paintings of pigeons to any art gallery, he tried an aviary society, then pawnshops. It would have dispirited him earlier in his career. But now his glory would be guaranteed, not through him but by his progeny. He even stopped visiting the brothels, instead depositing the savings into an ankle sock for Pablo to do with as he wished.

The proud Spaniard loathed France and would have preferred Pablo go to Florence or Rome. But he couldn't argue that the World's Fair saluting the arrival of the year 1900 wasn't the biggest event around, perhaps ever. That his son should have a painting hanging in Paris representing the nation of his birth? It was an honor—and an even greater opportunity.

When Pablo asked if the family could afford for him to stay abroad awhile longer so he might improve his odds of making inroads into Paris's famed art scene, Don José piled all his works into a carriage, save his only portraits of Conchita, and sold the canvases for a few pesetas each to the art school for the students to reuse. He began reaching into his dovecote when a pigeon came of age and strangling it before cleaning and dressing the breasts for the butcher. Doña María collected and rinsed the birds' plumage in sodium borate to sell to the women who made feather beds.

Pablo also contributed to the kitty with the money that Els Gats paid him that spring to redesign the menu after calls became deafening for Pere to employ a fresh cook and ingredients. A contact at the health board had tipped the tavern owner off that there might be an inspection soon, which aggrieved recipients of his salt cod stew whispered should be more like a raid. Pere and Utrillo also helped Pablo find other graphic work to earn cash. Carles proved equally adept at this, and their studio became a miniature poster-making factory.

"If you're going to get that good with a brush, you'd better teach me to stop speaking like an idiot," Pablo teased his friend.

"Poetry is mastering speaking like an idiot," Carles replied.

"And painting is mastering what, then?"

"Paint."

~

By Pablo's next visit to his parents' for supper, another letter had arrived. When Doña María went to retrieve it from her bureau, he was seized with fear.

What if there had been a mistake, a mix-up? What if he were not the recipient of an honor from the nation of France but rather one of the countless victims of its famously inept bureaucracy?

But the envelope his mother placed on the table was not red and princely. It was simple, tattered, and addressed in a familiar unsteady scrawl. He tore through the top and was pleased as ever to hear from his art school chum, Pajaresco. He'd gotten a substantial commission to paint a chapel's interior, he wrote. It would let him be free of his family's farm in Horta soon, and there was a gal in Barri Xinès tearing herself apart to see him.

Pablo replied immediately with the Paris news, imploring Pajaresco to join him and Carles. This other friend was from a different upbringing, he told Pajaresco, but they must've met somewhere before and would no doubt get along, considering now all three could be called budding artists on the move.

A slight unease hit Pablo after sending the letter. He should have asked Carles before inviting Pajaresco.

Later that night, Pablo found Carles in the studio, working shirtless, experimenting with oils. The overall structure of the canvas was reasonably composed, but Pablo saw the shading was not what it should be.

"Remember, fat to lean, and take care when you're laying the color, or you'll get eaten up," Pablo said. Another wave of regret washed over him; he'd sounded just like his father.

"Fat to what, and what?"

"It doesn't matter."

"I want to know."

"It means mind your medium and watch the cobalt or pure emerald greens. You have to wait to lighten a deep color. Otherwise, the dark will continuously swallow the light."

"You painters are a poetic sort, at least when you're talking about paint."

"Never mind that, Carles. I gotta tell you something, something important," Pablo said, divulging how he'd entreated Pajaresco to come along on their trip.

"And, so what?"

"So I didn't know if you wanted it to be you and me. You know! Just the two of us—and a thousand Paris belles or whatever you call them."

"I'm confident there will be plenty to go around."

"What if it isn't always the way it is now?" Pablo explained he wanted to make sure they got to have their adventure, together.

Carles reassured him the addition of one more companion would not interfere in their conquest of France. "After all, how many musketeers were there?"

"No clue. I just make pictures," Pablo said, looking again at the easel with Carles's canvas. "Fat over lean, blah, blah, blah. There's no right way. Everyone should paint like a child."

"It's getting hard to know whether I'm being complimented or insulted."

"A compliment."

"Suppose if I judge everything you say that way, then I'll never be cross."

"No, Carles. Don't ever be mad at me. I couldn't take it."

"OK, but two things."

"What?"

"First—and you've got to know this if we're to go to Paris—there were three musketeers in the book by France's most acclaimed writer, Alexandre Dumas, fittingly titled *The Three Musketeers*."

"Got it. On to two."

"Three. Didn't we just go over this?"

"No." Pablo grimaced. "What was the second thing you wanted to tell me?"

"Before we may go to Paris—"

"All right, all right. I'll read the book already."

"Don't. It's duller than it sounds. But it's not that. What I'm trying to tell you is I haven't mentioned our trip to my parents yet."

Pablo was confused. "Why?"

"My mother, she's not well," Carles revealed. "And Father is away, traveling on matters of which he cannot speak."

"She bad off?"

"Don't know. Doctors talk a language even poets find baffling."

Pablo told Carles not to worry. "I'll take care of everything."

CHAPTER 7

I

Paris, October 1900

W hat's that you say?" Carles asked, leaping over the divide separating train and platform as the light bounced off his shoe in
midair. Once beneath the sweeping glass ceiling of the Gare d'Orsay,
awe froze him.

Pablo, in front of Carles, hadn't meant for anyone to hear the three
little words he'd uttered reflexively. He replied that this merely had been
thinking aloud and set down his heavy-pile carpetbag, portable easel,
and a small brown case containing sable brushes and pigments he didn't
want to repurchase here—viridian, vermillion, antimony yellow, cobalt.

As the Parisian commuters at the station looked askance at him
and his friend, Pablo realized that the two of them must be a sight to
behold—one tall, lean, and pallid, like a Kajar scribe idealized on a
lacquer pen box; the other short and sturdy, with a sunbaked complexion and barn-owl eyes—each decked out in their matching custom-
made garb. When he inched up his hat's brim, the shimmering from
above warmed and anointed his face. Pablo couldn't help repeating once
more—this time loud enough for all to hear—"I am king."

~

Before leaving Barcelona, Pablo and Carles had gone to a tailor who smoked foul-smelling cigars and wore cravats. Pablo knew him through Don José and agreed to do a portrait of his family picnicking in exchange for his cutting identical suits for Pablo and Carles's journey—double-breasted corduroy jackets with tight wales of glossy black that would sling low past the knee and flare at the top so the collars could be flipped up to cover their necks when it got cold.

They'd boarded the train dressed in these inventions. After so many fittings, the material was like their own skin. Beneath, they wore starched shirts, oversize floppy bow ties, and pointy patent leather shoes that reflected ceiling and sky. Once inside the passenger coach in the Barcelona station, Pablo and Carles had arranged their belongings on the wooden benches to allow the two of them to sit across and at an angle from one another, better to stretch their legs. Carles extracted from his bag a red bandana with a paisley pattern, carefully folding it into a three-inch-wide strip and tying it around his eyes.

"What are you doing?" Pablo had asked.

"When I arrive, I want to be like a newborn infant squeezed from the womb. There will be up till now, then my life after I've seen Paris."

As the train had exited Barcelona's Estació de França, Pablo gazed upward through the mud-flecked window at the great continents of cloud drifting through the blue. The steam engine huffed and pulled them to the foothills of the Pyrenees, where cedars grew from the ground like daggers. He narrated the landscape to Carles as they progressed to fields of autumn wheat dotted by houses with red tile roofs and steepled white churches that looked from a distance no bigger than upturned thumbtacks. He lit Carles's cigarettes and split loaves of bread longwise, then tore off pieces to put into their mouths.

When night had fallen and there was nothing to see outside, Pablo cried, "Now you—paint me a picture!"

"Picture of what?"

"Of Paris! In words!"

Carles imagined aloud the museum halls, the gardens, the electric lanterns, and cancan girls with legs in lacy tights and garters of red riding round them. He told him how splendid were the women's dainty fingers, made for jewelry just as much as jewelry was made for them. They handed back and forth bottles of musky red wine with floating bits of cork and dreamed.

"You think it will look like it does in the posters, the Muchas? Lautrecs?" Pablo had asked.

"It can't."

"Liar! You do! You do think!"

"Well, why not?"

Pablo bought candied peanuts, and they lobbed them into one another's mouths. Carles, still blindfolded, nearly choked. His ability to aim a peanut toward the sound of Pablo's voice, however, was surprising.

As the train emerged from a tunnel, Carles asked, "How many women, would you say, have you gone to bed with?"

"How can I know? Not enough, tell you that. What I would like is to love them all, to recall the scent under every skirt."

The truth was that, outside the brothels, neither had known many women or girls intimately.

"You're going to have to pick up the pace," Carles said. "You're nineteen already, and there must be millions, no, billions, to go."

"If not, my curiosity will not let me be."

"And what about the tall ones, Pablo? What will you do when you get to them? Stand on a chair?"

"I am a great artist. Haven't you heard? They'll be up for anything. Perhaps you have seen something of me in the newspapers?"

"Can't say I have."

"Well, you should read more instead of drinking so much. I am quite famous in Barcelona, you know. Soon Paris, too."

That was also a stretch. But before they left, Pablo had enticed the lads at the newspaper who'd written about his portraits show at Els Gats to sneak a line into their publications announcing this latest development, that two of Barcelona's "most promising young artists" were departing to conquer France.

"There is no mountain I cannot climb, no woman with flames inside who won't burn to mount me," Pablo boasted.

"Your confidence is certainly soaring. Some ladies still, I hear, appreciate a bit of modesty."

"Nonsense. Modesty is for the modest."

After two days on the train together, bantering and sleeping with their legs propped up, the bells finally chimed, signaling their stop. Carles untied his blindfold right as a grandiose beaux arts station appeared. With a 370-room luxury hotel attached, the Gare d'Orsay was thoroughly modern and marvelously magnificent. It was as if they had ridden not a locomotive but a time machine to the future—a beautiful, electric, and lyrical future. The stationmaster in his red waistcoat and silk top hat came into view. Rows of eager porters waited behind him. As soon as the doors opened, a newspaper seller appeared on the platform with a wicker basket, waving rolled-up broadsheets and shouting headlines in French as the passengers alighted. Children ran up to their papas. Reunited lovers pressed into each other's chests and cooed. And Carles followed Pablo, who stepped off the train and proclaimed himself sovereign in the same instant.

So it was that the newborn and the new king found Paris at last.

～

For months, Carles and Pablo had planned their voyage to France— what they would wear, how they'd walk, what to order in cafés. But they wholly failed to set a course for once they'd disembarked from the train.

After stumbling around by the station, Pablo suggested that to avoid getting lost they follow the Seine. But it didn't take long for inland adventure to call, and they began scouring the Left Bank for the Latin Quarter, the only arrondissement they knew, thanks to *La Bohème*. Puccini's free spirits had drunk, loved, made art, and—in Mimi's case—died somewhere around here, albeit sixty years earlier in a fictional work.

If Gare d'Orsay had transported Pablo and Carles to the future, they now managed to wander far into the past. To their great surprise, much of Paris resembled a feudal grubland. How could these tumble-down buildings and overgrown lots belong to the city of Eiffel, of Ader? How should this decay coexist beside dazzling iron-and-glass gates leading to the brand-new Métro whirring underground, beckoning like damselfly-winged portals to other dimensions?

On a squalid block of short houses that smelled of livestock and a gurgling street drain, they came across a stump of a gray-haired woman. She wore a dress of homespun cotton, and a white flannel serviette covered her forehead like she'd wandered from a Courbet painting. She was haranguing a cabbage-seller who'd overcharged her.

Having already delved deep into a flask of rotgut, Pablo and Carles interrupted the woman's tirade to ask if by chance she knew of someone renting a studio. It was midmorning, and they'd been beating the streets and dragging around their luggage for more than two hours.

Why, yes, she so happened to own one right there that had belonged to her late husband.

They took a cursory gander inside these most rudimentary accommodations, gave her a deposit on the spot, and left their bags. Figuring the woman too old to be crafty, Pablo and Carles didn't think twice about the price.

Unburdened now, they sped through the city, sightseeing like ravenous pillagers, rambling like wild men, erupting with adolescent giddiness. They strutted up Avenue Denfert-Rochereau and ogled the

Fontaine de l'Observatoire, pretended to be buckaroos on the ponies spinning around the carousel in the Jardin du Luxembourg, pocketed bonbons and *pâtes de fruit* by the smeary handful from the chocolatiers in the Saint-Germain-des-Prés, traipsed back across the river over the Pont Neuf and explored the Île de la Cité until happening upon an immense cathedral with twin towers and buttresses flying everywhere.

"Dare me to spit on Notre-Dame?" Carles asked.

"Hawk on that brawny Frenchman guarding it with a carbine, why don't you?" Pablo countered.

"If he strikes me, what will you do? Will you forsake me? What about his rifle, if he shoots?"

"I shall write a poem to commemorate your untimely death."

"A poem? Why not paint the scene instead? I'm the wordsmith," Carles replied.

"Have you gone buggy? A painting?" Pablo said in mock disbelief. "Do you know how much blood there will be? It'll use all my vermillion."

When they grew tired, they found a bench on the Quai de Montebello to view the parade of young women strolling by and wondered how different were these ones than those back home. The same species as their Spanish counterparts, they decided, but evolved to suit an entirely different landscape. Here, women's faces were hung like lanterns instead of hidden. Each one walked as if every obstacle in her path would move out of the way.

"Belle! Belle! Je veux baiser!" Pablo waved to a lady whose heels clicked against the paving stones, garbling all the French he knew. She swiped the back of her hand across the bottom of her chin in a gesture Pablo could only presume indicated affection.

Carles wasn't wholly surprised at the severe limits of Pablo's language ability. After all, the southerner still spoke Catalan with a thick, halting accent despite five years of residing, on and off, in Barcelona. Luckily, Carles had studied French. His parents spoke it fluently. The vocabulary came easily to him. It was only his tongue's Catalonian lisp that now and again caused him to sound like a reptile reading Molière.

"You can't go around propositioning French women like that," Carles chided Pablo. "This land is civilized. You must have decorum. Or at least act like you do."

"Did you see the way she looked at me? That sign she made with her hand? I think she's keen."

"This is nothing like in your Barcelona brothels. French women demand respect, even the most hard-up grisette."

"What's that?" Pablo asked, guilelessly.

"Have you ever studied a book in your life? *Gri-sette.* A woman of low social standing, though quite conceivably high intellect, who may, time to time, commit herself to a unique arrangement with a benefactor. It's endemic to this land, though perhaps oriental in origin. Altogether a bit hard to explain. Something like a seamstress, I suppose."

"A seamstress? They sew buttons, don't they?"

"Not these. Not mostly, anyway. It can be a front."

"Front of what?" Pablo shook his head.

"Really, Pablo!" Carles said, tipsy, riled, and admittedly amused.

When it began to drizzle, they beat a retreat toward the old woman and then hustled through a doorway beneath a burgundy awning after the rain picked up, hoping to find beer, bread, and stew. The restaurant was loud and busy, and they sat down on palm-bottomed bentwood chairs at a little marble table, studying the hand-scrawled menu.

"Well, I'll be damned," a husky tenor coated in Cavendish and phlegm called out. The room was so dark that Pablo and Carles felt the broad hands of Nonell—the artist and regular at Els Gats—on their shoulders before they saw his face. "Really, are there any Spaniards left in Spain?"

"We'll all be gone soon. We expect America to invade any day," remarked Carles, before remembering he was a diplomat's son and someone might take him seriously. "Not really—that's a joke. For now, anyway. Good to see you, man!"

"To hell with America," thundered Nonell, having obviously downed a pint or thirteen. "Name a painter it has produced. Not one in over a hundred years who improved the canvas after he stretched it. I tell you, I don't think America is long for this world. No goddamned country will sustain itself without art, and none . . ." He broke midsentence to get a good look at Pablo and Carles, appearing surprised again to find them here. "And no man can last long without beer. Let me welcome you to Paris, gents," he said, whistling for the garçon.

Nonell hiccupped before adopting the tone of a museum docent. "Know what they call a place like this in French?" But before they could respond, he answered himself. "A bistro."

"We're Spaniards, not dullards," Carles said.

"Bet you don't know why, do you, wise guy?"

He thought about it. "No."

"The Cossacks," Nonell said. "They barked 'Bistro! Bistro!' to the city's poor restaurant cooks after sacking the place with the tsar, which is the same way they hurried their horses. Now, it's what everyone calls one of these joints to wet your throat and find quick grub before riding off."

"What'd they say at the cathouse?" Pablo asked.

"How I've missed you so," said Nonell, planting his wet palm on Pablo's head, messing its black mop of hair. "Look at you. I remember when you could hardly see over the counter; we thought you might be a mute. You'd sit in Els Gats with your fucking sketchbook, drawing all day. I hear you've got a painting in the Exposition?"

Pablo dipped his head slightly.

"Proud of you, little brother," he said, slapping Pablo on the back heartily. "Listen, where you jokers staying?"

"Just rented a place nearby."

"What? On the Left Bank? Why? How much you paying?"

"Six hundred francs."

Nonell held a finger to his temple and looked bewildered. "Are you off your onion? That's a small fucking fortune!" Across the river, he told them, they could nab a grand studio for next to nothing, have money left over for canvases, paints, and a bit of mischief, too. "Over by Boulevard de Clichy, where all the action is," Nonell said, adding that Montmartre—just beyond Paris proper—is a charming area, high on the hill with a laid-back, country feel. All the artists were moving in. "They got no tax on wine up there!"

"How's it called, again?" Pablo asked.

"What are you, an Iberian painter or a shepherd boy?"

"It's the hat," Carles said.

"Is that what you did in Andalusia?" Nonell pressed. "Sheep?"

"We had a certain fondness for the livestock," Pablo admitted. "But it prepared me greatly for when I had to make love with your mother. Always from the backside, she wanted—always! And I never let those outrageous chompers near my privates. Oh, I was too afraid!"

The booze had turned Carles devilish. "Nobody would mistake a blade of grass for a meal, Pablito," he said.

"You guys are idiots all right," said Nonell. "Don't stay here. It's a waste pile. Worst in all of Paris. Montmartre is the place—farmland but with cabarets. Renoir lived there. Painted the windmills. Hell, it's where Le Chat Noir was, before that went to pieces."

"Gone?" Carles asked.

"Long time already," Nonell shook his head. "See, you're no fucking dummy! Heard of Lautrec? Steinlen? Degas? Well, Montmartre, Montmartre, Montmartre. I'm telling you, it's where youse decadentes want to be. Yeah, too bad about the black kitty, it is. Kaput."

"You must think us far more fashionable than we intend," Carles inserted casually.

"They're already building the most beautiful church in France there, taller than fucking God," Nonell continued, slamming the bar top. "Pablo! Carles! Look, you've made me take the Lord's name in vain, for Christ's sake. If my mother knew, she'd whip me."

"Can she whip me, too?" laughed Carles.

"Watch your mouth, you funny bastard."

"Which way is Montmartre?" Pablo relented. "And how are we going to find a studio there?"

"That I can help with," Nonell hiccupped.

~

Tight in the bladder and light in the head, Pablo and Carles gave Nonell several hundred francs to rent his Montmartre studio—unseen but already palatially appointed in their imaginations—and set out to collect a refund from the old woman. After they'd managed to wrangle back half what they'd paid, she chased them out with a cleaver, yelling, "Swindlers!" The two cried with laughter and fled in the direction they believed north, the wind of mischief steering them and filling their sails.

Traveling up Avenue d'Antin, turning his head this and that way to take in every fresh scene, Pablo realized how very small Barcelona was by comparison. And dark. Paris, on the other hand, felt like a vast, radiant bouquet—a hub near the center of existence. Here, Haussmann's broad boulevards lined with town houses the colors of butterfat and chalk were somehow brilliant even in the overcast sky. Pablo further recalled how Andalusia was full of light, but there the rays become oppressive. All throughout Spain, which is to say all throughout his life, bright light had always been countered by a corresponding inescapable darkness. The land where he was born must have been predetermined to be a chiaroscuro country—one of demons, umber, cannibals, firing squads. And, perpetually on the horizon, was Judgment itself. "If Degas were a Spaniard," Don José would say, "his ballerinas would be clutching daggers." However, in this ancient city of the Gauls that Pablo'd finally found, the gods made each atom emanate its own Parisian glow.

~

"Sacré-Cœur," muttered a shabby street sweeper who spotted Pablo and Carles staring up a steep hillside at the gleaming white church covered in scaffolding, which stood at Montmartre's highest point. The two weighed-down pilgrims clambered up the slope's thousand steps with their bags slung over their shoulders as if they were traversing a mountain en route to some holy relic. Upon reaching the top, they were winded and dripping cool sweat, racked with aches and pains and blisters, and well drunk. They followed the road as it eased downward for a bit and came to a beige, brick, four-story building on Rue Gabrielle flaunting a red door.

There it was: number 49.

Not planning to return to the studio before leaving Paris, Nonell had given them a ring of keys. The lock easily turned. A giant mirror hung in a hallway just past the vestibule, beside mailboxes labeled with French names: "M. Papin," "Mme. Cocteau," "M. Leclercq." Pablo and Carles both halted in the yellow from a skylight above to stare at their reflections in the looking glass.

"It's us," said Carles, "in Paris."

"Honest folks pray for heaven. All painters want is a Paris studio," Pablo replied.

They bolted up the stairs to the third floor, reenergized, like kittens chasing moths. Pablo jammed another old-fashioned ward key into the brass hole. It rattled around three twists before giving up its fight. But the door stuck in the frame. Together, they threw their weight against the heavy oak and exploded into the apartment. And then came a scream.

Inside the ramshackle studio, strewn wall-to-wall with half-finished canvases, Bordeaux bottles, a hodgepodge of furniture, and a chaos of painting paraphernalia, was a woman with tawny tresses who rushed to gather the blanket from a daybed in order to cover her bare body. *"Police!"* she shrieked.

"Aleluya!" Pablo cried.

The woman pelted the intruders with pillows and beat them with bolsters that split at the seams. A flurry of feathers floated through the air, the room becoming a startled snow globe.

Another door swung open, and a second woman stepped out from the water closet, framed by the molding like a maja in the Prado. Her hair was blue-black and pulled into a pincushion bun. The straps of her hourglass corset loosely clung to her chiseled shoulders. Her eyes had such fire, her body was so statuesque, it frightened Pablo. Perhaps her next most conspicuous characteristic was an absolutely perfect French nose, slightly upturned at the tip. "Nonell!" he kept saying, over and over while being assailed by a headrest, even as he couldn't tear away his gaze.

"You know him?" the black-haired woman asked—to Pablo and Carles's surprise, in a throaty Catalan.

"Yes, yes," they pleaded.

"Wait till I see that bloody chinch!" She dug into a beaded handbag sitting on an easel's ledge and withdrew a narrow boning knife, its silver point gleaming through the falling feathers. "Let him suck on this!"

"Madam, allow us to explain," said Carles, summoning whatever diplomatic grace he'd inherited. "We are artists. It would be a crime against the law and good taste to kill us."

"Artists?" she roared. "You mean con artists, like your friend Nonell!"

"If you please lower your weapon," he beseeched the woman as she filleted the air, "I will give you the distinct honor of meeting my illustrious companion, the magnificent painter, Pablo Diego José Francisco de Paula Juan Nepomuceno María de los Remedios Crispín Crispiniano Santísima Trinidad Ruiz y Picasso!"

The syllables lisped gallantly from Carles's mouth, and Pablo bowed like a caped bullfighter, peering out from under his brow, shocked as anything that Carles could actually recollect his full-winded Andalusian name.

"This up-and-comer's prizewinning and tear-wrenching master-piece," Carles said, "which he's christened *Last Moments*, hangs at this very moment in the Spanish Hall at the World's Fair, the Exposition Universelle. We have traveled from our Catalan homeland to Paris to collect the laurels he so rightfully won." Cheekily, Carles added, "We can even arrange for you and your fair companionette an intimate visit, should you wish."

"I don't give a shit about you, this mother raper, or any of your Catalan countrymen. You can all choke on a fucking olive pit. And make sure, while you're at it, my good-for-dirt father is buried there besides. Now, I'm going to ask nicely, before I paint the walls with your bile. Where is Nonell? He's supposed to finish playing with his pictures today and pay us what he owes."

"Seamstresses," Pablo whispered to Carles.

"Models! Professional models for professional artists," she countered, punctuating each syllable with the knife. "We don't stand around naked catching a cold for free, *comprens*?" Her eyes, black and fierce as a bear's, looked Carles up and down. "And who the fuck are you, anyway?"

"I, my lady, am the poet Carles Casagemas," he said. "Betrothed to an austere life of vermouth, verse, and revolution, I'm a scribe wittier than Lucan, an enfant terrible more *terrible* than Rimbaud."

"I have no doubt you are terrible. How did you get the key to this studio?"

"We have rented it from Nonell, who said he shall be returning to Barcelona, posthaste."

"Without paying us? That chinch!"

"I beg your pardon, madam. But we have come as Nonell's emissaries, extending the promised sum—your most worthy fee, that is—for agreeing to arrive each day as our models and muses." He fumbled for a moment, as his ad-libbing had raced too far ahead. "Seven hundred francs, I believe. Yes?"

"You wretched twit! It's twice that! And what do you mean, 'arrive?' We have every right to live here! This roof, it is ours, rightfully ours, just as much as yours. That's the stinking deal—four hours per day of modeling, no more, no less, and paid room and board, if you can call this squalor a place for ladies to reside. It's what we agreed on. Nonell, was he drunk?" She paused, then added, "And why are you dressed like goatherds who won a carnival raffle?"

Pablo and Carles brushed the feathers off their corduroy pants and jackets indignantly.

"Your fine name, what is it?" said Carles, tipping his hat.

"My name is Bugger Off. We model for Nonell, not his petite bourgeoisie Spanish friends who're more broke than even him. You Spaniards come to Paris and think models fall from trees like rotting fruit."

Pablo was spellbound. Never mind even the flesh—beneath it this formidable woman was all nerve, and spine, and spleen!

"Madam, we'll pay your fair price for such very fair models. Have no fear," Carles said. "As a token of goodwill and recompense for this unfortunate incident, we shall in fact make the sum one thousand five hundred. And we should be enchanted for you to share our humble studio while we work, tight quarters though they may be. We'll do all we can to make you comfortable. We only hope you don't mind if in the process we make you famous, too."

"Fame? What do I want with that? You mother rapers give us two thousand francs or else talk to the eels at the bottom of the Seine," she said, waving the blade again.

From his trouser pocket, Carles exhumed an envelope. "Half now," he said, handing her the bills, "half when we're done."

She counted it, twice.

Once more Carles asked her name.

"Germaine Gargallo," she replied, aiming the aspirant double *L* with her lips like a poisoned blow dart. "That's right, half Spanish. Mother is French. Daughter is done with every one of these lousy countries." She motioned with her chin to the woman wrapped in a quilt. "Call her Odette," Germaine said of her partner. "But if you don't speak French, she'll have no idea what the hell you're saying."

Pablo could see Odette was perhaps a decade older, a flower in full bloom. Her hair ranged from zesty yellow to sunset floss. Her cheeks were plump and fresh.

Germaine announced abruptly they had business to attend to and could suffer here no longer. Odette fastened the back of the boning of Germaine's corset and threw a worsted gray sweater coat over her shoulders. Odette donned a long fur with nothing underneath and high boots. "We'll return in the morning," said Germaine. "Be ready with your little paintbrushes."

The door slammed.

Pablo turned to Carles. "Have you ever seen anything like it?"

"The daughter of the Eye of Ra," he mumbled.

"What?"

"Sekhmet, the Egyptian deity before whom all men tremble. Evil itself is known to jitter. My heart, oh, my heart, it aches!" said Carles, clutching his chest, smiling in delight.

"Heart? Ha! My knob is swollen like the Eiffel Tower, old man. I almost told her, stab me or love me, but please put me out of this misery."

"Careful. What if she'd gone for the groin?"

A devastating injury to have in Paris, they both agreed, shedding their jackets and swigging from the flask, exhausted after such a long journey.

In his poetic talk of ancient immortals, though, Pablo could hear Carles claiming Germaine to pursue. This left Odette, who spoke no common language with him. At least she was an impressive vision in her own right, although he still felt drawn to the one who'd brandished the knife. But how could he deny Carles anything? And, who knows? Maybe Odette would even teach Pablo a little French along the way.

~

Pablo and Carles awoke on the floor after dark, stirring slowly amid feathers and debris. Pablo found a candle and lit it to finally take proper inventory of their surroundings. The walls were the color of whipped eggs. A confusion of threadbare rugs lay over the scuffed parquet floor. There was a row of narrow casement windows that should let in decent light before noon. Canvases and ashtrays and empty bottles and painting supplies were scattered everywhere. Pablo placed the candle on a round tea table draped with faded pink brocade and spotted a clock on the mantel above the fireplace. They had no watch and no sense of time, though, and couldn't be sure it was really after nine until at least another minute passed.

Then, silently, each began gathering himself in a rush. They threw water onto their cheeks from the thin stream of yellowish liquid running from the washroom's faucet. They polished their teeth with powder, gargled brandy, used their jacket sleeves to wipe their lips, and ran out the door, lest they have to spend eternity knowing they'd slept through their very first evening in Paris.

Answering to grumbling stomachs, they ducked into an inn right off Rue Gabrielle. The dark wooden beams inside seemed to struggle to hold up the sagging ceiling. But they were grateful to have someplace so close at hand and ate *soupe à l'oignon*, tasting of pungent earth, and gulped goblets of acidic but tasty *vin de pays*. A buxom waitress brought a leg each of duck confit—so tender you could have fed it to a toothless baby—with sliced potatoes swimming merrily in golden fat.

When their bellies bulged, Carles paid the bill and asked the woman who'd served them where to find nightlife in these parts.

"It is for you two? Go down the hill, to the boulevard," she said.

Carles asked if she knew where to buy tobacco. The shops were closed, she told him, before rolling a cigarette herself, shaping it with wine-stained fingers, then running the tip of her tongue across the paper to seal it before smoothing and licking both ends again. She placed the cigarette between Pablo's open lips.

"Thank you," Carles said, slapping Pablo on the back to break his fixed stare.

"It's nothing," she replied.

"My companion won't soon forget your generosity."

Outside, Carles found a fancy umbrella leaned against the inn's wall and tucked it underneath his arm. They stood there, passing the cigarette back and forth, contemplating again this mysterious creature, the French woman, imagining hints of Merlot on the wet paper. How different were these than the demure ladies of respectable Spain still emerging from their mantillas! Here, women seemed to have no inhibitions, sometimes barely even clothes. He wondered aloud, "Have we wasted the first two decades of our lives?"

"In Paris, I would have never learned to paint," Pablo said.

"Can we even go back to Barcelona?"

"There's some nice ladies in Barri Xinès who may get lonely if we don't."

"Write them," Carles said. "Say, 'Come to Paris. Lonely feels less lonesome here.'"

As they smoked, Pablo began to recollect every woman he'd known or seen, starting with his own mother and aunts, who nurtured him like precious saffron—to the bathing hut at the beach in La Coruña, the coatroom in the cathouse in Barcelona, and beyond. But had he ever witnessed a glory greater than Germaine? Unexpected guilt tainted his mood. He was ashamed for envying Carles. But he couldn't deny the attraction he felt for the woman with glossy black hair—art embodied. For a brief moment, Pablo was inclined to tell his best friend this. Perhaps he'd understand. After all, given how close they'd become, their interest in the same girl should come as no surprise. Hell, they even were wearing identical outfits. But the notion of letting anything come between them made him think better of it. "Come on, Carles," he said. "The night, it's young."

It had started to mist. Carles opened the filched umbrella, clutching the tigerwood handle and holding it upright as can be. The two of them walked closely beneath the silk canopy, an odd pair because their heights were so different. Carles rested his elbow on the shoulder of his companion, and Pablo replied by wrapping his arm around Carles's waist. They strode off, looking just like an elderly husband and wife might.

II

Into the early hours, Carles stayed up, chronicling their escapades to the gang back in Barcelona.

He penned letters telling of how the dazzling had stretched far down the Boulevard de Clichy, with every option for inebriation, from sleek cabarets to ginned-up gin joints and rum bars with ridiculous names: "the Nothingness, the Sky, the Inferno, the End of the World, Les 4 Z'Arts." Outside the bars, streetwalkers hiked up their ruffled organdy underskirts to reveal even more thigh than the cancan girls did on stage. "But all these spots are tinselly and ill-suited to relaxation— someplace down-to-earth like Els Gats could make Pere a fortune here," wrote Carles. Popular also was a drink the color of distilled pond scum, he explained. Upon adding cold water, it turned cloudy and phosphorescent like a dusty milk jar holding a glowworm. The French and the many foreigners—Russians, Bavarians, Moravians, English, Corsicans, Basques, some Catalans—drank it with unchecked glee. Tonic wine, ales, punches, and fizzy quinine cocktails were equally en vogue and overpriced.

He described how a towering six-story windmill beamed at the foot of the hill, its blades studded with electric bulbs and flashing letters below announcing this revue as the Moulin Rouge. The noontime effulgence corrupted the sky all around, casting the whole area in garish purple light. "The structure is grafted on top of a music hall, like a corsage orchid might be made to grow unnaturally from a weed—perfect disharmony," he mused, signing off his last missive just as the sun rose and a rag-and-bone man was coming up the street with a donkey cart that was clacking and rattling against the stones.

Carles left to locate a *tabac*, a mailbox, a gift.

~

The models arrived early while Carles was still out. Though Odette understood no Spanish and Pablo no French, all he had to say was that lovely Italian word, *contrapposto*, and she knew exactly what to do, shifting her weight and assuming the most dramatic angles of the pose with no more effort than a bird perching on a branch. She held it without moving, as if her flesh were soapstone.

People who are not painters or models never understand how hard a job this is. Grown men panted from the strain. Pablo's best models had been his sisters. Lola possessed an unusual knack for stillness. Conchita never could remain in one place, but her flickering eyes lit up every drawing he'd made.

Countless times before, Odette had posed. Many painters' works even resembled what she saw in the mirror: her long neck and high forehead, a healthy frame with broad hips that earned compliments at every café in Montmartre, that garden-of-smithia hair. But no one had been able to adequately capture the thing about her she herself most admired—how she could say more with her eyebrows than all the books in the Bibliothèque Nationale. She was proud of those prominent crescents and used them to great effect in daily life. So when she pardoned herself to wet her mouth with Champagne and saw this was the first thing Pablo'd added to the canvas—these bold, bent streaks speaking volumes—she already felt a masterpiece.

~

Carles returned to the studio and found Germaine seated at the breakfast table, a mare's tail of smoke rising above a folded copy of *Le Sourire* that she held in front of her face. When she lowered the magazine, he fought to keep his nerves.

"So now you're going to make a poem?" she said, snuffing out her cigarette.

"A picture," Carles replied. He'd never even seen a professional poser before but wasn't about to cop to this fact.

"Where do you want me, and what shall I wear?"

He saw that across the room Pablo was painting a practically nude Odette and hesitated.

"You pay me to model, I model," Germaine reassured him, adding she knew people in Montmartre who could furnish them with any costume he liked to rent. "Marie Antoinette. Water nymph. Nun. Joan of Arc. Salome. Say the word."

"What about a Spanish goat tender? I could lend you my corduroys." He regretted at once the smidge of hostility in his voice, but it was the only way to cover up his fawning.

"Oof." Germaine sighed and then clicked her tongue. "You're not going to hold that against me, are you? You settled up. Now let's get on with it."

Carles silently extended a small package to her. "Mind putting this on?"

Germaine received the parcel he'd picked up on his morning jaunt, undid the knot, and delicately unwrapped the pink tissue. It was a broad plastron necklace of silver, turquoise, and malachite that might as well have been taken from a pharaoh's tomb.

"Cleopatra? You aim to paint a hieroglyph?"

"I thought you might think it was pretty."

"A gift?"

"If you please," Carles said, seeing that she couldn't hide her admiration for the heirloom he'd found in an antique shop by the apothecary. He was sure he'd won the upper hand.

"How should I wear it?" Germaine asked, fastening the necklace's clasp behind her nape and undoing the zipper of her dress with the same hand so that when she stood up from the chair, she was in nothing but jewelry, corset, and a pair of black walking boots with snow-white foxing. "Like this?"

~

"Most painters want us deadly quiet," Germaine said to Carles after a few hours posing on the other side of his easel. "Like they have some great wheel turning in their head that might go off in the wrong direction. Certain you want to keep talking?"

"The wheel will be just fine," he assured her.

"Good," she said. "Now, then, please answer for me why is it so many young creative types believe they have to come to Paris to give themselves a jolt?"

"You came, didn't you?"

"Ah, ah—I came to Montmartre from Paris. You'll see the difference after a while."

"All right," Carles pressed her. "How'd you wind up in Montmartre?"

"Simple—it was a lark. I ran away to the circus. My life had become worse than a cage. And I'd always wanted to do the trapeze, soar through the air like I was born with wings. A misplaced step ended that. Came within an inch of dying is what I did. But when I landed, it was in Montmartre. Now it's home," she said, confidently. "I do whatever I want here, be however I choose, love whomever I desire, become what I wish."

"Do you miss it?" Carles asked.

"The trapeze? Don't want that now. I'm very content to watch the show and get to know the performers, perhaps."

"Oh? Any old clown?"

"If a man can juggle a dozen bocce without ever dropping one, what else can he do?" Germaine countered.

"That what you want, a lot of balls?"

"Doesn't hurt."

"What else?"

"Wise. I want him to have figured out what it is he really wants, what's worth wanting, that is, and then know how to get it." She peeked up at the clock. It was nearly noon. "That's enough for today, no?" Germaine stood and pulled her dress up over her undergarments. She removed the necklace. "I'll leave this here. Maybe we pick up tomorrow."

"I thought you would stay the night? Didn't you say you lived under this roof?"

"No. I said we have the right to be here—we come and go as we please. Right now, I'd rather sleep beneath the stars. Don't worry. I have a key. You'll forgive us, but we've another appointment." Germaine's tone sharpened. "For you, for today, I'm a Cleopatra. She kills herself, right? What is it, snakes? Tonight, who knows? Maybe another artist will want to paint a picture where the sitter gets to live. C'mon, Odette. You through?"

Germaine walked past the canvas that Carles had been intently looking at when not ogling at her; it was completely empty.

"Hmm. I see I won't be Cleopatra after all."

"How do you know that's not you walking among the clouds? Next time you pose, I shall write a poem."

"Blank verse, I expect."

The door shut behind them, and Carles came over to Pablo and examined his canvas. It displayed Odette standing before a wall of twisted vine—the eyebrows more arresting than the Mona Lisa's.

"She fancies me," Pablo said.

"Who?"

"Odette, of course."

"Right. I can't make heads or tails of that Germaine," said Carles. "It's like my brain has been set to boiling. My heart? Up in smoke."

~

At night, Pablo and Carles set out in search of a simple, homey place to swill lager, somewhere rather like Els Gats. Pablo led them in the opposite direction from the too-loud, too-bright boulevard, and Montmartre became—as Nonell promised—increasingly pastoral. Patches of vegetables grew next to townhomes. There were henhouses and horse stables. Lots were planted with Pinot Noir and Gamay. Cobblestones deteriorated into barely paved roads. And yet when Pablo squinted, he could still see the Eiffel Tower's outline in the pink smog.

At the plateau's edge—the end of Montmartre—they found a very different milieu, first detectable by its stench. Here, hundreds of jerry-built tarpaper-and-scrap-wood shanties rose above brushland. The ground was spread with pot shards, broken furniture, soiled paper, and refuse. All around, rabbits darted, rats scrambled.

Pablo and Carles forayed further and noticed that a band of ragtag teenagers shouting and idly kicking a cart wheel back and forth hushed to conspiratorial whispers when they passed. Pablo felt his back tense. They'd wandered beyond where was wise, he realized. In the distance, he spotted a tavern's porch light, and they hurried to take cover.

Inside, it was hot and packed tighter than a steam tram at rush hour. Lanterns hung low from the ceiling. Faces hovered cosmically, floating and bobbing amid a smoky haze. The wait was three Frenchmen deep, each one chuffing at the barman. Pablo inched up on the balls of his feet to be seen. He couldn't tell who exactly this place was for. Every walk of humanity, it seemed—dockhands and roughs to bourgeois misters with pomaded hair, all looking to get drunk and grab a girl.

"*Deux absinthe,*" Carles called out, reaching two fingers above the crowd. A man built like a bulldog elbowed him from behind.

"Why, after you with the push," Carles said through his teeth.

"There's no queue here," the thickset fellow growled back. "Where you from, anyhow? Your French sounds like a lizard chewing."

"We come from Barcelona, on a civilizing mission," Carles said, placing the tip of his umbrella on the raw wood floor.

"A Spaniard, civilized? What a riot, lads. Didn't anyone ever tell you Africa starts with the Pyrenees?"

"I see we're in enlightened company, here in this supposed capital of culture," said Carles. "Nothing so welcoming as a big-mouthed bigot."

"Caught an invitation to come, did you?" the bullyboy said, four companions massing around him as he bumped Carles with his chest. "Or you just showed up, like maggots at a delicatessen on a hot day?"

Carles snatched an empty beer bottle from the bar and swung it at the Frenchman before the goons seized him and Pablo from behind. The original assailant squeezed Carles by the neck, and the crowd erupted at the promise of violence as the brute's meaty fist began to pound the wordsmith.

"Jean! Stop! They're with me!"

All froze.

There was murmuring, and then Germaine parted the throngs like an approaching dignitary. She wore a dark long-sleeved jacket and fitted bodice with a lacy jabot. Everyone appeared to recognize her. "What do you think you're doing?" she said sharply. "How will the circus receive any press if you pummel the magazine correspondents who've traveled to write about it?"

The man's grip was still coiled around Carles's neck. He looked down, nonplussed. "Correspondents? Ah, c'mon, these ain't nothing but Spanish bullshit rakers!"

"When bullshit is printed, it's called publicity, and it's damn hard to come by—got it?" Germaine said fearlessly. "Now let go."

"And what'll you spare me if I don't make *tartare* out of his face?"

"For one, another run-in with the constable—and just maybe I put in a good word with the foreman at the new church to get you on the masonry team for the next tier. He's a friend, you know. The wages, they're better than you got now, for sure."

Soon as the men released their grasp, Germaine spirited Pablo and Carles to the front door and began shouting once outside. "You have no business," she scolded. "Don't you know this is the Maquis?" Germaine uttered the word like the name of an awful disease, adding that the area was famous for lawlessness, thanks to the gangs that called themselves apaches and roved the dusty lots, terrorizing inhabitants. "It's not for painters and poets with their heads in the sky," she said, walking quickly down the road in front of the tavern.

"You stopped the fight in the first round," countered Carles, following her, wiping his nose on his sleeve. "For that ugly lout's sake, we thank you kindly."

"Lord, Jean sure pegged you right. You are a bullshit raker," she said, stopping at the entranceway of what appeared to be a nightclub at the top of the hill. Like the Moulin Rouge, there was a windmill attached to the building—but one that was old, quaint, and without flashing lights—rising above an outdoor orchestra stage. The doorman in a top hat recognized Germaine and waved them inside.

"And who says it was for his sake—or yours?" she added. "If you're murdered, how do I get the other half of my money? My sake. Always for my sake, else I wouldn't have bothered."

"That how it is?" Carles asked.

"A woman may choose to be a doormat or a goddess," she pronounced, leaving no doubt where she came down.

In the courtyard below the enormous windsails, the bandleader strummed along to a Gypsy tune, horns sounding at his back, moonlight making the sweat on his bald head glisten. The lilting music brightened everyone. Carles locked eyes with Germaine and, blood dripping down his cheek, motioned toward the open-air dance floor.

There was something so comical about it, her laugh turned to a nod. "But if you try any funny business, I'll give you worse than a black eye. Bleed on my silk? You're dead."

"Go on," Pablo encouraged them. "I'll find beer." As Carles and Germaine were swallowed up by the crowd, Pablo observed the way men's eyes followed her. He wound his way to the bar and ordered by pointing absentmindedly at the first bottle on display.

There was a loud rapping against the counter. "So Paris has claimed another," said a reedy voice by Pablo's side.

It took Pablo a moment before he could place Manolo, one more mislaid regular from Els Gats, whom Carles had pointed out long ago. He wore gold rings on his hairy fingers and a cropped burgundy blazer. Ever since dodging conscription, he'd drifted around. Manolo always had been an enigma to Pablo, a cool customer and perpetual schemer who gave the impression he was just about to vanish before a bomb went off. He was good company, though, the kind you wanted to stick around longer, right up till the bang.

Pablo asked Manolo, "You tell me. Is this city I've heard so much about all it's cracked up to be?"

"Sure, long as you don't crack up first." Manolo grinned with a mouth full of precious metal. "You've already found the venerable Moulin de la Galette, I see. This old place has what other spots can never reproduce: atmosphere. How long you in Paris?"

"Depends when they get 'round to giving us the boot."

"Should be all right, provided you don't have no wild anarchist uprising planned. That's what everyone suspects of Catalans, that we're here to assassinate a minister."

"An unfortunate reputation, for sure, but sounds more your brief than mine. What brings you to Paris anyway?"

"Same as everyone else. Cancan girls and a place to paint."

"You paint, Manolo?"

"Not these days. But I could. I am the concert violin in its case at night," he said. "Someday, God'll play my strings again. Till then, I only let beautiful French women manhandle me."

"How you make a living here anyway?" Pablo asked as he paid the bartender.

"Kidding me? I make a killing, not a living. I run a lottery."

"How's that?"

"You know, the tickets with the numbers?"

"I got what a lottery is," Pablo said. "But how does a guy operate one?"

"Every week, I print the tickets on fancy card stock—has to look nice, right? Then I charge one franc apiece."

"Where did you find the money for the jackpot?"

"There's no jackpot. Not in my lottery."

"What do you say to the people who bought the tickets, then?"

"I just tell them, 'You didn't win.' I say, 'I'm not the loser—you're the fucking loser. Now, you want a ticket for next week, or what?' In Paris, you gotta be tough," Manolo said, slugging back a *rhum de Martinique*. "You sell any pictures yet? You do real nice work, Pablo."

"Nah. We just picked up our models."

"What, Germaine? And let me guess, Odette and Antoinette? From Nonell, right?"

"Yes to all, except I never heard of Antoinette."

"One of Germaine's sisters, cute as a bonbon—and young, too," he winked. "You'll meet her. Germaine has lots of 'sisters.' That's what she calls them."

"I guess her father had a lot of daughters. She does seem to know plenty folks."

"Yeah, they all like Germaine. She takes care of people, so they're there when she needs 'em. Get what I mean?"

"Sure."

"For scratch, though, you can pawn off loads of paintings to tourists. Tidy lil' racket is what it is. Newspaper says there's fifty million here for the expo, from far as New Guinea. Paint any Spanish thing—a bullring, a flamenco—they'll eat it up."

"I did come for the Exposition, actually. I got an oil hanging."

"You, too? I just bumped into Ramon Casas. What am I, the only Spaniard without a painting in the Spanish Pavilion?" Manolo told Pablo he and some other Els Gats faithful were planning to pay a visit tomorrow. "Come along. Why not? Maybe make some connections. You know Manyac, right?"

"Who's that?"

"You don't know? He's an art dealer. Got good connections with all the galleries. From Barcelona but lives here a long time already. Manyac's a hustler, like me. I'll introduce you."

As Manolo spoke, Pablo couldn't help his eyes from drifting to Germaine and Carles spinning on the dance floor, her backside swaying like a metronome. Carles dipped her as the song ended, and Pablo fantasized about the pompadour-chignon she wore coming loose, all that hair tumbling down like a black flood.

The two returned arm in arm, smiling like children. Ever since that night at the cemetery after Els Gats, Pablo had harbored an abiding sympathy for Carles. Suddenly, though, he didn't feel too bad for him.

"Manolo, you know Carles?"

"Yeah, I heard about the cop in Barcelona you almost killed," Manolo said. "Jesus," he added when the light caught Carles's cheekbone, "you did come to Paris to start a revolution, didn't you?"

"No, no," Carles said, gesturing to his swollen face. "This was just some loudmouth."

"That's right," Germaine interjected. "Your friends up and decided to take a leisurely walk around the Maquis!"

"Then you seen the shanties where the anarchists run their newspapers out of," Manolo said, recounting how some were the real old holdouts from the Paris Commune, the uprising that briefly toppled the government a few decades earlier. "Remember what happened after that? Was a fucking massacre."

Pablo had never heard of it but Carles nodded.

"Anyway, I hope that ball-burner looks worse than you. Don't take shit from nobody, not here. Besides, I'm one of you guys, a Marxist—redistribute the wealth, I say." Manolo grinned, and then his face abruptly tightened. "Speaking of which, I gotta run. I see another happy customer who may have recently become aware that the watch I sold him—as I said, frankly—once belonged to a duke. Trouble is, the duke wasn't done with it just yet. So long, *chicos!*"

They spotted Odette nursing a wine flute at the end of the bar, and she joined them. Pablo was taking a sip of beer when Germaine sidled up and asked, "You want to come for a twirl, champ?"

"Not until you catch up."

She gave him a wry smile. "Do I look like the kind of girl who takes no for an answer?"

Pablo gazed intensely at Germaine and then everything around her, freezing the dance hall scene in his mind, capturing the men in high-crowned hats and ladies in aigrettes and how the flickering yellow from the chain of hanging lanterns skipped across the room. He worked out the means by which the pleated silk tucked beneath Germaine's broad black choker was draped over her chest, thrust forward by an S-shaped corset and placed just so. He fixed how her lacy white gloves grew daintily like night jasmine from her snug black jacket. Most of all, he recorded exactly the way Germaine's face shone in the gaslight and the marvel of how her smile appeared to emit a luster all its own.

Germaine shook her head playfully at Pablo, who was holding his thumbs and pointer fingers together at right angles in front of his vision to form an imaginary picture frame. "You don't quit, do you?"

"How about we make another deal?" Pablo proffered.

"Try me."

"You two ditch modeling and come to the Exposition tomorrow night instead? If yes, we waltz."

Germaine looked straight at him and shrugged. "So let's waltz."

The four of them—Pablo, Odette, Carles, and Germaine—took turn after turn gliding around the parquet under the aging windmill and the midnight stars, just as in a Parisian dream.

III

"I don't understand why the girls didn't come home last night," said Carles, attempting to knot his bow tie in the speckled mirror on the studio wall.

Pablo twisted the spigot of the faucet in the bathroom to rinse the turpentine from his brushes. A thin, cloudy yellow cascade poured from the spout into the basin. "Maybe they prefer clean water and sanitation."

"I don't believe I've seen your Odette drink anything other than Champagne."

"Right, and cherubs appear whenever Germaine grows thirsty," Pablo said, grinning.

"They never let her be thirsty," Carles replied.

"You're really falling for her, aren't you?"

"Plummeting," said Carles, shifting around to see what his fingers were doing in the mirror, while also reviewing the results of yesterday evening's barroom brawl. Fortunately it appeared that his face wasn't too bent out of shape after the beating he took.

"Easy, there," Pablo cautioned. "We don't know how these French girls are. You may be biting off quite a lot."

"I'm a big boy. I can manage my own baguette."

"As you like. I have my plate full with Odette—I can't bloody understand a word she says. My interpretation is 'make passionate love until we can't take it anymore.' That what you hear?"

"This is the trouble with me and Germaine," Carles said, ignoring the question and undoing the crooked bowknot to begin again. "One minute, we're on this deep level. And the next, she thinks I'm an idiot. You suppose it's because of the poetry bit? Some just can't see it. My own family, to start with. Should I have introduced myself as something else? Mother would have me tell everyone I'm to be ambassador or a legislator. But if I say that, it sounds so phony. I already feel I'm pretending."

"She doesn't strike me as someone who gives a lot of weight to titles. Seems more a libertine."

"I know, but that worries me, too. I'm beginning to suspect she's having relations with half the men in Montmartre. All the circus performers at least." Carles sighed heavily. "Oh, maybe I have bitten off too much?"

"Chew slowly and swallow," Pablo reassured Carles as he began working the canvas on his easel in front of him. "And don't think I didn't notice how you cut a swanky pose on the dance floor last night, either. I guarantee you Germaine did. I had no idea you could move like that."

"Get dragged to enough diplomats' balls and you will, too. It's silly—whoever dubbed this 'culture'? It's everything I'm against." Carles looked over at Pablo. "And what about you?"

"I just try not to step on anyone's feet."

"No, Pablo. I mean, do you feel sparks with Odette? Romantic kindling?"

"A romp, at minimum," Pablo replied, playing it cool. "Like I said, I don't know what other language we have in common! Listen, you and I just arrived in Paris. Let's keep our eyes open. And here's some advice about Germaine—you got to relax. You're too stiff. You said it yourself: it's as if you're playing a part in some play. Something has gotten into you. But it's not you. All the 'madam, this' and 'madam, that.'"

"Think so? Relax?"

"Yeah, she'll go for you, man—if you let her see who that is."

Carles made the corners of the bow tie he'd finally managed to complete crisp with his fingertips and excused himself. "Off to pick up a newspaper and cologne. I smell like a sailor. Need anything?"

"Yeah, ultramarine."

"What's that?"

"Only the loveliest pigment in existence. Think of the prettiest part of a peacock's tail."

"Where the hell am I going to find it?"

"Doubt you will. Beauty is meant to escape us."

"Indeed," Carles said, walking off. He paused at the studio's threshold and turned back around. He was quiet for a moment. "Tell me something. What do you feel when you paint?"

Pablo couldn't help but detect a note of envy in Carles's voice. "Didn't you declare once that painting is nothing more than dust and grease slopped on a rag?"

"Am I wrong? Doesn't mean it can't evoke powerful feelings, though. In the viewer or painter. You always appear so immersed in the picture you're making, yet serene."

In contrast, Pablo had seen the pained expressions on Carles's face as he scribbled in his notebook—a tortured poet wrestling his demons stanza by stanza. So often, Carles seemed to lose the match. When speaking, he always knew how to make his words dance on command. In writing poetry or prose, he did so now and then.

As for his own work, Pablo had not considered the question before. He was sure his brush never got the best of him, though, and supposed that's what Carles must see. But the *feeling* of painting? It came so naturally that Carles might well have asked him, "What does it feel like to be awake?" As opposed to what, asleep? All Pablo could offer Carles was a shrug.

~

Rambling up Rue Saint-Vincent, Carles stumbled upon a svelte, mole-eyed man in a porkpie hat daubing a canvas with the scene before him, as viewed—in the impressionist style—through foggy glass. From hacks to virtuosos, it was easy to see why any painter would travel to the quaint, stuck-in-time enclosure of Montmartre, its stubby chimneys smudging the sky irregularly just above the world's grandest city. There was life in every dead-end street. And Carles understood why Germaine chose Montmartre, too.

Now, Carles thought, as his eyes followed the pointed toe caps of his boots leading up the igneous cobblestones, how to resolve this impasse? She was not at all like those Spanish girls who yield when pressed and have no pushback, no firmness. He thought of how close they'd been on that first day when she posed for him, how he could almost feel the heat emanating from her and wanted to bundle himself in it. Why hadn't he allowed himself to reach for the body calling out to him? Did he fear he wouldn't stop? Or was he afraid he might not be able to get it started at all, as had happened in the past?

The origin of this unenviable condition was difficult to pinpoint. Its root, though, no doubt was tangled up with his ennui. Hard to say what comes first and in what order, right? Events conspire to induce sadness, then melancholy becomes its own disease. So we medicate ourselves. And then, poof! The flesh is sapped—another unhappy development, thus repeating the cycle. The world sags, the body sags, the world sags even more.

In any case, Pablo's advice was sound. At this point, it's best to relax. Nicer for the circulatory system so all the blood isn't dammed up in the head, with none left for any other organ.

It was also true what Pablo pointed out: ever since meeting Germaine, Carles had been playing a part. Couldn't he be loose? Be himself? In fairness, their introduction had been one holy hell of a mix-up. Time to unwind already. Devil may care. She'd adore that. Act like the French. Just her thing.

At the same time, Carles was peeved Pablo had been so didactic. What did he know of love? Had Pablo ever slept with a woman he hadn't paid for?

Bother, Carles reproached himself. He shouldn't think this way about his friend.

But there was also something about Pablo's paintings that Carles found at once miraculous and a bit like trickery, albeit feats performed by a talented magician. After all, could anything done with such ease be of value?

Whereas, while Carles led a materially privileged life, few knew suffering the way he did. His poems were proof. He poured himself into his writing to unearth universal truths, not to manufacture some trifle to acquire money. His anguish and what it revealed did not belong to commerce.

Carles retrieved from his coat pocket the amber vial and dripped a few drops onto his tongue. He'd tried to stay away from the drug since that awful night of the ball, but it was still the only antidote when depression bore down like this. He walked on, and a few blocks later, the world was already more bendy, he more fit to be plied.

He reached a *parfumerie* and found in the back an enticing eau de cologne, fragrant of violet and musk, ambergris and wet cedarwood. He bought it, despite the outrageous price, and dabbed his collarbone. In a cloud of pleasantness, he retreated to a cozy boîte with a shingled mansard roof on a hidden side street, like a capsule holding the lost charm of the Second Empire. Into a tumbler of rum, he stirred a few drops more from the vial with his long finger, which he licked. His thoughts slowed like a river after the rains calm. He sauntered back toward the studio, loose as a barn door swinging in the wind.

What? Jealous of Pablo? Ha! Never.

~

Each pair held hands while cutting down the hillside of the Montmartre Cemetery to meet the Els Gats crew. Speckled brown lime and purple ash leaves crinkled beneath their feet. It was in front of Stendhal's grave that Pablo, Odette, Carles, and Germaine found—standing in a circle, hands dug into their pockets or else cradling pipes—Casas, Utrillo, Pichot, Manolo, and some others from back home.

"Your tastefulness has improved considerably in Paris," said Casas to Carles as he sized up Germaine.

"I've always had taste, Ramon. It's my fortune to have found better company here."

"Careful." Casas nudged Germaine in the rib. "The only thing worse than a painter husband is a poet—they write beautiful vows but don't ever keep 'em."

"If all I cared about was loyalty," she answered, "I'd put a briard with bangs over the eyes on a leash and saw off its bollocks."

Casas twirled an invisible lasso in the air and lifted his voice to corral them into joining the hubbubing droves filling the Rue Caulaincourt viaduct, all marching to celebrate the new millennium at the mightiest exposition ever known. The crowd was made of both aristocrats and plebes who'd flocked here from around the world, many in their native garb so that Austrian knights in revers and cape sleeves walked shoulder to shoulder with Australian bushrangers in curled slouch hats.

During the journey, Manolo introduced Pablo to Manyac, the big-fish art dealer whom he'd spoken about at the nightclub.

"I hear we're going to see one of your paintings," said the man who wore a gambler's mustache and the finest grosgrain top hat Pablo had ever seen. It was angled slightly to the side, almost hiding that one of his pupils seemed more dilated than the other.

"If you like, I'll sell it to you," Pablo said bluntly.

"It's a religious subject?"

"A woman receiving last rites."

"Won't do, I'm afraid. The French have decided to be quite the godless lot. Pious art only reminds them of centuries of persecuting Protestants—and before that, the Moors. They're even having second thoughts now about harassing Jews. No, they will not buy that painting. It would hurt too much. Have you anything else?"

"How do you like Lautrec? Steinlen?"

"Which one are you?"

"Better than both. That style is easy. Except I do it with El Greco's passion and Goya's madness," Pablo boasted, hearing how his confident pitch echoed the way Don José touted him when he was a boy.

"I don't doubt it. Manolo said you were good. Long as your work has got a little carnality—provocative, magnetic, right up to the edge of obscene. But pretty. That, I can sell. You know, it's not impossible we could work out an arrangement. Put you on a contract?"

"What if I've already been offered one?"

"You? By whom?"

"Heaven. Hell. Maybe it's a bidding war."

"You're not actually religious, are you?"

"See my painting and you'll believe I'm divinely touched. That doesn't make me a believer—just a recipient, right?"

"Your bravado and blasphemy are both admirable," Manyac said.

Carles leaned over and whispered in Pablo's ear, "I do believe this eerie man is trying to part you from your soul."

Pablo cupped his hand around his mouth to reply, "He may be dangling quite a lot of money."

"That's usually how it goes, no?"

"Considering I've only got one, I ought to get a good price."

Manyac turned to Odette, whose arm was hooked in Pablo's. "And who is your companion?"

"One of the finest models in Paris," Pablo said, adding that she didn't speak Catalan.

"I'm sure you'll have no trouble fondling your way along," the art dealer mused. "It's rather too bad, though. You look so young and pure, maize still in the husk. Shame such an experienced creature should de-kernel you."

Pablo's eyes narrowed. Odette might have been slightly more mature, but she wasn't old. And he wasn't so innocent.

~

The Palais du Trocadéro, an enormous concert hall with tiered arcades, stood opposite the Eiffel Tower like an outpost of Byzantium facing off against modernity. The Exposition's pavilions filled the surrounding expanses of great lawn on either side of the river. Each building adjacent to the Palais was devoted to the peculiarities and progress of France's colonies and vassal states—the Transvaal to the Tonkin protectorate— and was done up in the architecture of that land.

As the group stepped onto the grounds, a rickshaw carting a pair of gasping English pensioners whizzed by. A two-man team in coolie hats raced them around, the gentlefolk holding tightly to the bamboo sides, saying plummily, "Oh me, oh my."

"Exploitation, right this way!" said Carles in a carnival-barker voice.

First the visitors found a monumental Cambodian wat guarded by seven-headed serpents and limestone lions wearing furrowed pompadours. The Dutch East Indies pavilion exactly replicated Candi Sari, a Javanese shrine from the ninth century, with soaring stone blocks carved with beatified bodhisattvas. Indonesians danced the serimpi to gamelan music and soothing bamboo flutes out front. Nearby, tourists bumbled through faux Cairo backstreets and makeshift bazaars. Over yonder, the subjects of a Dahomian king brought offerings in a staging of supposed life back home, both sexes in loincloths, which caused a sensation among the crowd, no one caring that these people were obviously freezing and would have given anything for a wool coat. In the Madagascar pavilion, schoolchildren and grown-ups alike were made to demonstrate the process of becoming civilized as they sat yawning in a classroom while a Norman headmaster, declared expert in such matters, discoursed unintelligibly about reading, writing, arithmetic, and how to wear shoes.

"Somebody ought to do that for the Spanish," whispered Pablo.

"Yes, the French are quite refined, at least before ten p.m.," Carles responded with an irritated rasp.

They crossed the Pont d'Iéna and headed toward the sounding of "God Save the Tsar!"—the Imperial Russian anthem. A table next to a Trans-Siberian railcar vended curious souvenirs of painted wooden dolls that hid one inside another, the smallest no bigger than a beetle and grinning with a tuft of yellow hair. Carles bought a set for Germaine, remarking, "It's like all of us, so many personalities vying underneath one façade."

He was sweating, Pablo noticed, and looked ghostly pale. "You all right?" he asked.

Carles didn't respond, and Pablo felt a pang of worry. He'd hoped Paris would distract his friend from this habit but feared now as Carles unbuttoned his shirt collar that nothing could keep him from that amber bottle.

Wending along the Quai des Nations, they stopped at a Mexican installation and drank a boozy slosh of fermented pineapple, toasting Bacchus with grappa in the Italian one before sipping cool plum wine atop a Japanese pagoda. The United States made its presence known with a theater showcasing Loie Fuller, a dancer who writhed and contorted with billowing white sails covering her body, imitating Salome before Herod. There was nothing to imbibe here save for the intoxicating movement of the wild woman.

Finally arriving at the Spanish Pavilion, which resembled a hastily constructed Gothic cathedral, each of their party was at least tipsy. On the steps, a gilet-wearing guitar player strummed incessantly, and *flamencas* in ruffled red skirts clacked their castanets and tip-tapped their heels. Other women in mantillas aired themselves with giant folding fans. The scene was meant to celebrate Pablo's homeland, but it felt like a mockery instead. He was visited by new empathy for the Dahomian king.

~

Inside the pavilion's first chamber hung Casas's painting, a long impressionist portrait. The subject—staring off into the distance through pince-nez glasses—was a famous music composer, Manyac quietly informed Pablo, who occasionally still haunted Montmartre, someone named Erik Satie. As Pablo dissected the work, he briefly thought he caught Germaine fixed upon him from across the room like a gazehound. Or was she looking so intently, so meaningfully, at the gilt-frame painting a few feet in front?

Further from the door, and a bit higher on the wall, Pablo discovered his own *Last Moments*. He was immediately swept away by a deluge of satisfaction. Then, as an arm curled around his shoulder, he felt himself ripped back to the place where he stood.

It was Casas.

They'd never shared even a sliver of intimacy between them, far as Pablo knew. It was strange to be this close, the dried fumes of Casas's cigar right beneath his nose.

"That, my boy, is how it's done. Painting's hard as breaking rocks— worse for the joints and back. You'll see when you're my age. Only thing to make this interminable fiasco worthwhile is to have your canvas mounted on the most hallowed wall where everyone damn well knows it." Casas paused. "And the money," he added, firing off a wink and that disgusting guffaw. "You'd be surprised how rich you can become with flax oil and a snip of hog's hair."

Casas's father had made a fortune in Cuba before he was born. He didn't need to burnish his wealth. Pablo was vexed to hear this man, whom every critic in Barcelona worshipped, speak only of the lucre of his profession. How could he be so callous at a moment such as this, one that Pablo wanted to cherish?

"Don't forget about the women," said Germaine, interrupting them from a few feet away. Pablo pivoted to face her and saw she was staring up at his creation. "Be honest. Don't you paint because beautiful women love to love great artists, feel their touch?"

She made no effort now to conceal the way she was eyeing Pablo. There was something especially attractive about the wisps of hair that protruded from Germaine's coif, softening her hard edge. Was it possible they might be intentional, too? Even her disarming features were ruthless, it seemed.

Pablo surveyed the room for Odette but couldn't find her. Instead, his eyes landed on Carles, who was wobbling around a one-to-twelve replica of the Alhambra. He looked like he might fall face-first into the miniature fountain, which was replete with a running trickle. Pablo thought about how one can drown in any amount of water.

As Germaine walked away toward a culinary display concerning the history of chorizo, Pablo began to follow her, almost as though her movement was commanding him. All of Pablo's life had been spent mastering his body, learning to control the eyes in his head, the fingers in front of him. What is a brush or palette knife but an extension of the hand, which itself is connected by a main avenue to the heart? The ability of body was what he offered the world. Pablo found Germaine's perfect mastery of hers—gained from modeling or who knows what—irresistible. He felt compelled to hold her, greet where that dark hair met the back of her neck with his lips.

Casas suddenly whispered in Pablo's ear. "I do believe she was making a pass at me."

At him! How could a painter be so blind?

"If that Carles hadn't already stuck his little flag in, I might take her behind that Javanese stupa for some fun."

Pablo shuddered to think of it.

"Let the lad have a chance, though. You know?" Casas continued, more magnanimously. "You also. My generation of prize horses has to make room for the colts sooner or later. I do hope you're taking care of that Frenchie with the high, round haunches. Had a bit too much Champagne today, but that can't be helped, can it?"

"Ramon," Pablo said, "we all could use more Champagne." He'd never directly addressed him, let alone by his first name.

Pablo retrieved Carles and exited the hall. The rest of the Barcelonans followed.

~

The blaze of five thousand incandescent bulbs pulled Pablo and company toward the Palais de L'Electrique. In the area surrounding it, every aspect of French art, culture, commerce, and science had a shrine. Inside the Exhibition de Viticulture, they downed the sweat of the finest Chablis grapes and tried *sirop de citron* stirred with Cognac. They sampled herbal liqueurs while nibbling pheasant flavored with juniper berries and delicately fried *cromesquis* drizzled with Villeroy sauce elsewhere at the Palais de l'Agriculture et des Aliments. A lecturer discoursing on the cultivation of drupes offered them paper cones overfilled with crushed ice and sweet *crème de pêche*, which they spooned into each other's mouths.

Hanging from the ceiling in a humongous display devoted to innovation were newfangled motorized flying machines that one day might sail through the sky in ways God had not intended for linen and steel. Humanity's biggest telescope was erected here, too, with which one could see the surface of the moon as clearly as if gazing at the banks of the Seine. A moving boardwalk paraded people along while they stood still. Powered automobiles were scattered throughout, promising to make carriages and coachmen obsolete.

"What will we do with the horses?" Pablo wondered aloud.

"Cut the reins and let them run wild," said Germaine.

"Cello bows," Carles hiccupped. "Glue."

By the time they were ready to leave, the bunch had drunk so much they were cakewalking arm in arm up the avenues like the minstrels outside the American pavilion. One or two peeled off here and there, into this tavern or that inn, this friend's apartment, or that bordello.

Eventually, only the two models, the poet, and the painter remained. Pablo offered to walk the women to wherever they had been sleeping. Odette protested she wouldn't take a step further than the studio tonight. Her feet had blown up like brioche in her high-buttoned boots.

Carles could barely stand.

When the four passed the full mirror in the vestibule, Pablo noticed Germaine eyeing him again. They sloshed upstairs and into the studio, where he lit a candle. Odette placed a bottle of sparkling wine to chill on the window ledge before plopping onto the chaise longue. She pried off her boots, sighed luxuriously, and announced that she was going to draw a bath.

Pablo rushed to heat water on the stove. Once hot, he proffered the kettle through the cracked door, barely avoiding a spill. There wasn't an inch of Odette he hadn't already seen. It was ridiculous. She said something in French and giggled before waving him inside. He entered, inhaling orange blossom and shading his eyes with his hand before leaving her soaking in the fragrant pool.

Germaine, meanwhile, stood over Carles, who was crumpled on the daybed. "He's going to be sick," she said.

"Nah," said Pablo. "He's like a horse. It must have been something that didn't agree. The plum wine—so sweet, you forget you're drinking."

"Or was it his habit?" she said. Pablo looked away, avoiding her. "You can see it in his eyes. They're all over Montmartre, people on the tincture. He's by no means the worst off. But he'll move to morphine soon."

When Pablo had first discovered that amber bottle jabbing his side in the middle of the night in Barcelona, he'd done nothing because he didn't know what precisely his hand held. Whatever this narcotic potion was, it seemed a fittingly romantic peccadillo for a poet. But after what happened at the Three Kings Ball, when Carles looked nearly gone, Pablo knew he ought to intervene. For a while, though, Carles seemed to be improving, the habit curtailed after he drifted out of love with his niece and he and Pablo began to spend more time together.

But now, Pablo asked himself, why had he not stopped Carles at the Exposition?

"He's not going anywhere but to bed," Pablo said.

"You're trying to protect him. Good of you, but you'll do him only harm," she said.

"Everybody has something to kill them, if they live long enough," Pablo said. But maybe he'd wanted Carles to become incapacitated tonight.

"What's your poison?" she asked.

"Besides turpentine fumes?"

"Would you give it up?"

"Painting? I'm bound to it, I suppose."

"And bound to Carles?"

Pablo told her how he'd once known no one at Els Gats, and Carles was the only soul who bothered to talk to him. He spoke of the studio in Barcelona he'd painted and they shared, of the sisters they both had lost.

"I am sorry for your mothers," Germaine said. "It's terrible to watch that happen."

"Carles is a good friend," Pablo said.

She asked, "But how loyal are you to him?"

"Thick and thin."

"You haven't ever seen thin, have you? Really down—really out? Where you'll do anything to make another day, sell your paints, your brushes, yourself?"

"Myself? Are you kidding? I'm trying to find buyers right now," Pablo said. "What else could selling one's art possibly be?"

Carles groaned. They worried over whether he might retch in the night and choke.

"You've got to get him on his side, at least," said Germaine. She slid her fingers beneath Carles's limp chest. "Go on. You push from below, and we'll turn him."

Pablo grabbed Carles by the knees.

"No, no. From where his weight is," she said.

Pablo hesitated.

"What is it with you men? You can be so stupid," said Germaine, grabbing Carles from under his hip at the pelvis. Pablo joined in, and they managed to flip him over onto his back. Germaine was close enough for Pablo to feel her breath.

Sitting on the bed beside Carles, who was out cold, Germaine solemnly undid her hair and raked her nails against her scalp. She blew out the candle and straightened to lie down without touching him.

Pablo crossed the room and lit a cigarette as Odette emerged from the bathroom and glissaded to the window to retrieve the sparkling wine from the ledge. She slipped onto the chaise, popped open the bottle, and drank straight from its mouth. After a moment, Odette's shadow moved again, her arm reaching in the dark toward the orange of Pablo's cigarette. He placed it between her fingertips and noticed how she was holding the blanket open like a cape. The outlines of the voluptuousness he had painted were like soft etchings in the night. He crept beneath the wing, and it closed around him, along with her wetness and body heat. He took the cigarette from Odette's lips and held it as far away as he could, leaned in, and found her face with his lips. She pulled his tongue inside.

Odette made no effort to keep their lovemaking quiet. More than once, Pablo caught her looking at Germaine across the room to see if her eyes were open, if she were watching them couple beneath the rustling covers. Pablo wondered what would happen if he sent Germaine just one glance of invitation. Would she come to them? Carles would never even have to know. After all, if Pablo were honest with himself, wasn't this his plan, why he'd allowed Carles to become so far gone at the Exposition?

But as much as he wanted it, Pablo just couldn't do this to his friend. He didn't dare fail a test of loyalty again, as he had as a child in La Coruña.

IV

Germaine woke in the morning with a headache. She'd drank too much, and throughout the night, Carles had tried to cradle her neck. At some point, she resolved to let him. It had felt nice to be held. One of those comforts she shouldn't allow herself, she knew, like napping when it was time to work or peeling a scab before new skin formed. At first, she'd only been playing a game with Carles, but by the time she sensed a simmering attraction for him, he was already head over heels for her. And now what? This was one of those boys, she decided, who may well become a full-throated grown man one day, a sumptuous lover far into his years, like a young wine so acidic that drinking it is like biting into a thornbush but which will mellow exquisitely given enough time.

Or else he might never mature. Quickly decline into something best poured down the drain.

One way or the other, Carles wasn't ready to be consumed.

Still, she couldn't deny certain moments when she felt a stirring. He was very handsome, or at least, again, had the foundations to become so. Carved cheeks. Eyes full of mysterious intentions. Tall. Taut.

And she did not doubt, when he was even half sober, Carles could be brilliant, a true poet who spoke what others wished to say. It's strange, she thought, how men, who aren't created all that different from one another, really, have such a range of faculties. Two, stood opposite, might look the same build—wiry and fit—but only the acrobat soars through the air. The other is ordinary. So, too, how's it some men make love to you so your loins are the fault line where an earthquake begins, and another is just a nuisance, the invasion of a bug? Tickles when it crawls on you. Leaves a mess to clean after you've swatted it.

There was something attractive, it must be said, about Carles's air of culture and sophistication. His upbringing had been so unlike her own. Yet he showed it off too much. Even when he quoted revolutionary literature and poetry or called to abolish laws and government and force the rich to the galleys to row, all this confirmed Carles's class and status rather than revoking it. An odd tension in him, she saw, one he had not worked out himself. In everything about him, Germaine felt tension. Or many tensions. Like many strings tied to many stitches that were still being pulled this way and that way till they become fabric.

Might she not allow Carles to love her and help him become complete? Perhaps, one day, would he be the sort of man she'd never had before—passionate, astute, charming, well-bred, able to provide for her? She was sure her ability to polish was equal to her capacity to corrupt.

By the same token, this whole line of questioning, she reminded herself, was so unlike her. This man did not exhibit what she prized.

Would he someday?

What did it matter if he didn't today?

No. She was not one to let herself be caught. She must be chased down and won. A fox has its wits, and it has pride.

The sun was just climbing in the window. Germaine suspected that after last night, Carles would rouse very late. But she couldn't go on lying there, thinking such thoughts. She grew restless. She craned her neck in bed and noticed the camel beneath the covers on the chaise had one hump, not two.

Where had Pablo gone? Sprawled out on the bed, everyone else asleep around her, Germaine was able to admit to herself, as she practically had to Pablo at the Exposition, that she felt something overwhelmingly bodily for him—something she didn't feel for Carles. She conjured his fragrance of turpentine and salt. The way he painted in great sweeps and powerful turns as if trailing a kite—motions his hands had become so accustomed to that they sometimes performed them even when not holding a brush. Germaine could peer inside him and see fertility, the magic bean that would grow and grow.

Yes, the surface allure was not traditional. Pablo was not tall, and he could barely articulate himself in his native tongue, let alone organize a sentence in French. But he exuded rawness. He really was a peasant from the Peninsula, as her father had been. The coarseness was genuine, that Spanish sultriness one dreams when imagining majas rendezvousing with secret caballeros and making love on the rugged plain with strange, swarthy travelers. It was there in his eyes, those big black orbs like the talons of an eagle that swoops down into the valley of your being and carries you, alive, away to some towering nest.

Yes, she wanted him.

And yet, Germaine could not tell if she had denied herself last night or if it was he who'd not given in. Perhaps both. But why? Did they fear they were courting disaster? That hadn't made her shy away before. Maybe he didn't really desire her. It was unlike her to be so uncertain about something like this.

Germaine noticed Odette turning beneath the covers, her shoulder jutting out and blooming goose bumps from the window draft. She poked her head into the open air.

"Have a good time?" Germaine asked.

"Oh là là!" Odette cried, stretching her arms above her head, before adding another *"là là, là là!"*

Germaine asked where Pablo was. Odette had no idea. She hoped he would return with breakfast. They got up and looked around. His paint box was gone. And the easel. Propped against the wall was the canvas he had been working on—the Moulin de la Galette, exactly as they remembered it from the other night: the hanging gaslights rouging the faces of the pretty girls in crushed velvet hats with iridescent feathers, their nicest jackets cutting sharp figures. Men in gleaming top hats undressing them with their eyes, twirling them around the parquet floor to the waltzing band. Germaine recognized herself, too, leaning into the frame of the painting from the side, grinning gamely.

It was downright mind-boggling! If Pablo did covet her, hadn't she opened the door at the exhibition and then again when they got home? Wide as day! She would have had him, with or without Odette. *N'importe quoi.* Think of how they could have played all night, like three snakes in a pillow slip, jostling and coupling—tripling, even! He seemed like someone who knew how to impose his will. Why had he restrained himself? Here was this painting he created only days after arriving in Paris. This was a man who could realize what he wished for. And if he wanted this, why not make it so?

But she knew. It was because of Carles. The two of them were too close. She had asked Pablo, "How loyal are you?" Loyal enough to not have done what he desired, what she desired—what Odette desired, for sure. (Although Germaine was becoming less apt to share.)

Carles rose and shambled to the water closet. A retching sound came from inside. It was horrible, like the possessed coughing up the devil. Then came gargling, a spit, toothbrushing, and face scrubbing. Carles exited, looking like a raised corpse. The mingling of his sickness and the ambergris of the cologne he wore made the queasiness almost contagious. He reached into the inner pocket of his coat and removed a cigarette case.

The three smoked in silence, like strangers watching the waves from a ship gallery, not knowing what to say or if they should bother to speak.

Eventually, Carles said, "Can I talk to you, Germaine?"

Odette wrapped a blanket around herself and withdrew from the room, bringing with her a book Carles had left open. It was in German, which Germaine knew Odette didn't understand a word of.

"About last night," he began.

"Yes?"

"I didn't mean to . . ."

"What?"

"No, I mean, I meant to . . ."

"Yes?"

"I'm having a hard time saying what I want to say."

"Well, I can't read your mind," she practically screamed, furious at him and Pablo and every bumbling, confused man she'd spent her life dealing with.

"Precisely why I write," Carles said, shutting his eyes and reciting from memory. "My heart is clouded. My brain is muddled. My blood beats in fearful, rhythmic thrusts. Everything is you." Carles's pupils moved back and forth beneath his eyelids, as though he were searching for something from within a trance. "The fault is yours for looking at me, for allowing yourself to be seen. Ever since, all I see is you. As I close my eyes, you come to life in a glorious vision of green and orange circles. My heart is heavy with clouds of lead and marble, threatening a storm, a storm that may yet come or may have broken out already within me."

In all Germaine's years, no one had ever spoken poetry to her before, and now once more she felt a softening toward this man. She might not want to kiss him—well, not at the moment, anyway—but she did feel warmth. There was something very beautiful inside Carles's poet soul.

"Are those words yours?" she asked.

"They are," Carles said.

Germaine put her hand on his.

~

Pablo became fixated on the question Carles had posed: What do you feel when you paint?

He began experimenting by interrupting his process to become aware of the sensation. Painting made him feel powerful, he found, like a matador whose face is wet from the breath of the bull's last charge but who is without fear, thanks to practice and superior skill. Pablo believed he, too, would someday hear the crowds roar. Even then, he wouldn't cease.

After long spells of staying up all night working, Pablo found he liked to walk the riverbank to come down from the high and watch the old men angle catfish. If he was feeling particularly edgy, he'd carry a portable easel to give himself the chance to do a quick outdoor scene on the way home that could be added to the stock of work he'd sell in the afternoon, following a nap.

It was during one of these early morning strolls that he stopped at a row of green wooden bookstalls lining the water. The vendors sat on folding chairs, paging old novels and smoking dark tobacco, apparently unbothered by potential customers. Pablo idly thumbed through a few titles, wondering if Carles's own work might someday land here. Pablo had long marveled at how Carles fought to transfer his loneliness onto the page through the bit of a pen. He had enough talent to be successful, for sure.

But what struck Pablo—who was still meditating on his own relationship with art—was how Carles's passion never seemed to render him strong.

Rather, poetry and prose were means he'd found to siphon off his suffering, lest he drown in it.

Did Carles envy him because of this?

Pablo reflected, too, about how his friend's ennui might be faring since arriving to Paris and becoming infatuated with Germaine. He'd even heard Carles reciting the very same poems to her that were written for his niece only months ago. In fact, Pablo reckoned it was these verses that won Germaine over. Still, he struggled to conjure the simplest of compassions for him. If Carles chose to grapple with his manufactured melancholy, then so be it.

A fissure had opened up in his friendship with Carles, and Pablo hated the feeling. He wished things between them would be like old times, that he could just content himself with Odette and the gentle pawing of sweet orange accompanying her.

But the image of Germaine lurked, keeping him from ever being satisfied.

~

Everyone was emerging from midafternoon naps a few days after the Exposition when Pablo entered the studio, arms full of Beaujolais, bread, and a strangled duck.

"Where have you gone?" Carles groaned.

"This is Paris. So I paint," Pablo said.

"Qui?" Odette called out from her chaise.

"You are my lone model, luscious," Pablo said, blowing a kiss, adding theatrically, "Today, I paint only the beastly things in my brain— toreadors, picadors, the final moment of the bull."

Pablo made a fire and boiled coffee, and the air began to fill with pleasantness. They drank cup after cup until they felt warm and alive and began talking, laughing. Carles told of when his father came home from a diplomatic congress with a modus vivendi and a gift from the heir to the throne of the Two Sicilies—a black mastiff, big as a sofa. It was the night Carles's mother was hosting Barcelona's wealthiest family and, not knowing what to do with the gargantuan beast, she locked it in the coat closet, where the dog attacked her guests' mink- and marten-fur stoles. Carles's mother howled and wailed. His father had to carry the animal all the way back to Naples to defuse a crisis between him and his wife.

Germaine translated line by line to Odette, and they all cracked up. They spiked their coffee with fruit brandy and smoked. Pablo patted the duck with salt and pepper and hung it by a string above the roaring fireplace. He twisted it round and round, then let it slowly unwind to roast evenly, as he'd seen hunters in Horta do. When evening came, they tore the bird apart and pulled up the fat from their plates with pinches of baguette, later nipping at mirabelle plums Pablo had hidden from them.

They sat on the rug and told each other of their childhoods in France, Barcelona, and Málaga. Of family, schools, first loves, broken hearts.

Pablo explained that his earliest infatuation was with a pencil and related how his initial kiss came from a girl who immediately raced away, her opera heels click-clacking down the spiral staircase of the Tower of Hercules.

"Why are girls always running off?" Carles joked.

"Did she ever go for you?" Germaine asked Pablo.

"Acted like I didn't exist," Pablo said. "But the memory, it's still there."

"The first streaking meteor you ever see vanishes, like all those to follow," Carles said. "But that's the one seared forever in the mind, evidence of other worlds."

Odette mused whether she'd ever seen a meteor. What's the difference between it and a falling rock? she asked. As a teenager, she'd begun singing to keep a roof over six siblings and contended that men at the nightclub had been dumb as boulders. If anyone were a shooting star, she was. But twinkling on stage turned to more behind closed doors. She recounted and burst out laughing as Germaine struggled to translate each sex act or body part that none but the French describe so well—how "one makes the madeleine cry" or what noteworthy detail might be placed in *la parenthèse d'amour*. Germaine scoured the studio for a map to use as a visual aid when Odette referred to a gentleman's testicles as Alsace and Lorraine. Determining what a man wanted, this was the hardest thing, Odette postulated. He wouldn't say and just expected you to know. And then it was awkward and difficult, and everyone might lose interest. Just imagine, she said, what would happen if a man walked up to a vegetable stand without knowing whether he wished for a plum or a leek and expected the seller to guess.

"So what does one do in that position, exactly?" Carles asked.

Odette told them, and Germaine translated: "When he couldn't make up his mind, she learned to do whatever she desired and found both parties always left happy." In the end, Odette changed over to modeling because it involved less drama. But Germaine said the same was true there. "For a few francs we're supposed to, what, compose the picture, too?"

As Pablo listened, he thought back to the first brothel Pajaresco had taken him to in Barcelona. He knew exactly what he was there for and yet had no idea. He'd felt not like a swimmer but someone towed away by the tide of arousal, tossed at sea and brought near to something resembling both euphoria and drowning before being suddenly and violently slammed into a sandy shore. All sex since had ended with a thud. Long ago, he'd imagined making love as in Renaissance painting, something transcendent instead of terrene. Pere had even suggested that in Paris, this could be so. How Pablo wished it. With Odette, he'd come close but not quite.

Germaine said she'd fallen in love once but declined to elaborate. "Temporarily I lost my most prized possession—liberty. Love's fun, but it was a price too high."

There was a disapproving look in Carles's eye.

"My greatest affair," Germaine proposed, "is with Montmartre—always handsome, full of excitement, and showers me lavishly with endless surprises. Who can compete?"

When the brandy wore down, Germaine slipped off her shoes. Pablo admired her long, narrow feet—a woman made for walking tightropes, he thought. He could see Carles moping after her homage to Montmartre. He watched Germaine notice it also, then saw how something in her softened, as if Carles's devotion—childlike and pathetic—tripped a wire inside her that forced a change in her disposition toward him. This, too, set into motion a cascade of jealousy in Pablo. He felt it flowing when Germaine leaned back to recline on the floor and rested her head on Carles's leg. She asked him, "Who was your meteor?"

"A young lady I petitioned to marry," Carles replied. "Had my father allowed me in the navy, she might have reciprocated my affection, or so I presume, since my offer was spurned for a lieutenant."

"You're the first anarchist to shed a tear because he wasn't allowed to die for a king," Germaine said, comforting him.

~

It had started innocently. A pose, a painting. But that was a blur.

When Pablo awoke, the bedroom was dark and hot, his flesh sticky, pressed against Germaine as she slept. He pulled away, and it was like peeling banana skin.

They'd been out cold—for how long, he wondered? An hour? The night?

Pablo went to the toilet. The urine was slow to come. Then it burst forth, followed by a pleasant feeling, the sensation of becoming again a channel.

For days, the studio had been full of brandied storytelling and nestling by the fireplace. But then the logs ran out, just as Paris was growing colder. Pablo went back to painting in the night and spending the day sleeping a bit before setting up on the street with his work to earn money. To his surprise, Carles had petitioned him for advice on how to do the same. Pablo told him to always appear to be laboring at an easel beside whatever paintings are for sale. "You must merge yourself and the painting into a memory that passersby will want to keep, then offer it to them for a price."

Carles had looked at him funny, and asked, "This is why you do art?"

"Absolutely not," Pablo replied. "But it is how to sell art—the reason I could afford to see bullfights in Spain."

Now, there was a washcloth hanging in the bathroom, and Pablo dipped it into the basin. He was cleaning his privates when he heard the door on the first floor of the town house shut. There were the clicks of footsteps—toe-heel, toe-heel—coming upstairs.

Pablo inhaled deeply, searching for the scent of sex, but smelled only that of fire embers combing through the air.

There was a jangling at the studio door, then the slide of the key—metal parts turning before the creaking of the hinge.

~

Carles poked his head inside the studio and was greeted by the aroma of burnt cedar. He laid down a bundle of logs on the floor beside ones already there. He was surprised to find Pablo curled on the chaise in the corner, quiet and alone. Pablo was usually painting or else cuddling with Odette at this hour.

There was no canvas on the easel, only those tucked nearby, their fronts turned to the wall. Pablo appeared fast asleep, his Parisian pet nowhere in sight.

Carles wandered into the other small room where was the only proper bed. Germaine was lying there in an immaculate, Caravaggesque slumber. He stood over her, watching her drift on a raft of dream. Gone was the heavy look she wore sometimes. He thought of how he could admire forever that perfect French nose as it flared gently.

The house was hot. Carles set his coat by the fire and pulled off his undershirt. He left his trousers in a crumpled pile on top of his shoes—flinching when the belt buckle hit the floor, hoping it wouldn't wake the sleeping painter, then scolding himself for caring. He couldn't figure out: Had he first become annoyed with Pablo at the Exposition or even before? Carles pondered this as he rummaged through his pockets for the most vital possession he owned and then placed it on the nightstand.

Germaine was naked, lying on her side, facing away from him. A breach in the sheets revealed a peninsula of flesh extending from ribs to ankle, an ideally placed cinnamon-colored mole adorning the crest of her pelvis. He'd never noticed it before, and now the spot seemed the totality of her. It was quite beautiful. He looked at the carved musculature of her long trunk, apparent in the smoldering orange light. He tugged at the sheet and slipped in behind her.

"Mmmh," she purred, pushing her round backside against Carles's middle. "Where did you go?" she groaned. "Painting in the other room?"

Carles reached past her head and pulled the hair from her face behind her ears. "No, no," he said.

She startled.

"I've been in the square all night, nearly froze. But I sold two canvases—eight francs. Bought firewood with it, although I see I'm not the only one."

Germaine recognized the voice, then the scent of cologne instead of sweat and spirits of turpentine. "Christ, Carles, where have you been?"

"I told you. I sold a watercolor of an old Spanish woman and another of a night sky to some tourists marveling at the marvelous Montmartre, where abide the artistes," Carles said, singing the last words sarcastically, showing off that he'd become a jaded local who mocked what outsiders thought of their enclave. "Artists and their muses, that is," he said, playfully. "What have you been up to, my dear?"

"Sleeping. In bed, all day. I have a terrible headache. Don't touch me, please. Can you go away?"

"Where to? Why?" He placed his wrist on her forehead. "You have a fever. What do you need? I'm not going anywhere."

"Yes, Carles. Bring me water. You can stay, but please, please leave me be. Why is it so hot?"

"Pablo must have made a fire before going to sleep," he said, getting up to fill her cup.

"Sleep? Where is he?"

"In the other room, on the chaise, knocked out. And all alone, for once. Where's Odette? They fuck like mice."

There was already envy in his voice. Germaine wanted to tell him that, no, Pablo is a man. "Odette's at her mother's," she said only.

"Drat. I didn't mean to sound cross. He's *incroyable*, Pablo is—why, he's like *le petit Jésus!*" Carles replied, handing her the water before glancing back toward where Pablo lay outside and then reaching to the nightstand for the cold glass object he'd retrieved from his pocket. "His work, it's miraculous. Yes, yes, he'd have us believe he's art's messiah. But why not? So be it. Art needs saving. I'll play along as apostle, one of the loyal ones. Hell, I'll even be a whore cavorting with the Christ," he proclaimed, drinking deeply from the amber vial and lying back on his pillow.

"It's what we all are," Germaine said, wetting her lips.

"What?"

"The whores." She promised herself then she would have no time for self-pity or its cousin, guilt. She rolled over in the heat and closed her eyes.

~

Pablo made sure he was gone before the first bells chimed. How could he face Carles, paint over what he'd done? He felt weepy, even as the cinders of desire still flared, his mind flashing with scenes of love, lust, and consequence.

To the Louvre's galleries Pablo returned each day, seeking refuge, pacing through the exhibits, wandering the museum's Egyptian halls, studying the frosty quartz eyes of the seated scribe who seemed to cast judgment. He froze before the plinth of Mantegna's Madonna to stare at the Tree of Knowledge carved into the throne the Virgin rests upon— where the serpent was curling round a limb, speaking to Adam and Eve. They looked so young, so dumb, Pablo thought.

Finally, at week's end, Pablo stopped fleeing before dawn and coming home after midnight. He returned to painting in the studio, resolving as he cleaned his brushes with solvent, the thin colors swirling down the drain and the fumes biting his nose, to wear the face of the Sphinx, to act like nothing had transpired.

Germaine, he knew, would do the same.

V

There was no sign of Pablo or Carles when Pajaresco got off the train from Barcelona at noon, though he'd sent them word of his arrival time by post.

Pajaresco searched every track, waiting until the station clock reached two. The gray sky outside was brightening, even though the sun was past its pinnacle and would soon fade. Days were short now, Paris more wintry than Spain. He decided to find Montmartre on his own.

On the steps of the Gare d'Orsay, Pajaresco lit a cigarette as the wind picked up. He cupped the end with his hands to keep it from going out, this strange city crystallizing around him. The suit he'd had cut by the same tailor as Pablo and Carles—from the exact same panther-black corduroy—was not nearly warm enough, even with the collar flipped up. Nonetheless, with his waves of flaxen hair, strong jaw, and farmhand's build, he knew he looked quite dashing in it.

But the further Pajaresco walked, the more frustrated he grew at being adrift, so far away from a warm room and hot food. Knowing no French, all the traveling Catalan could do when he encountered someone on the street was say "Montmartre" and stand dumbly while they jabbed a finger in one direction or another. In this way, Pajaresco climbed up Boulevard de Magenta, past garment shops and the monument at Place de la République, and turned left at Boulevard de Rochechouart, where the light-colored buildings with clay roofs began to be replaced by wooden settlements with straw ones. Finally, atop a high hill, he could see the low base of a wide, bone-white structure enmeshed in scaffolding. A few odd builders lurked about like garden spiders. The air up here was misty. The sky was darkening.

"Montmartre," Pajaresco said to an itinerant.

The man gave a cheerful, toothless smile, his gums purple and withered as prunes. He pointed to the ground beneath them.

"Forty-Nine Rue Gabrielle," Pajaresco said.

The old tramp grabbed his crotch—apparently misunderstanding.

Pajaresco quickened his pace again. After more than two hours, he came to the address and knocked on the building's red door. There was no answer. "Pablito," he screamed. "Carles!"

There in the entranceway, Pajaresco stood for a long time, swearing and begging mercy on his poor feet, becoming wetter, colder. He crouched and wrapped his arms around his knees, sipping the brandy he carried from Spain to keep himself from turning to ice.

As the church bells announced the vespers just after five o'clock, the door opened in a whoosh, and Pajaresco felt a kick to his rib.

"Fucking vagrant!" shouted the man stumbling over him. Pajaresco leapt up in alarm, his fist cocked behind his ear. But it dawned on him who this fellow Catalan was. "Where the hell have you been?" Pajaresco said. "Were you upstairs this whole time?"

"It's you—from Barcelona," Carles said, confused. "What are you doing here?"

"You two begged me to come. Remember? Why didn't you answer? I've been out freezing my prick off. You could have maybe considered meeting me at the train so I'm not walking around France like a goddamned fool."

"I was asleep. And how was I to know?" Carles replied.

"I mailed my train time. You didn't get it?" Pajaresco squinted and looked at Carles's pale face, his wobbly eyes. He'd heard stories about him. "What's wrong with you?" he said scornfully. "You might have noticed my letter if you weren't such a fucking dope fiend."

They turned to the shouting of Pablo coming up the street with a woman on each arm, one blonde and one brunette, and another younger one with fiery red tangles skipping just ahead. He charged up the steps like a bull and pressed his face into Pajaresco's belly, laughing with such buoyancy that it seemed to lift them into the air. Pajaresco flung his arms around his old *amic*.

"When did you get here?" Pablo asked. "I'm gladder to see you than anything."

"I brought the brandy you like, but it's half gone," Pajaresco said.

"In Paris, we will drink so much absinthe, you'll want your head back. And the women here? Pajaresco, who saved my life in Horta, you have no idea. They are not of this world but from above it."

Pajaresco saw Pablo's three companions were busy inspecting him, and he straightened his already sturdy posture, puffed up his brawny chest.

One, introducing herself as Germaine, kissed Pajaresco on both cheeks.

Another called Odette outstretched her hand and cooed when he pressed his lips against it.

"And last but not least," Pablo said, "I give you the adorable Antoinette, Germaine's sister."

"Pretty family," Pajaresco said.

"You should see the work we've done since we arrived. Lautrec? No one will talk about him anymore. Paris is to sing of me alone—except for El Pajaresco!"

"You paint?" Germaine asked Pajaresco.

"I mess around. But I'm no Pablo Picasso. He wrote me about those joints with the cancan girls, though. I'm going to pin him down to teach me how to get the garters and lace just right."

"Why leave the studio?" said Germaine. Pajaresco was enticed by her eagerness but saw how it made Carles's already hard brow turn to a scowl. Pablo also looked taken aback. Carles seemed to notice this as well and glanced sideways at him.

"Antoinette, she can model anything, if you like," Germaine said.

"Should say I do," Pajaresco replied.

"Then," she said, "you must do."

~

That night, Germaine led them along Rue Ravignan to a little boîte with peeling plaster walls inside. The dim light created a pale-yellow background that they became silhouettes against, like streaks of Chinese ink on tree bark. They quaffed cider, and Pablo and his art school chum recounted their adventures in the wilds outside Horta. Pajaresco told of how he'd tracked a boar along a mountainside. "When I put the gun up to my shoulder," he said, "the bastard charged. Came so close, I could feel its whiskers."

The girls hung on every word. Carles sat at the corner of the table, stewing.

"Haven't they great big teeth?" Germaine said.

"More like tusks!" Pajaresco crowed.

"You were almost eaten by a pig?" Carles sniffed. "Sounds like Sancho Panza."

"Who?"

"From *Don Quixote*. The book. You've heard of it, no?"

"I wasn't doing a whole lot of reading at the time—just running like hell."

"Sancho is the buffoon," Carles said. "What is it you paint, again? Landscapes?"

"Some," Pajaresco said, massaging his chin. "Not mostly, lately, though. Just finished painting a chapel, floor to ceiling. Received a real nice commission. But I like a landscape, now and then, sure do. 'Cause it don't have too many people to get on your nerves."

Pablo ordered a round of mint cordials. "Something to sweeten everyone's mood," he said. The barman's belly was big as a cassoulet and shook like aspic as he rustled behind the counter to gather teensy crystal glasses. They toasted to them having all made it, one way or another, to Paris.

If Carles had been paying attention instead of fretting about Germaine falling for Pajaresco, he'd have registered that the newcomer had a clear affinity for the sprightly Antoinette. Beneath her auburn ringlets, her face had something of the East, from Moscow or even further. Pablo could tell it was driving Pajaresco mad. He also wondered if Germaine actually enjoyed watching Carles becoming jealous. Did she like seeing his own envy grow, too—part of some game she entertained herself with, the people around her nothing but playing pieces made of ivory and bone?

The barman informed everybody that, with regrets, he must kick them out so he could sleep a few winks before his infant woke with ceaseless wails. "But what can I do? She's my little girl," he said with fondness.

Germaine inquired about the man's wife, and after a few minutes of her easy chitchat, they all had another round poured in front of them.

～

Carles' ire steeped in the alcohol, giving it more bite. This is what women want, he told himself: menfolk who regale them with shotshells and swine.

His hatred shifted, however, when he thought he noticed Germaine's focus steal over to Pablo, the two exchanging looks. Had it really been what it appeared to be?

"We go now to another place," Germaine said to Pajaresco, clapping her palms together. "Will you come?" As if there was any doubt.

"You lead, ma'am. I'll follow," Pajaresco replied.

Carles trailed behind, steaming underneath his flipped-up coat collar.

The lot of them tromped up the street and stopped in front of a dark bungalow, without even lights in the window. Germaine ushered them inside, where a piano player's hands raced across the row of zebra keys, becoming two soft blurs. The musicians were leftovers from the Romanian pavilion at the Exposition that closed after running out of money, she explained.

Pajaresco and Odette carried drinks from the back, and they all squeezed to fit around a table no bigger than a crepe pan. Something nudged against Carles's knee underneath. His first reaction was to jerk away. But he caught himself and discovered it was Germaine's leg that was suddenly crossed over his, the warmth of her thigh heating his own. He inhaled her jasmine perfume.

How can this woman be?

Who—and what!—was she after?

Why'd she insist on torturing him?

He wanted her so, so bad—even if she were the most perplexing person he'd ever encountered.

To think, just an hour ago, Germaine was eyeing Pajaresco like she could gobble him up. Then it was Pablo whom she'd enthralled. And now, it was as if she were Carles's real mistress, as if the piano bass line had rattled the cork from her heart. Perhaps she was his. He should never have suspected that Pablo might betray him.

"Says she thinks she could be a painter," Germaine said, translating to Pablo and Pajaresco as Antoinette—who'd abandoned her limited

Catalan—compared their métier with decorating desserts. "Something about spreading the paint over the canvas she would enjoy."

It was clear to all now how Pajaresco was transfixed by her.

"When she was a girl," Germaine continued, "her mother would make tortes, and she would mix the butter, the sugar, and the pink dye to make—how do you say?—frosting, which she'd spread with a spoon."

"*Magique!*" Antoinette said.

"Lucky spoon," Pajaresco added.

"We've told her she should become a pastry chef," Germaine said.

"If I gave you a canvas, what would you paint?" Pablo asked her.

"Tortes!"

Even Carles laughed, and Germaine was pleased with this. She firmly believed there was no melancholy that music, libations, and a pretty face couldn't cure. In Antoinette, she saw the naïf she'd once been, and it agitated both memories of her past and a maternal tenderness. Sometimes, this is what she felt toward Carles, too, in a way she'd never been compelled to feel so acutely before. It's funny—she'd always been convinced that having children was a trap, and now here she was, mother to a grown man who wanted her as a lover.

Germaine had watched Carles brooding all night. She knew he probably thought she was trying to torture him. That's what men always think when you're having fun, isn't it? But it's just the opposite—to be free is hardly an affront against anyone. It's what we do so that we don't have to always suffer the thumbscrews. Whatever Pablo thought, that can't be helped, either. If these Spaniards want to rut and lock horns over her, that's their own damn fault. They're the ones who barged into her life and made a feathery mess. Days ago, she'd decided the only thing to brighten the situation was being herself.

"We have known Antoinette since she was little," Germaine said, leaning into Carles, which she saw startled him. "She's like porcelain, so smooth."

"They're both your sisters, those two?" Carles asked.

"Closer, closer than sisters. Odette has learned the art of refinement, though she still may lack tact sometimes, especially when she's drinking, which is always. She's a complicated creature happiest with simple distractions: Perfume. Champagne. Cigarettes tightly rolled for a lady's mouth. Bathing in luxury or something that feels like it. A man who fucks like a demon."

"Antoinette," she added, "practically is a child, but then she'll surprise you. Earnest. Talks to everyone. Says whatever she's thinking. But everything moves around her, like water."

Carles replied, "Nothing wrong with honest hearts."

"Until they get you into trouble."

The flood of music flowed, and so did the beer. The gypsy guitar's thumping solo and the singer's wild arabesques eventually appeared to carry away Carles's moodiness. Germaine felt his posture loosen, his body inch closer. She walked them arm in arm through the crowd to dance, but she was aghast as he let the other couples moving onto the floor just pass in front of them. "You can't do that here," Germaine said. "We in France have to impose."

"On whom?"

"Me, to start."

"You?"

"Yes, I may push you away. Or may take you in. For me to decide. But I want to see what you're made of. That is French. See how I take as I please? Do as I please. Give as I please. I always know what I want, even if it's only to play. I will not hesitate."

Carles appeared thrown.

"The people, look at them," Germaine said. "They don't care. 'Get out of my way,' they say. 'I'm dancing. This space on the floor, I want it. I need it.'"

"You sound like a dedicated Nietzsche acolyte."

"Is that how the Spanish try to sound smart, or just you?"

"What you're telling me is the French are bad people but know how to get what they want, for their own good or *the* good?"

"All people are bad; all are good. But the math is a lie. Ten times good is less than one part bad."

"How are you divided?"

"*Moi?* I don't worry about such ridiculous things. I see good in everyone. But, then, what's the use? The bad ends up weighing more. So it's better to not worry, have fun, let someone else debate the right and wrong. There are no rules to this game."

"Are you old enough to be cynical?"

"You see a face you think is young, but inside I am a hundred-year-old woman."

"Even more stunning, then."

"And what I'm telling you, it's not cynicism. Just the antidote."

Germaine noticed Pablo and Odette and Antoinette and Pajaresco doing something like the quadrille—even if it was in the wrong time to the wrong music—and she couldn't help pointing at them gleefully. She saw Carles beside her was still clinging to his beer glass. She grabbed it from his hand and set it on a table off the dance floor. "You're a lush, you know that? One day it will catch up with you."

"Is that you being good?"

"I never said I didn't care."

Before Germaine even realized it, they were turning, slowly. Her hands were clasped around Carles's waist, and he cradled the low part of her back. She brushed the ends of her fingernails up his side and felt him shiver. He clutched her tighter, the way she wanted him to, moving his palms against her hips, harvesting handfuls of her corset. He put his cheek next to hers as they spiraled around, and she pushed her face beside his until their lips docked. He pressed slowly forward, and she parted her mouth, letting him inside. Germaine was aware she very much wanted to be made love to. She tickled his tongue with hers while they revolved like an empty carousel at the fairground. She pulled with her mouth and tried to unravel his flesh beneath her palate. Then, she suddenly stopped to say, "Why aren't you kissing me?"

"Am I not?" Carles asked, looking befuddled. "Teach me, will you?"

But Germaine pushed him away by the collarbone with both hands. "I won't teach a Spaniard how to kiss, if he doesn't know."

"Tell me, how does a French woman want to be kissed?"

"Why don't you read about it in a book?" she said, tearing back to the table and downing her beer. In that moment, she saw the truth for what it was: she'd fallen for a man who was determined to resist her and hooked another who had no idea how to have her.

How was it that she—who'd sworn away guilt, promised to live belonging to no one, pledged to have no obligation other than her own satisfaction—had not freed herself from this entanglement? She didn't need the money this badly. She kept a roof over her head, even if it were not ideal.

The power of infatuation had puzzled her before, but she detected now an array of arcane forces acting upon her. Why, for one, could she not smother this nonsense motherliness? Not only this, she could hear echoes of a previous situation that had pinned down her free spirit. The safeguards she'd put into place had not functioned right. She was not only bound by the present but also the past.

Germaine sat alone amid the piano music during a slow tune, rummaging through her thoughts, opening locked boxes deep within her and dusting off the contents to stare at them. Did she really know herself?

VI

The magnetism that pulls human bodies together is greater than the moon on the tides, Pablo was learning. It draws weary heads onto strong shoulders, hardened hands through satin hair—always seeks to shed layers of costume separating flesh. Fighting it is fencing the wind.

The trouble is, attraction may not begin for two people in the same way, nor is it required to bear upon them simultaneously or at an equal rate, so that lust may burn for only one. In Carles, Pablo saw firsthand how this leads to the saddest of states. His friend was at the studio less and less and out of sorts when he was around.

Pablo and Germaine, on the other hand, felt the same force of desire during each modeling session and whenever they were under the same roof. Every day, Pablo couldn't help his yearning. He avoided being alone with Germaine, lest glances bloom into another traitorous, dangerous night.

When Pablo invited Carles to join him at the Louvre one afternoon to browse the Franco-Flemish collection, then, it was both to flee Germaine and to selfishly keep Carles from her. Except that while they strolled through the museum, Pablo could not stop thinking about Germaine, her disarming humor and consuming stares. Of the way when her lips curled into a silent smile Pablo could almost hear the sly thought crossing her mind. He was dead certain Carles could think of nothing else, either.

After walking past so many paintings of flowers, beggars, and Lady Madonnas, Carles finally said, "I'm in love."

"With Bruegel?"

"To hell with him. With Germaine. It's a flood, and I'm drowning."

"And what will you do?" Pablo asked, feeling his stomach sink. He thought to gently remind Carles of how a hopeless romance had nearly been his undoing before. "Don't forget, love can hurt."

"With my niece, you mean? That was ages ago. Who can say what was going through my mind then? I was a kid, a dolt."

Pablo wanted to ask, And now?

But Carles was already rattling on. "Germaine must feel it. I know that. It flows from me to her."

In fact, Pablo could see she was starting to absorb instead Carles's disquietude, the way a nurse might catch the cold of a patient in her care. She was drinking more, slept late, didn't seem herself. She was losing that blush of activity, the rapture in her eyes. Her nose no longer stood at attention quite so much.

Pajaresco's arrival a couple weeks ago hadn't helped. The studio had become a mad place. He frolicked in bed with Antoinette day and night, devouring her from top to bottom like a croquembouche. She seemed happy to oblige, as if the repetitive act of loving were a process of sloughing off girlhood.

Needing to show off his own virility, though, Pablo nearly kept pace. He and Pajaresco often made love to their mistresses at the same time, sometimes a few feet apart. This shared ritual affirmed them as intermediaries of divine womanhood and provided the household with its music, even though to Carles and Germaine it must have been an agony, Pablo conceded. From their bed in the other room, he never heard shrieks of joy.

If nothing else, sex was a comforting distraction for Pablo from the two people who'd become his obsessions.

More and more, though, he was concerned about Germaine. A few times, he'd woken in the night to find her outline haunting a window frame. His greatest hope and fear was that she stayed for him.

"Have you told her?" Pablo asked Carles.

"She thinks I'm joking. That I don't know what I want, when that's all I know."

Pablo paused them in their steps. "And have you . . . how close have you got?"

Carles wouldn't answer.

Jealousy overcame Pablo. How could Carles waste the opportunity to lie in such a bed? He had no right to fumble what Pablo wanted so badly. "That hair," he said, "her nose, those eyes, those breasts, for Christ's sake!"

"Of course! More than anything, I want it all, but the flesh, it no longer responds."

Pablo speculated that this problem must stem from what Carles was ingesting: the booze and the evil genie in that little vial. Carles had become as much a slave to his analgesics as he was to Germaine. To add to the chaos at 49 Rue Gabrielle, Carles had found that Odette, a natural and perpetual tippler of Champagne, was always a reliable companion on the road to inebriation.

"Just take care," Pablo said to Carles as they left the museum.

For everyone's sake, he thought.

～

A week later, Carles stopped Pablo in the hall outside the studio. "All I've had is a cordial today—no morphine. Sober as a monk," he said, reaching for encouragement.

"Morphine?" Pablo barely knew what this was, only that Germaine had referred to the stuff as if it were laudanum's ogreish cousin.

"Soon, I will be like a bull."

"Very well, friend. I wish you the victor in this love sport of blood."

"You mean blood sport of love, don't you?"

"No. I got it right."

But Pablo doubted Carles would stay sober any more than he'd cease his devotion to Germaine.

Listlessness was spreading in the household like a contagion. Germaine and Odette spent their afternoons drunk, with Carles passed out on the chaise. Pajaresco and Antoinette were seemingly the only people fit enough to stand, and they were most often horizontal.

Even that pairing, though, Pablo envisioned heading for a dark turn. Pajaresco had begun seeking out other French morsels in the bordellos off the boulevard, exploits that he detailed to Pablo as if recounting a boxing match.

"You sure Antoinette's not going to be in for a rude awakening?"

"That's what learning is, isn't it?"

Arcadia, Pablo was coming to realize, shares a thin border with hell.

VII

As weeks went by and 49 Rue Gabrielle became an icy morgue, the city itself remained coquettishly fascinating to Pablo, meticulously unraveling its charms. Each time he set out to paint, there was more to admire. The nursemaids hurrying dawdling girls in white cotton bonnets by the hand in the Sixth Arrondissement. The mustached coachmen in high hats with dangling pom-poms swinging back and forth as their dappled gray horses trotted along cobblestone. Society women in feathered toques leading little poufy dogs who decorated Avenue Montaigne with almost cute filbert-sized *crottes de chien*. How was it possible that the midinettes balanced huge wicker baskets of batiste and brocaded fabrics on one hip in the narrow, crammed lanes? Or that intimately tangled lovers who would have required drawn curtains in Spain were on display as commonly as soft cheese?

Other times, Pablo ventured past the perfumed paths of Le Jardin du Luxembourg to join Manolo for a *café Turc* and plates of honey-dripped sweets bejeweled with jade-colored pistachios. They sipped and nibbled, sucking peppermint smoke from an oriental water pipe.

Some afternoons, they convened at the cafés along the boulevards with an array of influential Paris consorts who gesticulated with cigarettes and traded gossip, secrets, and witty insults. The chief of these gatherings was always Manyac, the dandyish art dealer whom Pablo warmed to since the man always lavished his works with enthusiasm, complimenting him for having such a penetrating eye. Finally free of Don José's shadow, Pablo saw his prospects growing like never before. He knew now exactly how Casas had come to Paris and returned to Barcelona a self-assured artist.

Pablo began to avoid the studio in the same way he'd once kept away from his parents' home back in Barcelona. Germaine and Odette and Antoinette were barely part-time tenants now, attending only when their other means of making a living in Montmartre came under pressure or if it was cold; they always returned when it was very cold. Whatever separate accommodations they had, Pablo surmised, must be insufficiently heated or else very drafty. Even when the fire in the studio was out, at least the walls were thick. This, if nothing else, kept them tethered. Come spring, he doubted they'd ever see the girls again. While he was still lovestruck with Germaine, something told him this would be best.

As for Pajaresco, his carousing had become a frenzied, full-time campaign to earn the adoration of every adulteress and prostitute in Paris so his name should forever be recorded in the city's scandalous lore, a Don Juan for the Gilded Age.

Carles also disappeared often and at odd hours to places that only the devil knew. If asked about his whereabouts, he'd reply that he'd gone to the Théâtre Montmartre. But Pablo knew this was a lie because he frequently set up his easel across from this scruffy company that performed melodramas, and he never saw his friend coming or going. When Carles was around the studio, he nodded off midsentence. Pablo alternated between guilt and resignation over this.

With winter bearing down, Pablo likewise felt both anticipation and anxiety, for he understood that the studio would become filled again.

He'd walk home, noticing his breath in the air, knowing that Odette would be waiting for him. Maybe, he hoped, along with Germaine.

But each frost that brought the models back to the studio meant friction. Once, Carles fell chin-first into a bowl of Provençal soup that Antoinette had fashioned with care. Odette laughed, said it looked like Carles had been scraping the bottom of the bidet with his teeth.

"You're a dirty little dishrag, you are," Carles muttered, the broth dripping from his beard and eyebrows.

Even though the modeling agreement between painter, poet, and hired muses had eroded over time, what was not forgotten was the money—Pablo and Carles still owed the second installment, as Odette continuously reminded them.

Carles came home one afternoon badly bloodied. He'd been robbed by a phalanx of apaches, the gangs who struck out from their base in the Maquis, he said—lost his wallet while escaping with his life. It stalled talk of debts for a while. But how much more could they hold out? Pablo's and Carles's savings had been worn to nil. And Pajaresco already pitched in his share, long spent.

There would be a reckoning, Pablo sensed.

~

December removed the last leaves from the chestnut trees, and a slick enamel covered the pavement and left the hills of Montmartre like toboggan chutes. Cruel Atlantic gusts swept up from the Bay of Biscay, making sleet pellets sting like horseflies and blowing dogs off ledges. On a Thursday during Advent, the snow began in earnest. It didn't let up.

Germaine, Odette, and Antoinette hunkered down. Being at the studio must have been favorable to frostbite, even if not by much.

Pablo and Odette had been treating one another as conveniences. Each was growing bored. And at this point, his relationship with Germaine was more frozen than the Seine. He feared the thaw more than the ice. But the merciless weather forced both Pablo and Carles to suspend their excursions. Even Pajaresco came back, announcing that while in the middle of an afternoon delight at a Moroccan-themed bordello, the owner had ordered the women to drop the last of their seven veils so he could hurry back to Saint-Denis to bring the livestock in.

And so, once again, everyone was bunched together under one roof.

The drinking—to warm and to numb—started one mid-December morning when they awoke and every window was piled up with white, the only light coming inside grainy and muted, almost unsuitable for painting. The world beyond the rattling glass was howling wind and metal shovels scraping the sidewalk as men futilely tried to clear the way for emergencies. The studio's occupants lacked provisions other than booze, though. All the boulangeries and patisseries and *boucheries* and crémeries—and, to Carles's dismay, *drogueries*—had drawn their shutters the night before. There was only a thin, sour stock that Germaine had brewed from the turnip, carrot, and leek Pajaresco managed to procure after braving the elements all the way to Pigalle, paying exorbitantly for root vegetables so mealy they weren't fit for rodents.

The pipes froze at five-thirty in the evening. Afterward, water had to be obtained from the powder accumulating on the ledge outside. Flushing the toilet meant using freezing hands to fill a saucepot with snow and then waiting for it to melt by the fireplace.

By the next night, everyone was as depressed as prisoners. Pablo and Odette nuzzled for warmth, as did Pajaresco and Antoinette, the brandy like fresh accelerant thrown onto their desires. No one dared shed any clothes, though, lest they catch a chill that turned to bronchitis. They loved each other through their fly fronts and by girding their knickers, while Germaine and Carles once again shared a passionless bed.

~

The six sat at dinner, spoons going up and down to their mouths like the wooden figurines of an elaborate cuckoo clock. They'd been cooped up for days. Carles and his bowl were deadlocked in a staring contest when Antoinette asked, "Won't you eat anything? You look ill."

Odette mimed from across the table as if she were downing the contents of a vial.

"Taking medicine?" Antoinette asked. "Do you need a doctor?"

"Bah, he is a licensed surgeon of the soul," Pablo said, "his pen a scalpel." Pablo remembered with some sadness how he'd once believed this.

"A surgeon?"

"*Un poète,*" Odette practically spat.

"Tell her the regimen of Champagne you prescribe yourself for loneliness," Carles said to Odette with sudden alertness. "*Et de ton cœur endormi,*" he recited, staring at the cold window across the room. "*Chasse à jamais tout dessein.*"

Hearing this doleful proclamation, Antoinette asked, "Whose lines are these?"

"Penned by Verlaine," Carles replied. "To a woman he loved deeply, Mathilde. Before he fell for another poet, Arthur—does that shock you?"

"She's brought up in Montmartre," Germaine said, cleaning the stewpot's edges at the sink with her fingertips. "You couldn't shock her with electricity."

But something in the poem did appear to frighten Antoinette. "Yearning," she said, nervously, "should not be chased away from the heart. Love, if true, is never in vain."

"I'm surprised you haven't taught her your cynicism," Carles chastised Germaine.

"She'll learn on her own, from men," Germaine said.

Carles looked into Antoinette's eyes. "What if I told you I was in love, madly in love, filled every moment with the boldest desire," he said, his voice faltering before picking up again. "I pray sometimes to God, who may be cooling in his grave, but I ask that my longing be embraced. Do you hear me?" Carles said, turning to shout at Germaine. "A love not in vain!"

Pablo placed his hand on Carles's shoulder, but he brushed it away. "This, old friend, is not a good idea," Pablo said, shaking his head. Everyone was too drunk, he knew, the air they'd been stirring in too thick.

Laughing uncontrollably, Odette snorted when the Champagne bubbles hopped up her nose.

"But Germaine is . . . ," Antoinette started hesitantly. "She's married."

Odette added in French that on top of that, she'd heard Germaine was having an affair with a circus performer, one of the lion trainers. *"N'est-ce pas, mon chou?"*

Carles pounded his fists on the table.

Antoinette translated for Pajaresco. "Bet she tamed him," he whispered.

Pablo was stunned by this news. So many screws inside him felt suddenly loose.

Odette explained that Germaine likes a certain sort of man. *"Un bête!"*

"What's that?" Pajaresco asked Antoinette.

"A beast," she said softly.

"Is there any other kind?" Carles managed.

"Some's more beastly than others," Pajaresco cracked, adding a little whistle. "You know, men who've got more balls to haul?"

Carles jumped from the chair and tackled Pajaresco out of his, toppling both of them onto the floor. Antoinette screamed. Odette's glass shattered. Pablo grabbed at Carles to pull him away. Germaine dropped the pot she was scrubbing to help. But Pajaresco was already out from under Carles, landing his knuckles square into Carles's nose. The sounds of bone mashing cartilage were terrible. Carles reached for the broken stem of Odette's Champagne glass and gripped it in his hand like an ice pick. Pajaresco scrambled and armed himself with a fireplace poker, taunting Carles to advance.

Above the clamor came a banging. *"Ouvrez la porte!"*

The two men stood across from one another, breathing deeply, their eyes bursting to fight.

"Inspecteur de Police!"

Carles snatched his coat and scarf from the back of the chair and dashed to the water closet.

Germaine patted down her hair and climbed downstairs to open the red door. Standing outside, snowflakes clinging to his grenadier mustache and falling from his stiffly peaked cap and oilskin watch coat, was a uniformed detective.

"May I enter?" he said, already ascending the steps. The inspector barged into the studio and pivoted his head around, noting the glass on the floor, the fallen chair, the general disarray.

"So sorry for the disturbance, Officer," Germaine said, trailing behind. "There was a mouse."

Pajaresco, the fire poker in his hand, smiled awkwardly.

"That is not why I am here," he said. "Who lives at this residence? All you? Under one roof?"

"My friends, they are painters," she said, reaching to turn over the canvases stacked against the wall.

Pablo prayed she'd not flip over the one he'd painted of Germaine on their night together, but she luckily chose instead a still life—a white jug full of blooming jasmine.

"Which of you is Carles Casagemas?"

They looked at each other, and Germaine shrugged. "Who?"

"Your friends," the rigid man motioned to Pablo and Pajaresco with a sharp outstretched finger. "They speak?"

"Not in French."

"What's their mother tongue?"

"Catalan."

"That name, Casagemas, is of the same origin."

"I couldn't say."

"I can. It is. Unfortunately, the region has become poisoned. Outlaws have killed scores. From Barcelona springs a particularly vile and violent strain of this terroristic scourge called anarchism. A most serious threat to our safety in Paris, to the Republic." The inspector said he found so many Catalans living in this apartment—in what can only be called desperate conditions—troubling.

Germaine asked for his pardon. Since the snow, her housekeeping had not been what it should. "Forgive me, sir, but these men are not terrorists, not anarchists."

"What of this Casagemas? What sort of man is he?"

"I wouldn't know."

"Does anyone?"

No, they shook their heads, after Germaine translated.

"Should you uncover who he is," she said, "you'll tell us, please."

The inspector eyed them suspiciously. "Monsieur Casagemas has been writing articles for the incendiary leaflets that proliferate among the shanties on the Maquis," he said. "We've foiled a dastardly plot. Can you be certain the men present are not involved?"

"They are painters, not fighters, sir."

"Better brushes than bombs, though best is they stay in their own country. There's plenty artists in Paris, too many in Montmartre. And you, madam, what is it that you do?"

"I and my sisters, we're seamstresses."

"You know these men how? Something intimate?"

"No. We have modeled to make a bit of extra money, keep us fed, warm."

"In other words, seamstresses, plus a trifle more?" he said. "I bet you cut a bloomy figure. Your sisters, too. In my day a painter—Detaille,

Meissonier—drew up glorious scenes of French triumphs. The models were war heroes, not women doing laundry and God only knows to scrape by." The inspector looked Germaine up and down and picked the rest apart with his eye. "This young one looks more a shepherd than a painter," he said, frowning at Pablo.

"He has his flock," she said.

The inspector wandered through the studio, moving around the blankets on the chaise with his baton and examining the kitchen for signs of stronger stuff than Germaine's broth. He opened the water closet door, and they held their breath. He turned the faucet handle carefully. A yellow trickle streamed down into the slime-covered basin, which appeared to disgust him so much that he left the room.

"All right, then. I have reports of comings and goings at odd hours from this residence. It can be said that my suspicions have been piqued by its unclean state and unkempt occupants—questionable women and Catalans, no less. Do not be surprised if I pay another visit. In the meantime, report any sign of a Carles Casagemas at once. He is wanted in connection with a grave investigation."

"Sure we can't offer you tea?"

"I would not drink from that sink, madam," the detective said, shutting the door behind him.

As the clacking of the nails in the man's bootheels against the stairs grew faint, Pablo rushed to the water closet. It was empty. There was a slight draft on his bare wrists, and Pablo noticed from the narrowly cracked window a trail of fabric running to a knot tied around the foot of the tub.

Pablo yanked open the sliding frame. There was Carles, three feet below the sill, dangling. His teeth chattered as he held on for dear life. The blood from his nose was hard, his hands nearly frozen. Pablo hoisted him inside, and they threw snow into a pot and heated it by the fire. Carles groaned when he dipped his fingers to defrost.

"Writing for the anarchist rags in the Maquis?" Germaine fumed. "What were you thinking? Do you want to be locked away?"

"Wasn't writing. Translating. French to Catalan, Catalan to French." Carles shivered.

"You and your messed-up little friends," Pajaresco said, "is trying to louse up the whole world, ain't you?"

Pablo pulled Pajaresco away and sat him down.

"Words with meaning, verse or prose, cannot help being revolutionary," Carles said. "They must reach every man, woman, and child."

So this was how Carles had tried to distract himself from craving opiates and Germaine, Pablo thought. He'd had enough. This misadventure must end—for all their sakes. "Tomorrow we take the overnight to Barcelona," Pablo announced, "after I attend to something important in the morning. Be packed before I return, Carles."

"*L'argent,*" Odette cried.

"Don't worry," said Pablo. "You'll get your money."

Germaine was biting her lip, watching Pablo, her eyes, usually so inviting, telling him nothing.

Antoinette held Pajaresco like a squirrel hugging a tree, but he pushed her away and put his arm around Pablo. "Look, if you need cash, I can cut back on my, er, pastimes? Paris girls is a helluva lot more expensive than Barcelona."

"Hold on to it," Pablo said. "Stay here, at least till another train. It won't look good to have three Catalans boarding at the same time." Someone, he reasoned, might suspect they were plotting to do God-knows-what and alert the gendarmes.

Pablo wanted Germaine to tell him he didn't have to go. But neither of them would admit to one another what they felt, he knew, and there was no time left to wait around. Carles walked silently to the window, squinting as though he were trying to see beyond the frost.

PART THREE

CHAPTER 8

I

Madrid, March 1901

The first bullfight of the season in Madrid, held the first Sunday weather allows, marks the conquest over winter as definitively as the pink-and-white almond blossoms arriving overnight in the Parque del Buen Retiro.

Pablo sits midway between the front row and the rim of the soup-bowl-shaped stadium, where the tickets are cheap and the sun shines all day. The section would be a brutality in mid-July, but it's welcome warmth for Pablo now, as the high-plateau air is still cool and flinty. He wishes for a scarf and Manzanilla tea.

The illustrations Pablo churned out for the debut of *Arte Joven*—the magazine he has been working on—are finally done as of last night, the proofs sent to the printer in time. Whether or not the irreverent writings and images will spark creative fire in this artistically stifled capital, Pablo cannot say. But it is a worthy endeavor, even if the bushy brows of the conservators at the Prado are not moved. Since arriving in Madrid from Málaga almost two months ago, he has spent many nights hunched over a shaky table of unfinished pinewood in the garret on Calle Zurbano—rented with money from Manyac, the Paris art dealer who granted Pablo a monthly stipend in exchange for rights to his paintings for the next year, which was the only deal he could clinch in the nick of time to pay off Germaine and Odette. But the India ink and pastels for drawing and shading the magazine's pictures have cost more than every Madrid meal he's eaten. There also have been many trips to the plaza to try to recover his mind, sort it all out. Nine days have passed since Cinto came rushing up to him there with the grim revelation of what happened in Montmartre.

By attending this bullfight, a staple of his childhood, Pablo hopes he will find reprieve from the ensuing shock and confusion. He remembers how, when he was a boy, his father used to take him to the novilladas and hoist him up on his neck like a Barbary monkey climbed atop a palm tree to watch the young, chiseled toreros in sparkling, brocaded suits as they learned to master the mighty animals racing at their hearts with deadly horns. He recalls how Don José taught him to heckle when their capework was clumsy or vain. But when the matadors were brave and graceful, when the animals charged, and they whipped the muletas away as horns passed inches from chest and cheek, together father and son would erupt, their eyes welling with victory and joy.

"It is no different than for a painter," Don José would say. "All the time the canvas is trying to murder you. Your brush is all you have to defend yourself against a beast."

Indeed, those bullfights made mortality real for Pablo at an early age. Pablo would beg to meet the bullfighters after the last toro was killed. Once, as Pablo was perched on a matador's knee, he noticed the rip in the man's gold-stitched jacket. The wound was patched, but blood oozed from the sides of the bandages like vermillion from a tube.

"It's nothing," the man said, "incidental." He pulled down his shirt collar and showed the boy a horrific crater just beneath his clavicle, where, the previous fighting season, an oversized Miura bull plunged his horn in like a harpoon. "That right there, that bull almost did me in. My life flashed before my eyes."

When the man said it, Pablo imagined flipping through a stack of old canvases, surveying the painted scenes. But how many pictures could you see before the blood drained, until everything went dark?

The wind at the stadium in Madrid picks up, jostling Pablo back from the memory. It feels too early for the first bullfight, the air still too frigid. He buttons his overcoat and flips up the collar. If there's one thing Pablo hates, it's the cold.

Carles must be so cold, he thinks. Dreadfully cold. Did his life flash before his eyes? Pablo wonders. If so, what did the canvases he saw hold? In how many of them was Pablo?

When Cinto brought word of Carles's death, it was not exactly pain or sadness that Pablo felt at first; rather, it was a knowingness. Strange, isn't it? He'd spent more time with and grown closer to Carles than anyone. He pondered whether the injury of what transpired in Málaga—where they'd fled after France, the police inspector, and all that had gone wrong there—severed what bound them together. But in the days that have followed Cinto's dark news, Pablo has been assaulted by a rush of memories, a band of escaped genies. Some are from the distant past. Other recent ones from his voyage down south are so vivid, they have a way of overwhelming everything else, even the present.

While Carles had knocked himself out before the train even pulled out of Paris, Pablo recalls, he stayed awake for the whole ride, watching the scenery unravel in reverse, a roll of canvas painted with hills and fields and towns and little churches' eager spires rising beneath the scythe-shaped moon and yellow stars. He was thankful his fidgety friend had his medicine to dose himself with. Pablo even envied Carles's anodyne, wishing it could quell his own hatred that burnt over so many opportunities missed.

They stopped in Barcelona long enough only to eat Christmas dinners with their families and scrounge a little cash. Word was there'd also been raids against anarchists and sympathizers here. They grew restless again, wary this was no place to linger.

Worse, the letter so feared by Pablo's mother had finally arrived—he was being called up for military service. He'd again have to think of something quick, as Manyac's monthly payments wouldn't let him buy his way out of enlistment in time.

Meanwhile, Carles was pining for Germaine like a cat at the window, mewling to return to a baroque love affair he'd created in his mind, fancifully referring to her as "my wife." Pablo suggested they both carry on to Málaga, clear their heads and hearts, hang them out to dry in the pounding rays of al-Andalus. He also held out hope Carles might be weaned off laudanum there and their friendship could be repaired, forgetting how the bright light of Spain is never without corresponding shadow.

~

There are three matadors to fight six bulls today. With all winter to fatten up, the beasts are gargantuan. The bullfighters' bellies bulge, too, after months of gorging on the lavish spreads set before them at every stop during the off-season, each day they are alive another cause for celebration, their exercise limited to hotel beds and boudoirs.

Still, both the matadors and bulls cut striking figures: the stiff-backed men with bejeweled capes draped over their shoulders; the monstrous mountain ranges of savage muscle, with needle-sharp horns hovering ominously above evil, burnt-brown eyes.

Even the bulls' roan-colored hindquarters are impressive feats of nature only outdone by the scrotums swaying underneath.

As each man enters the ring, he bows before the president, seated in the best box, and the brass band's paso doble is drowned out by the booming crowd.

~

When Pablo and Carles arrived in the city of Pablo's birth, Uncle Salvador's household was unprepared to greet these two unshaven young men, with their scraggly hair and worn clothes of strange proportion. Carles, raw-boned and pale as a phantom, claimed to be a poet and revolutionary. In the library, he retched inside the loud horn of the Berliner Gramophone, yellow bile dripping as the recording turned.

Pablo decided to shell out for a shared room at a *habitación* by the port.

"What are you doing in Málaga?" the squinty concierge asked.

"My family, we are from here," Pablo replied.

"They don't want you?"

Pablo assured the woman he and his friend would be no trouble.

"He doesn't look healthy," she said, nodding toward Carles.

"The water hadn't been too kind, that's all," he told her.

They were heaps of trouble, though, from the moment she rented them a small apartment where they could smell the sea each time a breeze sailed through the window. Whenever Carles wasn't passed out or writing love letters to Germaine, the neighbors complained about the Catalan madman calling out, *"Per què? Per què! Per què?"*

∼

The first fights prove predictable. The clown-like banderilleros jab sashed barbs into each animal's back to correct its movements and aggravate its temper. Mounted picadors invite the bulls to charge their horses and then lance them with spears. The matadors do the killing, hiding the sword behind the red muleta and waiting for just the right moment to drive it between the shoulder blades straight through the heart.

Sometimes at a bullfight, especially in Madrid, when both the bulls and the men battling them are superb, the fight is art, grand as opera, delicate as Japanese silk screen. Or else, as on this day at the stadium, when Pablo has come to regain control of his stampeding thoughts, during the slower moments the spectacle wears thin, and it becomes too apparent what the audience is really watching: doomed animals chasing a cloth.

∽

Pablo tried to bait Carles's passions away from Paris with the choicest temptresses of Málaga, but his besotted friend had no interest in the chicken ranch where the wizened madam known as La Chata presided with a cigarette perpetually planted between her crepe-paper lips. It was here that many years earlier Pablo had followed his father after church one Sunday and stood on a milk crate outside the window to see the women kissing Papa.

When Pablo took Carles to the local watering hole, where hardened *campesinos* drank shots of moonshine and ate fried mullet, guts and all, Carles nearly got them both clobbered, accusing the man sitting at the bar with a *navaja* knife poking from his work pants of not speaking Spanish correctly and being inbred. Pablo saved their necks with a few well-placed Andalusia-isms and many pleas of *perdón*.

All the time, Carles was either starting fights or else out cold from that poison he drank. To think Pablo had once admired—looked up to—this man, who'd been the spitting image of a youthful romantic poet right here in living, breathing, snarling flesh and perfectly creased clothes!

Carles had become a shade of himself—it was steeper than Don José's decline. Only a last shred of loyalty was keeping them together, like the root strands anchoring a loose molar. Unable to summon compassion, Pablo felt mounting disgust.

∽

The final bull enters the ring, and the crowd hushes. It must weigh a ton and shows less fright than the sun has of sea. Murmurs spread—the balls, they're ripe as honeydew!

Fresh from the gate the animal charges, aiming its master horn directly at a banderillero's vitals. The paunchy man, who should have quit the sport long ago, leaps over the railing and into the first row. Two others flap their wide dress capes—saffron on one side, magenta the other—and draw the bull, twisting themselves away just before it arrives.

~

When Carles lectured Uncle Salvador at his New Year's Eve dinner table about Catalanisme and proclaimed Barcelona's superiority above backwater Andalusia, Pablo's patience splintered. The family patriarch had chipped in for his tuition to art schools in La Coruña, Barcelona, and Madrid. Now Pablo was coming home to beg money so he might not lose his fingers in Spain's next disastrous war. He excused himself and Carles, returned to the hotel, and shut the door behind them, before pouring equal portions of brandy into coffee cups.

"Drink, you imbecile," he told Carles. "Where do you get off insulting my family?"

"Nothing of the kind. I professed pride for my homeland. Each is entitled, no matter if he is right or wrong."

"And what if you are wrong—wrong about everything? Wrong about your pride, your poetry, and wrong about Germaine?"

"My poetry? Are you my judge?" Carles's brow twisted as if it were being wrung out. "And what's Germaine got to do with this?"

"Your love poems are worse than tripe."

Carles held his cheek as if he'd been struck.

But Pablo knew how a wounded animal could suddenly grow ferocious, a bull rising again in the ring.

"My verse," Carles snapped, "is a higher creation than your tiresome pictures—those which are devised to sell, mere paeans to profit. No, I've not learned to whore myself as you have, friend."

Pablo's big eyes narrowed to knife edges. "Who do you think you're in love with, a virgin?"

"Germaine may not be a saint, but she's no whore," Carles shrieked.

For the life of him, Pablo couldn't figure out how Carles had gone from wanting to be the poet laureate of the damned to dreaming of some goose-game life with Germaine. "And do you really think that's what she would have?" Pablo interrogated Carles. "Darn your socks, suckle your babies? You said it yourself—she's making it with half the circus, which Odette confirmed. She has a husband, for Christ's sake, who she didn't bother to tell either of us about. How can you be so dense?"

~

Picadors trot from the corral on blindfolded draft horses, one liver-colored, the other slate-gray. Their assignment is clear: do something to attenuate the strength of this hellish creature or else the matador will surely die.

The lanky, unseeing horses parade around the ring.

The bull's eyes lower and fix on the right side of one of them. The beast dips its neck and tears across the clay. Its head hooks after impact, ramming the horns into the horse right up to the ring's wall. The picador astride the shocked mare thrusts his lance into the bull's back along the spine and digs in with all his strength. The bull jerks up again and lifts the horse into the air, piercing deeper. Red grows, absorbing the horse's gray coat.

~

Carles paused and drew back his neck, scrunched up his eyes, and chewed for a moment on what Pablo had said about Germaine's husband. "Why the hell should she tell you? So you can paint him?"

"She might've told me so I didn't make love to another man's wife."

Carles looked confused. And then it dawned on him. "You made love to . . . you fucked her?"

"What's the difference? Just one more," Pablo cried. "Wake the hell up. Germaine doesn't love you. She detests you. And so do I."

Carles flew into a rage then. "If you ever go near her again, think of her face even—"

"You haven't the will to destroy anything but yourself," Pablo said. "Not to make anything worthwhile, either."

"How do you know what I'm capable of? You think you're God!"

"I know what you aren't capable of, and so does Germaine."

~

The bull rattles back and forth, tearing the horse open. Its bowels leap out like a cobra escaped from the snake charmer's basket. The mare bares its teeth in agony while galloping away, dragging a tangle of guts behind. If horses could pray, this old nag would ask for the knackery.

~

The cup Carles hurled at Pablo flew past his ear and crashed against the wall, scattering porcelain and making the leashed dog outside yowl, which hid Carles's weeping, a soft quavering song as he lay on the floor, his cheek against the tile. Pablo stepped over him and walked back to his uncle's home to rejoin his family at the table, promising that the stranger who had disturbed them would not return.

~

Hidden within his cape, the matador brings his curved sword up high above the bull's lowered neck, then drives the point down, straight through the aorta. The animal kicks and bucks before dropping to its knees. It goes limp, and the crowd roars.

II

While Uncle Salvador had given Pablo money to escape the draft and travel to Madrid, the man resisted petitions to contribute to the art magazine Pablo is working on. He accepts that no more funds will be forthcoming from Málaga.

Pablo's partner in this publishing venture is a Catalan named Francisco Soler. His family has lent support to *Arte Joven* from the fortune it made selling an apparatus to cure all manner of ailments, rheumatism to nervousness. Chiefly, however, the device promises to rid the afflicted of that most worrisome hobgoblin: impotence. As with death, even men who have no reason to be anxious about its proximity live in mortal fear this numbness might strike at any hour, leaving them limp, without meaning, legacy, or joy.

The machine's construction is simple and undeniably effective—at least no one seems to doubt that some effect is happening. It consists of a wide leather belt interlaced with copper wires connected to a motor coil that the wearer straps around his midsection. A codpiece-like diode dangles in front, which must be fitted and affixed, too. Jolts of alternating current to the groin then invigorate and revive the region in a procedure that recalls raising the Frankenstein monster, only in miniature.

It's been a smashing success in Barcelona since the Soler family got the patent two years ago. Now they are aiming for their medical miracle to likewise inspire Madrid—conveniently paralleling the aspirations of Pablo and their son to induce an appreciation for contemporary art and culture in Spain's capital, long in a state of repose.

In the end, though, *Arte Joven* fails to find any other advertiser besides the Solers and is expected to fold after the fifth issue. Fortunately, Pablo has other developments to occupy him. Two letters from Paris arrive, along with a postcard and an envelope from Barcelona.

The first is from Manyac. As Pablo sits in his garret in Madrid, he pictures the elegantly attired Montmartre art dealer hovering over the embossed ecru stationery, his writing hand carefully slanting each character, curling the tails just so. Pablo has thought a good bit of him recently. The excitement of signing his first contract still lingers, even though he's begun to believe he should be earning more than the agreed-upon monthly sum. As Pablo reads the letter, he imagines the long fingers on Manyac's other hand plying his mustache's corner, which is like the soft bristles of a fine-tipped kolinsky brush.

Good news, my charming Pablo. A very reputable gallery owner in Montmartre named Vollard—hung Manet, Renoir, Gauguin, among others—wants to give you a show, along with a promising Basque whom I also introduced him to, though I believe he will prefer your output. Of at least fifty works! Can you do it? Be on your way already, Pablo. Celebrations in order! Also, I have not received a parcel from you this month or last—are you painting? Have you received my payments? Write me at once, please. And then hurry to Paris!

The second letter is from Germaine. Pablo slits open the cottony envelope with a palette knife and removes the pink paper. He holds it in his hand momentarily before shredding it without reading a word.

Ever since learning of Carles's death, a creeping anger has replaced his desire for Germaine.

The next is a halftone postcard from Barcelona showing off a smoldering *vedette* making eyes at a hand mirror. Pablo knows before he turns it over who it is from. "How 'bout it?" is all the card says. It's signed "Pajaresco."

Pablo thinks of how urgently he'd like to see his friend from Horta. Cinto had brought few details about what happened to Carles—he'd found out from his brother in Barcelona, who'd gotten it from Manolo in Paris, who was never a stickler for facts. Most valuably, though, Cinto did impart that Pajaresco was also on the scene that night. Pablo desperately wants more information.

The last letter is from Pere, who is writing to let Pablo know that Casas will stage another exhibition at Barcelona's prestigious Sala Parés. But this time, Casas had deigned to share the space with Pablo's work. Pere has underscored three times this is Casas's idea, not his own. The painter has insisted, he writes.

Pablo's heart flutters, and he forgets all his troubles. Will he really don the same spotlight as the most well-known contemporary artist in Barcelona, if not all Spain, in the city's most respected gallery? That, Pablo thinks, is the power of having been to Paris. Ignoring the one-year lease on his apartment after just a few months in Madrid, he packs his belongings to abandon a place he never learned to love or despise. Pablo writes Pere to let him know he's on his way. He also scribbles a note to Pajaresco, accepting his tersely worded invitation.

CHAPTER 9

Barcelona, April 1901

Long ago, Pablo had memorized the paths of Barcelona's narrow, doglegged alleys wending between churches, guild halls, and high buildings, a barely navigable tangle that Catalan counts plotted centuries earlier to ward off sackings by the Moors.

But now, he is getting hopelessly lost in the streets of his youth. Since the invasion of the news about Carles, Pablo's head has been a mess—has itself grown into a maze. It takes him an hour to reach the dank hideaway where he agreed to meet Pajaresco so they can talk freely. His old friend is ducked in a corner and jumps up from the table. They find themselves in an awkward trap, not knowing whether to embrace, shake hands, or merely nod; be happy to see one another or still be in mourning. Pajaresco orders jars of Cuban rum to smooth things.

There is just enough small talk before Pajaresco comes out and says he has to tell Pablo what the hell happened. "It's eating on me like vermin."

This is music to Pablo's ears.

~

As far as Pajaresco knows, after Pablo and Carles left Paris, the police did not visit the studio again. But he wished they'd hung around more.

Apaches laid claim to the entire zone, and one night, Pajaresco scarcely avoided being garroted from behind by thugs.

The models all went their separate ways, with barely a goodbye. The last time Pajaresco saw Antoinette was right after she'd charmed a pastry chef into letting her train at a top kitchen in the First Arrondissement, hoping to someday earn more money baking wedding cakes than by modeling painters' virginal brides.

Soon, Pajaresco moved into a shared living space on Boulevard de Clichy a couple blocks from the Moulin Rouge. The apartment's lease belonged to none other than Manyac, but he was regularly gone for weeks on end and would allow Catalan artists to stay in his absence cheaply or even for free. "Dropped by asking for news of his Pablito now and then," Pajaresco says. "Sometimes, Manolo was around, too. I considered myself a passing guest."

But a postcard eventually arrived there for Pajaresco—from Carles. He wrote that he'd taken a steamer back to Barcelona after Málaga and was Paris-bound now. It specified what time to fetch him at the Gare d'Orsay. "I thought about letting him wait there, like I done. But it ain't my style. Even if I kicked the shit outta someone, I'll still buy him a pork chop if he's visiting town."

On the day of Carles's scheduled arrival, Pajaresco said he found Germaine on the platform, holding in her fingers an identical postcard. He tipped his hat and plunked down beside her. Her other hand was buried inside a bear-fur muff. A boater crowned her head above a black shawl.

"Carles wrote you?" Pajaresco asked.

"Every day. I never forget to wind my wristwatch," she replied dispassionately.

"Love fallen from its perch?"

Germaine flung him a razor-sharp look.

Listening in the barroom to Pajaresco recount the story, Pablo pictures Carles approaching on the train from Spain with absolute clarity. It's as if he's right there with him, the countryside villages passing outside the window, the autumn foliage that blanketed the hills on their first trip to Paris gone now, each little house naked.

He watches how, as the engine pulls into the station, Carles scans the platform, searching for Germaine's shape, which he knows so well.

What is Carles thinking when he spots her silhouette, head tilted slightly back in that gypsy shawl? But Pablo knows this, too. Carles hears the whistle and the brake hiss and realizes he'll have to disembark any moment and speak to this woman who has consumed him. Is his hair fixed? He nervously licks his palm and presses down the unwieldy bangs and grabs the corners of his collar and pulls them taut from under his coat.

But what can he say? He's already filled a thousand pages.

"Woman of my life," maybe? Not convincing.

"I am a fool for you," perhaps? Too foolish.

"Marry me already!" A touch, what's the word, direct?

"I forgive you for what you've done." He isn't exactly in the position.

Germaine cranes her neck as Carles's car passes the bench where she is sitting with Pajaresco. Carles sees she's seen him.

Wearing the cutaway suit of olive-green velvet that he's carefully selected, Carles alights clutching a leather attaché and a fancy tin of pink marzipan. Be like a leopard, he tells himself. A thrill runs through his being when he notices Germaine's pupils increase into fantastic black gems growing just for him.

"I told you I'd return," Carles says.

"So you did—and you have," Germaine replies.

"You look more ravishing than when I left."

"It's been a long ride. C'mon, we'd better find you someplace to stretch out."

This is Carles's chance, and he wastes no time. "How I want to be alone with you. In the woods, where are the birds and the wind and the oaks, they hear only our whispers to one another. Or on the waves, in a little white boat, the billowing sail carrying us further out to sea, as we chase the horizon."

"We'll go get coffee," she says, biting her lip.

"Each day I've been away has been like living not at all, as if I've vanished from myself."

She adds, "And a croissant."

"Live with me," he says. "Be my wife. Be my love."

"Where? Look, Carles, you can't. You just can't have me like that."

"There's nothing in this world I need besides you—not poetry, not prose, not painting. You are the greatest line ever written or drawn."

"But, you see, I don't love you. Do you understand? I get a say, too, you know?"

"Not yet, you don't love me. But you don't know me the way I know you."

"You're right. I don't know you. But you do not know me, either. You just know what you think you see. I'm not some lyric in your mind. We're like pieces of two different puzzles. They don't fit. They never will."

Carles bows his head, and the starched white collar creeps up on his neck. His bangs fall onto his brow.

"You're a good writer," Germaine says. "A fine painter. And here you are in Paris again. You'll find it's a place where things happen far more wonderful than even me."

The three walk to Montmartre in silence. But, as they approach the butte, Carles begins to tell a joke about a friar, a mule, and a magistrate. They all laugh a little before stopping at the door to the apartment. Pajaresco says Carles can stay while he gets sorted out.

Germaine seems surprised when Carles doesn't even try to invite her inside. "How about a pastis on the boulevard?" she asks.

Pajaresco responds with a don't-look-at-me shrug.

"I won't be long here," Carles says.

"Nonsense. Why? You don't have to go anywhere else," Germaine says. "You've just arrived."

"Paris, this isn't the place."

"Everything is here—or in Montmartre, at least."

"Not for me, not now."

"Give it some thought, would you? See a show. Have a waltz. A drink. Have some fun. Don't do anything rash."

"Thanks. I will. I mean I won't. You know what I mean," Carles says, even pulling off a smile. "Do one thing for me, though. I'm tired. I don't want this to be our goodbye. I want to celebrate, a toast to each of us finding something new."

"I'd raise a glass to that. Where? When?"

"Soon. I'll write you."

There's a pause in Germaine's breath.

"No. I mean I'll write to let you know where to meet after I've got rest. And then I won't bother addressing you with any more silly letters. That's over now. I promise."

"Oh, you haven't bothered me, Carles. It's charming, actually. Just your way. You're a poet. You have so much in you to say. And it's lovely. It is. I'm just not the one to say it to."

That night, Carles stays awake at a draft table in the apartment's corner. He doesn't write poetry in his notebook or a love letter on the stationery he's bought. Rather, they are screeds. When he is done, just before light, his wooden legs rise from the chair, and he walks gingerly to a window overlooking the Boulevard de Clichy. Outside, above the white Haussmann buildings and plane trees, is a half-sleeping purple sky encroached by that daily menace. Carles wishes the violet were sweet and everlasting, but soon it is overcome by the steady warping of the spectrum to azure—another crushing day. The dawn chorus of blackbirds begins to sound and so does the chirruping of a thousand house sparrows flying from gutters and streetlamps. There is no escape.

~

When Pajaresco wakes, Carles is gone. He's absent from the apartment the next morning, too. A courier with a message sent by pneumatic dispatch turns up. Carles has written to say he's departing Paris and requests Pajaresco's attendance at a farewell in the evening at L'Hippodrome, a bistro a few doors down.

Pajaresco couldn't be more relieved. Three people in an apartment barely bigger than a birdcage is too tight, especially when one is Carles. Under the wrap of that tortured poet façade, there were those high-caste manners Pajaresco detested. And something about Carles always made him uneasy.

At 7:00 p.m., Pajaresco arrives in the cramped corner restaurant to find Carles, Germaine, and Odette, plus a couple other Catalan acquaintances, sitting at a zinc-topped table. Apparently, everyone received invitations via *la poste pneumatique*. Carles orders a feast that would make all the starving artists and fashionably slim bohemians in Montmartre writhe with envy. Buttered bread and radishes. Frisée and lardons topped with a gently poached egg that resembles a sea creature escaped over the side of aquarium glass. Glistening pork shoulder with stewed chestnuts. Seared *rumsteak*. Crème caramel. Orange peels in black chocolate shrouds. With every new dish, there is more wine; Carles makes sure of it.

Little tulips of brandy and hot Chartreuses follow dessert. They all reach over the table to clink glasses, Germaine to Carles's right, Odette to his left, Pajaresco directly across from him, flanked on either side by the other Catalans. Carles stands to make a toast. Pajaresco, who can't understand polite French—a language that always sounds to him like a flamingo trying to pass a billiard ball—has no idea what he is saying.

Carles is wearing the same crisp, notch-collared cutaway sack coat of shimmering green velvet that he stepped off the train in.

Everyone's tipsy at this point. The girls snicker when his voice rises loud as a stage actor, as if he's speechifying to an imaginary balcony in the cozy restaurant.

Pajaresco spots Germaine noticing something poking out of Carles's pocket, and she playfully reaches toward him. The letter falls onto the table beside the glazed china bearing the last chocolate-coated *orangette* that no one has been bold enough to claim. She leans forward to inspect to whom the missive is addressed, and the smile on her face goes crooked—before it is wiped away by instant sobriety. Pajaresco cranes his neck to look closer and finds that the name on the envelope is that of the prefect of police. Odd, Pajaresco thinks, as he bastes a spoonful of custard in the well of sweet, vitreous caramel gathered at the edge of his plate. Suddenly, Germaine bolts under the table, disturbing the setting and knocking over at least two wineglasses before scrambling up behind Pajaresco, who is about to shovel the custard into his mouth just as Carles turns and politely says to Germaine, now crouched behind the back of Pajaresco's chair, *"Voilà pour toi."*

The glint of the barrel rising in Carles's hand seems to move across the disheveled table as slowly as if it were traveling through gelatin—such a pretty little pistol, Pajaresco thinks, admiring the engraving fine as lace, the ivory grip. He can feel his brain churning as it calculates the trajectory of the arc of Carles's arm, and the balls of his feet push from under bent knees, catapulting him forward and upward, with Pajaresco's outstretched fingertips reaching Carles's wrist just as the gun explodes in a room-shattering bang.

He feels the hand clenching his chair from behind go limp. The body it belongs to falls to the floor in the very same instant the custard that was flung into the air from his spoon splatters back onto the plate. Carles looks down at Germaine, licks his lips, and reaims the gun. He says, calmly, *"Et voilà pour moi."*

By the second blast, the restaurant has all but emptied of patrons. Odette is frozen. Pajaresco has dived on top of Germaine, his body covering her like a pile of clothes. The two other Catalans at the table are yelling as they try to plug the hole in Carles's temple from which blood is gushing out. It's futile, and they cup their hands beneath, as if they could capture every drop to later funnel it back inside him.

A frantic waiter approaches with a policeman, and they drag Carles to the pharmacy across the street to find help, his limbs like a marionette's, the tablecloth wrapped around him soaked crimson.

~

At this place in Pajaresco's retelling, Pablo can't contain himself any longer and interrupts the tale that has filled his imagination. "Was there nothing you could do?" Pablo asks, more pointedly than he'd meant to.

"I did do," Pajaresco says in a ruffled voice. "I jumped on top of the woman in case he fired at her again. Ain't that enough? I was half blind from the gun that went off not two inches from my face, couldn't hear nothing in neither ear. I still got ringing, and my eye isn't right yet."

"What happened to Germaine?"

"She was more than all right," yells Pajaresco. "Carles didn't but graze her. Looked like an orange caterpillar climbed along the back of her neck. She comes up, and what's she do? Kisses and hugs me after using me for a shield," Pajaresco tells him. "I reckon if your boy Carles had one more bullet he woulda liked to send it my way. Never did see eye to eye. I thought he was a little pompous, frankly."

"Let's not speak ill of the dead," Pablo reminds him.

"Look, I didn't mean nothin'. I just been through a bunch, is all."

"Was there anything else? Another letter?"

"Yeah, one to the king of Spain, one for the pope."

Pablo had hung on to the prospect that there may be more than only Carles's anarchist ranting to authorities, that there might be something addressed to him, even if it were a single paragraph of verse.

"If there was one more bullet," Pablo tells Pajaresco, "it should have been for me. This, it's all my fault."

"Yours? What'd you ever do to him? You was his friend. I'm the one almost broke his skinny nose at the studio. But I'd say it was that Germaine's doing, if anyone's."

Pablo thinks back to the way Málaga ended, and then to Paris, and he asks himself how could he have succumbed and slept with Germaine, been so reckless? Yes, long ago he had warned Carles about the pistol, but that hardly made him less culpable. Again, temptation had led to disloyalty.

"I was not a good friend," Pablo says.

"Hell you wasn't," Pajaresco huffs. "Always done right, far as I know. Nobody's perfect. Can't be. Wouldn't want to be. Life's like paintings. Perfect don't catch your eye. It's that smudged-up canvas that's all kinds of wrong that does."

Finally, Pablo feels the waited-for sting, the hurt of understanding how he'd ruined his own best friend.

"But you, you were a brave man, Pajaresco," he says, "More than she, or I, deserve."

They each throw back their rum. It is a while before either speaks.

"Excitement over these past months has got me about worn out," Pajaresco says eventually. "Time to head home to Horta and clean up. Fill the purse."

"Why don't you come back to Paris instead?"

"Nope. That's one place I won't be revisiting. Them lionesses play too rough. I'll stick here in Spain and find me some pretty kitties that don't do nothing but purr when you pet 'em."

"I hear you."

Pajaresco lets his gaze drag along the tabletop awhile before picking up his head and asking Pablo if he might want to snatch one by the tail right now at the cathouse down the street, "for old times, you know?"

"You never change," Pablo says.

"Sure I do." Pajaresco nods. "I'm blinder and deafer now."

～

After another two rums, Pablo gives in. The friends leave the hideaway and creep through an alley to a red lantern resting on a window ledge on Carrer d'Avinyó. It's early still when Pablo and Pajaresco arrive. The bagnio is quiet. The crone who greets them is wrapped in a cloak of night-colored gabardine. There's something about her movements that gives the impression she may have been a fine figure long ago, before her left eye was ghastly marred.

She leads them to a countertop, where gherkins that look like digits snipped from a mummy's hand, drab olives, and a sweating rind of manchego sit beneath bell jars like laboratory specimens. She motions to the tapas, but they wave her off, patting their bellies to indicate they'd already had supper, couldn't possibly handle another a bite.

The procuress shrugs and continues to a stage curtain of crushed orange velour. "Maybe you'd like a little dessert," she says in a creaky groan. "Nice and juicy. Nice and fresh. Just for you."

Pajaresco inches back the fabric.

Two figures behind it immediately halt whatever they were doing, hiding any expression and striking poses that seem part mannequin and part mantis. The one with her hair pulled into a Psyche knot has both arms folded behind her neck. She heaves forward her bare chest. The other mimics this, though she clings to a sheet with one free hand, draping it above her powerful thigh. Each of their eyes intently move and adjust like the aperture of a camera lens capturing its subject.

Nearby on the stone floor is a bowl of fruit—musky grapes, a yellow apple, and a half-eaten melon that another woman squatting beside it just put down, her chin dripping with the sticky remainders. She lifts her gaze, seems to be sizing up the potential customers as much as they are judging her. She is intriguing, almost in a runic way, Pablo determines. But the manner in which her shape is underlit by the oil lamp on the ground is briefly terrifying.

And what, he wonders, do these viewers think of him—how does Pablo Picasso measure up? Is he the man he'd hoped to be or just a coward? An artist or an amateur? Deliverer or treacherer?

A fourth woman draws back another set of drapes partitioning the room and emerges to see what the madam wrangled from the street. She appears perplexed by Pajaresco and Pablo, dashed perhaps with a streak of pity. The quandary also distorts her face.

Every painter in the Louvre or Prado has painted prostitutes, Pablo thinks. But what's before them here is not some dreamy, idealized scene. It is far more strange, possibly sinister, and altogether intimidating—like something fearsome bubbled up from the dark center of the universe, a place where past and future are interchangeable, and everything and everyone is far while also near. But for what purpose are they here now—to woo him away?

Pajaresco chooses the woman with the juice-stained chin, which relieves Pablo because he found her chiefly disquieting, like she saw something beneath his skin he'd meant to keep hidden. His heart is pounding, he realizes, understanding the extent of how deeply he's been disturbed. To be done with it, he nods toward the one who has just entered. She has the most laconic air about her, and he can't bear to maintain a conversation with anyone right now.

The last time Pablo went to a brothel was the night he learned of Carles's death from Cinto. He'd marched to Madrid's red-light district, thinking of how Carles had once read from a history book detailing ancient peoples' practice of ritually purifying their souls at Aphrodite's temples. But the experience was far from erotic or purgative: he paid a fee he could ill afford to lie beside a woman twice his age and fall asleep on her breast, nothing more, as she held his head beneath the flea-infested blanket on the yellowed sheets of the bloody mattress in a dirty room. In fact, Pablo had made love to no one since Paris.

Now, this dreary evening back in Barcelona is turning to be much the same. He lies in his undergarments beside the odd, ruminative naked woman, thinking to himself of how in his youth the unmoored bathing hut in the sandy shallow had swayed in the tide after the Galician beachgoer ran up the steps. He and the prostitute cradle each other without exchanging words. Pablo's thoughts continue to wander, and he contemplates the particular way Germaine had smelled. It was mostly the perfume she wore—jasmine, he supposed—but also hay. He remembers the other smells of his night spent with her: that of the smoke from a burning fire, the sweat, the lust, and the embers combing through the air. Does greed have a smell, the way anger does? Carles had a scent, too, Pablo recalls. No matter how infrequently he bathed or how much brandy and God only knows what else he'd drunk, Carles always smelled like a clean, cold river. That's how Carles was the night Pablo found his friend unconscious on the sofa at the Barri Xinès brothel that he hated. Or when he'd nearly fallen over the railing at the Three Kings Ball. That's how Pablo knew Carles would be all right even when he already looked gone, that it would be all right. Because Carles had not smelled like he was going to die, not the way Conchita had. There was no faint emanation of decay.

Pablo himself is in need of reviving now. In the past weeks, his body has grown weary all over. At first, he figured it was scarlet fever again. Hope sowed that his planned return to Paris in a matter of days would restore him.

There is another disturbing development Pablo has noticed, though, part of the reason he's reluctant to remove his undershorts now. He recently discovered a chancre on the tip of the bulbous part of his penis, like a ladybug perched on a tree gall. It has not bled or oozed. But the notion that its putrefaction is growing and might soon envelop him entirely infects his thoughts every still moment. Pablo knows of the diseases sailors get, of the French curse, Paris's revenge. It makes them mad. And, far worse for a painter, it makes them blind. He worries this is what it could be. He is not special, Pablo thinks. He is as doomed as the horse or bull in the ring was. Or Carles.

CHAPTER 10

I

Paris, May 1901

There is no response to Pablo's knocking on the door to Manyac's sixth-floor apartment on the Boulevard de Clichy. He gives a gentle push, and it creaks open before swinging shut again, as if trying to eject him.

Inside, four stern-faced men are seated at a round table on the far side of the room, a plaid deck of cards distributed among them, the players locked in dead-eyed stares.

Pablo recognizes Manyac's waxed mustache beneath the shadow of a gray felt homburg. He is wearing a checked wool waistcoat with his necktie loosed. His back is to the wall. Pablo waves to him.

The art dealer had been so ebullient in his recent letter that Pablo is shocked when he doesn't move a muscle or offer a greeting. Pablo failed to announce his trip, but isn't this a pleasant surprise? Or is Manyac irked at him? The man has always been hard to decipher. And he has a way of making Pablo anxious, especially in light of their budding financial relationship. Pablo has long accepted creativity as a natural gift, but he is doubting his own business acuity. The gushing tone of Manyac's correspondences has led Pablo to become increasingly suspicious that the one hundred and fifty francs he gets per month is a swindle. Maybe he's worth twice that—why not? Or, then, might he be worth only half? Nothing at all? So hard to know.

If Manyac was not happy to see Pablo, though, he should appreciate at least that in Pablo's hand is a portfolio stuffed with all his best recent work, owed to Manyac under their contract. He'd become so excited to get it to him, he even skipped his own show with Casas in Barcelona and boarded the next train heading north. Shouldn't Manyac be overjoyed at both? He's a difficult one, all right. An uneasiness has planted itself right above Pablo's navel and is starting to grow.

Pablo looks around the twin rooms without partition. The watermarked plaster is covered with risqué chromolithographs advertising cabaret performers, the froth of their white petticoats blooming around pink legs kicked high. Chéret, Mucha, Grasset, Lautrec—all surreptitiously peeled from the sides of Paris shops and kiosks and public urinals.

Finally, Manyac darts his eyes and tilts his head to the side to beckon Pablo. He looks a bit older than Pablo remembers, maybe in his thirties. Pablo traverses the room, and Manyac whispers something. Pablo kneels close to Manyac's lips to hear. The other card players sigh. One slams down a notebook he was using to keep score, sending stacks of poker chips clattering all over the table.

"You'll have to excuse me, my dear. Delightful to see you," Manyac says, barely moving his thin lips and granting no readable expression. "I happen to be engaged in a rather fraught game of high-stakes silent *manille*. If I speak much more, I fear my good-natured opponents might become, shall we say, cross."

"Sounds no good."

"For now, it is not, Pablito. For now."

Back in Barcelona, Pablo had witnessed this intense card game at the gambling dens in Barri Xinès. It is similar to *botifarra*, but with a deck of only thirty-two cards. No one is allowed to talk or signal in any way to his partner across the table. Even in that unsavory and violent district, however, Pablo hadn't seen the rules regarded so gravely. It dawns on Pablo he'd made a particularly grievous faux pas by passing the other players' revealed hands and then crouching to chat conspiratorially with Manyac. He is embarrassed and a little afraid for them both.

Manyac tells Pablo to put his things down and come back tonight. He'll be a prized guest. "Now, and I beg your pardon, but you'd better scarper. The gentleman to my left was a soldier of fortune in Tonkin and is said to have killed a man by lashing his torso above a fast-growing bamboo. Imagine that for a moment, would you?"

Pablo hisses at the thought of what this mercenary might do to a card cheat.

"Precisely," Manyac says.

Leaving his portfolio and carpetbag, Pablo sets out for coffee. He is exhausted after the train ride from Barcelona and fears he might doze off standing up. He'd made scant preparations for this sojourn in Paris, as his last living quarters in the city materialized so precipitously, and fatefully. Only now is Pablo considering what it will be to spend a night in the very Paris apartment that Carles occupied before his suicide. But he doesn't have any other options. He wouldn't dream of staying with Germaine, not after what she did: tempting and deceiving everyone, toying with them, and then putting Pajaresco in the cross fire.

From him, Pablo had also heard that two days after Carles shot himself, Odette decided she was through with Paris and hopped a train to Belgium, mentioning something about an uncle who fashions brass instruments there. Too bad, Pablo thinks, imagining a waft of pleasing citrus following her to Brussels. But then, maybe it's fitting that Pablo is here, near the scene of the crime. Even in death, Carles's life is intertwined with his.

Despite how much Pablo needs a dose of caffeine, and all that's brewing in his mind and weighing on his heart, he does feel exhilarated to be back in *La Capitale du Monde*. He's even committed to improving his French and trying to think in the language. After a short walk, Pablo finds an outdoor café and sits beneath a green canopy, watching the women on the street, both the done-up ones and those who artfully wear their disarray. Somehow nothing in Paris ever seems out of place, even the hodgepodge. It's all so much livelier than anything in Spain. The arc lights, omnibuses driven by dapper coachmen, metros whirring underground, and a sweet odor of singed track grease from the electric trams. The engrossing silhouettes of grandes dames with so much plumage their hats look ready for flight. The flashy boulevardiers prowling like urban tigers. Those rouged ladies working the sidewalks outside the cabarets. He's been gone too long.

Yet when Pablo stirs the bitter espresso with his eyes closed, listening to the warble of pigeons above the street noise, the sound makes him think of his father, and his recollections veer away from France and back to the ride his family took across the country from La Coruña to Barcelona when he was a boy.

On the way, Don José made them briefly disembark in Madrid. Doña María and Lola went to the Puerta del Sol to haggle with stall-sellers over folding fans. His father and he headed to the Prado.

They marveled at Velázquez's portraits, analyzed Goya's lunatics, licked their chops at his *La Maja Desnuda*. And they shared a laugh for the first time in ages over Hieronymus Bosch's *The Garden of Earthly Delights*, in which a bird-daemon on the third panel of the triptych gobbles a man headfirst while shitting a flock of magpies. Don José called this an accurate illustration of his own personal hell.

When his father left to use the latrine, Pablo drifted to a gallery where El Greco's saints were on display all in a line, a murdered row. Pablo admired the *figura serpentinata* coiled in each scene. But he also noticed something special while observing these martyrs' hands. In their long, slender fingers, bent in ways that seemed to defy joint and bone, he saw the shape of pigeon toes. Pablo still remembers the way he puzzled over this surprise. How many birds must Spain's adopted painter have composed before he knew their secrets? In spite of all appearances, Pablo ponders again now, could it somehow be true—had Don José stumbled onto a channel to mastering human form by contemplating pigeons so long and hard? Was he not a washed-up dauber, as everyone said, but instead an unsung master?

But then Pablo remembers what happened as he stood staring at El Greco's famous imagining of *San Sebastián*—the faithful's elongated golden abdomen bound to a tree trunk and pierced by a hail of arrows, his soft gaze tilted almost Magdalene-like to eternity, as if he loved the Christ more than anyone knew.

Pablo had been transfixed—caught wondering if the hands clasped behind this martyr's back were not those of a dove—when Don José reappeared, startling him with a backslap, sneering, "I wouldn't leave my son alone with that gamy ol' Greek for too long."

While exiting the museum, they passed by Goya's chalk sketch from the Peninsular War of a lynch mob chastising an invading Frenchman. The soldier was lashed to the ground, naked below the waist, squirming while the guerillas buggered him with a crescent-cutter. Upon spotting the crude picture, Don José cawed, "Bet he didn't mind it as much as they thunk!"

At the time, Pablo forced himself to raise a smile.

When Pablo finally returns to the apartment at night after wandering Paris all day, the card players are gone, and Manyac has dozed off. He plops onto the settee in the corner and falls fast asleep.

~

"I call it the second-best cigarette of the day," says Manyac, standing above Pablo in the morning, smoking—his voice silky and firm, like taffeta.

Pablo rubs his eyes and sees a silver case extended in an open palm near his head. "Go on," says the art dealer.

"I won't say no," Pablo replies, removing one of the tightly rolled cigarettes and letting Manyac light it.

"You realize I'm going to bring you today to meet someone who will change your life?" Manyac says, taking a deep drag before settling on the scroll arm of a sofa across the room. "He's very special in Paris, Vollard is. One day I suppose you'll owe me a share of gratitude. Not for inventing you, of course. But for, let us say, announcing you to the world."

Pablo is silent as he inhales smoke both from his cigarette and the haze expanding in the air.

Manyac asks Pablo his age and then whether he understands what it means for a nineteen-year-old to exhibit at a gallery here.

"I have a show up with Casas right now at the Sala Parés."

"Barcelona is for hacks," Manyac croaks. "This is fucking Paris. You do know the difference, don't you?"

Pablo is quick to nod.

Manyac tells Pablo to get dressed and sort his portfolio. "Put anything too studied in the back. Vollard hates that sort of dreck. He wants feeling. Wants pretty," Manyac says. "He wants something he can sell."

The plan is they'll double Pablo's stockpile before the show. Manyac can furnish him with whatever he needs: models, booze, opium. Pablo is learning his host can be even moodier than Carles, although Manyac's swings are of a different kind, seesawing from charming to tyrannical in the same breath. "I'll be out strolling for the next hour. Be ready when I get back," he says.

Pablo fills a pitcher and pours it over his head above the basin to wash his face. He scrubs his eyes before a mirror and pulls back his hair. It's the first time he's had a good look at himself for a while. He's gotten thin. And he will have to do something with the wispy mustache above his lip—shave it clean or make it neat. Pablo uses his undershirt to dry himself. He stands by the window and stares outside, looking across the boulevard lined with plane trees, thinking of how Carles might have peered from this same spot on his final day.

As Pablo is scouring the card table and every other flat surface for a stray cigarette, he notices a pile of canvases leaned against the wall. They are his, ones he painted in Paris months ago before everything turned upside down. Pajaresco must have brought them here for safekeeping.

He riffles through them, each facing inward except one, which is unfinished. The face is unmistakable to anyone who knew her, though.

It all comes back, like a riptide.

During those heady days on Rue Gabrielle when Carles was dissolving just as Paris revealed its wonders, Pablo painted each night, all night. Only then could he count on no interruptions. The crisp of the nocturnal air enlivened him. He would strip to his undershorts and set up an easel in the front room with the fireplace or lay the canvas against the wall there and crouch, becoming entranced in his work, allowing his brain to process all he had seen during the day, working it onto the canvases, breaking only to fetch a cigarette or when the ache in his back and thighs summoned him. Then he'd fold his arms tightly and rock his head side to side, viewing the work from different angles, before squatting again to resume his thoughts with the brush.

Pablo was immersed in this routine late one evening when he realized Germaine was standing in the doorway, having watched him for who knows how long. He sucked in a breath of smoke and said she shouldn't sneak up. "I thought no one was home."

"Women like surprises—flowers, earrings, a fragrance. Men don't like to be caught off guard," Germaine replied. "Even when it's something they wanted."

"Men don't know what they want."

"Most men," she said.

They fell silent for a moment, then Germaine spoke aloud what both must have been thinking. "Sure, that's what he tells himself. Oh, and he says it to me, all the time, 'I adore you. I worship you.' Says it's my fault for looking at him, letting him see me."

Pablo asked what she was doing awake so late.

"I've got an ungodly hangover."

"From the other night? Shouldn't you have cured it already?"

"Thought I did. Must have been in remission," Germaine said. Looking down at the scene of Spanish dancers Pablo was working on, she asked, "How come you never ask me to pose?"

Pablo said he could paint her into this canvas right now. "Just like that, carry you to Barcelona faster than the express."

"As you like. I've Spanish blood in me."

"Who is really Spanish, anyway?"

"Gypsies and Moors," Germaine said knowingly.

"I've a little Gypsy blood in me," Pablo countered, thinking back to Horta.

"Why am I not surprised? There's something different about you," Germaine replied, nibbling on her bottom lip.

"Let's get a fresh one," Pablo said and retrieved a blank canvas. He directed Germaine to perch on the armchair and turn her chin ever so slightly. "I want to see your eyes."

She rolled them sarcastically instead. "Do you have any idea how many times I've struck this exact pose? No variation. No novelty. I thought you'd be a bit more, you know, inventive—might imagine something exciting."

Pablo couldn't help imagining plenty.

"Ever been on a Friday morning to Place Pigalle, where all the models are gathered 'round the fountain?" Germaine asked. "They even call it the Model Market—like we're ripe produce! Painters saunter up there to pick and choose, as if sorting aubergines and cabbageheads. But careful if you go," she warned. "The models might be a little snappish, cruel even. You'll find all types, though—Moses, Jupiter, Venus, Napoléon, Marie Antoinette. And every one of the commedia dell'arte gang. Probably more than a handful of Virgins. Think of it: you're Jesus's mother all day, a naughty lil' minx at night! What a life, right?"

Pablo asked, "Still have the necklace Carles gave you?"

"I do, and I rather like it. Don't you?"

"And how do you like Carles? He's mad about you, you know?"

"I'd rather not say right now."

"How Egyptian—like the Sphinx!"

"A kitten who knew her craft," she said.

"Have you ever seen the Egyptian galleries in the Louvre?" Pablo asked, to which Germaine nodded. "The Chaldean ones, too," he went on. "The gods and the paintings on the walls, I find them fascinating. They remind me of people I know sometimes."

"And the goddesses?"

"Yes," Pablo said. "Funeral goddess. Vulture goddess. Goddess of scorpions."

"And of magic, and of love. Et cetera, et cetera. Not everyone is wicked, you know?"

"And the cat-headed goddess? What is it? Motherhood—and war?"

"Fertility," Germaine reckoned.

"But also war?"

Germaine borrowed Pablo's cigarette for a puff.

"And why should the models at the market be cruel to me?"

"Maybe not to your face," she told him. "But why not? They spend a dozen hours bent into some mad pretzel pose to please the painter. What, and then have these louses chinch your pay, when it's only a few sous to begin with? Haven't models got the right to be cross? The worst is they try to seduce you once you've got your clothes off, like you're some little idiot."

"So we're the wretched ones, then?" Pablo asked.

"You're sweet. But you, you're still young. Just wait," Germaine said. She reached for an open wine bottle on the sill of a warped window that never quite closed and held it upside down above a glass. Nothing came out, and she landed the bottle back in its place with a thump. "It's nippy in here. Have anything else to warm a lady before I freeze?"

Pablo poured his stash of brandy into two teacups and threw one of the hefty cedar logs he'd bought that afternoon into the fire. It started to crackle. "When you went to the Louvre and saw the Egyptian, what struck you?"

"The men and the women and even the animals, they all have such nice, calm faces, no matter if they're killing or dying. Don't even open their mouths."

"Maybe they know something we don't," he replied, handing her a teacup. "The art in these galleries is called primitive. But it's not, I think."

"What do you mean?"

"On those walls, artists with no names did something quite special. It's because they didn't paint to please. It's not just for people to look at. It was more, sacred. A ritual. A struggle for survival."

Germaine looked intrigued.

Pablo explained it was as if back then, the painters were ordering the cosmos. "Life, death, creation, destruction, all of it. Just with pigments dashed on stone walls."

"Now that's some poetry," she said, clinking her cup against his. Germaine took a sip and set down the porcelain. Her eyes lit up then, and she said excitedly, "C'mon! What'll it be? Order the cosmos, or at least the scene in this room! A little creation? A little destruction? Hint of both? Tell me, what shall I become tonight?" She leans closer to him. "How do I pose? I can do my face. I've got on only cold cream and rouge."

"You like to pretend, don't you?" he said.

"Are you kidding? I love it," Germaine said with a twitch of her nose. She made him promise not to tell anyone, though. "Business is business, after all."

"A professional."

"Consummate," Germaine said, her eyes serious again. "But I always imagine I'm somewhere else. It's all play. Every model likes to pretend. A trade secret, I suppose."

"What if I were to paint you dressing up, then? Looking in the mirror, putting on your powders?"

"It is a sort of pretend, too, isn't it? Being a lady," she said. "A parlor game."

They moved to the small bedroom, and Pablo began working up a canvas that showed Germaine in the flickering light as she angled her neck before a standing vanity. His brushstrokes were slow, until the bristles barely shivered against the plain weave. He knew then how Carles felt, he who had fallen into the trap of making believe with Germaine ever since they met but couldn't keep up with a master of the sport. "Pretending is fun," Pablo said, almost to himself, "until it's not fun at all."

Germaine pulled out the pins holding in place her loose chignon, and a black curtain of hair fell and rushed around her long, golden neck. "What if you painted me, I don't know, unpretending?"

"Go on."

"Well, I'll remove my rouge, see? And the powder. And . . ." She unfastened her cotton-and-bone camisole from the back.

"Thought you were cold?"

"So right," she said, plunging into the bed in nothing but her laced corset, burying herself beneath the eiderdown.

"But how will I paint you?"

"You'll have to come 'neath, too, I suppose," she laughed. "Bring your brush!"

"And Carles?"

"What about him?"

"He'll be home soon."

"He's been gone all day. Probably found some little chippie whom he'd rather make love to."

Pablo played dumb, the brush in his hand shaking.

"It's not for lack of enthusiasm on my part, either. I'm no dead herring, you know?" Germaine stared right through Pablo. "Come now," she said, flinging what remained of her garments across the room. "Carles will thank you for saving me from catching a deathly chill."

Pablo knew his decision was already made. And he understood what he was doing. But nothing in this moment mattered besides what awaited beneath those covers. He put down the palette and obeyed, diving just as he'd leapt after the school of glimmering fishes when he was a boy in La Coruña, finally catching what had enticed him.

∼

In the blackness of the bedding's cave, Pablo grazed his cheek playfully against Germaine's bare stomach. He sowed a string of kisses from navel to neck within the mystery of the feather-filled duvet. He kneaded the arches of her tightrope-walking feet, then moved up her calves. She hugged the pillow and curled onto her side. He skated behind her knees with his lips all the way up to the cleft of her derriere and felt her body melting as if in a hot iron pan. He reached around her and swept his palm up the length of her thigh, curving it between her legs before dragging it through the valley of her breasts to the mouth that nibbled his fingers.

∼

Germaine stretched her arm under the blanket and searched blindly, like a hound hunting a burrow. She pawed at a clump of wiry hair, tugged for a second, and then scoured again before discovering a pair of evasive ornaments. She girdled the web of her hand around them and gently squeezed, feeling the dangling skin tighten like a creature in a tide pool as Pablo gasped. She trailed her fingertips along the protrusion guarding these jewels and giggled in her head because his penis was bigger than she expected, silently musing once again how women more than men enjoy surprises. With her thumbnail, Germaine circled the bulbous glans, puffed up like hen wings, and ran the tip of her forefinger down the narrow ridge of flesh. As he rose from the cavern of the blanket, his dark eyes caught the flickering light and then met hers. She guided him inside her.

~

Pablo proceeded attentively at first, before adopting an oarsman's rhythm. He pushed in and out of the inlet and felt himself expanding, as if his blood was increasing in volume.

~

Germaine's hands clung to Pablo's biceps. Then she lowered her grip to his elbows, feeling the pulsing of his veins inside the soft creases. She clasped her ankles behind his body, absorbing him as he moved. The wind through the crack of a window picked up, and the room quivered and hastened. She swept the back of her forearm against the stubble of Pablo's cheekbone and held it there. Color was rippling through her, emanating from her sex. With her other hand, she drew him nearer. He was deep, but if only he could reach just a bit more, touch some new part of her, closer to the pith.

~

They were fucking so hard, the feather vanes of the quilt began to grow and bud at the seams. Their bodies' movements slid the two of them to the mattress edge. Pablo saw a drip of sweat roll from his nose onto Germaine's cheek. The singing of the bedsprings and basso buffo of the floorboards were one song. But just as they were both on the verge of climax, they tumbled onto the ground.

With the fitness of a show rider, Germaine flipped over from bottom to top, and they pinwheeled across the rug.

She suddenly was above Pablo, like straddling a motor. It was as if she were piloting some marvelous experimental flying contraption that bests gravity and birds. Pablo pumped harder, and she felt a sensation in her abdomen as they took off into the clouds, leaving France far below, the lighted boulevards of Paris becoming mere yellow lines in the etched face of the distant, gleaming metropolis. At the edge of the stratosphere, there was an explosion that jetted from her center up through his back and down her legs, rolling through their shoulders and shooting through every fingertip, scattering a frond of sparks through the embrace of the sky.

Floating down into a deep, dreamy opium-like spell, where pink light danced to *mélodies* saturating the night air, Pablo knew this was the communion he'd always imagined, that he wanted since he was a boy, one for and of the gods.

~

Remembering all this months later, before the very canvas that began the episode, that night feels to Pablo like a lifetime ago, Germaine someone from another era, and Carles now cold in the ground.

Pablo stands in Manyac's apartment on Boulevard de Clichy, awaiting his patron's return. He has been hoping to visit Vollard's gallery to see what promise, what newness, lies ahead. The memory that has been awakened by the painting, he both wants to recapture and bury it. How everything has happened so fast. But he can't help hearing again the echoes of desire.

Until, that is, Pablo wonders if it had been Carles who flipped over that canvas from the pile during his brief stay in this apartment before he killed himself.

A wash of sobering guilt comes, just as it did months ago when he woke right before Carles reached the top of the stairs. Pablo also feels feverish, his limbs suddenly weak. He thinks of that sore he noticed in Madrid. It has gone away now. But when will it return?

Manyac arrives home, cradling a long paper bag in one arm and a pale cream Pomeranian in the other. "What's its name?" Pablo asks as Manyac and the powder-puff dog brush past him with a growl.

"Cat," Manyac replies, removing a baguette. He slices it in half with a tomato knife and splits it lengthwise, slathering the inside with butter and layering on top a goopy glaze of pure strawberry jam.

Pablo hasn't eaten since buying from the news-butchers aboard the train a stale roll that sopped up an oily fried egg. His stomach is acid. He is salivating now at the sight of breakfast and the warm yeasty smell in the air.

Manyac dries a plate from the zinc-lined wood sink and plunks the baguette on top. He pulls from the daisy-colored icebox a frosty glass carafe, pours into two coffee cups three fingers each of Armagnac from a brown bottle, and adds a splash of grapefruit juice before handing one to Pablo and drinking the other in a gulp. Onto the floor he sets the bread, which, to Pablo's horror, the toy dog gobbles up.

"Why haven't you dressed yet?"

Pablo gazes down at his modest but neither stained nor tattered trousers of thick cotton, collarless shirt, and duster jacket.

"I am dressed," he protests, more shrilly than he meant to.

Manyac's face blanches as if he's stepped into excrement in his velvet slippers.

"I can close the top button," Pablo says. "You won't even see the rest."

"It's not the coat! It's the whole everything! Jesus, you look like a chimney sweep." Manyac pounds his fist. "And here I am, trying to sell a sophisticated picture-maker whose paintings ought to command top rate from an esteemed gallery owner? He'll think we trade in rags and pewter. Is that what you want to make? Bric-a-brac?"

Only half the sum Manyac paid him this month remains, Pablo announces, and he has no other clothes. "Maybe we hold off till I can afford a tailor?"

"Vollard is not a man you keep waiting," Manyac retorts. "He makes or breaks a painter's career. If he excuses himself to the loo, you offer to unzip him and hold his prick to piss!"

~

Manyac has no doubts about how suave he appears in his scarlet-red four-in-hand silk tie jauntily tucked into a stiff shirt with a pointy collar, a habit he developed when he was the promising son of a well-heeled manufacturer of lockboxes, safes, and vaults back in Barcelona, studying his father's trade and making money hand over fist, before it all grew too dull and, well, Spanish.

Even earlier in life, Manyac had, like Pablo, been an art school dropout and, like Carles, held an avowed affinity for anarchism. Or his own interpretation of it, anyway.

"Too many laws," Manyac regularly tells his coterie at Paris's sidewalk cafés, "serve only to keep riches in the hands of fools instead of visionaries." He goes on to detail how bygone notions of good and evil prevent a painter from making great art—or, in his case, reselling it for the highest price. "Society, particularly throughout Spain, is full of constraints—manacles for your wrists, a muzzle on your jaw, a Dominican rosary 'round your neck, and an iron-grip codpiece squeezing the gonads like an olive press." Only in Paris could Manyac have a chance at being a happy libertine, satisfying himself aesthetically, philo-sophically, and financially.

As to the latter, Manyac has been a quick study in the cutthroat business of trading pictures. Lately it's been recompensing handsomely, as he has applied the tried-and-true tricks of the trade.

1. Never pay more than one-third of what a painting is worth.
2. Always reject the price the painter initially asks, not countering before he appears visibly desperate.
3. If you find just one painter who is young, very talented, and too thin, stake your claim with a long-term contract. You've uncovered a gold mine.

The other essential ingredient in this business, Manyac insists, is looking the part—always. "Sheep's clothing is for lesser wolves," he's apt to repeat. "I prefer couture, really."

Now, he strokes his beloved mustache as he considers Pablo, then twirls the ends around his forefingers.

"No, no. This won't do," Manyac says, finally. "But I shall not let you let us down," he adds before hastily repairing behind a Chinese screen. "Get out of those bone-grubber's clothes—I have just the thing!"

Manyac returns clutching a pair of hangers, the one on top bearing a straight-cut suit of worsted black-and-blue diagonals. In the other hand, he holds a pair of varnished button-up oxblood boots. "The trousers may be long, but we'll pin them," he says. "The jacket ought to fit. Can stuff newspaper in the shoes, need be. Shouldn't be bad, not at all."

Eyeing Pablo's cotton knickers, Manyac asks if he wants a fresh set. Pablo shakes his head.

"Are you sure? Take those off and have one of mine. It's just been laundered."

"These are fresh," Pablo responds.

"Very well," Manyac says, suspending the suit from the top of the folding screen. He undoes a starchy dress shirt from the other hanger and tosses it to Pablo. "I remember when I was young as you once, a yearling growing into racing shape—fitness up and down." With a flick of the wrist, Manyac's plush top hat sails through the air across the room, right into Pablo's fingers. "What a glorious ride it was."

~

"Stone's throw from the birthplace of Claude Monet," Manyac remarks, hustling them to a gallery in the Ninth Arrondissement, just below Boulevard Haussmann. Sixty years on, very many of the first-floor leases within the thick-slabbed, nicotine-colored buildings of Rue Laffitte are held by galleries of all sizes, some smartly curated and others in curious disarray. Manyac ushers Pablo inside the one belonging to Vollard, and it turns out to be a mix of the two styles—a single, methodically packed square room with very finite wall space for mounting frames, which consequently means canvases by Renoir, Gauguin, and Cézanne are leaned on top of one another on the floor. The air is redolent of geranium oil and yellow paper. The owner, Manyac tells Pablo, descends from a long line of aristocrat adventurers and convicts-turned-sugar-planters who colonized the isle of Réunion—a blip off of Madagascar. Vollard is a crafty kestrel, Manyac has warned, his ability to spot value and connive ways to extract it without peer.

When Pablo catches sight of a large, frumpish figure paging through a stack of canvases in an old-fashioned three-buttoned swallowtail coat, however, his first thought is how Vollard appears extraordinarily uncomfortable in so much heavy-grained wool. His face is glazed with sweat, and his rosy-beige skin seems to be pleading for a bush shirt and drill trousers.

"What have we here?" says Vollard to Manyac, his eyes roving around Pablo's own oversize clothes and borrowed top hat. "A dancing chimp? Can he paint? If not, does he play an instrument? An accordion? Jew's harp?"

Pablo begins introducing himself, but the man cuts him off in his lilting, tropically tinged French. "Ah, ah—I want to speak to the organ-grinder, not the monkey."

"Why, can he paint? Does Rodin sculpt in bronze?" Manyac sallies. "Ahem, this right here is the little genius I've mentioned. You've already seen a sample of his work, and you liked it very much."

"You have? I did?"

"Yes, twice over."

"When?"

"Just a few weeks ago," Manyac says. "When that physician was browsing the gallery."

"What? Who?"

"A doctor of venereology, I recall. You know—Cupid's diseases. Nasty stuff."

"Jog my memory with one of the little creep's arrows, why not?"

"Well, you were boasting of your acquaintance with van Gogh again, retelling for the umpteenth time the story of his self-portrait with a bandaged head. How he'd read the bible verse that says if an organ causes you to sin you must lop it off before slicing his ear with a razor to give to a prostitute. Or some such—I can't be bothered trying to follow anymore."

"Why'd he nick his ear?"

"The sound of the prostitute's voice piqued his immoral curiosities, one suspects. For Christ's sake, it's your bloody tale."

"I should think it more lasting if he'd scissored off both his balls. Ear's not really the root of his troubles, is it? Or perhaps he's mad."

"Eek! That's precisely what the physician said! One look at that other painting of his, that right there," Manyac says, pointing to a cramped little bedroom done up all in blue that looks like the walls are closing in, "and he cried that this painter must be tortured in the brain by a bacterium."

The picture dealer stands, gawking quizzically, as if Manyac were the mental case.

"This is all an act of yours, Vollard," harrumphs Manyac, "because you've second-guessed whether you ought to give an exhibition to the remarkable young talent I've brought you. Really, you should reconsider. The boy's phenomenal, likely to make you and me heaps of money."

"What's this doctor's name, the one who treats the privates?"

"What does it matter? Enough with your games!"

"What's the man's name, I say!"

"I don't recall. Same as some saint."

"Patron of what?"

"Sodomy."

"Close! I'm almost inclined to award the question to you," Vollard cries with maniacal amusement. "His given name is Louis—the guardian saint of France! Now, what's the surname? Let's see . . . on the tip of my tongue," the frisky man says, tapping his balding head with a long fingernail. "Ah, yes! It's Jullien—Dr. Louis Jullien. That's it. 'Have a bout of something ghastly in your pantaloons? Why, make no apologies. The good Dr. Louis Jullien, master of venereology, will see you soon!'"

The art merchant is busting up laughing at his own joke. Manyac appears unamused. Pablo is confused, though he commits the rhyme to memory.

Vollard recovers eventually and says, "So it's very fine to see you again, my Spanish friend, but I must say you're losing both your touch and humor. Now, you assert you've a prodigy with you. But I fear he'll see me no more commerce than that other painter from the Peninsula you brought. Let's have the proof!"

"Go on," Manyac prods Pablo. "Show the man. He'll need nothing more. He's not blind—mostly."

Pablo unzips his portfolio on the ground. He carefully removes the unstretched canvases depicting a simmering dwarf dancer three heads in height, cancan girls revealing tantalizing frill and flesh, sultry-eyed Spanish *cantantes*, and bravura scenes of bullfights done in yellow and red.

"Not bad—mostly," Vollard says. "You'll get you a show after all, Manyac. We'll bill this one together with that Basque. And I might arrange for several leading—to where, I don't know—critics to sit for portraits by the lad to drum up press. The works would be offered as gifts, naturally."

"A tried-and-true tactic," Manyac assures Pablo.

"Of course it is," says Vollard. "Every writer's in love with himself."

Pablo looks on as the two carnivores wrangle over the gallery exhibition's details. On one hand, he is flattered by Manyac's public praise. But these dealings also raise even more skepticism about how he is being handled. Manyac certainly stands to grow richer from this than what he pays Pablo as a stipend. And if Pablo's work is good enough to nab winning looks from an impresario like Vollard, then he's sure to be worth much more.

This wariness about being cheated, Pablo knows, is only more to weigh on him. Meanwhile, his fever has worsened at the gallery. His appetite is gone, there's a sickliness in his muscles, and his head feels consumed by dark clouds moving fast, waiting to burst.

∼

In a harshly lit antechamber of a nondescript building beside the train tracks leading to the Gare du Nord, a short, brown-haired secretary presides over a leather-top desk bearing a clunky stenograph machine. She uses it for recording notes whenever the doctor charges off in a dust cloud of oration, which he demands be documented for his review and ultimate consideration in an appropriate journal, be it in, or not in, his delineated field. "I am no shire horse with a set of winkers on," Dr. Louis Jullien is apt to say. "I'll trot where I please."

In science, pseudoscience, politics, and society elsewhere, many wild theories float around, he contends. But so many esteemed idea-makers should stop attempting to peer into the soul, analyze our early childhoods, or palpate headbones, scanning for abnormalities, perversions, or tell-all convexities and lumps. He declares they ought to instead limit their field of vision to a microscope's eyepiece. For Dr. Jullien, one of the most accomplished venereologists in all Paris—where this line of practice is in considerable demand—increasingly believes that everything ailing humankind is caused by bitty creatures, nefarious as they are ubiquitous and elusive to all but those with the most acutely trained eyes using the highest grade of equipment. "Even bad dreams may have as their source a virus," he says. "Kill the cause, end the nightmare."

The trouble is, due to all his dictations, Dr. Jullien has been spending less time at the microscope. As with preparing manuscripts, culturing tissue swabs, and even some examinations, this is now more often a task completed by the secretary, who's known no other occupation since she was Dr. Jullien's patient as a schoolgirl and came into the employ of the office because she'd no other means of repayment. By this point, she has more learning than some medical doctors of high degree.

Pablo, by way of a city directory uncovered among the detritus left behind by so many comers and goers in Manyac's apartment, has arrived at the office on the morning after Manyac brought him to visit Vollard. He only hopes the physician who advertises that he can cure "all maladies of love" might save him. After all, if Dr. Jullien had diagnosed that other mad artist in Vollard's gallery from his brushstrokes alone, what better place to seek aid?

In the waiting room, Pablo finds a cherrywood bench, where a couple patients are idling—not surprisingly, a stout sailor in a striped *marinière* sweater and an old lecher whose nose is as caved-in as a fallen theater marquee. The man's every feature seems to be disintegrating. Sadly, there's also an adolescent gal in a Windsor chair opposite them, legs crossed. Pablo knows she'd rather be in purgatory than here.

The secretary is full in the face and not unattractive, with flush lips recalling poinsettia leaves and alarmingly feline eyes. A Latin cross studded with clear crystal rhinestones dangles from a thin gold chain just above her neckline.

"Good day, young man," she curtly says to Pablo, although she appears to be no older than he.

"Is the doctor in?"

"Do you have an appointment?"

"I need treatment."

"What do you seek to remedy?"

"I'll tell Dr. Jullien, please."

"Tell it to me first, or not at all."

"In my country, we call it the French Disease."

"And what sovereign is that?"

"Spain."

"If in your country the infection of which you speak is more common than in France, and the limited statistics available suggest this be the case, should you not call it a Spanish disease instead?"

"But we're Spanish?"

"Well, don't look at me. That is no fault of the French." She asks if Pablo has money to pay the doctor. "This isn't a charity, you know?"

Pablo nods.

The secretary scans a ledger with the names of disorders, the corresponding prices of treatment to the right of each one.

"Let's see, syphilis . . . syphilis . . . syphilis . . . ," the woman says in a loud stage whisper as she draws her finger down the page.

Pablo stands there bashfully, pretending everyone in the office can't hear her, even though there is no escaping that they surely can.

"Yes, there we are—the Spanish Scourge. Fifty francs. Pay and be seated."

When it's Pablo's turn, the secretary guides him into a back room beyond a sturdy door with frosted glass. The doctor is stuffing tobacco into his pipe at a pedestal desk cluttered with tied-together papers and notes stabbed on spindle files. He is a long, angular man, with a neat beard and prominent ridge in his brow. Pablo can't help thinking how much he looks like Don José at his easel. The resemblance troubles him. On the opposite side of the office, there's an examining table with stirrups and a glass cabinet filled with brown bottles arranged around a bronze mortar and pestle. Beneath this is an index of many drawers. A menagerie of medical equipment—microscopes, calipers, scales, shakers, canisters, chimneys, steam traps, meters, tubing, drips and a bain-marie—is assembled on a center table beside a carriage clock. Dr. Jullien stands up and briefly stares at the clipboard the secretary gave him before telling the patient to hold out his hands.

Pablo shows the doctor the newly formed freckles that appeared on his palms before he left Barcelona. They scared him almost to death.

"Anywhere else?" the doctor inquires. "Shoulders, chest, how about the feet?"

Pablo shakes his head.

"But you noticed an ulcer, didn't you, near your groin? About a month or so prior, am I right?"

He nods.

"And a fever, nocturnal headaches? Intercostal rheumatoid?" Dr. Jullien asks, impatiently adding, "Pains in your ribs, son. Does it hurt there?"

"Yes, yes."

"No matter. We can fix you. That's the dilemma—the grandness and curse—of modern science. Your generation, given its predispositions, should be very, very thankful for the medicine of these times. Innovation couldn't have arrived at a more necessary moment. Although it's difficult to distinguish the originator, the chicken or the egg? What do you suppose, boy?"

"Chicken or egg?"

"Yes. Did science mature to treat the immorality of our desires, or did we kneel to temptation soon as we knew consequences might be evaded? Did the chicken come first, or was it the embryo from which it hatched?"

"The rooster?"

A smile interrupts the doctor's exam. "Why, you've a mind on you after all! Most of your ilk haven't any—complete ciphers. This generation is full of them. But you may have a gram of that precious gray matter yet. And we aim to preserve it, we do. Nooo, no, you needn't wind up like one of those lunatics in the street, for whom we also could trace back what ails him to some trollop who infected his loins ages ago."

Pablo's nose uncontrollably jumps.

"The advances we've made," Dr. Jullien begins again, as if feeling the simmering of his intellect, the ideas and words flowing like liquid inducted through an alembic, "enable us to peer into the world of molecules, view the very etiologies of what sickens us. What causes those spots on your hands? At this very moment, your body is like a flax crop being decimated by countless locusts. Only on an infinitesimally smaller scale, that is, yet, conversely, infinitely numerous. An outburst of a bacterium, as opposed to a migratory insect, is doing terrible things inside you." The bubbling boffin allows himself to cool a moment, muttering regret that his secretary has been out of earshot, before adding, "In theory."

"Theory?"

"Not mine alone! It's simply a fact that's yet to be proved, like many of the truest facts."

"But you aren't certain?" Pablo presses.

The doctor explains that in this case the exact microorganism has escaped identification. "It could be so many horrendous little critters,"

Dr. Jullien says, a billion bogeymen infesting the closets of Pablo's being, creating chaos and destruction everywhere they lurk. But, he confesses, no one knows their shape.

"Something suspicious has been studied by me in plasma, something almost serpentine," the physician explains. "But I cannot confirm it in regard to the pathogenesis of the symptoms manifested." He seems unaccustomed to being interrogated by a patient, and his brow stiffens. Then, a frisson fills his face. "Have a seat," he exclaims, pushing Pablo down into a swivel chair and wheeling him to the table arrayed with instruments. "I've an instance of something related, something really remarkable," he says, bending Pablo's neck over the tall brass microscope. "Ghastly, too!"

Dr. Jullien unlatches a small filing box on the table and removes from it a rectangular glass slide. He rushes to the cabinet on the room's other side and yanks open a drawer before returning with a clear phial containing a dollop of pale yellow—like a melted droplet of the moon, captured and preserved.

"There, take that, an excretion from the urethra of my previous patient. You may have seen him exiting," he says. "A very, very rangy fellow. Head almost can't fit beneath the door. Every inch crawling with the clap. Wife has it, too. She's even bigger than he! Frightening, isn't it?"

Pablo nods.

"They swap it back and forth, like polo players on great vast horses, bumping the ball around with their mallets. No way to say who gave it to whom first, carrying on as they do. But"—the doctor raises a forefinger—"neither tells the other one they come to me. Nooo, no. They each found me in-deee-pen-dent-ly," he sings, one beat at a time, "after experiencing acute symptoms of blennorrhea—mucus discharge, accompanied by irritation of the meatus.

"That's the power of publicity, thanks be to my ad placed in the city directory. Best investment I ever made, after my microscope—and

Madame Jullien, that is. So far, the unhappy couple haven't both arrived on the same day. That'll be a holler! When we call the police, tell them to bring their game rifles!"

The doctor gives a hoarse laugh before turning serious again.

"Such is the condition of the modern age," he says, and sighs. "The decadence, I call it, for which, remember, lad, the root of the word is 'decay.' No morals, not a one, not anymore."

Once the exuded purulence is smeared onto the slide, Dr. Jullien lights a safety match and draws it to the tobacco protruding from his pipe's bowl before lowering the flame and holding it beneath the glass rectangle. After the specimen is dry, he applies a dribble of methylene blue from an eyedropper before sandwiching it all together beneath a thin translucent square and placing it under the microscope. Pablo struggles to raise enough of a smile to show he's a good sport as the doctor switches on the instrument's newfangled illumination mechanism and adjusts the knobs of the armature.

"Go on. It won't leap from the slide. What do you see?"

Pablo shutters his other eye and squints to glare through the eyepiece, and suddenly he is peering through the ocular into a frigid blue planet. Shifting shapes and formed masses drift by one another like cobalt-filled clouds on a white background, an inverse of the sky.

"Where am I?"

"Inside the pus!" the doctor screams with delight. "That's the magic!" He proceeds to narrate Pablo's journey, guiding him to the globular structures, slightly darker than the rest. "Looks like a harlot's puckered lips?"

"Yeah?"

"That's her! Little Missus Blue Monster."

"Have I already been kissed?"

"No, lad. Should you be so lucky. You've something far nastier. Makes those *Neisseria gonorrhoeae* look like playthings. You've got the syphilis," he says, expelling the syllables like a sneeze. "She's one real tricky devil!"

"Are they 'she'?" Pablo asks.

"It is not known whether these microorganisms are gendered," the doctor explains. "We can't say until we've seen her with our own eyes."

"But you did it again, said 'her.'"

"Just a way of speaking, son. In my mind, they're hordes of tiny treacherous tarts, preying upon mankind."

The doctor gives Pablo two needles of arsenic, one in each arm, and—for good measure and good science—an injection of silver nitrate administered via a catheter of vulcanized rubber directly to the urethra. "You're lucky, boy. If the chancre were present, I'd have excised and cauterized it to jugulate the infection. Seems to have receded on its own. Clever, isn't she?"

Now, they must treat the affliction internally, the doctor imparts, to prevent further penetration of the microbes before they infect the nervous system and gobble up the very seat of consciousness. "Protect the brain!"

The physician writes a script for Pablo to bring to the dispensary: a preparation of two grains of bichloride of mercury, to be taken orally as a prophylactic until a follow-up visit. "Fear not," Dr. Jullien reassures Pablo as he walks him to the door, throwing an arm around his shoulders. "There is no cure per se, but treatments, delivered on an ongoing basis, can keep you from suffering the worst of it. You may even lead, for the most part, a perfectly natural life up to the end." The doctor drones on about side effects, but Pablo has stopped listening. Right, he thinks—or does he say it out loud?—just make it till we die.

~

The trains nearby are sounding as Pablo leaves the office with the afternoon heat coming on. His loins ache. His heart could bound from his chest and ride away. There is no doubt how he contracted this malady. It must be Germaine. His head feels like it is growing bigger and bigger, and his legs are like soft spaghetti. His belly cramps, and his bladder is full, but he is afraid that loosening any cork will mean surrendering all control. Pablo heads toward the engine horns until he is hobbling along a narrow pasture of brome and sow thistle littered with discarded rail ties. He clings to a chain-link fence that runs parallel to the tracks and river below, thinking of the blue world beyond that microscope's eyepiece. Pablo remembers how colors, any of them, had not been his first love, how when Don José brought him that japanned tin, the watercolors got in the way of the lines. All he had wanted to do was draw. But the bottle of blue on Papa's high shelf was something splendid. The Virgin, she always wore blue, like the statue on Aunt Pepa's altar. And this is why they'd wrapped Conchita in that gauzy wool swaddle of the same color. If only it could have rescued her. But why had he not been able to save her instead of yielding to temptation?

Memories spin along with everything else, like swirling pigment and linseed.

The sour smell of wet, rotting lumber pickles the air.

Pablo leans into the fence grating and vomits onto the tracks, the locomotive's whistle blaring as he empties his bladder and bowels at the same time.

Hours pass before Pablo is strong enough to stand. Remembering dreams of twisted masses of cobalt and indigo, he thinks he must have been out cold for a while. His tongue feels cemented to the roof of his mouth. He tries to wash his clothes along the banks of the Bassin de la Villette, the fading sun bouncing off the water. They are hopelessly ruined, though, and he lets them drift away and float corpse-like down the canal. But Pablo refuses to return to Manyac's apartment in his wrung-out underwear, which is the only garment he's standing in on the outskirts of Paris, like a lost savage. Should he spend his last francs on some cheapjack getup? Or scrimp and buy a pistol to finish off

Germaine? She's done him irreconcilable harm, he thinks, his head still pounding. And she did even worse to Carles, who'd had the right idea firing at her before he bungled it, bless him.

It's one thing to get a thrill out of pretending but another to go on letting someone else pretend.

At a flea market nearby, Pablo ignores the stares of passersby and purchases a pair of bib-and-brace overalls with his last bits, reasoning he can always strangle Germaine for free.

~

Back at the apartment, Pablo tells Manyac he was accosted by apaches who stole his clothes, and the man is as sympathetic as a priest, taking his *papuce* to be fitted for proper garments, treating him to a lunch of *blanquette de veau*, and granting him next month's allowance.

Still, Pablo feels uneasy around Manyac and plans to avoid him when he can. He will work at night and sleep during the day, communicate through left notes. The art dealer seems happy enough, so long as one canvas after another for the upcoming show piles up.

When he isn't painting, Pablo struggles to focus on anything but fury for Germaine. He's convinced himself it is she, not he, who led the greatest friend he's ever had to end his life with a lump of lead. So, too, she—presider of a million microscopic she-demons—has forever altered Pablo's predicament, infecting him with this onerous, fatal perhaps, disease. What terrifies him more than death, disfigurement, or dementia, though, is that this wretched curse might blind him.

But each time Germaine's statuesque outline appears on the horizon of Pablo's imagination, so, too, returns that inevitable attraction. "I'm like a pigeon devouring poisoned grain," he repeatedly hears himself think. During that one night of seduction—which, frankly, even Saint Anthony would have succumbed to—she hammered a stake into his soul.

The only part of the letter Germaine sent Pablo in Madrid that he kept is the upper-left corner of the envelope. On a moonless night, he hunts down the return address and finds a dwelling space on the second floor of a decrepit warehouse on the edge of the Maquis. Pablo climbs a wooden ramp, the kind used for machinery and materials to be rolled up and down on hand trucks. The air smells of tar. Pablo bangs on the rickety plank-and-batten door. He digs his fists into the pockets of his coveralls, which have become a uniform of sorts.

The door flings open, and there she is, in a pink satin robe. She looks almost exactly the way he remembers her: hair loose, eyes and lips unpainted. But her middle is puffed out like a beignet.

"You got my letter," she says in a paper-thin voice. "I don't leave my house. No one knows."

Germaine leans into Pablo and clasps her arms around him.

He feels his anger melt until it drips down his legs, pools at his feet, drains through the ramp's wooden slats, and falls two flights to the dusty earth, which absorbs it, making it disappear like winter snow.

~

Opening night at Vollard's gallery on Rue Laffitte is packed, the stifling air and free-flowing Beaujolais loosening collars and purse strings.

Pablo worked like a dervish for weeks and has produced dozens more paintings than the Basque headliner, Iturrino. There is no vacant inch on the walls, no room for frames even, just edge-to-edge paintings, floor to high ceiling. Displayed everywhere are Pablo's colorful café socialites, his absinthe drinkers, his grandes dames gliding across the grass at Longchamp, his chorus girls, his spent lovers with arms draped over brows. Hanging in the middle of the wall facing the entrance, a mysterious creature with blue-black hair leans forward as if she'll crane right out of the picture, her eyes inviting the viewer everywhere. There's also a smaller work nearby in which a disemboweled horse is laid out in a sunny Spanish bullring, its head resting on the limp carcass of the toro just slain.

The paintings aim to excite the senses but are also executed in a range of styles—from thick, slithering lines to bright, boiling whirlpools of color; watery caricatures to smudgy pastels; fierce raids of the brush to languorous harmonies—as if to say to each and every one who witnesses them, "Name your fancy, and I can please you beyond compare." There's even a dashing impasto self-portrait inscribed "*Yo*, Picasso," in which Pablo has donned a flamenco's white ruffled shirt, a saffron scarf trussed around the neck, and gibbous hither-come-I black eyes.

Pablo stands in the back of the room, taking it all in. He is impressed that the real insiders and trendsetters of the city's *milieu artistique* have flocked to the gallery, habitués of posh arrondissements mingling with bohemians, as easy to distinguish from one another as show dogs among mongrels.

The denizens of high society and bourgeoisie Paris file in with bowler hats and walking sticks, striped wool and cream linen, and two-tone spectator shoes—their dangling gold timepieces swishing back and forth as they travel picture to picture, rubbing their chins. They come cresting through the crowd in fitted and boned bodices, bishop sleeves, and two-inch-tall Louie heels, accompanied by paper parasols, glass beads, and clattering metal spangles, their fingertips extending beyond the openings of lace mittens to point to the risqué portraits of reclining courtesans with garishly carmined lips. Oh, the way these prized guests to the gallery act demure—drawing back, coolly analyzing Pablo's images of sin!

Pablo savors what he imagines is going on inside their heads. How his paintings make them wonder for a moment what it would be like to lie naked on a bed, a stranger working the canvas above you, tracing your outline, studying your flesh, extracting the essence of what your body has to say and preserving it for all of time in line and shadow, color and oil. One lady even gathers in very close to a painting, clasps her hands behind her back, turns down her mouth, and clenches her eyes in a squint before Pablo hears her make a little humming sound and sees her appear to sniff the canvas, as if expecting to detect a whiff of sexual intercourse.

In turn, each time Vollard approaches one of the society mavens, Pablo sees his glance rove from earlobes, to neckline, to wrists, to fingers, as the gallery owner conducts an audit of her jewels to estimate the size of her probable spending allowance. He adjusts his praise accordingly.

Manyac also carefully eyes each arrival, and Pablo watches and guesses how his sponsor is mentally subdividing the well-dressed into private buyers and competitors, those savvy secondhand dealers who seek to snap up anything that might interest collectors in a few years' time, ideally at a much-appreciated rate. All the while, he must observe the dilettantes keenly to know what bait they're biting at today.

As for the bohemians who ramble in, many are young, thin, unwashed Spaniards paying tribute to one of their own. "Adds a sort of authenticity," Manyac says.

Then, there are the critics. Pablo is learning that potential purchasers won't trust their own instincts until they are confirmed with tomorrow's ink. Entreating these tastemakers to give a rapturous review is one of the secrets of Vollard's success, Manyac says, a talent he's pristinely nurtured over the years. He laid it out to Pablo once: "The public, see, is highly susceptible to persuasion by a noted critic who says a certain artist is good. But it is impervious to the same overtures by a gallery owner, who cannot tell an audience directly it must pay for a painter's works."

Luckily, for the most part, critics are as pliable in the hands of a talented dealer as the public is impressionable, Manyac has assured Pablo. In this case, some of them Vollard has wheedled by having him paint their portraits before the show. He says that for those who too easily wash off so much soft-soap, there is always, as with many bullfighting writers in Spain and opera columnists in Milan, the option of outright bribery.

However, such wooing clearly eats into dealers' profits. For Manyac to call an exhibition a success, then, means that the newspapermen didn't require too handsome of a sum just to dash off a reasonably well-embellished review.

And, by this standard, he says, Pablo's debut in Paris will do nicely.

Gustave Coquiot, who cost time but not much fortune, agrees to remark eloquently on the momentum and tenacity of Pablo's eye and brush hand, adding that the new artist "wants to see everything and say everything." He will grant him this likelihood in the review's flattering closing sentence that promises all the world should be hearing of this young man soon. Another critic will write an even more gracious phrase to lodge in readers' ears, branding Pablo "the painter, wholly and beautifully the painter."

In all, more than half the works sell, many of which were cranked out in the previous few days. Indeed, Pablo learns that one of the reasons he appeals to Manyac and Vollard is his manic and unfathomably quick means of production. Why, if calibrated properly, Pablo might spit money faster than the mint, he overhears them say to each other.

By the end of the night, Pablo has downed several glasses of wine, and everything seems to shimmer and move. He marvels for a moment at how never in Don José's life did his old man see a triumph such as this. But then, Pablo thinks—also a little drunk on himself—even God had to wait for his son to achieve what evaded Him.

II

The diners cramming the sidewalk tables along the Seine sparkle with *grand air aristocratique* like so many plump swans loitering atop the finest real estate on the Left Bank. This is not where Pablo expected to lunch.

But after inquiring twice with the maître d' whether he was indeed at the place called Le Voltaire, Pablo sits down at one of the cane-backed Louis XVI chairs and tries to fake belonging. Manolo, the puckish Catalan who'd introduced him to Manyac before Christmas, said to meet at noon so they might catch up.

While Pablo waits, he gapes at the Louvre just across the river. Inside that building, he thinks, resides the biggest art collection on earth, with masterpieces representing the entire lineage of human creation.

Since the gallery opening on Monday, Pablo has experienced an acute postpartum comedown. He's fallen from floating on top of the world into a vacuum where he mourns Carles, fixates on his own precarious health, and can't help but think of Germaine locked away in that warehouse cubbyhole, her middle expanding.

If this weren't enough, Pablo still hasn't seen a bit of extra income from the show. How long will he be able to get by?

As Pablo stares at the museum on the watery horizon, all his troubles are pressed beneath a more complex quandary, however—the contents of the building also constitute countless years of artists' lives. Many never saw anything approaching the acclaim their names have enjoyed since they've been dead or an ounce of what their works have earned. So what, really, is the point?

How long, after all, did Dürer spend in a mirror rendering his self-portrait with a thistle, and how much more time layering varnish for the colors to hold?

How could Michelangelo manage to keep *The Dying Slave* alive in his mind for the years needed to complete it with a chisel and mallet?

And the real pyramid-builders depicted in hieroglyphs on stone and acacia wood—their likenesses now entombed behind display glass—how much had they given of themselves? Everything? Clearly these artworks are cherished, since Napoléon bothered stealing them from a faraway desert—this lucre that is not gold but rather pigment imbued with mysterious value. But why?

How come art exists at all? And why do artists do this and not something else? There must be more to it than prettiness or hoped-for esteem. As he'd once suggested to Germaine, maybe so many academics, drawing instructors, art dealers, and critics corrupted what the ancients naturally understood. Perhaps "primitive" artists comprehended far more than today's tastemakers can imagine—that there's something in humans' will to create the universe depends on.

Manolo sits down across from Pablo, excusing himself for being late. "A little something kept me," he says, removing a straw hat from above his deep-set eyes and placing it on the table. His hairline has begun to creep away from his thick brows. "What, you're not going to ask me her name?"

"Actually, I hoped you might be painting for a change."

"I'm more of a sculptor," Manolo says, carving the air with his quick, soft hands. "But, really, you gotta do what's hot—oils, waters, exotic ink, smears of goose shit—whatever's selling." He points at a pair of imaginary patrons and barks, "'How's that? Double portrait with both youse? Coming up. A Grecian urn? Yeah, m'OK. I got one right here.' You know how it is."

Manolo orders two dozen oysters from a harried waiter. "You can never tell when you might get a pearl," he grins. "Know where I learned to eat those?" he asks in his reedy Catalan. "Not any fancy restaurant." He tells Pablo about being a kid with no money and nothing in his stomach, humping through gorse and mud to where the Llobregat enters the sea—a half-day hike from Barcelona—before reaching straight into the sludge. "But the shell, it's sharp, see? So I tried not to cut my wrists."

"You almost made poverty sound tasty."

"Gotta survive," Manolo says, tapping his temple, "with wits."

"I always figured you was slumming it at Els Gats."

"You kidding? I was a dog with no pack after Mama died. Smartest thing she ever did, dying," Manolo says. "My father didn't even see his real kids, let alone the fuzzy illegitimates. I was a tramp. Studied every hustle. That's an art, too, you know?" Manolo's face belies that he doesn't believe Pablo gets it. "Anyway, how's Manyac treating you?"

"Kind of an odd fellow. Awfully particular. But he comes through," Pablo says, telling Manolo about the show at Vollard's. "And the money, it's not bad, I don't think. Or pretty-not-bad, I guess."

"Vollard, huh? That Creole's gallery is tops. He knows how to pack 'em in. That's what it's all about in Paris—publicity." Manolo rattles on about how cabarets increase their business by paying Lautrec to make posters. "Then the dancers close their eyes and give that gimpy freak a backroom treat to look pretty in the pictures so their salary goes up. The artists and dealers, what do they do? Shell out for nice press to push their prices up. Everything's publicity, understand?" Manolo takes a drag on his smoke. "And Manyac, he felt you up yet?"

"Never," Pablo shoots back, lowering his voice as the waiter slings the oysters onto the table. "So that's his game, is it?"

"Him, he got lots of games." Manolo shrugs. "Likes manille, for one. Ain't half bad, neither. Takes talent to cheat where no one's saying nothin', everyone's all eyes, all the time. Ripping off picture painters, that's two."

Pablo wonders if something transpired since last fall for Manolo to sour on Manyac. Or maybe Manolo was just in on the scheme at the time.

"As for the other, well, you're smart. He's faster than a barracuda and more slippery, too. He'll want you to work for that little stipend. Fine, if your pictures sell. If not? He'll want something else," Manolo says, dangling the live mollusk over his gullet before slurping it down and kissing his fingertips.

Pablo looks nervously at the platter and reaches for one of the half shells.

"See, I'm watching out for you, OK? You look more innocent than guys with a halo for a hat."

"I . . . am not," Pablo contests, swallowing the oyster lodged in his throat.

The waiter returns, huffing from sprinting around the restaurant, which has filled up since Pablo sat down. Manolo orders Rouen duck—young, plump, pressed, and roasted, served in sauce made of its own liver. Pablo asks for the cheapest thing on the menu, a hard-boiled egg nestled in mayonnaise. He can't help worrying he'll soon be completely broke. Paris is too hard to predict. And his friend—should he call Manolo that?—seems to be issuing a warning.

The food arrives, and they eat and drink listening to the music of the crowd until the silence between them becomes awkward. Pablo is still thinking of the Louvre's relics and masters—about how if it represents ancestry and parentage, then who will decide what's next? He finally says, "You know, in art, I think we have to kill our fathers."

"Just don't forget," Manolo responds without pause, as if he's been waiting for this ball with his racquet, "to grab what they got on them."

A puzzling thing to say, Pablo thinks.

Manolo wipes tarragon from his lip with the tablecloth. "My papa held a general's rank in the war of '68," he begins. "Comes home from Cuba and hears I'd run afoul—a mix-up, naturally. So he sends some hard-nosed MPs to bring me back in cuffs. 'I seen your ol' man slit a guerilla's throat with a shaving razor,' one of 'em says, talking about how they got orders to throw me in the brig. Pretty rich, coming from a philanderer and a deadbeat, right? But Pops is a decorated guy. He don't give a shit. Anyways, first time in a dozen years I seen him, not since I was pulling on his pants leg to stand. I'd hated him, letting me live like a wharf rat. But I bust out in tears—it's the Ebro River, times two! I says, 'Take me away! Lock me up for what I done. But before I go, give me just one thing. Let me touch my papa, who survived the war. Because there was a time when I thought he's dead as a Danish king, and I had nobody to look after me but the street.' The officers who got me by the arms, they was even bawling."

The story touches Pablo, who can't help thinking of Don José. "Did your father understand what you felt, everything all pent-up?"

"The general went to waterworks, too—tells 'em, 'Release the captive, my son.'" Manolo rubs away the droplet that's gathered at the corner of his eye again. "It broke me to pieces. Next thing, we both take two steps in and wrap our arms around one another like a pair of wet seals."

"Can you even imagine what's it to become someone's father?" Pablo asks Manolo, thinking of Germaine, wondering again what he has been wondering since he found her in the doorway. "Fine, if things work out and life is going in the direction it's supposed to. But if not?" Then Pablo just doesn't know. "So many years, I felt the same way— despised my own papa. But what sort, I ask myself, could I be? What would I teach anyone? What do I know?"

"You knocked somebody up, didn't you? One of them models?"

Again, the words from Manolo are quick, like he saw Pablo's response coming. Pablo hears them, but his thoughts have drifted back to La Coruña and the sting of Don José's hand as it crashed into his cheekbone that awful night after painting the pigeon's claw, how his father had foretold suffering for everyone he would encounter.

"I'll bet it's Germaine, eh?" Manolo wagers.

Pablo doesn't respond, instead turning to look down at the mayonnaise on his plate, now littered with yellow crumbles of egg yolk. He recalls how Carles hated the stuff.

Manolo yanks the waiter by the shirtsleeve when he passes and orders more Champagne and a chocolate soufflé with crème anglaise, which vexes the sturdy man in a bow tie and too-tight waistcoat. Diners should order this at the meal's start, the waiter fumes. It would be at least another quarter hour before dessert will come now.

"Take your time," Manolo says magnanimously. "Relax."

The waiter disappears, and Pablo asks Manolo if after he and his father embraced, things finally got better.

"Sure, I ran like the lil' bastard I am."

Pablo squints. "Why?"

"'Cause I stole his watch—solid gold, crusted with gems, all types! Rubies, diamonds—every broad at the bordello got something that sparkles that night, and I ain't just talking about my pearls. I had more *farranaco* than I could hold with three arms!"

Having been chiseled into spilling his deepest anxieties, Pablo feels like one of Manolo's unlucky lottery customers. "And just one little prick, right?" he bleats.

"Hey, that's me," Manolo beams, tilting his head as he excuses himself to take a leak.

"You're something else, Manolo," Pablo says bitterly. "Tell you what, by the time you get back, I bet I steal the air right out of your soufflé. Happy?"

"Now you're learning, kid. You wanna make it as a painter in Paris, don't trust nobody, and use your wits."

A warm breeze comes, and Pablo's eyes wander to the steadily flowing Seine. Germaine, he thinks, she's like Manolo, in a way. Born into a hardscrabble life but found ways to survive. These past months must have been miserable for her. Someone else would have disintegrated. When Pablo had reached for Germaine's neck with his lips the other night, he'd found the scar from the bullet that grazed her, a purple silkworm crawling sideways from her collar.

And that—that was the very same throat he'd wanted to strangle? In his anger, Pablo had been blinded to the fact that Germaine was already bruised by life, love, circumstance, men's desires—be it Carles's or those of her husband, whoever and wherever that man is. He'd probably been the one who infected her with this hideous disease when she was a mere girl. Yet Germaine, she never played the victim. Quite the opposite. Pablo recognizes that even if he'd gone and tried to kill her, she never would've let him. She'd have scratched his eyes, gored him with that boning knife in her purse. Because Germaine never betrayed her own strength.

Except for in that single moment, when she was standing in her robe, sobbing into Pablo's shoulder. There was a split second then when he felt nothing holding her up but him. It was the same instant his anger thawed.

The bronze church bells strike the hour, and Pablo awakens from his thoughts right as the steam-powered smell of brown butter and cocoa hits the air. He looks at the empty chair where Manolo was sitting and realizes he's been gone more than ten minutes, and his hat evaporated with him. Who wears a straw boater to the loo?

Why, that son of a bitch has run off and left Pablo with the check. This will clean Pablo out for the month. And now he has to pay Dr. Jullien for that god-awful medicine. Would he need to ask Manyac for an advance—have to owe him? Pablo rubs the back of his neck, and his eyes search for the restaurant's exit. The soufflé is advancing toward him fast on the gleaming silver tray balanced on the fingertips of the burly waiter, tilting straight at him, building from the ramekin like the snake head climbing from the charmer's basket, escaping like the guts of the horse. Pablo's limbs tingle. He curls his arms over his ears. Everything is madness. This hulking Frank is about to attack with the soufflé, Pablo knows. He panics. He leaps over the sidewalk railing and darts away like a grazed animal.

"Monsieur, wait!" a voice calls after him. Pablo can hear the rapid footfalls beating the pavement in his wake, faster and faster, until someone yells, "Stop, Gallego! Thief!" Pablo races along the quay, dodging hapless tourists and the booksellers who line the riverbank, knocking over their green boxes, copies of *Candide* spilling everywhere.

Pablo spots the Pont Neuf's archways dapping across the river and bolts for it. He crosses the first half of the bridge to the Île de la Cité and ducks into the Sainte-Chapelle, kneeling in the huge Gothic church as inconspicuously as he can, bowing his head, shoulder to shoulder with others begging for mercy or benediction before an altar with dozens of flickering candles. He makes the sign of the cross.

Cobalt-toned light rains from every direction in the thirteenth-century nave made of long fillets of stained-glass window stretching toward a high ceiling. It once had been the reserve of the king and other palais penitents and was where France's holiest relics from Christ's passion were reposited, including the thorns that tormented the Lord's weary head. Pablo had pondered this crown as a boy when he was bent down before a life-sized crucifix at Aunt Pepa's blood-strewn shrine. He'd watched and mimicked the woman, seeing she was different than the rest of the family, her eccentricities tolerated in Don José's household because she'd amassed eldritch powers through a steadfast devotion to God and the saints. Even Doña María didn't dare invade her holy closet, save to chase away the copal- and rockrose-scented mice feasting on idol offerings. She hardly spoke to mortals.

Aunt Pepa had allowed Pablo to wander in, though. During the rare times when she wasn't dived into prayer, she would tell him stories of the lives, deeds, and gruesome deaths of martyrs and teach him recitations to slake their thirst, receive their blessings, not allow evil to be sown. At her behest, he drew Paul's inverted crucifixion, Cecilia's beheading, Catherine stretched on her breaking wheel—all of which the old woman added to the altar, like sacred talismans.

"Be ready, child," Aunt Pepa implored him during his growing up. "You never know when it will be your time." Even then, Pablo understood.

Now, though, God's kingdom and the foibles of His creations—shaped in the chapel's one thousand windows of glass shards and lead ribbons surrounding him—are almost blinding. Pablo is awash in the unsparing light, frightened. His own end feels too near. What awaits then? He looks straight up at the vaulted blue ceiling spangled with sharp, bladelike fleurs-de-lis—a heaven where souls might ascend to be shredded.

No one's safe, not even the good, Pablo thinks. He can't help reciting his childhood prayers until the words blend into a continuous keen. He feels ridiculous and wishes to recall instead just one poem Carles composed.

III

A former model with whom Germaine is acquainted can concoct a powerful blend of pennyroyal tea. There's also a sundries shop on the boulevard vending "lunar tablets" promising to return regular menses by the next moon. "I just couldn't, though," she'd uncharacteristically confessed to Pablo when he came again. But every day, Germaine's body tells her that time is of the essence. If outside appearances weren't enough, she feels within her a maelstrom.

On the Friday after his gallery opening, Germaine meets Pablo at noon near the Gare du Nord at the medical office of a Dr. Louis Jullien. The Spanish painter appears to have worn his least wrinkled clothes.

Germaine, however, woke at dawn to attire herself—putting on a serious-minded but fashionable navy blouse with leg-of-mutton sleeves and training her hair to rise in an impressive tower above a tortoiseshell comb. She pinned to her bodice a sparkling ornament of assorted marcasite flowers that dances in the light as she moves. She might be broke and broken, but no one would know it. Not today.

She sits together with Pablo on a cherrywood bench in the drab waiting room. Thankfully, the little secretary with feline eyes calls them back quickly. Dr. Jullien is a tall, odd, talkative man who's quite full of himself. He appears to recognize Pablo and seems to inquire about her carefully, as if he's tiptoeing around something. Pablo introduces Germaine as his cousin.

"Verboten," Dr. Jullien declares when they tell him what they're here for. "Absolutely not. Have you read the law?"

She can feel her face ice over.

"Look at the woman, for crying out loud!" the doctor says. "Have you tried listening?" He points to her belly and proffers Pablo the stethoscope.

An impulse to tie the rubberized tubes around the man's neck and throttle him nearly overcomes her.

"Palpate the abdomen. Go on, feel," Dr. Jullien says. "It'll wake if you nudge it. Nothing I can do at this point, not now." He babbles on about how he could lose his practice, end up in prison. "Have you ever seen the medical facilities inside Le Santé? Nothing but bush doctors. They have no microscopes. Nooo, and no!"

Germaine hasn't "read the law," but she knows it. Every model does. The dilemma is that the quickening happened to her weeks ago. From just a simmer, her body has become a boiling pot, a mysterious hand deciding when it stirs.

And despite her best efforts of concealment, of wearing ever-thicker clothes, more layers, Germaine knows what she must look like. At first, she'd eaten hardly anything at all, hoping the problem might resolve itself, but it was no use. As her abdomen got rounder, and her skin got thinner, the movements became even more obvious. Now she's afraid to be naked even when she's alone. She certainly can't model. How she will make ends meet is anyone's guess. And beneath so much wool, someone still might see. The most frightening thought is the possibility of her estranged husband finding out. He has a way of learning where she is, what she's up to. Would he try to hurt her if he knew? Men can be unpredictable. Germaine often finds herself reflexively gripping the knife in her purse.

"Have you no obligation?" Germaine yells at the physician.

"It's strange, in a way," Dr. Jullien says, introspectively. "You are, after all, infected—by a mere single cell, certainly not one of your own. Spermatozoa are very much alive, with a tail steering them, much like flagellates—eukaryotes, bacteria, et cetera." The doctor appears to have excited himself and asks in a burst whether he can prepare a microscope stage for them to view. When Germaine and Pablo remain silent, he shrugs disappointedly and continues.

"And now, what you have inside you, it could almost be considered a tumefaction, that is, an abnormal growth in your uterus, swelling at an exponential rate. Can you imagine, a sarcoma that goes from the size of sand to the weight of a Sunday roast in forty weeks?"

But Dr. Jullien cautions them that in this case the fetus is almost certainly malign, having been contaminated with syphilis.

The implications of the news sink in for Germaine.

"Pardon!" he turns to Pablo. "You said she is your cousin, didn't you? But that really doesn't mean anything? I mean, you could have easily . . ." The doctor is stepping all over himself trying to discreetly inquire who the father is. "Why, it's you, isn't it? What's your name, again? Pueblo? Pedro Picado? Paolo Piccolo? Pincho—"

"The father is dead," Pablo replies. Germaine feels a churning inside.

"That is a problem. For him, I suppose, too. Well, madam," the doctor says as he turns to her, "it may be a blessing in disguise. If what we're dealing with were hereditary syphilis, oh, that's a grievous condition. The lesions. Pustules. Hydrocephalus. Deformations of teeth and bone. Sometimes, the infant has hardly a face at all."

"You do nothing for these women?" Germaine asks, her blood pressure soaring as she becomes irate. "Is it not a crime to refuse a patient in need?"

Dr. Jullien appears flabbergasted. "My obligation is to practice medicine and advance science within the laws of France," he says. "To honor the Hippocratic oath of 'do no harm.'"

Behind him, Germaine notices a petite silhouette beyond the frosted window. The door swings open. It's the cat-eyed secretary. "Your manuscript, Doctor. It's done," she says, waving a ream of paper bound with gleaming brass fasteners.

"Yes, yes, very well. Bring me my pipe, and you can read it to me," Dr. Jullien says, adding with a dismissive flick of the wrist that he is through with patients for the day. "And where were you a moment ago? I was extemporizing about a most fascinating comparative study of the motility of human sperm cells and their anatomic analogues in the bacterial kingdom."

"So sorry to have missed it, Doctor."

"You should have got it down. Were you that busy?" he chides her. "Now please see the Spaniards to the door."

Germaine aims a poisonous stare at the physician as the secretary leads them away. While they pass through the waiting room, she braces for the sinister glances they're likely to encounter stepping out of the venerology office.

Behind her, she hears someone right on her heels, though. The secretary has rushed out onto the street and places a hand on Germaine's arm. She extends a slip of russet paper pinched between forefinger and thumb.

"What's this?" Pablo demands as he turns around. "A bill? No service has been done—it has been a disservice! We owe nothing, not one centime!"

Germaine opens the small folded square. Written on it is nothing more than a time: eight o'clock.

∾

Germaine and Pablo find a shabby boîte located below street level to count down the hours. The cement floor is damp. The area between a pair of mouseholes is a rodent thoroughfare.

Pablo fetches two glasses the shape of blossoming dog roses, absinthe filling their bottoms. From a carafe on the table, slick with condensation and the oil of so many handlers, Germaine pours ice water. The emerald-colored liquor clouds over with an auroral glow. They clink glasses. Neither of them can come up with a better toast than "to health." They sip in silence for a time, staring.

"Thank you," she says, at last.

"For what?"

"You're here."

Pablo has been following her eyes. He's studied how Germaine has watched the mice scamper back and forth before disappearing inside the crevices in the plaster and then popping their twitchy heads back out again later. He knows what she is thinking, he's convinced. It's the same thing he's wondered—what is the invisible life of the tiny creatures behind those walls?

~

The secretary opens the entrance of the physician's office before they even knock and whisks them through the antechamber and behind the door with frosted glass, double-locking it. The only illumination inside is from an oil lamp. A set of gleaming steel instruments is lined up in a row on parchment. She turns to Pablo and says, "If you faint, then I'll have two patients."

"He won't," says Germaine.

Wearing an apron and Dr. Jullien's stethoscope, the secretary wastes no time in telling Germaine to remove her clothes. She eases Germaine onto the table and into the leg supports. She begins cleaning the skin with iodine. She pulls on gloves and probes Germaine with her fingers.

She pours brandy into a beaker and drips a tincture into it with an eyedropper. She fills a pump with a mix of distilled water and fine salt. She unrolls a sheet of gauze and inverts over it a metal canister until the white cotton becomes translucent.

Pablo had not made his hesitations known about whether or not a secretary could be trusted to perform such a task. But as he watches her work—with quick, deft, silent movement—that concern subsides. It's clear she's absorbed all the gynecological knowledge and experience required.

Still, as she inserts the rubber tips of the stethoscope into her ear, there is a moment when something else, a lingering doubt about whether there might not be some other way, seizes Pablo. When the secretary places the device's diaphragm on Germaine's stomach, he feels an urge to grab it away. But the woman has already removed the instrument.

"There is no heartbeat. The fetus is dead," the secretary says, turning to the clock. "I don't know how long, but sepsis may be imminent. The patient is at grave risk. We haven't got time."

Pablo's eyes lock with Germaine's. Contrary to the secretary's call for haste, it's as if everything, everywhere freezes. He thinks, If I'm ever to do anything correctly, let it be that she cannot see this fear.

"Are you ready?" the secretary asks Germaine.

The two women exchange nods like cavalry officers preparing for an unwinnable assault, and then the secretary holds the gauze over Germaine's mouth until her eyes bat and shutter. Her limbs go limp. The secretary gives the cotton to Pablo to administer again if Germaine wakes.

Pablo hasn't been anyone's assistant for years, not since a class way back at La Llotja when he was the junior member of a sculpting team. He remembers standing in awe before a slab of Calacatta marble worth its weight in silver. Despite all the bodies he's ever seen and painted and made love to, none have looked anything like the one resting before him, legs splayed open and in stirrups. It is at once foreign and intimate, breathtaking and disquieting, hard and vulnerable.

The secretary inserts a bivalve brass speculum inside Germaine and then instills a saline solution with a steel pump. She places the round end of a lubricated glass rod inside. After a few minutes, she inserts a different one, slightly larger. She does this several times. And, just as when Pablo watched in amazement as the senior sculptor chiseled away at the slab of deep-veined stone, he is impressed with the secretary's poise and exacting technique. But once she reaches for the serrated forceps and double *crochet* resting on the parchment paper, those thoughts dissolve, and so does his courage.

From here on, Pablo tries everything to make certain he sees nothing besides Germaine's sleeping face. His mind flees to years earlier in Horta with Pajaresco, when late at night someone knocked at the farmhouse's door. A family friend was inviting the two art students to watch an autopsy. A girl had been clinging to her grandmother when lightning struck. Pablo and Pajaresco arrived at the country doctor's shed, and the dead girl and woman lay side by side on a rough-hewn table. The faces were bloated, hair singed and matted, lips stiff like duckbills. The fat, cigar-smoking coroner sliced open the old woman's clothing to reveal the damask pattern of her blouse ironed into the skin and then placed a bone saw atop the child's skull. Pablo averted his eyes as red speckled the shed's wall. He puked his dinner onto the floorboards and could stand the autopsy no longer.

According to the clock on the table, the procedure to remove the fetus takes less than an hour, but it feels like an eternity. Pablo breathes a sigh of relief when it's done, having managed to prevent himself from viewing what is left behind. But no sooner is this air exhaled amid the chloroform fumes than he begins to understand that whenever he ponders death from now on, he'll be haunted by the phantom of mangled limbs and viscera that his mind will create for what he assiduously refused to face. There will be no salve for this, no way to ever go back.

~

Germaine is weak. She bleeds often and has developed a fever over the past days that they fear will turn for the worse. Pablo stays with her where she lives above the warehouse. He admires how she's converted this hovel into what looks like a Moroccan majlis, with hanging lanterns and moiré silk draped from the low ceiling. But he understands now why during the winter she'd always returned to the studio on Rue Gabrielle each time it became cold, even after everything had unraveled there—this place has no heat, no stove, and no ventilation, aside from what comes up from the uninsulated floors. And Pablo gets why, if Odette lived anywhere similar, she immediately drew a warm bath upon arriving at the studio, lying in it as if she'd found heaven. Pablo became itinerant by choice. He could go to his parents' home if needed. That is not the case for these women.

From a café nearby, Pablo fetches hot water and administers Germaine strong tea and spoonfuls of bone broth. He rips apart pieces of *pain de mie* and feeds them to her, followed by licorice drops from a yellow tin. He places his fingers behind her ears and draws her close, pressing her gently against his chest, moving his hands up and down her back as if smoothing wet clay. There's something new in this, a *tendresse* he's not experienced before, one absent erotic desire. She seems to realize the specialness, too.

On the fifth day, though, Pablo wakes on the straw mattress and finds Germaine squatting in the corner of the small room with her elbows bent around her knees. He asks, "What's wrong?"

When she removes her arms, there are wet spots on either side of her nightgown. Pablo is fazed. He had no idea it was possible for women in these circumstances to lactate. He gets up and starts toward Germaine, feeling the impulse to comfort her. But as soon as he moves, she casts a look so stern it forces him to back away.

"You were good to me," Germaine says in a clear, firm voice. She stands up and walks to within a few feet of him. "I forgot what that was, to be cared for. But it's time to leave."

"Why would I go? I don't want to," Pablo protests, shaking his head. "Tell me how to help you."

"If I desired company all the time like this, I would have lived my life differently. Done things differently. Been different."

Pablo pats down the pockets of the pants he slept in and determines he possesses all he came with—keys, a penknife, a small roll of bills. He buttons a shirt over his chest and opens the doorway that he'd found Germaine standing in only weeks ago, knowing he won't see her here again. They stare at one another, and he begins to softly repeat the line he's heard her say over and over since they first met—"A woman may . . ."

Germaine kisses her finger and covers his lips with it, then finishes her own vow: "choose to be a doormat or a goddess."

Outside, in the morning light, Pablo is certain this had been some sort of love.

~

When Pablo travels to Vollard's the next day, the man he wants to see is nowhere to be found. Manyac has instructed him to retrieve any unsold works, but how, Pablo thinks, could the owner just leave the gallery unattended? Might some ruffian not come by and help himself to stacks of Renoirs?

There's a pungency tracking through the air, however, as if the paintings of Tahitian villages that Vollard keeps displayed in the rear have sweated jungle spice. Pablo has the sensation he's been picked up by the collar and flung off to a wild, undiscovered land. Something brushes by his legs and curls around his ankle like a python. When he looks down, the mangy orange tail of a tabby cat is roped around him, and he reflexively jerks his knee. The animal darts away. From the corner of his eye, Pablo sees it slip through the narrow opening of an egress he'd not noticed before. He follows the kitty down a twisting staircase to a cellar. The passageway is thick with the smell of kaffir leaf and turmeric. A pair of ugly, gape-mouthed Polynesian statues carved from teakwood guard either side of a patina-covered doorframe at the bottom of the steps. Beyond these tutelary deities is a clandestine room with a long mahogany table lined with Trafalgar chairs and a dozen settings. A mantelpiece supports a cast bronze statue of a lithe nude, her hair covered in a caul.

Hanging on the opposite wall is a painting, the only one down here. It's hard to tell if the object in the canvas's foreground is a giant cypress or a towering black flame. Pablo gathers nearer. There is so much movement within the picture frame, he finds he cannot stare at any single point for long. In the distance behind the dark spire in the center, though, there's a valley with little houses nestled around a high-steepled church, not unlike scenes Pablo witnessed from the train window as he rode with Carles through the Pyrenees. The buildings, limned in black, are the same vivid blues as the painting's sky—Prussian, ultramarine, cobalt. Lanterns in their windows create little boxy panes of bright yellow. Above the horizon, amid spinning eddies of foreboding cloud, shine bright, magnificent stars. Pablo examines them from only a couple of inches away and can tell they were made from quick, curving flicks of the artist's wrist using thick impasto. There is an urgency in these manic brushstrokes that Pablo admires, the whirling together of rapid streaks of pure bold color squeezed straight from the tube. The blues are intense, the mood rueful, throbbing, eternal.

"Don't punch a hole through the thing, would you? It's not mine," squawks Vollard, suddenly at the entranceway behind Pablo. "Just a little something borrowed from a collector friend."

"I have never seen anything like it," Pablo, still mesmerized, says at last.

"I expect not," Vollard replies. "If you can paint the same, though, perhaps you'll become rich before this man's estate does. A Dutchman, dead now, a suicide, I believe. They never found a note. Brother's wife handles all the works. There's rather a lot. She's quite the promoter. Publicity, publicity, tsk. Trying to milk the departed for all he's worth after the trouble he caused them."

"Why did you hang this here in the . . ." Pablo fumbles for the word. "What do you call this place?"

"Haven't ever seen a dining hall buried below an art gallery before?" Vollard chortles. "Your Manyac has designated it the Cave. Another of my eccentricities, I suppose. Everyone acts as if I'm cuckoo for putting a little pepper in their pot. Indeed, you've found me rousing a curry for a Bavarian noble and his whole bloody county. If they're expecting it to be bland, well . . ." Vollard pushes up his lips and offers a *je-m'en-fous* shrug.

"To answer about the painting, I like to look at it from time to time. You see, I find this work an intriguing proposition, a vexing philosophical question-and-answer, spread out as if by a rolling pin. I'm told it is the view in early morning hours from the window of the mental asylum where the painter was committed. Only thing is"—Vollard smiles devilishly—"he left out the bars."

Pablo recognizes the brushwork and cramped composition, but also how both something torturous and transcendent are conveyed. He's seen this artist before. "This is that painter you spoke of with Manyac on the first day, the deranged one with syphilis."

"So some venereologist says. The fellow's name was Vincent. Gave him a showing a few autumns past. One way or another, we can rest assured it was a lady who made this madman mad—quite beautifully so, I'd say. Whether she infected his head with the thought of her on some evening in Arles or if she poisoned his loins with a disease that went from bollocks to brains, I wouldn't venture to guess."

Pablo thought of how the doctor had insisted on calling the organisms under the microscope "she." "Is that always the way it is," Pablo asks, "with women, I mean?"

"You'll find out in time. They are, after all, the spice of life—the sweet, the sour, the bitter, too. The savory, the intriguing, the acidic, the scalding hot. I could go on." He looks at Pablo as though for the first time. "Now, what is it you came for?"

"My paintings."

"Ah, yes. All the ones that did *not* sell. Hardly worth taking, you know? What was good, it's gone. And as for the rest, might as well cover them with gesso and reuse the canvas, if I should be blunt."

"You don't like them?"

"Does that surprise you? No one else did, either."

Pablo can't find a way to disagree.

"Tell you what. I'll take them off your hands, save you the expense of coach fare home, and purchase the whole lot for seventy-five francs, shall we say? You can't easily stuff them back in your shiny portfolio now that we've put them onto stretchers, can you?"

"No. I want them."

"Go on, then. I haven't more time to waste. There's every blasted German in Paris to feed."

Pablo loads the paintings into a car and rides to the apartment on the Boulevard. He uses the last of his money to pay urchins on the corner to help him up the six flights. When he sets them down inside, however, he's shocked to find on the table his allowance from Manyac for the next month, plus an extra hundred francs that his patron has given him due to the show's success. Pablo hastily snaps up his fancy top hat and runs downstairs to fetch the first horse driver he sees to carry him to the Folies Bergère, the Ninth Arrondissement dance hall he's never been able to afford. Pablo takes a box seat there alongside the financiers. He spends his money as fast as a reckless gambler, downing *vin blanc cassis* and watching the burlesque dancers shed their clothes like rolling snakes, the audience stomping and howling for more.

Is it true, Pablo asks himself, that women are what make men mad? Lead them to reach for a noose or gun? He drinks and watches, pondering the question and the performer's miraculous thighs, meaty and thick. Perhaps he, too, will lose his mind. The thought fills him with ironic cheer, then it leaves and comes back again, all in little more than a moment's time. His mood undulates this way, bobbing up and down. But what, Pablo asks himself, makes women mad? It must be men. Yes, women prey on men. Men prey on women. But something else is devouring us all, which is impossible to escape. That painter whose tortured night scene seethes now in a basement below Vollard's, he must have known this—we're not just prisoners of temptation, but also Providence.

~

Pablo stumbles back to the apartment at midnight after Bastille Day festivities, all of Paris having become a raucous tricolor. For the past week, he's tried everything to rinse away the ill temper he's felt in body and mind, to escape the acute melancholy growing ever since Madrid: booze, showgirls, cinema reels, and those restaurants that people in Spain rave so much about upon returning from France, as if godly ambrosia had been discharged directly onto their plates.

Manyac is thankfully not home. Pablo leans back on the settee and stares up blankly, reflecting on how his aim had once been to conquer Barcelona. He'd done that. Then, he'd meant to win over Paris. Now that, somehow, appears plausible. Not even two decades old, he's opened here at a top gallery. Yet he is powerless to dispel this gloom.

In the empty white of the ceiling above, Pablo envisions how Carles's eyes would wrinkle at the corners when he'd laugh at a wry joke, the creases reaching almost to his hairline. That, the temple, is the place where he shot himself, Pablo thinks, imagining a hole one can run a finger through. He pictures that same head trapped in a wooden box. What would Carles have said about the paintings Pablo displayed at Vollard's? Might Carles again have branded him—as he had back at the Málaga hotel—a sellout? The same rotten thing Pablo figured Casas for? And that which Don José contrived for Pablo to become?

Pablo beetles across the room to an untouched canvas leftover from the flurry of work he did before the show. He opens his paint box and selects the lead white and bone black and squeezes them onto the palette, not knowing what to make or where to start. He swirls them together on the board into a glaucous murk and covers the entire surface of the painting. Then, he reaches for more of the tubes—the Prussian, the cobalt, and the ultramarine—and idly begins to layer on color.

IV

Pablo scrapes the rough skin between lip and chin till it turns pink and raw. He is standing naked in an ironstone basin at the break of dawn, the bathroom around him redolent of laurel water and candlewick. The handheld vanity keeps fogging up. The razor is freshly stropped. He flinches when he nicks himself just below the ear. The drop of blood hits the pool at his feet, echoing against the wall tiles like the sound of a porpoise click. The bright scarlet spreads in the liquid, contaminating it.

Pablo's freckles on his palms have faded, but he still recognizes the outlines, shoals beneath the surface. He has felt weaker by the day. Maybe the physician's treatment is failing, he thinks as he sets down the mirror and reaches between his legs. He rolls his privates around with thumb and forefinger until finding where the ulcer appeared. There's hardly a trace. The snake has receded, off into its burrow again. Slithering inside him. What will Dr. Jullien say when Pablo sees him later today? What will be his prognosis? Pablo cups his testes in one hand, straining to remember if the folded flesh always was dotted with evenly distributed bumps. He recalls how Vollard had suggested it would be better to scissor off the root of one's troubles and sneezes. The razor clanks against the floor. Pablo gawks at his reflection in the blade. The herringbone pattern of the tiles around it vibrates in a continuum of tiny rolling waves.

A trail of wetness follows Pablo as he exits in a towel. It's still almost black in the hallway, with only a faint blush of purple from the window. The cheeping of sparrows announces morning coming. Pablo bends at the knee beside the pile of canvases sloped up against the parlor wall. Behind it is the crevice where he stashes his valuables. A shadow moves against the plaster nearby and startles Pablo. He turns and finds Manyac stretched out on the settee behind him, a crystal tumbler in one hand. In the other is a narrow, unlit cigarette. Pablo didn't hear him come home, figuring he'd been swept away in Bastille Day reveling.

"Something different, eh?" Manyac says, aiming the tip of his boot at Pablo's still-drying canvas leaned up at the front of the pile—a young man's profile, painted in quick, hard strokes of pure black, white, and blues. The hair is wild, face slack, eyes dreamily closed. A dark patch is opening at the temple as he falls. The painting's motion and rhythm resemble the dancing flame and ethereal whorls of the work Pablo discovered in the gallery's cellar.

"I see you've been up all night," Manyac says, pointing to a stack of pastels on moldmade paper resting on a side table by the settee's arm. They both turn to one of the pages that must have floated onto the floor while Pablo was bathing. The subject in this picture is the same, wrapped in a shroud, lying in repose, his bloodless body rendered again in frigid shades of blue. "Must be that poet friend of yours—the maniac who shot up the restaurant at the end of the block, eh? Don't think there will be a market for it, frankly," Manyac says, adding he won't object so long as the rest of production keeps coming along. He places the cigarette in his mouth and tells Pablo he has a contact, an American, who may be interested in his works. "The ones that are more fungible, or, shall we say, more lively? Who knows, another show may be in the offing."

"I don't want a show," Pablo says in a flat tone.

"Don't want what?" Manyac coughs with startled incredulity. He strikes a match to light the cigarette.

"My work in the gallery, it's shit," Pablo says, still in a crouch, staring at his bare feet, tightening the towel around his waist.

"Oh, stop," Manyac says, swatting at the smoke in the air. "Don't be so critical of yourself. Though your modesty is becoming. We sold half. Next time, we'll do more, much more." Manyac tells him they can command higher prices, too. "Picasso won't be a newcomer any longer. He'll be on his way to being established, desired."

"I don't want those things, either."

"All right. We can ride the *primitif* thing awhile longer. The man-child crawled to Paris from the Iberian wilds, making fantastic scenes of cancan dancers and winking whores. They're very fine, you know," Manyac says, an orange ember tracing an arc in the purple light and arriving a few inches from his lips. "Why, even Lautrec would be jealous."

Manyac exhales a smoke ring. "But it won't last," he says. "Someone younger, more intriguing, from someplace more exotic than Barcelona, will come along and paint prettier petticoats than even you. Hard to imagine, right?"

"I guess."

"Come now, why so glum?" Manyac says, rising and placing his palm over Pablo's brow, like a priest anointing the baptized. There's a buzzing in the air. The smell of Manyac's arm is resiny, like the perfume of a tree wound. Those manicured fingers that created such delicate cursive letters rake their way through Pablo's hair.

"I should leave."

"Nonsense. Where will you go?"

"The doctor."

"Aren't you feeling well?"

"No. I don't think so. I'm not well at all."

"Any way to make it better?" Manyac asks, running the soft pad of his thumb across Pablo's frozen-in-place lips and inserting the tip of his salty fingernail just inside.

Pablo braces for a fight when he tugs away. But Manyac lets him. He rushes to dress behind the Chinese screen and makes a beeline for the door.

"Hurry back," Manyac says. "After you've cured your melancholia. You've scads of work to do. I need something besides dreariness. You know, painting that actually increases the value of the canvas?"

~

At the physician's office, the secretary is stone-faced, betraying no inkling of what they'd done together. "Pay and be seated," is all she says.

Pablo takes his place on the cherrywood bench, grumbling to himself about how Dr. Jullien's treatments are adding up. Nothing remains from the extra money Manyac gave him from the opening. Hardly anything is left from his monthly allowance. What a word, Pablo thinks— *allowance*. How did it come to pass that his health is dependent upon the physician who forsook Germaine, and he's beholden to a satyr for his daily bread? This is a captivity worse than living under Don José.

If only Pablo could deal directly with the gallery owners—no mediator taking a cut, or more than his cut—then he could be independent. He might even be able to paint subjects with depth, meaning. He could stuff the pocketbook while giving succor to his worm-hollowed soul. If, that is, his body doesn't give way first.

When it's his turn, Pablo perches on the examination table and readies himself for a dire new verdict, one as bad as he feels inside.

"Am I dying?"

"Surely, lad. How soon, that is what my profession endeavors to tell," Dr. Jullien says, pouring a dilution into a sturdy glass syringe. He then screws a three-inch needle onto the tip. "In your case, the prognosis is at least fair. No discernible signs of deterioration. No new symptoms. All that is required are routine treatments and the absence of further complications," the doctor says as Pablo rolls up his shirtsleeve. "You're still young. What, you're some kind of a writer, are you not?"

"A painter."

"Knew it was something on the fringes."

Dr. Jullien remarks that Pablo is lucky to find himself in Paris, of all places. He may even meet a fine young lady here, not the impure kind he's so far been acquainted with. "A few more doses, and it's entirely possible to approach the hymeneal altar with health regained—preserve hers, too. Thanks be to science!"

Pablo winces as the doctor plunges the needle into his arm, filling it with fire. The doctor slowly compresses the hypodermic, and Pablo tries to busy his mind with anything but the pain. He hunts around the room before pointing to a brass apparatus resembling a bilge pump connected to two tubes of black India rubber and howling, "What's that?"

"So glad you asked. For this may be the instrument to revolutionize medicine. In each man and woman, we have a volume of five liters of blood, you see? Lose two, easy enough to do, and you're done for. But"—to Pablo's horror, the doctor stalls in depressing the syringe and wags his finger in the air—"what if I could give my blood to keep you alive? Of course, you could not give me your blood because it's got the syphilis. Or you might try, I suppose, but I'd not want it. Soon, though, there will be better diagnostics for that," he says, mercifully pulling out the needle and placing a gauze pad over the seeping red. "Imagine, to be able to transfuse the very vitality of life? You can see the ready application in the operating room. Even a top-notch surgeon's sure to lose lots of blood."

Pablo breathes heavily, trying to calm himself as Dr. Jullien goes on about how at the office his bread-and-butter surgeries are mostly limited to nips, scrapes, and lithotomies.

"But in my position at the Saint-Lazare, that's another story. I am the only Frenchman who performs more than one thousand procedures on genitourinary organs each year," he says. "I'll be applying to patent a brilliant metrotome I've rigged up for amputating the cervix during a hysterectomy."

Pablo has no idea what the doctor is talking about. He scrunches up his face in confusion while continuing to grit his teeth.

"Cut the womb, it means. Complete removal. Rut it all out after it's become corrupted. By venereal disease, quite often. Sarcoma sometimes. For my prison patients, women who can ill afford children, this has the added benefit of being highly effective birth control."

The pain starts to subside, and Pablo asks, "They're locked up?"

The doctor acts as if he can't believe Pablo has never heard of Prison Saint-Lazare. "Why, Marquis de Sade was incarcerated there during the revolution," he says. "All women and girls now, though. Confined for lunacy, degeneracy, indecency, or, often, mere indigence and crimes of need. More of a sanatorium than a jail."

Pablo detects a strain of unexpected compassion in the doctor's voice as he recounts that their offspring, female and male, can also be found there until they're old enough to become state wards. "The majority of inmates are stricken with something venereal," Dr. Jullien says, adding this may—or may not—be the cause of their state of mind. "Chicken or the egg again, right?"

Pablo thinks of how disheveled and twisted his own thoughts have become ever since Madrid, how his memories run amok. He asks, "They have syphilis, the same disease as me?"

"Some do. Some do," Dr. Jullien says. "I've sympathy for many of the women—victims, really—they've often done nothing to bring upon themselves these redoubtable maladies. Rather it's the libertinism of their husbands or erstwhile fiancés. So many a coward wrecks a girl before marriage, then doesn't have courage even to go through with the rite. How she suffers—the sores, aches, blindness, madness. Not to mention stigma for the condition itself. Don't get me wrong; plenty of floozies in there, too."

An idea awakens in Pablo as he imagines these women hidden away in prison—or infirmary or whatever it is—and how in them he might find subjects more worthy of attention than what he's been pecking about for on Paris's streets. He looks up and says, "Can I view them?"

"For what?"

"To paint."

"They're ne'er-do-wells, harlots, and loonies, not a bowl of fruit. Why should you paint them?"

"Make the world see they exist."

Dr. Jullien looks excited by this idea. He points out he's been doing the same for years, frankly, in his written volumes, which have been published even in Spanish. "But the beauty of a picture is it needs no translation," he says. "Then, the symptoms of this ignoble era might be recorded in the very visages of its distempered lives, could be made readable by the gouges and pro-truuu-sions of their disfiiigured flesh!"

The physician pauses, considering.

"Let's arrange it," he concludes, shoving the needle into Pablo's other arm.

～

A stocky guard with shaggy gray hair stands at the gate of the Saint-Lazare holstering an ancient flintlock pistol. He ejects a stream of saliva that lands beside Pablo's feet. The man pats Pablo down, then scours his easel and box of painting supplies for anything that could be made to slice, saw, garrote, or puncture. He confiscates a palette knife but lets him keep his brushes, after snapping them to be two inches long, incapable of seriously damaging an internal organ.

The guard leads Pablo through the partitioned courtyard bordered by tall walls darkened by centuries of dirt and carbon. "That there," he says, pointing to a round island of soil with a few huddled orange azaleas amid the paving stones, "was the guillotine." His face is so rough, utterances of any sort are a surprise, yet he seems proud to know this gobbet of prison lore. Or is he remembering the contraption with fondness, Pablo wonders, having once been the executioner? The Saint-Lazare's main building has four floors of barred windows plus a row of dormers eyeing out from the slate roof. Its most notable feature seen from a distance, however, is an adjoining dome-covered chapel rising over the rural landscape.

Inside at the admitting desk, which is surrounded by iron mesh, Pablo meets Mother Superior. Framed by a dark veil, her pale, grave face and double chin are almost inseparable from the high-necked white guimpe beneath them. Pablo hands her the note of reference that Dr. Louis Jullien, the prison's esteemed medical laureate, gave him.

"Why should I allow you to disturb these women?"

"Art's good for the soul," Pablo replies.

"So is solitude. Silent contemplation. Prayer," she says. "Wherever did you learn to speak such atrocious French?"

"No words in my paintings," Pablo assures her.

Mother Superior looks long and hard at him. She consents for Pablo to paint the inmates but only in public. "Make no effort to be alone with them. Don't speak more than the minimum. They've nothing to hear from you, and you nothing from them. Understand?"

"Yes, Your Holiness," Pablo replies with his most beatific smile, before begging one more question. "How do I know which women have syphilis?"

"They're marked by white bonnets, easy to spot."

"Those aren't nuns?"

"Hardly."

The head of the congregation and her second-in-command chaperone Pablo down the hall to a large chamber with high ceilings and muted sunlight bending through leaded glass pocked with tiny bubbles.

Row upon row of women crowd around long wooden tables—sewing, darning, doing needlework, and making lace. The room is a whir of turning treadles, scissor snips, and whispers.

In the corner, Pablo locates a group of condemned women by their telltale white bonnets. He strides over, easel under his arm, supplies in one hand, the other planted beneath his chin. The prisoners, unaccustomed to strange young men meandering the premises, look both curious and cautious as he circles.

Pablo clears his throat and begins unfastening his easel, pulling out each leg, tightening the wing nuts to keep the hinges in place, positioning the picture stand—all with the speed of dripping treacle. Quite aware he has an audience, once everything is in place, he theatrically hastens his movements, mixing paints on the palette with a flourish, fluttering the brushes, and snapping his wrist with each stroke like a flamenco, displaying the showmanship he perfected before his mother, sisters, and aunts.

The convicts at the Saint-Lazare appear spellbound. Except, that is, for the seated woman closest him, who instead busily ties little knots of white thread to make a tatted trim. Like Pablo, her fingers are fast and deft, her eyes black beneath wide-set eyebrows. She couldn't be more than thirty. Her face is slender, cream-white, and unstirred. A squat companion speaks softly into her ear. The woman shakes her head, gives a dismissive French shrug, and carries on.

After an hour of painting, Pablo hears a handbell chime outside. Scores of women rise and head toward the exit to take exercise, walking together in a line along the courtyard's perimeter.

Pablo continues to work amid the clamor. The woman he'd been depicting, the same who'd ignored him, is the only one remaining seated.

"Why me?" she says, without turning.

"The light chose for me. Without it, I can't work," Pablo says pointing upward with his brush to the latticed window casting a diamond pattern on her face. "Blame the sun, if you must."

"I see I'm not the only fatalist. Who are you?"

"They must have told you a painter was coming," he lies.

"I stopped listening a long time ago, but so I see. What did you come to paint?"

"In Spain, artists can't help specializing in heartbreak or loving madness."

"That's what everyone says. I'm going mad."

"Today?" he jokes, looking to the wristwatch fastened above his hand holding the palette.

She coils the extra length of thread that's still on the needle back onto the spool, appearing to be mulling him over. "It wouldn't matter if I didn't want to be painted," she says, "would it?"

"You could please recommend someone else, maybe?"

"Another zany, you mean?" When the woman looks up, the hatched light catches her pupils, and they shimmer like polished onyx. She points to the girl sitting outside, clutching her ears, rocking, and pivoting her head like a crazed dove. "Could always try her."

"Don't think she'd stay still," Pablo says, before adding, "and, if I may, you're nice to paint."

The woman shows no sign of registering the compliment as she nimbly pries apart the knot at the end of the needle with her incisors. "Did you know that I don't think I've ever seen anyone with bigger eyes than yours," she says. "Perhaps somebody ought to paint you instead?"

"If your brushwork is anything like your lace-making, I'd be delighted. Paris is full of so-so artists, you know. I've hardly met one who can hold a candle to me. But you appear to have skill, technique."

"Aren't you cheeky, Bugeyes."

There's something about the delicate movements of wrist and neck, Pablo thinks, that gives the woman the air of a deposed royal under lock and key, a tsarina, or a Medici. Awaiting the hangman, yes, but still bold and genteel. He is reminded of Germaine. A moment ago, his showy painting demonstration gave him a rush of confidence, but with this memory, it quickly departs. He begins to pack up his easel and notices she has seen the canvas, a reflection of herself—solemn, stately, stoic, beautiful, and washed in blue. Pablo thinks he's won her over with it.

"If you come again, I'll have nothing to do with it," she says, however, returning to disinterest. "Paint a dead cat."

Early the next day, Pablo wakes and heads back toward Prison Saint-Lazare, stalking from Montmartre to Boulevard de Magenta and passing the bridal shops near the Place de la République, all the way to where civilization ends and men with reeking wheelbarrows unload their haul of horse droppings onto giant mounds. Pablo has noticed these collectors trailing carriages—rake in hand—in the city's center. Way out here, he finds the depository granting them five francs per load. Grape and wheat farmers purchase this fertilizer, after it is cut with night soil, for their fields. Five francs is about the same as a model's wages for a day, or, Pablo calculates, apparently what Vollard thinks one of his unsold paintings is worth.

This is the route that Pablo follows to the institution each morning for weeks. Soon, he gets to know the signs of the affliction he shares with many of the inmates. Most of the women are in much more advanced stages of the disease or have worse cases of it. Should he consider himself lucky or doomed? For example, the palm freckles that may appear after inoculation sometimes render the flesh like toad skin. Had he suffered the same, it might not have let him paint. Further along, there are the soft, sunken noses or the jaundice that makes the whites of eyes look like buttermilk. Vision usually begins to deteriorate at this point. Necrotic sores dot and swell and curl the brows of the patients. Then it's uncontrollable contortions, incoherent rambling, hallucinations—and eventually, death.

~

After a while, the woman whom Pablo painted on the first day quietly consents for him to set up an easel at her side and capture her mood as she works. It's odd, but he's never learned her name. By the time he realizes, he is already calling her in his head "the Bronzino"—after her likeness to the portraits by the late Italian mannerist whose subjects always appear to be lancing the viewer with their eyes. Perhaps, he thinks, it is this resemblance that has led him to adopt that era's style of flat backgrounds, warped proportion, allusive meaning, and inscrutable faces. Sometimes while painting her, he feels they are cantering toward one another on horses in a jousting match. Each speaks little, establishing a pattern where words are not, as Pablo promised the Mother Superior, required.

When the Bronzino does address Pablo, however, she calls him Bugeyes. It is an unexpected intimacy. She is chief among a handful of women he paints at the Saint-Lazare. After their breakfasts, she sits for her portrait while spinning webs of lace as complicated as basilica ceilings.

In the afternoons, Pablo heads outdoors. Never particularly enamored by the impressionists—a disinclination planted by Don José, he hates to admit—Pablo doesn't seek to capture the complexities and fleetingness of sunlight, despite what he told the Bronzino about his dependence on it, which is true. Rather, his excursions to the flagstones in the courtyard allow Pablo to pretend he is focusing on the canvas before him while instead furtively viewing the shaded portico where the children play. Pablo takes care to avoid watching the wet nurses work, although he notices how their faces appear rigid and unyielding, like the bars on the infirmary windows. It is the children who fascinate him. Ranging from three months to four years, they are allowed to see their mothers one hour each day, in the evenings, depending on good behavior. There is something infinitely sad to Pablo about the notion of being born into a prison. It both irks and tugs him.

With few exceptions, the incarcerated women whose young also reside here are the best behaved. Other punishments—reduction in rations, ice-cold hoses, forfeiture of exercise, cross-irons around the ankles—are all ineffectual deterrents compared to the threat of refusing to let a woman see her child for even a day.

When Pablo asks Mother Superior whether he might be allowed to paint the children, she doesn't say no. He reads this as acknowledgment that, after a month, he's become a Saint-Lazare fixture, and the women and nuns, on some level, accept him. He isn't allowed onto the portico during nursing and is barred from the newborns' crèche but otherwise comes and goes as he pleases.

One late-summer morning, Pablo, in an unusual outburst, recounts to the Bronzino how he watched the kids romp outside the previous day. "They drew black squares on the pavement with a charcoal nub and pitched a bead of glass inside," he describes excitedly. "I couldn't believe it—here they are, all running, chasing, having more fun than me back in Montmartre!"

"Not all," she says.

Pablo did not realize there were others.

After this, he learns from slyly questioning the children that there is another enclave of the prison he's not visited. Stowed away here are *les petits monstres*. The children tell tales of these cloistered creatures: the incisors rough and irregular like broken almonds; yellow skin covered in spots; rent, lipless faces with craggy noses; bowed, brittle legs and shins.

All Pablo can think of is the fetus Germaine carried, the one he didn't have courage to view. His invented visions of these children begin to haunt him. He and Germaine hadn't any good option, if there were a heartbeat, he tells himself. This is what the child would have suffered. The images float alongside Conchita and Carles in the gauzy blue eternity of his nights.

∾

Pablo is preparing a canvas when the Bronzino glances over at the portrait he painted of her the previous day. She is staring at the long, wispish fingers and abnormally stretched neck of the figure against a smooth background. "It's as if you're trying to extend me," she says.

"I'm experimenting. The style is from ages ago," Pablo responds. "Back when painters from Florence to Spain were reaching to achieve perfection in any pose. They were continuously refining, challenging themselves, like scientists searching for truths that no one had succeeded in discovering. But they had no more equipment than paints, brushes, and their eyes."

"It appears a bit bizarre, don't you think? Does my body really look so tortured?" she asks, setting down her bobbin.

"That was never my intent."

"And all your works since you've come to the Saint-Lazare, they're blue."

"Does it bother you?"

"Are you asking if I wish for you to paint in a different color?"

"Would you like that?"

"In life, we only act like we're free to choose," the Bronzino says, closing her hands around the swath of lace she's been making. "But there are no choices. I learned that here."

The woman's eyes fix on her pitted fingernails. She's begun to see the signs, she tells Pablo. Felt them, too. How her brain is more scattered. The people she is speaking to, who move inside and outside of view—they may not really be there at all.

Pablo looks down at the holes in the lace.

"Bugeyes?"

"Yes."

"You can't come back after today. I don't want you to see how I am."

A sadness fills Pablo as it sinks in that he is being banished from the only place in Paris he's felt at home since the studio he shared this past winter—and by the first model who's inspired him since Germaine.

When the bells ring, they part and meet again secretly upstairs, against every prison rule, in the grated cell in an attic dormer where the Bronzino stays—as opposed to the common, lice-infested sleeping quarters—a privilege afforded to her because of her unrivaled needlework. She grants him this intimacy for his final picture.

There, beside the barred window, she positions herself and loosens her bonnet. Grecian black locks emerge. She folds her arms, stoically, and Pablo imagines how she will fit into the canvas's rectangular borders. What shall she be? What feeling should he convey? The sun is filtering through the prison window, but the first thing Pablo does is change it to the light yellow of a moon in the early evening.

"You might have taught me to paint," she says.

Pablo remembers how he'd instructed Carles long ago. "And I could have learned to make lace."

She replies with an anemic smile.

Hours pass, until day really has become dusk. Pablo finishes. The figure on the easel is long and elegant, cloaked in blue, and turned away from the twilight beyond the cell. Her keen gaze beneath scythe-like eyebrows sees fate clearly, what it is to be made to briefly exist.

Now there's a record of who this woman had been while she was sane.

The window painted on the canvas has no bars.

~

Without Pablo's trips to the Saint-Lazare, he finds himself with Manyac much more. His penury and even the elements conspire to keep them close. Pablo has no money and no credit at the cafés or boîtes, and autumn rains mean trudging through mud and then finding nowhere to paint outdoors.

After the exhibition at Vollard's, Pablo expected work. But no one else has offered him a spot on their walls or bought his paintings. Pablo suspects this is due to Manyac deploying his influence to divert interest away—to make Pablo more dependent, obedient, pliant.

And Pablo's contract with Manyac, he learns, is nearly impossible to circumvent. At last, he manages to secure a single commission to illustrate a magazine but only after resorting to using a name he hasn't signed with in years: Ruiz. If Manyac found out, he could charge Pablo with breach. But it's the only way for him to land enough cash to live with a shred of autonomy. Even in good weather, there are no longer World's Fair tourists around Paris whom he can impress with bullfighting scenes.

Every day, it seems, Manyac lords over Pablo more, regulating how he dresses, who he sees, what he eats and drinks—taunting him like a lover. Until Pablo relents and becomes one.

Pablo will ask himself why he does this. He concedes it may be a product of being sent away during the past six months by both Germaine and the Bronzino. Or raw, physical need—combined with the strange magnetic force proximity exerts, plus Manyac's relentless baiting. But most importantly, Pablo decides, this is not Manyac having his way. Rather, Fate is having its own.

For Pablo has become resigned to the idea that circumstances are not ours to control. Yes, he's being exploited, his youth taken advantage of in more ways than one—just because he's from Spain doesn't mean he's an imbecile. But the light in a room, the colors we find there, these are not ours to decide. There is no stopping the tide or holding on when it tears away. It's just as the Bronzino said: in life, we have no choice. There is always death, that's true. But death is a certainty, not a decision. Instead, we imagine there's the power to choose while we're alive, too afraid to admit soon there won't be this consolation. Freedom is a mirage.

Pablo can't even deny the response of his flesh when Manyac caresses him. And, to be really honest, nor is he Pablo's first lover of this kind. There was that boy who appeared at the mouth of the cave in

Horta long ago. It was different—very different—of course. He'd felt so drawn up in this stranger who'd shown him something miraculous: the paint running through the ground. And, besides, Pablo tells himself as he clenches his fists and watches the gold fringe hanging from the tufted divan sway pendulously to Manyac's rhythm, what else is Paris for if not to expand one's passionate repertoire?

~

Manyac gleams with conquest and treats Pablo well. The cantankerous taunter has subsided; he has become again the affectionate man who'd sent flattering letters to Madrid. He sings Pablo's praises all the time.

As winter goes by, Pablo hears whispers about their relationship. But Manyac is the one in Paris whom every Spanish artist hopes to know. He promotes them, makes connections, finds avenues. Despite other faults, Manyac takes care of his own—so they all must envy his Pablito, whom he takes care of best. Pablo even cuts a little mustache, just like his keeper's. And he is showered with gifts—stylish clothes, trips to restaurants and cabarets, and even to the Palais Garnier opera to watch Saint-Saëns stage *Les Barbares*. From front-row balcony seats, they witness the Goths storm Italy and a vestal virgin relinquish her vows for the mercy of the invading chieftain. Manyac and Pablo quietly hold hands during the duet between the agile mezzo-soprano and the golden-toned heldentenor, these harmonious passages floating up to them and an immense sparkling chandelier that refracts the flames of the pillaging on stage. How light dances sometimes, Pablo thinks, and elsewhere it is still and settled, pondering its next move.

~

There is a knock on the apartment's front door one afternoon, more than half a year after Pablo first entered it. Reaching for a bath towel, he listens to Manyac receive a telegram from the postman. A moment passes in silence before Manyac's crystal tumbler shatters against the hardwood floor.

"Coin, encouragement, guidance, finery, and connections—in-valu-able connections I gave you!" Manyac wails.

Pablo recalls how the art dealer once revealed that there was no creature in Paris he'd ever loved besides his Pomeranian and him.

"I even lent my home. And this you'd do to me?"

Fog had gathered on the mirror during the bath. Pablo dries himself with the terry cloth before rubbing the glass clean. In the reflection, a tiny smile rises. He knows from Manyac's sobs that the giro transfer from his father must be complete. The money from Barcelona for train fare to come home is now available at the Société Générale on Rue de Provence. It's true, he acknowledges: Manyac's cunning granted him higher recognition than any unknown twenty-year-old artist in Paris should aspire to. Eventually, Pablo might feel a twinge of remorse. He'd known he was deceiving Manyac and never loved him in return. How must the man feel that a messenger should come without warning to snatch his happiness away, granting him no choice in the matter?

But that, Pablo thinks, is also Fate at work.

CHAPTER 11

I

Barcelona, January 1902

Pablo hikes from the station with his belongings slung over his shoulder. The entire train ride, he fretted about facing Don José, agonized over how his father would critique his latest works and needle him about his time in France. But when Pablo unzips his portfolio at home, the old man slouched in an armchair in the family's salon merely nods at the paintings. He must be nearly blind now. Pablo surveys his father's face for other signs of the venereal disease they might share. It's not unlikely Don José would be afflicted—the goat has only patronized Spain's brothels since before Louis-Napoléon.

Would Pablo be gladder if the clear deterioration above and below Don José's brow were of the more typical variety? That is, only the familiar hand of age that leads babes to adolescence, then middle age, and so on, promising accomplishment before robbing youth with every swipe—hair, sight, tautness in cheeks, vigor in loins—until nothing more remains. What, anyway, could be left of this tired manqué who's seen a life of sadness after losing his beloved Andalusia, his most beautiful daughter, a cherished career, the steadiness in his wrists, and the respect of his only son?

Doña María guides Pablo to the kitchen table, bemoaning that Lola is away and can't be there with them. She sets a steaming cup before him. The clank of the porcelain echoes. It dawns on Pablo how quiet the apartment is. There are no pigeons floating around, leaving feathers and ghost-white droppings everywhere. Pablo's mother—already preparing dinner, although it's before noon—explains that the dovecote on the roof is empty. "Your papa couldn't take care of them," Doña María tells him, picking up a mortar and pestle. "I opened the cage and said a prayer."

Pablo is astonished. Those birds are all his father might have had. They are inseparable from both Pablo's memories of Don José and his own childhood, the family having carried the oldest pigeons here all the way from Málaga. Pablo can clearly recall features of individual animals as if they were blood relatives. He could have picked them out of a flock just by the way they moved.

A snippet of conversation returns to Pablo as he inhales the steam from the chamomile tea, an exchange at Els Gats he'd once had with Cinto, back when his friend was attending medical school.

"Tell me something," Pablo said then to Cinto. "How about hands and feet?"

"What about them?"

"Painters always get them wrong," Pablo remembers saying. Then they laughed at how so many society portraits leave one hand outside the picture frame and have the subjects tuck the other into a waistcoat, avoiding the trouble altogether.

Cinto pointed out, though, there was good reason painters struggle with these extremities. In a hand there are twenty-seven bones—twenty-six for a foot. With two of each, that's half the bones in the entire body. Together, it's also hundreds of joints and ligaments. "But the thing that makes them even more unusual," Cinto had said, "is fingers have no muscles."

"How can that be?" Pablo asked incredulously.

"All you do with your hands is controlled by tugging and relaxing in the wrists."

"Like strings on marionettes?"

"Precisely."

"Would that be true also of birds? Say, pigeons?"

Cinto had looked puzzled. "I am not studying to be a bird doctor, thank God. Why do you ask?"

"No reason," Pablo replied. But, just as when he'd seen the twisting hands of El Greco's portraits in the Prado, he wondered then what if Don José had never forced him to paint pigeon toes for countless hours? Might Pablo have failed each time he attempted to render a man or woman offering an outstretched palm, a gentle stroke of the hand, a beckoning finger? As Pablo sits at his parents' table, this memory makes him rethink Don José yet again. If only things had been different, who might his father have become? Pablo feels a tide of regret for both of them.

Looking up from his reverie, Pablo finds Doña María staring from across the kitchen counter. "You're too thin," she says, shaking her head while pulverizing ingredients into a fine paste. Pablo goes on sipping tea as she prepares to fatten him. She moves to mixing finely chopped pig neck with spices before rolling giant meatballs. "And where is your Paris wife?" she asks, holding a moist finger in the air, bits of wet pork clinging to it like grout. "I want grandbabies, Pablito. Hear me? They can speak French, long as they eat Spanish."

It's clear as daylight Pablo can't tell his mother or father anything of the life he's lived during the many months that have passed since they last saw him beyond that there was a gallery opening, and it went swell. Nor can he bear to stay here. Pablo excuses himself and leaves in search of a studio to cadge, lying to his mother that he will be home in time for dinner.

At Els Gats, Pablo asks around and learns that Angel Soto—the family friend whom Don José hired long ago to model a novice priest administering the Eucharist for *Last Moments*—has a studio his parents rent for him. Apparently the occasional painter and full-time lothario has produced no paintings there, though. Pablo isn't surprised. The building is located next to the notorious Eden Concert cabaret and Barri Xinès red-light district. Pablo remembers how when Angel was his model more than a year ago, he would pose as a cleric all afternoon only to repair to a brothel at night, sometimes still in his cassock. Pablo accompanied him more than once, just as he had earlier with Pajaresco. He even took to calling his fiendish companion "We're-No-Angels" Soto.

When Pablo knocks on Angel's door, this old acquaintance is happy to let a talent like Pablo share his atelier. "It'll be like I'm legitimate," Angel says. The living arrangements are modest but suitable. Angel is surprised, though, that Pablo is much less inclined these days to join him in his libidinous exploits. Pablo can't say it to Angel, but brothels remind him too much now of the women in Prison Saint-Lazare and the consequences they endure. These days, if he paints prostitution, instead of giving the women lush, bright, décolleté attire and coaxing looks, the scenes are drowning in shadow. The women sometimes are crouched low, their arms curled around themselves. They often avert their eyes, unable to face the viewer's cruelty.

Instead of partaking in seedy nightlife, Pablo nurtures a habit of slipping away just before sundown to walk the beach near the cemetery that Carles once brought him to, setting up his portable easel a few yards from the shoreline. He paints here amid the damp, spumy, nocturnal air, projecting from memory inhabitants of the Saint-Lazare onto the cooled sand—stealing them away from their prison, freeing them to wander barefoot in the slanting yellow moonlight against a backdrop of a collapsing cerulean sea and sky. Loosed from fate, they hold their children close to their lips. As always, both mother and child in these paintings are shrouded in Mary's sacred blue.

As Pablo fills up these canvases by the sea, Germaine also drifts through his thoughts. He didn't try to find her again after she sent him away, but he's heard she's taken up with some other artist in Montmartre. Pablo wants to be happy for her. And yet he can't help feeling hurt and angry that she chose someone else. A million times he's tried to distill what exactly he feels for Germaine, or she for him. Was it a great love shared—something beyond even that? Or, in the end, was the attachment all about Carles? After all, he had invested in her his desire, his poetry. Was she to Pablo a mere contact relic, revered because she touched a martyr? He doubts that, knowing Germaine emanates too much of her own magic.

But after a month back in Barcelona, Pablo's mysticism continues to recede, the nihilism he gained in the Saint-Lazare filling its wake. Late one Sunday night, beneath the moon, he falls asleep on the beach inhaling salt mist after painting Germaine in the bonnet the women there wore, the sound of whistling air filling his head.

~

In late winter, a wind begins to blow across the Mediterranean from the Maghreb, and a great fog sometimes rolls over Barcelona as the warmth fans over the cool, choppy sea. Pablo awakes in a thick blue-gray haze. He can't see his own feet. There is a deathly quiet, as if mist has swallowed all but a waxy light. No din at the ports, no gulls.

This fog, Pablo thinks, is thicker than the dreaded one of La Coruña he'd experienced as a boy, or any other. It has a different, speculative quality. Everything around him feels shapeless now, not yet drawn. He stumbles in the uneven sand and falls, remembering how after living under Manyac's regime had become insufferable, he'd begged his parents for money to return from Paris to Barcelona.

But with his fingers inched into the cold grains, Pablo intuits there is something else that pulled him back here. There have been brushes with success, although no guarantee more will come—just as it's unclear whether he is heir to a master or the son of a hack. He'd needed to be closer to where art first began, felt natural, before Don José drilled into him what succeeding means or Paris tried to impose its own definition.

Pablo stands and attempts to angle inland through the haze. It's hard to say where he is. He locates steel tracks laid into the pavement and follows them, knowing the *tramvia* will lead to the city center.

A clanking in the distance breaks the silence. The noise becomes louder, and Pablo jumps to the side, fearing the emanation is the bells of a streetcar about to flatten him. But the sound isn't moving fast enough. And it's too big, like a clattering of many objects striking metal rather than one chime. Pablo finally makes out the base of the Cristóbal Colón statue and turns up La Rambla. It's early but shops should be open. Where are the flower vendors? The canaries and parakeets packing brass wire cages? The macaque monkey? Two figures whoosh through the cloud around Pablo, their faces streaming blood. He walks on and now hears clambering and shouting.

The fog thins, revealing a crowd. The metallic sound he heard is spoons clanging against casserole dishes. Protesters are chanting, holding pickets with caricatures of politicians and fat-cat industrialists. Pablo's studio is on the opposite side of a barricade. He learns from others on the street that the area by his parents' apartment on Carrer de la Mercè is also besieged. Even a church may have been set on fire. Among the aggrieved masses he finds metalworkers, factory laborers, shop-weavers, tradesmen, stevedores, housewives, cooks, waitresses, lame veterans, and farmers who'd fled to Barcelona because the land back home is dry, their crops dead. There are anarchists and nationalists, communists and Catalanists, liberals and reactionaries, *progressistes* and *collectivistes,* acolytes of Marti and freemasonry, Marx and human rationality, hayseeds and intellectuals. All stripes of the disenchanted are on one side of Spain's first-ever general strike that began with grumbling at a metal foundry but has grown to encompass every perceived

inequity leveled by the powerful against the rest of the population. Even
the circus handlers are outside agitating, the howling apes beside them
banging against pots with hand and foot.

On the other side of the street, there is a cavalry regiment.

Amid the waving and shouting, Pablo sees some of the strikers fling
stale bread at the soldiers. A bucket of slop is aimed. Soon the air is filled
with detritus and stones.

There's a crack-crack-crack.

Then, screams.

Who's been hit? It's a cacophony of frantic cries.

The crowd eventually determines that the flashing muzzles fired
only into the sky. But Pablo has a sinking feeling. In the commotion,
he flips over the barricade and darts to his building. He desperately
fumbles for his keys for a panic-stricken moment before hurriedly turning the lock, pushing inside, and slamming the door behind him.

After a long, twisting climb up the grungy staircase, Pablo watches
the scene below from the rooftop and sees a shadowy figure sprint by
in a balaclava and strike a horse in the jaw with a club. The animal
stumbles like a dazed boxer. Its rider nearly falls off before regaining
control of his steed and charging through the crowd in a flurry of hoofs.
Troops of every variety arrive until half the street looks like a mosaic of
combatant uniforms, hats, and armbands.

But the opposition is also swelling.

Pablo spots a pair of guardsmen, easy to distinguish in their *tri-
cornios* of polished black leather, the brim's back upturned—giving the
appearance that bone-eaters have perched atop their heads, waiting for
carrion. They are scanning rooftops, looking for snipers. He shelters
inside the studio and prepares a canvas. He can get some painting done
in between viewing through the window slats.

The sun is soon low again, the situation outside taut as piano
strings. Provisions in the studio total one box of Ceylon tea, a half-
eaten canister of hardtack biscuits, two casks of Monastrell wine, and

one large bottle of cheap brandy. After two days, he'll be famished, Pablo concludes, but he might be drunk for five.

When Pablo hears footsteps coming upstairs, his skin crawls. The knob and spring bolt turn.

As the door opens, Pablo is standing in his britches, smeared with oil paint and clutching a palette knife as though it were a broadsword.

"You look ready to defend the Peninsula against the infidels," laughs Angel. He's brought an accomplice with him, a chubby rounder named Josep who claims to be an artist of some sort. They're both swinging gin flasks between their fingers.

"Would you believe even the whores are on strike?" Angel says.

"I didn't think it would go that far," Pablo admits, genuinely shocked at the disruption to the city's order.

"What do these gals want, a nine-hour workday?" Angel muses, plopping onto the threadbare sofa, narrowly avoiding a protruding spring. "Like they don't enjoy every lovin' minute!"

Pablo finds this company and its commentary boorish, unsalvageable, and out of place with everything going on around them. He thinks of the women he met at the brothel when he stayed there for a couple weeks in the coatroom during his teens—some had turned to prostitution after the textile factory they worked at closed down or a boss needlessly fired them. And then of those at the Saint-Lazare. Pablo wishes his visitors would disappear before remembering the studio belongs to Angel, even if his frequent carousing means he's hardly here.

By evening, warfare has rung out below. Authorities and rioters exchange ambushes—baton and bayonet versus broom handle and brick. When union toughs arrive baring jackknives and cleavers, however, the city's forces switch from crowd-controlling knee knockers to full-lead bullets. There are dead and wounded on both sides.

All night, Pablo hears rifles fire in response to potshots. He tries to focus on the canvas, ignoring not only the chaos outside but also Angel and his friend, who deal cards and page through a raunchy magazine, comparing the bodies of the women inside both to conquests and planned endeavors, telling stories from the illustrious battlefield of *amor* they've created in their heads.

Early the next morning, when Pablo looks through the shutters, the streets are covered in spent cartridges, glass, horseshit, and blood. Intermittent gunfire and the scampering of heels have replaced the song-birds. Smoke, dust, and the aromas of cordite and burning tar hover between ground and rooftop. He hears in the distance pans banging—the sound that preceded yesterday's carnage. As the clattering becomes louder, Pablo braces for violence. This cycle lasts until Thursday morning, when Pablo perceives on the ground outside the window something new—little dots growing in the gory mess like pointillism. There's a giant noise in the air. At first, Pablo thinks they've brought out the cannons. But a terrific deluge from the sky opens, and he understands it was a thunderclap.

At week's end, Pablo braves the elements and finds a newspaper at the corner *tabac*. The front page shows the dreaded general who'd viciously put down uprisings in Spain more than a decade ago before his talents were called into service against Cuban guerillas. Now, with martial law declared in Barcelona, he has been redeployed here. Anyone suspected of inciting violence has been rounded up and sent to the dungeons of Montjuïc so they can be persuaded to identify coconspirators. In the newspaper, the military commander gives credit to himself for saving the nation.

Pablo will go on firmly believing, however, that these hostilities that left more than a hundred dead and many more wounded were finally brought under control not with gun barrels but by the rain. It's one thing to be shot at. That happens so fast, the consequences are so unimaginable, human brains can't fully comprehend it, he decides. But all animals instinctively avoid a storm.

~

When the water subsides and debris has been washed from the streets, Pablo joins many familiar faces at Els Gats. They've come to regroup and trade tales of what they witnessed or argue about who's to blame. Several men wear dressings or scars. Ongoing food shortages mean few items on Pere's menu are available, no doubt a blessing in disguise.

The beefy owner of a butcher shop is throwing back Italian grappa like it's sweetened milk—saying he's never been so afraid as when he visited the slaughterhouse today and was greeted by a half-starved mob.

"They'd blood in their eyes. Cried, 'Give us meat, or we'll take it,'" the butcher recounts. "But it wasn't seven in the morning yet. There's no pork—just sheep, chickens, pigs, all waiting to be slit." The man says he started stocking his store as a lad. Slaughterhouses are like a second home. "But I's scared, for animals and the drudges working the carving line. When crowds get a frenzy, there's no telling."

A youngster yelps from behind: "The multitudes have a right to demand rations."

"Piss off already," the butcher shouts at the high-pitched boy.

Another waspish regular chimes in that during the uprising, he saw somebody nearly torch city hall. "I couldn't wait for them to roast up every last crooked barrister."

The room grows tense.

Pere, who's been quietly smoking a pipe by the cash register, turns and asks the butcher, "Where's the steaks on a fellow anyway?" It elicits grins, and he passes around his best brandy. "Starve if we must; we needn't be sober, too."

Anything but that, they all agree, downing their glasses. The mood improves.

Pablo doesn't know how many total hours he's spent at Els Gats, but not since the night of the shadow puppets has he seen Pere give away a drink for free. Like those around him, Pablo's been shaken by these past days. It feels good to be back at this tavern. Pablo is even oddly glad when he spots his old nemesis Casas stride in. Until he realizes the painter is scalding mad.

~

"Fear my brush!" Casas shrieks. For the past three hours, he's been railing to the men, calling the ruling classes in Barcelona curs.

There is hardly anyone whom Pablo figured less likely to defend the workers and poor than Casas. How could a painter who'd made a career out of kissing up to every benefactor who might grant him prestige—and who'd given Pablo the most venal advice imaginable about art back at the World's Fair—be the one calling out the establishment? All Casas's work that Pablo has ever known has appeared aimed at making a rich livelihood—dashed-off portraits of patrons' wives and mistresses in whatever style brings the most money and favor. And now the man is snarling at the very hand that feeds him?

"It's same as the time of Goya," Casas proclaims. "If no one engraves images in the public mind, how will they be remembered, addressed?"

Apparently, Casas was once a very different sort. After the painter's own bohemian stint in Paris, Barcelona's powers-that-be branded him a bête noire for depicting the executions of prisoners and other tableaus designed to ruffle bourgeoisie sensibilities, he tells the people in the room. When he worked up a devastating scene showing the precise moment before the most infamous bomb blast the city had known, he was cast out of every gallery. Each viewer who saw the painting glared at the crisp details of the schoolgirls' white dresses and veils as they left the Basilica de Santa Maria del Mar, thinking only of how the procession would soon be enveloped in red. Only later did Casas climb his way back into gallery owner graces with soft portraits of high society.

But now Casas promises to return to his rebellious roots. Just as the great Goya swore off courtly commissions to immortalize how a firing squad sliced apart rows of peasants, this week's events have inspired

Casas to shine light on the government's atrocities—consequence be damned. "In my studio at this moment is the canvas I've done up of a guardsman charging down innocent bystanders," Casas says, slamming his brandy onto the table. "If they hang me from a rope in the plaza, one of you can take a photograph!"

That line to a bar full of painters is classic Casas condescension and bombast, Pablo thinks. But under the circumstances, he forgives this slight. In fact, quite unexpectedly, Pablo swells with regard for the man he's long despised. He wonders whether Carles knew of Casas's revolutionary past. Before Paris, what Carles aspired to do in life was write poetry and prose to strike against inequality. Was he aware, then, that Casas had once done the same in paint? Just as perplexing, how could Pablo have not known this about Casas before? Or maybe he ignored it somehow, the same way he'd stop paying attention whenever Carles was spouting off about politics.

What's different today is that Pablo has seen injustice firsthand—not only on Barcelona's brutal streets but also in how the uncared-for women at the Saint-Lazare are led to lives of want, illness, scorn, and agony. If Casas feels the call to act, shouldn't he? Or, as Germaine once implored Dr. Jullien, does Pablo have no obligation?

While seated at Els Gats across from the table he once shared with Carles, Pablo pledges to forgo making pictures formulated to merely please buyers' eyes, as Carles accused him of on that awful final night in Málaga. Pablo will not sell out. He will exert his brush and a lifetime of perfecting technique to portray suffering that goes unnoticed and use his talent to assault decorum, awaken the public's empathy, stir its soul.

Pablo will seek what Carles sought, before he became consumed by desire.

~

Hair and beard grown long, Pablo renders every misery, painting with the zeal of an itinerant preacher who wills himself to the mountaintop so his voice might echo below.

He paints blind alms seekers.

He paints alcoholics.

He paints singing prisoners.

He paints street sellers and their scrounging children.

He paints broken, heaped-upon housewives.

He paints wizened Jews in tattered trousers.

He paints old shoremen with sacks weighing their shoulders.

He paints wandering, babbling lunatics.

He paints rheumatic troubadours.

He paints the decrepit.

He paints sickly prostitutes.

He paints desperate mothers.

He paints young women crouched in pain.

Each wretch and sinner, the sediment of humanity, Pablo paints in only lonely blue. He endows these canvases with emotion and resonance that artists for centuries reserved only for saints and wealthy patrons.

Pablo combs the city streets, seeking his subjects. They are easy to find, even if they're hard to look at. But he tells himself he must not be frightened by the leper or be stunned by the naked, shriveled breast or the faces rotted by disease. He will walk among them and display their plight, making it impossible to ignore.

After months of illustrating people whose demise is near, Pablo wakes one morning on the studio floor, gathers himself over a cigarette, and determines the only logical next step.

Wearing his white machinist coveralls, carrying a small canvas and his paint kit, Pablo sets out for the Hospital de la Santa Creu, which is undergoing a renovation to transform the grounds into a sprawling, brightly colored modern monstrosity. At its heart, however, remain formidable Gothic cloisters with high pointed-arch ceilings dating back five hundred years.

Pablo has come here to see Cinto, who is busy with the frenzy of his intern year. In addition to bringing a stash of painting supplies, he also roves the halls with a small gift tucked under his arm. Passing by an examining room, Pablo spots his bespectacled friend hovering over an amputee and the man's almost widowed wife, straining to sound authoritative as he admonishes, "Better to remove the limb than perish the patient."

A great, awkward smile grows on Cinto's face when Pablo approaches the door, and he abruptly excuses himself.

The two escape to a citrus grove in the hospital courtyard, sharing a pipe, reminiscing over old times, and chatting about Paris life. Cinto confesses he's jealous Pablo spent so many months there. Despite the tragedy of Carles, Cinto idealizes the fabled place as at once sinful and divine.

"True," Pablo confirms. "But my soul is Spanish, always." He asks Cinto if he's seen his drawings in the newspaper, *El Liberal.*

"Are you kidding? I've been filling my scrapbook. You're quite the star."

"I couldn't care less about that," Pablo replies.

"So what do you want, then?"

Pablo hesitates. Should he tell Cinto the radical idea that's been steeping in his mind? How not only artists but practically everybody today has gotten it so wrong, not seen the scale of the problem? No, it'll sound too insane. "Change," he says instead.

"Change what?"

"Everything, up and down—that's the matter."

"Is this why you've been painting all those blue canvases of the dispossessed? I don't know if that's going to get the attention of the king, to tell you the truth. But it's noble."

"No, no. Think bigger. See, this is what kills me. People think too small in Spain." Pablo doesn't want to sound so angry. "Sorry, Cinto," he says.

But Cinto seems unperturbed. "Well, look on the bright side— there's hardly any place with a greater supply of downtrodden. What exactly are you after? You want to do what, change the world?"

"How about the universe? Now do you get it?"

"Are you OK, Pablo?"

"Take Paris, for instance," he replies hastily. "There's plenty of pain, gobs of it, just like here. People suffer everywhere. That's the issue. What I'm talking about is the whole canvas, not just one corner. Like I said, everything—the misery of being alive but understanding it's not for long, that you're sick and getting sicker, and soon all you'll be is forgotten."

"This is about Carles, isn't it?"

Pablo is silent for a while, still reticent about divulging all that he's deciphered. He says, finally, "I'm just tired of being a pawn."

Cinto looks deeply into Pablo's eyes, studying them. Then he glances down nervously at the neatly bundled white box under Pablo's arm. Cautious, he says, "What's that?"

"*Tortell,*" Pablo replies. "I brought it for you."

"Because you come to a hospital, you bring sweets? I'm not one of the invalids, you know."

"How come we always bring dessert after people are ill?" says Pablo, raising a smile, trying to cheer up the conversation. "Ounce of prevention is worth a pound of cure. Didn't they teach you that?"

"Pastry prophylaxis! I love it! And you, Pablo. You make me laugh," Cinto says, motioning them to a stone bench beneath an orange tree where they scoop fingerfuls of the chewy confection into their mouths. Pablo brightens briefly, until sinking at the thought of the tortell he'd once carried to Carles's mother. The frail, unwell woman had sat between two classical urns in her extravagantly appointed stateroom. Her lips were sealed, the face above them unmoved. Pablo had to summon every crumb of charm in his being before she agreed to let Carles go with him to Paris. After the suicide, Pablo'd heard she nearly died upon receiving the news. Carles had been reluctant to inform his parents of the trip because of her weak heart. And Pablo broke it—after assuring Carles and his mother he'd take care of everything.

Cinto studies him again. "This *is* about Carles," he says. "Look, there's a question you need to ask yourself and answer honestly. Would Carles not have burnt out sooner or later, no matter what you did? And, by the same token, your suffering is not going to last forever. That's what we see in physiology. A genesis and a lysis."

Pablo kisses the sugar off his fingers and squints. "A what?"

"It means dissipation. Disintegration."

"You mean, like, we're all going to die?"

"Well, yes. But there's another side. And I want you to think about it. The principle dictates that a patient with a terminal disease will eventually expire, but it also says temporary symptoms affecting him might disappear because the microbes causing them die off. Everything has a beginning and an end. Whatever pain and guilt you feel, it will abate with time."

"So will I," Pablo replies.

"And me. But the relevant diagnostic question is where in its natural arc is the organism—beginning or end?"

"How much more can I take?"

"A fair bit," Cinto supposes. "Call it a doctor's hunch."

"An intern's, you mean."

Cinto slaps Pablo on the back, playfully. "Still a doctor—and thanks for the reminder!"

"Do me one favor?"

"What, you didn't come just to make certain I had pastry today?"

~

A row of granite slabs draped with white linens fills the basement morgue. Icy air encircles Pablo and Cinto.

"Preference?"

"Not moving," Pablo replies, unlatching his easel. Pablo has asked Cinto to sneak him inside so that he can finally face death. He remains haunted by not having looked straight at the autopsy of the girl and grandmother who were struck by lightning in Horta when he stayed there with Pajaresco or at the fetus that Germaine had carried.

Cinto raises the corner of the shroud that covers a patient who came in the previous day.

Pablo asks, "How'd she go?"

"Complications of a gynecological surgery," Cinto says.

"A hysterectomy?"

"What, are you taking up medicine in your spare hours?"

"Let's just say I've spent far too much time lately in doctors' company. They're starting to make me sick."

"No offense taken," says Cinto.

"Present company excluded," Pablo adds.

"The woman came in with her husband, experiencing pain," Cinto recounts. "But the problem was too big. This was her end."

Pablo peers on squeamishly before applying dabs of lampblack to his canvas, limning the face of his subject in dark, thin strokes. He questions his friend while filling in the outlines. "Don't you think people should be attacking the causes? Not the symptoms?"

"Doctors do," Cinto says, sitting down on a stool, watching Pablo work. "We're always examining, testing. Discern the disease, then prescribe treatment."

"The disease is not the cause," Pablo says.

"I don't follow."

"Search harder. Look for the roots," Pablo tells him. "You said it—everything has an end. People are always dying. Disappearing."

"So you want me to cure death? Tell me how."

"Are you really asking the painter?"

"Listen, what you're describing is entropy. I get your point, though. Let me ask you," Cinto says, rising to hold out the nickel-plated end of his stethoscope to Pablo's chest. "Why did you see so much of Paris doctors?"

Pablo recounts for Cinto his trips to Dr. Jullien, detailing the injections he received and the pills he's been taking.

"That's a substantial dose of mercury," Cinto says. "I can write you a script for something else to relieve the symptoms without so many side effects. It might even improve your state overall."

"Figured I deserved to be queasy," Pablo says.

"I've never seen you like this," Cinto says. He taps Pablo's head with the tip of his finger. "What's going on up there?"

Pablo has been working on this synthesis for weeks while painting so many people on the edge. He finally decides to lay it out. "All around, everyone's ill, miserable, dying. And we all know someday, not far away, that's going to be us. But we go on about our days like fools, ignoring the basic truth."

"Yeah, so you said. And what should we do?"

"Fight back."

"Fight? Against who?"

"God."

"Huh?" says Cinto.

"Hear me out," Pablo pleads. He'd worried that explaining this to even a close friend would be too hard—how the memories and events since Carles's suicide have changed him. "You were in Barcelona for the general strike, yes? What I'm saying is, it's time for a real revolt. Not against the monarchy, the elites. Against the true source of suffering. No more prayer, candles, veneration. None of that shit. Starve the rotten geezer, the one who made this infinite disaster and expects thanks. Assault *Him*."

"In other words, no more taking death lying down?" Cinto says, amused.

"Serious, man!"

Cinto hushes Pablo, delivering a reminder that yelling is sure to get them caught trespassing in the morgue.

"Don't you see what I mean?"

"I'd say you've been perseverating nonstop about death for far too long. Also, you may want to avoid inhaling the embalming fluid down here too deeply. Tell me, do you find yourself picturing your own death a lot?"

"All the time," Pablo says, finishing layering the painting with a wash of thinned Prussian and cobalt.

"Well, knock it off," Cinto tells Pablo. "When you die, you won't be around to see. Nothing to worry about," he says. "But I'm concerned about you right now, while you're still very much alive."

"I have to get out of Barcelona, don't I?"

"Go the hell back to Paris already. This place is no good for your head."

CHAPTER 12

I

Paris, October 1902

S pose we could top 'n' tail, but it really don't feel right, you know?"
says Josep, bouncing onto the room's only bed. This leaves Pablo
the dusty floor.

Angel's chubby sidekick has accompanied Pablo to Paris, and after
less than an hour, Pablo is already sick of the sour-mouthed man. With
barely enough cash for a few meals, though, Pablo needed any way possible to defray the trip's costs. He'd scraped together train fare by doing
illustrations for *El Liberal* while still in Barcelona, but that left almost
nothing to put a roof over his head once here. So when the two of them
arrived together and Josep offered to spring for a pensione—but insisted
it be on the Left Bank, where he claimed "all the real artists" live—Pablo
could hardly decline.

As for not wanting to share a bed, Pablo knows just what Josep's
getting at. He wonders what stories he's heard.

Indeed, the prospect of facing Manyac had helped keep Pablo away
from Paris. Never again would he be somebody's indentured servant
or bauble. He can't wait for that whole ordeal to fade from memory—
his own and everyone else's. It was in fact the news that Manyac had

decamped France altogether, along with Pablo's one-year contract end-ing, that freed him to return.

Once settled in at the pensione, Pablo leaves to head over the river. Packed inside the portfolio with him is his finest recent artwork portray-ing the destitution of so many lives in Barcelona and the hopelessness of the Saint-Lazare. During his stint back home, he'd seen clearly that the human conflict is no smaller than a war against fate, natural order, God—whatever word you use for that which has chucked us onto earth only so that we may molder. Standing now midway across a bridge leading over the Seine, Pablo stares down at the slow-moving water beneath him and strategizes how to win over the Paris gallery owners. They alone possess the clout to make his works reach audiences far and wide. They also can grant him the financial means to restock his supplies—ammunition for the long campaign, as it were. Only in this way might Pablo create art endowed with meaning instead of canvases that merely tickle the eye, as he seeks the power to reshape the cosmos.

~

A bell chimes as Pablo enters a gallery at the end of Rue Laffitte. The shop is neater and more elegant than Vollard's. Every picture is mounted behind conservation glass in florid frames that are thought-fully arranged.

A man with a slicked-back widow's peak and well-ironed morning suit approaches Pablo, asking if he is looking for someone.

"You," Pablo replies, assuming the cutthroat confidence he'd seen Manyac wear.

The glittering chain of a skeleton pocket watch twirls in the gallery owner's fingers. It and the wax in his goatee and the rolled gold of his glasses gleam all at once. "Whatever for?"

"You run this joint, right?"

"How might I assist you?"

"Au contraire," Pablo says. "Today, you're a very lucky man. For I am a distinguished painter from Barcelona who's displayed at top galleries both at home and right here in Paris. Accompanying me is a handful of works, which would be ideally suited for your discerning clientele."

"A Spaniard, eh?" The owner asks, "Have any bullfights? Ladies in mantillas? Flamencos, that sort of thing?"

"No," Pablo says, "only paintings far more original and vastly more moving. They possess what we call in my country *duende*—the raw, essential feeling residing at the depths of every man, woman, and child's soul. This is what I offer, in oils and pastels. Like to see?"

The man appraises Pablo up and down, then centers on the watch face on his chain. "Try me after lunch."

"Excuse me, but this will be more satisfying than even your croque monsieur," Pablo says, revealing from his portfolio a blue work showing a gaunt woman staring back from a prison cell.

"What on earth? I've lost my appetite."

"I painted her at the Saint-Lazare," Pablo says, trying to contain his irritation.

"Goodness, have you washed your hands? I don't want my customers to become infected."

"Another may be more to your liking," Pablo volunteers, reaching inside the leather case again.

"You say you've exhibited in Paris? I can't fathom where."

"At Vollard's, just up the block."

"You mean *our* Ambroise Vollard? That old coot must've lost his feathers. Why don't you go sell your pictures to him, then? Perhaps he has some depressed clients desiring the portrait of a wan harlot whose last john hanged himself."

Pablo is appalled by the man's callousness. He blurts out angrily, "Is art not always about sadness?"

The man's squeal spirals into wicked laughter. "Art is always about business, my unworldly little shaveling, and that can bring great, great joy," he says. Tears of mirth must have formed, because the gallery owner removes his glasses to wipe his eyes with a silk pocket square. "Tell you what," he says, a few notes appearing as if by sleight of hand, "here's twenty-five francs."

"My painting could sell for four times that," Pablo responds.

"Not for the shriveled trollop." The man lowers his eyebrows and draws back his neck. "For everything. I don't need to look at them, either. I couldn't bear it, in fact."

"You must be mad."

"Or not mad enough."

"I'd rather find a gallery with a spoonful of respect for art," Pablo says as he fastens his portfolio.

"Just a teaspoon," the man replies, the money having disappeared. "Wouldn't want anyone to choke."

The bell above the door clangs on Pablo's way out, and he remembers how Paris can be so unkind.

He soldiers on to the gallery next door. It's shabbier, more of an auctioneer's warehouse offering paintings alongside other artifacts. Interest in Pablo's work, though, is no more forthcoming.

It's the same all along the block.

After a dozen rejections and twice the cigarettes—smoked with the nerves of a corrida bull pacing in the corral—Pablo sucks it up and visits Vollard's.

The frowzy man has his eye glued to a jeweler's loupe when Pablo comes in. He's arched over a browned, vellum-bound manuscript atop his fruitwood desk, some acquisition for the gallery's antiquarian offerings, Pablo guesses.

"A sixteenth-century ship's travel log," Vollard says without looking up, preempting the question he must have felt looming after hearing footsteps. "The ending might be abrupt—the crew was eaten by cannibals in the Solomons. Some may find it tempting, nonetheless." Vollard finally drops the eyepiece into his lapel pocket, observes Pablo, and drily says, "Well, well, what fortune brings you by?"

"This is indeed a lucky day," Pablo replies, trying to muster the bravado he displayed earlier.

"Merely a matter of speech," Vollard responds. "Wouldn't do to say, 'Curses, why has this bothersome monkey disturbed me at such an inopportune moment,' would it?"

"Let me rephrase: it's *your* lucky day!"

"Appears that things already are spoiling."

Pablo hastily unzips his portfolio, and Vollard pages through the canvases, making faint groaning noises. "Let me ask you, how can a cheery little fellow paint with so much oppressive dreariness? And why all in blue? Have they no other paints in Spain?"

"These scenes represent what life is really like," Pablo proclaims.

"Miserable, you mean?"

"Often, no?"

"Don't have to rub it in my face, do you?" Vollard rebuffs him. "What do you imagine would be the market for something like this— who's the buyer?"

"Have you any clients with stirrings of a human soul?"

"You've seen them, right?"

As for blue, Pablo pointed out to the man that the painting downstairs he so admires is the same color.

"I've got rid of it. Returned to its owner. Had to. I couldn't sleep. Found it disturbing, like some sort of voodoo," says Vollard. "Besides, it wasn't all blue. Used a good bit of yellow, too."

"Bloody yellow! That's all you need?"

Vollard recollects that he showed a Spaniard once who'd painted in all yellow. "Or was it saffron? Manyac brought him also. Did scenes of cretins on some hilltop village in the Pyrenees. Your country sounds like a truly terrible place. Whatever is wrong with Spaniards? Don't ever let me go there, will you? Or have I been? That's right, I have. I caught listeria."

Pablo asks, his agitation flaring, "What is it you want me to do to my paintings?"

"Don't do anything for me, please, but depart," Vollard replies. "I'm dying to find out if at the conclusion of the ship's log we learn the taste of human flesh."

"You're a scoundrel!"

"Say something that offends me, why don't you?"

"You're an imbecile."

"Only to receive you again. Off now. Return to your country, as your Manyac already has."

Pablo hauls his portfolio back to the morning's first gallery, finding the owner returned from lunch, sandwich crumbs dotting his goatee.

"I'll take it."

"Take what?"

"The twenty-five francs."

"Fifteen," the owner says flatly, the folded cash already out.

"What! It was twenty-five just a few hours ago."

"Should have nabbed it then. I've been to the café and the bordel since. Neither's provisions were free. Had more for my money with the croque monsieur, but that's another matter."

As Pablo treks back to the pensione where Josep is letting him bunk—his load much lighter—he wonders if Manyac has poisoned the well at every gallery in the city just to spite him.

∽

Disillusioned he may never show work again, Pablo decides to consult Max Jacob, an art critic he first encountered at Vollard's exposition months ago. The urbane but eccentric Breton magically appeared at his gallery opening in a long jacket with braided edges, blowing smooches at Pablo's paintings and trumpeting, *"Quel génie!"* Manyac naturally begged Max for a calling card and even invited him on another occasion back to the studio for *un apéro* and rillettes. But Manyac soured on his guest after Max spent all night smoking the sweet-smelling kif he'd brought along, lavishing his hosts till dawn with impressions of Sarah Bernhardt.

Pablo kept in touch after returning to Barcelona, however. He appreciated Max as a learned writer who prized the Symbolists, as Carles did. He was also tickled by the doodles that found their way onto the backs of Max's postcards. And Pablo very much enjoyed Max's poems—whimsical like nursery tales, lyrical as a chansonnier, sardonic like epigrams, suggestive as an exposed leg, more mystical than the Catholic Church.

Now, back in Paris and needing help reentering the art scene, Pablo searches Boulevard Voltaire for Max's address, eventually locating it above a flower shop. He climbs a flight of stairs and finds the door to flat number 5 slightly ajar. Pablo spies through the crack a hefty gent in an overcoat of fine Bowmont wool seated with his hands palms-up on a table. Max is sitting across from him, studying them intently. Around Max's neck hangs a bronze *hamsa* amulet studded with garnet and turquoise. On his head is a giant plumed turban woven with cloth of gold, like a swami from the Raj might wear.

"It's not good. Not at all, I'm afraid," says Max.

"What? What can you make out?" the eager man anxiously replies in a cigar-smoker's growl.

"Right there. Your love line. See it?"

"Yes, yes, go on."

"Fate has not been kind."

"Fortuna, you mean?"

"You know her?"

"Well, you said . . . what is it, for God's sake? Have mercy, would you!"

"Let me ask, Ever been in love before?"

"Of course I have," he says, digging into the ticket pocket of his coat and then hunting around in his trousers in a panic before finding his wedding ring still on his finger. "I'm a married man," he exclaims, holding up proof.

"Makes no difference. Think hard."

"She's beautiful, a dream, my wife is. Caring. Given me three fine children. And I received a liberal dowry from her parents, in the tannery trade, you know?"

"What do you feel for her?"

The man goes silent. He pours his head into the very hands that exposed his vacant heart with their cruel pink lines. "Nothing!" he cries. "I'm a wretch. I've been to the brothel more than I've been at her side, not cared for her as I should. And the children, they're pests! How I have little to live for."

"Precisely as I feared," Max says, even toned. "Your love line is hopelessly formed. Does love mean anything to you, anything at all?"

"Surely. I want love, I do! Don't say it's hopeless," he blubbers. "I want to be wonderful to my wife, give everything she desires! What, pray tell, can be done?"

Max prescribes that after returning home the man should place a cascade of orchids on his wife's bed and wait. When she sees him there, he must kiss her, "and not like a concupiscent ogre, molesting her lips," Max exhorts. "Rather, bring one arm behind the small of her back and lean in, gently placing your mouth onto the corner of her neck. She will say, 'What are you doing?' You will reply, 'Only what is in my heart, *ma jolie*. I cherish you, your every atom, and if you will allow me, I want to love you now as I promised on our wedding day.'"

"Can this cure whatever it is you see?" the man pleads.

"Without love, nothing is possible, and with it, everything. Once you let love into your life, you'll have no need again to consider your palms."

"I'll do it. I will! I must!" Reinvigorated, he thanks Max profusely and strews a fistful of coins and bills across the table.

Pablo, unable to believe the mounds of francs, accidentally lets out a gasp.

"What was that?" He turns, spotting Pablo's big eyes through the cracked-open door. "What has he heard? That I'm a profligate, a frequenter of the bordels? Think of my good name!"

"Nonsense," says quick-witted Max. "This is my assistant. He knows the rules: absolute confidentiality, at all costs. Your secrets are safe. Besides, you're a changed man now."

"That is the truth," he agrees.

Max calls to Pablo, questioning whether the required items have been procured. "The untainted deck of Tarot de Marseille? Quicksilver and brimstone for my alchemical experimentations? Spool of crimson string specified in the Kabbalah?"

Yes, Pablo signals three times.

"Most excellent," Max says, adding he's intuited that a breakthrough is nearing and he'll have to send Pablo out again later for tincture of henbane and a bottle of eau-de-vie to calm his head. In the meantime, Max beseeches his customer to forgive him, but he has a pressing obligation to purify via telepathic means the spirit of a very pretty young woman who's in great distress since her fiancé left her. "Practically beside herself. She's bed-ridden, can't even bother to be dressed."

"That sounds dreadful," the man says. "Shall I pay her a visit? Bring one of your potions and see she takes it? Keep her company until she is strong enough to put on her clothes again?"

"Quite all right," Max replies, the peacock feather looming over his head like a third eye. "I have complete psychic ability to ordain her convalescence from right here. Besides, don't you have other matters to attend?"

"What? Oh! At once! My wife, she is waiting for me!"

"For far too long, I should think." Max cautions him that in his case he cannot intercede from afar. "Only you can cultivate love in your hearts. Do her your duty."

"Indeed, thank you, Monsieur Max! I'll sing your highest praises to Monsieur Poiret."

That would be very fine, Max tells him. "Paul, he's such a doll. Or the doll-dresser, as it were. Godspeed!"

The repentant philanderer tips his hat to Pablo as he rushes off.

"That was remarkable, Max!" Pablo says, stepping inside the apartment in the visitor's wake. "How did you manage? Quite a lot of money, isn't it? All for palmistry?"

"I ought to have a handsomer commission from that rascal's wife, I reckon. But it's for the good, one supposes. Lovely to see you! I had no notion you were back in Paris."

Pablo apologizes for not writing. "It all happened so fast. I just had to get out of Barcelona. My soul was sinking, and my head wasn't right," he says, studying the red Indian wallpaper of Max's apartment, its woodblock design a many-layered parade of ridden elephants, wedding umbrellas, and palanquins.

"You sound like one of my patrons. Need we cook up some occult medicament to brighten your disposition?"

"Will it work?"

Max removes his turban and roots around inside an oak buffet standing next to the table. "Let's just fix what you really require—a good, stiff drink." He pours Cognac and absinthe into a pair of snifters, halves a curlicue of mandarin peel with his teeth, plunks one end in either glass, and pronounces, *"Tchin-tchin!"*

Pablo takes a mouthful and almost heaves it onto the battered Persian carpet. "Some kick," he tells Max, setting the drink down to cough.

"Used to be Lautrec's favorite libation—*un tremblement de terre,*" Max reflects. "I was heartbroken to hear of his passing. Pound-for-pound,

I can't think of a greater artist. How come they talk about boxers that way and not painters?" Max says, peering down at Pablo's own thinned frame. "Why, you're not very tall and lean as a sand cat. And the finest painter who's come through in years, I'd say. How's it, then? 'Pablo Picasso: The New Greatest Pound-for-Pound Artist Alive!'"

"Yet somehow I could hardly recoup the cost of my canvases on Rue Laffitte just now," Pablo confesses.

"What'd you want with that place?" Max scoffs. "Those gallery owners wouldn't know art if it kissed them on the balls."

"The only way they'd recognize it," Pablo muses.

"Why in God's name are you so skinny? Food in Spain must be worse than I fear or else they're all out of it. I'll admit it was meager here as well, for a while. Weeks passed when all I'd eaten was the fruit at the bottom of a cocktail."

Max's career in art criticism had come to an unceremonious end when he wrote that the late, great painter Meissonier—renowned for his abilities to transpose the exact details of equine musculature—had known his horses in the stable intimately. His finances got so bad, he took to working as a window dresser in a department store. "I figured at least I'd get discounted," he was wont to say.

Instead, however, a top designer for the House of Worth, Paul Poiret, came by shopping for ideas one afternoon when he noticed Max behind the glass, practicing reading palms on the mannequins during his lunch hour. The couturier introduced himself and asked if he might send Max clients with a penchant for the occult, have their fortunes told.

Max's new gig as a psychic doesn't surprise Pablo. That sort of crazy thing is always happening to him. He's met just about everyone famous in Paris and has better stories than even their publicists. And he's an absolute riot once you get him going with impressions. Jane Avril to Sada Yacco, Max can reproduce the high kicks and affectations of everyone on the Paris stage. He even wears a dress and makeup better than most.

Max insists on giving Pablo at least enough cash to buy paints. He also refers him to an acquaintance, a sculptor named Auguste who may be of some help at the galleries.

"Thank you, Maxie. I'm going to crawl out of this mess."

"You've got the right attitude, *mon prince*. Don't hesitate to call on me, anytime," Max tells Pablo. "We'll see you crowned yet."

∼

Auguste, it turns out, doesn't have a gallery contact, but he does possess something as valuable—a cheap bed to rent. Not only has sleeping on the cold floor become intolerable, Josep is openly speaking of charging Pablo for the pleasure.

Pablo moves into the attic suite that Max's sculptor friend keeps in the jaundice-colored Hôtel du Maroc over in the Saint-Germain-des-Prés. The once-elegant town house now has more fleas than a grey-hound track and sells rooms by the hour. Auguste's accommodation is an absolute sty, but it's cheaper than staying on with Josep. Suddenly money is everything.

Weeks pass by like the scenery outside a slow-moving railcar. Pablo continues painting blue portraits of the poor and lonesome in the corner of Auguste's bedroom but sells nothing. The gallery owners have caught on that each day he is bringing them the same canvases, reused. Pablo contends not only with rejection but also their ever-deepening mockery. What cash Max gave him is long gone. Lunch and dinner is yesterday's baguette. Breakfast is a loaf from the day before soaked in water. Pablo's direst conundrum is how short he's become on paint, and the colorists won't offer credit to foreigners. Soon, he'll have no way to make new work. And what other commodity does he have to improve his circumstance? Pablo is not so different than his subjects now—grossly thin, fearing disease because he hasn't money for medicine, clinging to a thread.

Even if Pablo did have fresh supplies, production at the Hôtel du Maroc has proven difficult. While he is grateful for a place to stay, Auguste's bigger-than-life sculptures and endless array of poached carving wood clutter the hatbox room they share. And the sculptor himself is as towering as the Colossus of Rhodes. He's so whopping large, Pablo conjectures, there is simply too much to wash without wasting all day, thus he simplifies by only scrubbing the necessities, and only once in a while, long ago having become immune to his own odor, which resembles spoiled potato soup. Any apartment Auguste enters feels immediately constricted. One this small is a breathless squeeze.

~

With nowhere else to paint, Pablo takes to sneaking to a disused slurry pit below a corridor on the first floor that leads to the hotel's back garden, which is covered with frazzled vines. Each night, Pablo climbs through a trapdoor and descends a bowed ladder to set up his easel, laboring by candlelight under a ceiling just high enough to stand. It's chilly down here. Rot and cat piss linger in the air. There's barely more room than upstairs with Auguste, but at least it's private. The smell is also preferable.

On a particularly blustery autumn eve, Pablo works up a portrait of a grizzled man selling mistletoe with his emaciated boy underfoot. He remembers how last December the *marchands de gui* arrived with fresh sprigs of the plant after it had sucked the life from poplar trees all season. Every annum, these roving men string up their leafy, parasitic stems onto poles and vend them without irony to passersby to hang in the home for New Year's. Vollard rejected that anyone would buy scenes of suffering, and Pablo wishes now he'd ticked off all the ways people relish tokens of others' misery. A better question, Pablo thinks, is whether the portraits he's painted over the past year have captured people's humanity or chronicled the inhumanity in everyone? Or perhaps, like in some Eastern saw, these two are really one.

Long after midnight, when Pablo can't keep his eyes open, he ascends the shaky ladder and unlatches the overhead door that opens to the building's rear.

Blocking the path to the stairway leading up to the hotel's first floor of rooms is a pair of rough, bleary-eyed men. One is tall and gangling, with a long and wrinkled face. The other has a broad brisket, short limbs, and a ripe, red complexion. Standing beside them is a woman with a mountain of plaited silver hair.

"The hell is this? A furry rabbit up from its burrow?" the thin man says to the red one—in Spanish, to Pablo's surprise.

The men's clothes appear thrown-on, their profiles slick with sweat and grease. The woman's powdered curls are a wig for sure, Pablo sees, just like those getups worn at the Model Market so painters can snag somebody to pose for their period piece of Marie Antoinette. Besides this, she has on little more than ill-fitting undergarments. Pablo looks closer. Beneath layers of opaque foundation and round stamps of rouge on her cheeks, Pablo detects wax-filled pockmarks and traces of stubble. He is sure that in the morning she will return to dressing as a man.

"You heard him," says the stocky red fellow, his breath reeking of wine, his teeth dark with its stain. "Who's you?"

Pablo recoils. "I stay here," he says.

"In that hole?"

"In the hotel."

"What room?"

"What's it matter?"

"We'll escort you."

"Not necessary."

"What you got there?" The slender, wrinkly one says, pointing to the canvas and French easel in Pablo's hand.

"It's a portable get-out-of-my-way contraption," Pablo replies.

"Funny. Never seen a Spaniard paint in Paris before. They all come to either fuck or get fucked."

The stout man jumps in. "No, wait a minute, eh. Here we are in France, maybe we ought to have a little art and culture with our jollies, no? Now I'd quite like to borrow this little bunny's kit and paint his nice, fluffy tail. Got the room for another quarter hour, after all." He motions to Marie Antoinette and asks, "How much we rent this one for?"

"Five francs."

"All right, what'd you say about that? How's five francs for a rabbit portrait, Mr. Rabbit?"

Pablo is frozen.

"Just take a few minutes to paint you," says the thin man. "We work fast, real fast."

"Ten francs," the stout one says, before flashing a burgundy-stained grin. "Or scamp back down to your bunker, and we'll ferret you out."

Pablo's eyes are wide and crazed as they search for an escape. Or what will he do if there is none? His thighs are shaking like noodle pudding, which is probably why when Auguste lumbers by and sees the four of them together, he turns and speaks up before heading to the stairway, despite his philosophy to live and let live. In one hand, the sculptor holds a rusted bow saw, and in the other, a tremendous bough of gnarled linden he hacked away under the cover of night.

"You all right?" asks the giant.

"That a tree you got there?" Pablo manages.

"Yup, for now," Auguste says. "I figure I'm going to carve it, though."

"Can I give you a hand?"

"Could get the door, I suppose."

No sooner, Pablo has hotfooted past his tormentors. He bolts over to Auguste, slips beneath the huge man's arm—rank putrescence hanging down like an invisible curtain—and races upstairs.

~

The next morning, Pablo departs the hotel before even the owner's nippy dog is awake. He wends his way through the Left Bank toward the pensione where Josep still resides. Pablo can't stop trembling, though. No, he couldn't possibly spend even one more night at the Hôtel du Maroc, he thinks—not after what nearly happened to him. Perhaps Josep might let him cadge a little more time on the floor, he hopes. If he could just pull himself together there, maybe he could get back on his feet.

Finding the man who accompanied him on the train to Paris not at home, though, Pablo lets himself inside with a spare key he hung on to and waits. After an hour, Pablo decides it wouldn't hurt anything if he uses the bathtub. He soaks in the warm water and dries with one of the pensione's towels, which seemed stiff and of inferior quality when the two travelers arrived a month ago, but now after so much time without a clean bathroom or linens (Pablo had even resorted to wrapping himself in canvas), the threadbare terry cloth feels plush and divine.

There is a fresh boule on the table. Pablo's starving and can't help but pinch off a sample of its wholesomeness. He finishes the entire loaf without pausing. Guilt seizes him, and he stuffs the fallen crumbs into his pockets so there will be no trace of evidence when Josep comes home. He can go to the boulangerie to get another, he thinks, before remembering he has no money. Pablo notices beside a crumb that escaped him a scattering of loose change; it must have fallen from the trousers folded onto a hanger just above. Pablo tucks it into his pocket, too. What to do with it, though? Buy Josep a new loaf of bread or one for himself? Does that doughy son of a bitch really need it more than he does? And what about paint? What will Pablo do in Paris when he runs out of paint? He doesn't want to even think about it. His mouth has turned dry. He reaches for his ears and rushes outside in a panic.

Pablo once believed he knew what deprivation was—but not like this. This is what Germaine warned him of, this is what it means to be "really down, really out." Now, he has nothing, and he fears there is no bottom. Who knows what he's capable of?

~

Hours later, Pablo's blistered feet are searing. With each step, he's accepted more of the awful truth. If Auguste had not come home, Pablo would have been the one wearing the wig. He'd have ended up taking the Spaniards' ten francs, or even if it were only five. How many times in Pablo's life had he said the word *whore* with disdain? Never did he treat the women at the brothels badly, but he'd looked down upon them.

But how is he any better? What, besides, had he just resolved to do with the canvas of the mistletoe seller? Cover it all over in white to work up the loveliest of scenes, people laughing in the prettiest hues, that's what. If Pablo could find just one measly buyer, then he could eat for a few days.

But what would Carles have said to him?

What would he call him now?

A sellout, that's what Pablo is. And a whore.

Pablo arrives at Max's door a whimpering puddle of tears.

"Come in," says Max. "I've just read the fortune of the *maître-fromager* at a restaurant in the Bois de Boulogne, and he's paid me all in Brie. You must have some. And wine!"

Max is the kindest soul Pablo's ever met, he thinks. When he offers to take him into his home as long as needed, Pablo cannot refuse.

They have one narrow bed between them but arrange a schedule whereby Max works at the department store during the day while Pablo sleeps, and Max gets a few hours of shut-eye at night when he's not watching the canvases fill up and reading poetry amid cannabis and ether fumes.

Of course, Pablo hoped to put to rest the sniggers in Paris about his relationship with Manyac and any lingering question about his manhood by letting a *sortable* little swallow perch on his arm at all times here, the type of gal who alights on up-and-coming artists. Sharing accommodations with Max, a man as masculine as a scallop shell made of soft butter, will do little to further that end.

But being with Max is so comfortable. It reminds Pablo of his time with Carles. Maybe there is something in a poet's blood. When Max reads aloud in the night, the words dance like fireflies. When Pablo is overcome by distress, there is someone there to commiserate, someone who feels also how this world is not made for artists. A painter, a poet, or a troubadour—they are as ill-suited for this earth as a wooden Indian in a wildfire, Pablo thinks, remembering Horta and that mysterious boy who'd materialized without a flock but had a master's brush hand and then wandered away just as easily. Pablo wonders what it would be like to be a painter left in the bush, how it would be different and the same as being so broke in Paris.

Ensconced in the protection of a new patron, Pablo sets to work, starting with a pastel of a pair of brightly colored, pretty ladies. He walks it up to Pigalle in search of Madame Weill, an elfin Frenchwoman who wears baggy trousers and men's frock coats and governs a diminutive gallery there. She is a friend of Manyac's, but she had been kind to Pablo during his first trip to Paris. She has an art dealer's eyes and wit but can't suppress her good nature, no matter how hard she tries.

Madame Weill isn't in, though. Pablo leaves a makeshift calling card on her doorstep, along with—as a token of friendship—the pastel. If she likes it, there will be plenty more, he writes.

While Pablo does not care for the work, he is enough satisfied to have made it in the service of a gallery owner with taste and a pleasant demeanor. While he waits for her reply, he returns to painting the blue-hued scenes of the downtrodden—his truer and higher calling. One day, he keeps telling himself, the world will value them, too.

~

The palette of the city's promenades lined with liberty trees is changed over from bright yellow to orange and crackling red. Roast chestnuts scent the cool air. A week after moving in with Max, Pablo has felt a whiff of the Paris magic again.

One evening, he receives a note from Madame Weill and reads it over dinner. On the strength of Pablo's work, she's agreed to have an opening at her gallery, splitting the proceeds down the middle. Pablo is so overjoyed, he frolics with Max around the table as if the tin of beef standing on it were a maypole.

But the show lacks sufficient advertising and is not the success Pablo hoped for. When it closes just before Christmas without a single painting sold, Pablo falls into despair. What good is talent without a smarmy salesman like Manyac to prop you up? Madame Weill might have discriminating taste, but in the art world, banditry outduels nobility every time.

Max also hits a wall. The department store dismisses him for insubordination and fondling the mannequins. Max blames the incident on the ether flask he routinely sniffs for inspiration, an excuse that fails to win his manager's clemency. Max's lucrative trade in telling fortunes also dries up after he forewarns an uppity lady dispatched by Poiret that she is guaranteed a premature demise. The clothier refuses to send anyone else, claiming shoppers preoccupied with death seldom order custom clothing that takes up to a year to construct. "But I saw it plainly in the cards," Max protests. "And what about funeral attire?"

Being gay and Jewish in the aftermath of the back-to-back scandals of Alfred Dreyfus and Oscar Wilde, Max would have difficulty finding work no matter what, without adding his untimely honesty and cultivated eccentricity. He probably could have had a successful theater career, Pablo thinks, but instead Max pursues jobs below his intellect and talent. Pablo encourages his friend in his highly inventive poetry, although Max has difficulty focusing on it for long. Occasionally, he falls into depression, from which he tries to bounce back by clowning and serving up jokes at his own expense.

Standing at his easel one day, as they both seem to be descending into a worse melancholy, Pablo asks his companion to recite something as he paints. The apartment soon fills with Max's stentorian tenor declaiming Mallarmé's "L'Azur," the Symbolist verses about a poet who longs to create something beautiful but can never escape the taunting of the majestic blueness forever hectoring him from above.

How could one hue be so ideal and also so cruel, Pablo asks himself, pondering once again the color that has occupied him for the better part of a year. Pablo can still hear Carles revealing in the graveyard how an empty feeling was always chasing him, never letting him be. This must be what he meant, Pablo understands.

"You and me," Max says, appearing to see Pablo smarting, "we've felt the trials of our craft, the bleakness. Yet we are called to transcend. Every time I just can't bear it, though, I look away and see you constantly laboring, painting glorious blue canvases. You're doing it, my dear. Your art, someday it's going to mean more to people than you know. Don't hate me for being jealous."

Pablo stares into the streaks of Prussian against a misty background on the canvas before him. "I never drew or painted like a child," he confesses. "Some artists, they can do only one thing. Landscapes. Portraits. Birds. Before grown, I could paint everything, any style, easy as giving milk. My father was the painter, but I moved ahead of him. Soon, there was no master. I had no peer."

"Heavens," Max whispers.

"But now, painting only makes me lonely. Yet I can't stop. So it feels not like strength but a curse. I try to breathe onto canvas the reality beyond what most people care to view—sickness, want, mortality. But this has made me as blue as the pigment, sad as the pictures."

Max's head is floating in a cloud of cigarette smoke on the other side of the room. Pablo can just make out his mouth, serious and narrow as he asks, "Why haven't we ever read your palm?"

"It's covered in paint."

"As it should be," Max says. From a hip flask he pours ether onto a handkerchief and tosses it to Pablo across the room for him to clean his hands. They move to the bed and sit together, legs folded into pretzels, knees barely touching. Pablo uncurls his fists atop a paisley cushion with frilly trim. Max reaches for his pince-nez and slides them up and down on his face like he is focusing a microscope. He traces the tell-all creases of Pablo's hands with his fingertips.

"The Mount of Mercury, it's prominent," Max says. "Means you're intelligent, obvious artistic aptitude. The line of the head, it forks and disappears. That signals to me you're prone to caprices, flights of fancy, and yet are dominated by preconceived illusions."

Pablo asks anxiously about his health, and Max peers over his lenses.

"The hepatic line is divided, a sign wellness will be indifferent, seriously failing as you reach the end of days. As for the luck line, I see a brilliant beginning, then a stumble. But there's a change of fortune to come, perhaps at thirty. Always give or take a few years. It's not an exact science."

"Oh really?"

"Shhh. Quiet! Do you see this?" Max says, pointing to the base of Pablo's left palm. "Then as we go higher, all the other lines arise from that crevice, like the spark of a firework shooting up and exploding in the sky. Only in very special predestined persons does one witness this kind of a living star. It will turn the sky its own color, leave its own image."

"And my love life?"

"This side of the heart, simply magnificent. Lust, sensuality. It's abundant. You're absolutely showered with it."

Pablo smirks.

"On the other side of the heart line, I see disappointments, brutal ones. It frightens me," Max says, knitting his brow. "Your greatest feud, Pablo, it's not what you think. You're convinced you're battling a higher power, but the real fight is against yourself. Besides, an artist should not have such hate for a fellow creator. It isn't right. Do you remember what I told the man who came to have his palms read on the day you arrived? Nothing can be won without love. With it, you'll have everything."

∼

After months of handwritten *reconnaissances de dettes*, Max loses his lease with the landlord. He and Pablo pack their belongings into a steamer trunk and load it onto the borrowed cart of a rag-and-bone man. They move into a much shabbier attic nearby, which is even colder, as if the walls are stitched together with thread.

Max tries his hardest to banish the glumness of the frozen garret with song and an array of analgesics and stimulants he's stashed away like a wartime supply of essential medicines: troches of Turkish opium, Vin Mariani coca wine, and a curious confection—gooey and sweet—of mortared coriander seed, fig, cinnamon, honey, and a scarab-sized glob of buttery hashish, which he claims once sustained and illuminated saints wandering the Sahel. Pablo and Max rarely have proper food. One night, Max brings home a scavenged sausage, but it is so rotten, it explodes upon hitting the pan.

Christmastime is always harrowing for Pablo, ever since Conchita. Around the holiday, a lull falls over the apartment. Pablo and Max awkwardly bump into one another, stuck inside their attic; anyone on the frozen streets far below the windows risks damaging their lungs.

Pablo eats Max's mystical fudge to be happy for a time, before euphoria lifts and forlornness returns with new urgency. He scolds Max when he performs the cancan.

"That's all right, *mon prince*," Max says. "Alas, even Helen could not cure her son's grief with *pharmakia*. How I know you don't mean it. But please don't forget to laugh with me."

~

Only dim light penetrates through a vicious snowstorm outside. The stove glows meekly. Max and Pablo are burning the only kindling left— sketches and notebooks of poems. Max lights a cigarette from the flame and unlatches the casement windows overlooking an arctic landscape. A noisy gust flings the panes open and blows in air so cold that the paint on Pablo's palette stiffens and becomes unworkable.

Shivering, Pablo scrounges the linings of his coat pockets to cobble together a mix of tobacco and wool lint to roll a wire-thin cigarette. One after another, wooden matches flare and extinguish in the fierceness. Pablo walks to stand in the bracing stream of spindrift pouring in. Max extends his cigarette to him. The two ends meet. He and Pablo puff together in the wild wind behind cupped hands, staring outside, beyond the window frame.

There is the sound of a snow shovel. They squint, searching for the narrow pavement five stories below. But there is no way to see. All is a whiteness, without up or down, depth or distance, a blank canvas with no delineation, no color, no gradient. Pablo senses the void calling Max just as it is summoning him—the ultimate victory that chaos may have over artists.

Pablo recalls when he was young in Horta and sliding down the cliff to what he believed would be his end in the ravine. If I die and never create again, he thought as he fell, then the very thing I traded Conchita's existence for will have been lost in vain. He also has another life to account for now; he left Carles wallowing on the floor in Málaga because his friend's despairing had become too much an impediment. Pablo pictures the emptied bodies of him and Max spread out in the white below, a pair of red cutouts on a silk screen.

This is his last chance to save anyone, Pablo understands. He clamps down the window in a whoosh, cutting off the cold current like the head of a serpent, and pronounces, "We must not think that thought."

Max appears taken aback. But then his eyes turn winsome. He smiles that crooked Max smile. "I knew you wouldn't let us go, *mon prince*." The poet closes a blanket around himself, walks back to the stove, and places an inkwell on top to thaw.

II

The air is warm around Germaine when she opens her eyes. The bed and covers are soft. Outside the window, fine-grained snow speeds by, and she hears the faint calls of a brave Montmartre street vendor selling candles on the corner for twenty-five centimes.

Germaine flops her forearm beside her, expecting to touch the long, firm frame of Ramon Pichot, the Spanish artist who she's been seeing, but he's not there. She recalls a metallic buzz in the dream she was just roused from. In waking life, she thinks, the doorbell must have sounded. Maybe he went downstairs to answer it. The second-floor bedroom around her still feels full of "Moni"—her pet name for Pichot—crowded as it is with wall-to-wall bookshelves, his countless volumes watching over her from their perch like curious forest creatures surrounding a visitor to the meadow. Could one man possibly read all these? It's just like him to live in a library, she thinks.

Germaine stares up at the medallions in the pressed-tin ceiling and remembers how Moni surprised her after they made love last night, saying he'd earned enough between Barcelona and the latest sales of his paintings in Paris to buy this old boardinghouse.

"It could be ours," he said.

"Is that what you want?" she asked.

"Only if you'll have it with me."

Germaine was silent for a long time, thinking of how funny it is to be with a man she actually believes knows what he desires. And the biggest surprise of all? It's what she wants, too. Yesterday the new year came, and now for the first time in memory, she isn't turned off by the notion of sharing her life with someone—or at least up to a point. Moni is so unlike every other artist she's known. She swore away cupboard love long ago, but this is different. Moni's bookishness does remind her a tad of Carles, minus the strife. And his paintings sometimes share a strange Spanish quality with Pablo's. But Moni is almost a decade older than Pablo or Carles before he died, and her Moni is so much more a grown-up. She doesn't feel trapped with him. She feels freer.

Still, though, it would have been foolhardy to not even negotiate. So when Pichot made his proposal in bed last night, she eventually turned to him and countered, in her most professional tone, "All right, monsieur, you buy this building, but I dress up every inch in sumptuous rose and transform it into where all Montmartre comes for an aperitif and a bit of play."

"Is that all?" he said. "Done."

A gust of wind rising all the way from the foyer and the sound of a shutting door interrupts Germaine's memory. She hears footsteps tromp upstairs. Pichot enters the bedroom, covered with white flakes. He pulls off his sweater, removes his boots, and shakes dry his curly beard. In the corner of the room, he sets down a black leather portfolio slick with melting snow.

"Was there a visitor?" Germaine asks sweetly, noticing the concern on Pichot's contemplative face.

"Yes, an old friend of sorts from the tavern in Barcelona, another painter."

"Left you with quite a lot of work, did he?" she asks, pointing to the familiar portfolio. "Why didn't you invite him upstairs for a Cognac to warm up?"

"I did. He wouldn't have it. Refused to even come inside. Said he must hurry off. He wanted to sell me all his paintings for a ticket home to Spain. Muttered something about still being at war but having to beat a retreat. Lord knows what he was talking about. There's no fighting here or back home."

"And you bought this from him?"

"No, no," Pichot replies. "I gave him the train money and told him I'd simply keep the work safe until he's back in Paris before long. He seemed to think he might not be returning, though. He looked as if he hasn't eaten, washed, or seen the light of day in weeks. It's a shame. Superbly talented, he is."

"True," she affirms.

"Right, right, of course. You know Pablo through Carles," Pichot says before glancing away and clicking the cheek behind his crooked teeth with a look of regret. "Sorry, love."

"Yes, I do, a bit," Germaine replies. She remembers how she once told Pablo that he'd never known hard times. "You say he appeared thin? Pale?"

"Like a wraith."

Nobody flies before falling, she thinks. "Tell me, did he have with him a small brown case and a box, or was he planning to pawn those off, too?"

"His supplies, you mean? That's all the luggage he had, actually. I'm rather worried about him."

"You needn't—not so long as he's still painting."

CHAPTER 13

Barcelona, January 1903

L ate at night, Pablo slips into the bedroom in his parents' apartment on Carrer de la Mercè that his mother keeps perfectly intact in case her son should ever materialize.

In the morning, Pablo opens his eyes and for a moment can't figure out where he is. The crucifix on the wall and framed pictures of animals he'd drawn as a child remind him. He leans over the bedside and peers down to the spot he peeled off his clothes before falling asleep. But there is nothing.

In the corner, gleaming like the coats of two Labrador puppies, are Pablo's shoes. They hadn't been shined in ages. He climbs from bed and reaches for the doorknob, then realizes he can't enter his family's living room stark naked. Also, the floor is freezing. Could he not escape the cold even here on the Mediterranean? He sinks barefoot into his now-glossy brogues and tears the bedsheets away to wrap himself.

Doña María is at the breakfast table, reading newspaper headlines to Don José, who can no longer make out the type even with a thick magnifying glass.

"Pablito!" his mother cries, jumping from her chair, rushing him for kisses.

But he sees his garments draped across the balcony and runs toward them instead. Leaned up against the railing is the broom Doña María used to beat the layers of dirt that had collected, dried, and colonized Pablo's unwashed trousers and jacket.

"Mama! What have you done?"

"I clean. I clean." She shakes her head, mystified.

Pablo kneels on the balcony, gripping his hair, squeezing the corduroy to his bare chest like it were a drowned child, crying, "The dust! My Paris dust!"

The street people below crane their heads upward to watch, signing the cross in memory of whoever was this lost Dust.

Pablo weeps for his treasured particles—microscopic talismans from a faraway city that was supposed to make painters into great artists but has been so merciless to him—until his mother is also in tears. He retreats to bed, unravels himself and lies naked, cursing himself, cursing God.

~

When Pablo wakes again, he smells a current of savory stew. He at once wants to sit for a meal and yet thinks he couldn't bear it. He loves his doting mother but doesn't know how to speak to her anymore, and his father is all but sightless, stuck in the doldrums, nearing his end. It tortures Pablo to see Don José like this. Pablo regrets telling Doña María he must rush out again before dinner. But he leaves to find someplace to paint other than here. On the train back to Barcelona, he admitted his latest Paris campaign was a failure. He hopes there's still a battle here that he can win to turn the tide of the war that has ravaged him.

Through word-of-mouth, Pablo learns that Angel, the dedicated bon vivant and sometimes-artist he last shared a studio with, has taken over the old spot on Carrer de la Riera de Sant Joan that Carles once leased. Angel occasionally uses the space for an evening rendezvous and rarely lifts a brush there. Pablo asks to move in.

The trompe l'oeil images that Pablo painted floor to ceiling three years ago—a Turkish castle's furnishings, the seraglio of courtesans—no longer glisten seductively. Now, the women's eyes burn with awareness, accusation. One even has Germaine's stare.

The davenport where Carles stored the pistol is still here, too. If this were not enough of a memento mori, leaned against a wall is that huge canvas, *Last Moments*, the picture that brought Pablo and Carles to Paris and to Germaine in the first place. The paint is cracking in places, stained and faded.

When Pablo stands still, he can almost hear Carles's voice, see him traipsing about the room in sorrowful robes, his head oozing. Pablo borrows money for supplies and works almost nonstop in order to distract himself, rendering the peasants whom Barcelona has been less kind to than Babylon was to Judeans.

After two in the morning, when Pablo is sleeping on the floor one night, he hears a click, and the doorknob turns.

Spilling through is Angel, his good looks debased by a fervid, animal intensity as he flicks his tongue into the mouth of a redhead in black stockings he'd picked up. He appears too drunk to care whether Pablo is home, and possibly too gone to notice. Pablo rustles the covers loudly so the woman won't trample him with her spiky heels.

Angel directs her to a wooden prayer bench that he'd mischievously pilfered from a church. The woman arches over the sloping shelf made for a lectionary book, extends her neck, and presents herself. Pablo can't bear to watch and pulls the blanket over his head. But it does nothing to muffle the desperate, grisly sounds. The entire studio seems to be hurtling toward apocalypse.

Then, the noises abruptly cease. There is only asthmatic breathing and a thin pant. Pablo peeks through the weave of the linen and sees Angel fall off his lover and onto the floor, a glacier sheet calving to sea. From the trousers riding around his ankles like shackles, the man retrieves a cigarette.

He calls out to Pablo, "Want one?"

~

After bearing the horror of having to listen to him copulate, Pablo convinces Angel, who's deferential to superior artists, that he must announce his debauchery so Pablo can make sure to be absent. But the episode lingers with him. Sex, after all, is the very source of human life. And yet something about it seems so calamitous. How can each person be the outcome of such an act? When Pablo is in the throes of passion, does he appear evil?

While vacating the loft, Pablo often escapes to the quay and watches the boats, just as he did as a boy in Málaga. Except in that fishing town, the same vessels that leave come back at day's end. In Barcelona, a shipping hub, they go and may never again be seen. Pablo feels that, for as long as he can recall, he's been drifting. Taunted, tempted, and now he is wracked. Pablo sometimes collapses in exhaustion into his blue dream, where he is visited by the faces of the people he's lost. In his sketches, he begins to add to the composition the frames and easels and studio in the background of the drawing, showing both his subjects and the labors of the artist, rendering scenes from his own life within the paintings on the page—pictures within pictures.

Pablo's other redoubt is the old, high-ceilinged café across from the opera, where the slouchy waiters line up against the wall, wearing bow ties and black jackets, like a row of vultures. Pablo is sitting there one day, staring through the window as they surreptitiously shovel into their mouths platefuls of greasy fried eggs. A towheaded girl walks by outside in her middle-school uniform. She's about how old Conchita would be, had she lived. Pablo wonders if this is what she'd look like now. Beside the blonde girl is her dark-haired classmate. Pablo shrinks down

Germaine to this tender stage and puzzles over what she might've been like back then. How, he contemplates, did she become who she is today?

~

Pablo returns to the same colorist each week. The old man pauses at the cash register one afternoon, and the smell of sea and vinegar from a plate of *boquerones* he'd no doubt eaten for lunch swims in the air.

"You know, we have other colors," says the man, who wears a faded red *barretina*, like Catalans of yore. "I could show you some, if you like."

Pablo tells him that's all right.

The paint shop owner asks if Pablo's eyes are OK.

"My eyes?" Pablo says, anxious he is succumbing to his father's disease.

"Can you see what you're painting? It's nothing but blue."

Pablo tries to think of some way to ease the fellow's concerns without going into a long explanation. "The sky, it's in every picture."

"But it is not always blue. Gray. White. Black. Orange. Even pink."

"Do you make pictures?"

"No."

"Ever thought about it?"

"If I paint, who will run my shop? That's for a different kind," he says. "I hope to always have plenty customers, though. And not just for my business. If there are no painters, I fear for this world."

~

At the beginning of May, a few months after returning to Barcelona, Pablo finds the lingering pungency of strong cigars in the studio. He concludes Angel must have been there with a coterie of *paios*, doing the devil knows what, their deeds hanging around the loft now like specters.

As usual, Pablo toils into the evening, continuing to draw scenes of a painter's work. Outside are distant flashes of lightning without thunder, as if a menacing rain is coming. As he sketches, Pablo keeps returning to what the colorist said about a world without artists. Also echoing is a conversation he had with Germaine long ago, from when they were riding inside the carriage after the procedure, headed back to the cubby where she lived.

"Why'd you tell that doctor the father is dead?" Germaine asked.

"How can you be sure it wasn't Carles?" Pablo replied.

"It couldn't have been," she said, looking at Pablo strangely. "You already know why."

"What about your husband?"

"Haven't let him lay a finger on me since I was seventeen."

"And the circus performer, or lion tamer, or whatever?"

Germaine's lips peaked ever so slightly into a simper. "Don't think it was hers, either."

She was right—Pablo never really doubted he was the father. He only thought of it as Carles's sometimes because everything between them was so knotted. As they rumbled along in the victoria, Germaine, still weary, reclined on the cushiony lazyback. Pablo felt the deep desire to kiss her, to land his lips where Carles's had been. Guilt and remorse for the deaths of his friend, his sister, and this brief life that never held a breath of air in its lungs had become one. And they were all tangled up with labyrinthine affections for Germaine.

"I couldn't help that I didn't love Carles," she'd said after a pause during the carriage ride. "Or what he felt for me. I wanted to. I did. What can I say? What could I have done?"

Thunder sounds, but in the blackness of the window, there is still no rain. Pablo turns to look at *Last Moments*. In the face of the painting's old woman receiving final Eucharist, he believes there are prescient hints of an elderly version of Germaine. Superstition overtakes him, and he determines to cover the painting up in many coats of white. Pablo rises and adds layer on top of layer onto the canvas, as if repeating ritual ablutions.

The room has filled with spirit of turpentine and some other urgent vapor. Pablo's head feels like a heated porcelain pot. His body itches from the top of his scalp to the inside of his legs, from the rims of his nostrils to the bend of his neck. Underneath his fingernails, his skin crawls. He feels the vibrating just before the boil. There's a current of cool night coming through the window, but he is dripping with sweat.

Something begins to command Pablo's hands. He furiously adds to the sketches he's been working on, black dust floating off the pages, torn sheaves of paper littering the floor. With each stick of charcoal, the idea that's emerging shifts, changes form, evolves, decides what to be.

Then, it's as if the tube squeezes itself onto the palette and the brush dips into a Prussian blue lake on its own volition before finding another of cerulean, and Pablo begins filling the white. Before he knows it, he is spotting and smearing, daubing and smoothing, muddying and blackening, limning and highlighting, jabbing and licking, shaping and scraping, working, reworking, pouring, turning, buttering, borrowing, reordering the cosmos—painting.

Pablo's mind races as he works. Evil is entropy. Entropy is evil. The ancients knew this, as did the masters. It is all around us and also a snake buried within, stirring in the gut. It is everyone's sickness. There is no option of avoidance—to resist every temptation or with an ultimate sacrifice. This is the nature of life. The lone way to fight entropy, to regain control, Pablo understands, is to create. That is what the colorist meant, why he fears a world without artists. To become one, then, is to join with the divine. Pablo has cursed God many times, but in this moment, he doesn't feel a rival but an equal, charged with the same responsibility to keep the universe from being overrun.

As the canvas fills, Pablo empties. He gives his last drops to that lost creature who has inhabited his dreams. When Pablo steps back, he sees his work is complete and that it is good.

Emerging onto the street, Pablo is vital again, the blue sky resplendent in the light of the yellow sun. The trees are budding, growing. He walks by Els Gats, even though it has recently closed, with Pere off on some wild trip somewhere. A mongrel with no collar sniffs around the door, and Pablo squats down. The dog comes to lick his wrists, to nuzzle its scraggly ears between Pablo's knees.

~

For the first time in weeks, Pablo returns home to his parents' apartment, finding his sister Lola back from school. She greets him with a love peck on the chin. Together, the two relish their mother's food, a cold white soup of garlic and almonds marbled with olive oil that suspends a halved green grape like an embedded eye of jade. Pablo spoons greedily, lavishing Doña María with praise and murmurs of satisfaction.

When Pablo hauls the new painting up to show his father, the old man palpates the canvas and its hardened brushstrokes as if he is reading braille. He searches the air with his unsteady palm. Don José finds Pablo's arm, and his long face spreads into a fond, toothless grin. They've not touched in years. Pablo lays his hand on his father's, their fingers overlapping. Don José offers to prepare a canvas for him, and Pablo agrees, believing that after a lifetime of practice, his father can do it no matter what. This is how he wants to remember the man—his first teacher, the one who provided him with means. For Pablo knows that when he leaves Barcelona next, this time it will be for good.

Just as he and Carles did long ago, Pablo begins inviting their band to consort at the studio. They all drink and chat like old times, whispering to one another admiration for the huge and hypnotic painting hung there, repeating what they've always known—that Pablo was among them but not of them.

The world on the canvas is that of a dream. A splotchy blue-walled chamber is illuminated obliquely. In the background, there are two more paintings—pictures within the main picture, chapters to the story, just as Pablo had been practicing sketching, folding in multiple

meanings, collapsing time, as if teaching himself how to construct ori-
gami hieroglyphs. In one, frightened lovers cling together, powerless
to stop calamity. In the other, a weary woman mourns her loss alone,
touched by the chaos of death both outside and from within.

When Cinto first sees this work by his friend, he comments on how
these two embedded pictures bring viewers into Pablo's process of creation and let them feel the power and uncertainty of the transpiring act.

On the left-hand side of the main image that fills the large canvas,
a couple occupies the space near an arched entranceway, cast in the
cool, crepuscular light. The young man stands forthright in nothing
but a loincloth, his face astute but resigned. It is Carles. Naked, resting
her head on his shoulder, is Germaine. In her eye is the same reasoned
knowingness. Carles's arms are at his side, but his wrist is bent upward,
the forefinger extended, pointing across the way to the right half of the
canvas where another figure has entered the scene—a stolid, thin-lipped
matron, barefoot with broad toes that have crossed many beaches and
deserts. She is clad in a tunic that is the deepest of blues. This woman is
cradling at her chest a new baby. It is swaddled in the folds of her gown,
protected there from all suffering, sleeping in peace.

What the observers who view this painting will not realize until many
years later is that in the first sketches that Pablo made amid the growing
thunder, the man holding Germaine was not Carles. It had been himself.
But when it came time, Pablo altered the scene, as one grafts a flower.

No one who sees this painting in the studio will leave without
speaking of it everywhere. They will conjecture and tell tales of what it
means and allegories they claim to know. Cinto, though, will tell them
they are wrong. This is something different, something they cannot
understand, though they already feel.

Finally, one of Pablo's friends will ask him, nervously, "What's it called?"

Long ago, he stopped naming pictures. For this, however, the title
came to Pablo while he painted.

"Life," he says.

PART FOUR

CHAPTER 14

I

Paris, April 1904

Pablo stopped in the Place Ravignan—a tree-lined square near the top of the butte—to fix his hair. He'd promised his mother he would do this, even in Paris.

After pocketing his comb in the smart suit Doña María sent him in and petting the head of the mongrel dog he'd secreted aboard the train from Barcelona, Pablo rapped his knuckles against the double doors of the single-story building front just east of the plaza. Its walls were buttercream stucco. White *volets* hung off the window frames.

When no one responded, he let himself in. A prehistoric smell permeated the darkness beyond the threshold, a mix of dampness, flora, and dust.

On the outside, the structure appeared to only have one floor. But inside, a staircase led downward, and twisting passageways branched off to more stairs and sudden drops into dark abysses.

Pablo and the dog proceeded gingerly, and the floorboards shifted and creaked beneath them, wobbling as if they might give way. It took quite some time to find the designated studio. How, Pablo wondered, could he become lost in such a small building? He was soon slick with sweat and out of breath from lugging around his carpetbag and easel. Just as he set down his belongings, he heard a pick sliding across the tight coil of guitar strings.

From behind a partial wall emerged a lean, copper-colored man, his hair twisted into a bun. He spoke Spanish. His name was Fabián, and apparently he was left behind by Pablo's sculptor friend, Paco, who'd written to tell Pablo his Montmartre studio would be free soon, as he was preparing to brave the no-man's-land of the Maquis if that meant being able to construct his own kiln. Pablo was ready for a fresh start and had replied to say he'd be there in a week.

Fabián asked Pablo if it were all right to stay on a few days longer, adding that he could sleep on the floor. Pablo looked around and thought it a strange offer because the large room came with no bed for either of them. But he nodded.

The man said little and turned out to be good company. The chords and notes of his guitar-playing filled the air and became the score of Pablo's afternoons.

There was a miraculous total of thirty studios in the building. Invisible from the plaza, the back side descended a steep cliff of four flights. There were peculiar carve-outs and vacant shafts one could plummet through if not careful. Each inhabitant made some specialized form of nectar in his or her chamber. There were painters and poets, writers and sculptors, models and musicians from all sorts of nations and backgrounds—Polish, Russian and Jewish, Catalans and Basques, French, Germans and Dutch, a Berber, and a Japanese.

A handful of older tenants dated back from before Renoir ushered artists and bohemians into Montmartre to reside amid the peasants who already had inhabited it for decades. A vegetable-seller rented a studio below Pablo. He dried carrots on a roof dormer. During winters, when nothing grew in the soil, he collected mussels from the Seine and sold them from buckets kept inside his room.

All the people living there became intimately acquainted, as there was only one bathroom—nothing more than a hole in the ground guarded by a homemade door and latch that rattled when the wind blew. There was also just one water pump, and many times, it was faster to go and fill a pot from the fountain in the plaza.

The building once had been a piano factory, and it had other lives as well, each constructed on top of the other like a French metropolis erected over a Capetian capital, layered above a medieval city, founded on Roman ruins, and so on, down to time immemorial. The architecture and furnishings, therefore, were as organized as archaic scrolls. The walls were perpetually mildewed. It was drafty in some corridors and stifling elsewhere. As summer grew hotter, the only way to breathe was to escape outdoors.

These accommodations were not always easy living, but the camaraderie of misfits made up for the convenience they lacked.

Pablo roomed with the dog who'd found him outside Els Gats, a cat he adopted from an alley near Notre-Dame, and a family of white mice who were longtime occupants of the studio. He cared for the mice like stranded refugees, keeping his favorite in a desk drawer, feeding it crumbs. He spent many afternoons in the chestnut-tree-filled Place Ravignan that the front of the building faced, relaxing with a pipe and passing around wine bottles with Fabián—who moved into another studio and whom Pablo taught to paint—and Manolo, who had escaped his sentence in the Spanish cavalry by riding to the border and selling his horse and rifle to a Gascon for train fare to Paris. Max also began trekking all the way from the Left Bank to join them, until he decided it would be easier to take an apartment only a few doors down. And Paco came around, too, perpetually merry, bringing bread and sardines, along with stories of his friend Gauguin's early days.

In the night, every night, Pablo painted, completing and refining pictures from the past. He also took up etching, his first big work a zinc plate of a spartan table setting shared between a gaunt man and his wife, their arms wrapped around one another tenderly. Everyone on the butte knew him as the talented little Spaniard with big handsome eyes that were filled with something heavy and captivating, the one who dressed like a mechanic and painted in only blue. Pablo, however, felt himself looking for new subjects now, another mood.

For money, Pablo had discovered a gallery on Rue Laffitte that he'd somehow never noticed before. It was little more than a bric-a-brac shop, run by a retired professional clown named Clovis who was keen to amass the works of undiscovered artists. Pablo managed to sweet-talk him into agreeing to hand over ten francs per painting—and then regularly appeared with almost more than Clovis could keep up with. Even Manolo gave Pablo kudos for this. It wasn't a lot of money, but Pablo's studio only cost fifteen francs per month. The arrangement allowed Pablo to avoid the hardships of his last trip to Paris, to maintain a virtuous cycle—make painting, sell painting, buy more paint—and to have a modestly gay time.

There was a farmhouse tavern that Pablo frequented called Le Lapin Agile. The owner, a bearded man named Frédé, strummed old, oddly stringed instruments that looked to be of his own invention and sang folk songs. During the day, he led around a donkey cart selling fish. At night, he was musician, barman, troubadour, and cook. Frédé kept a pet raven, and after Pablo saw the man's daughter press her lips against its dark crown one day, he asked to paint her with the bird. He started by adding a flat background of ultramarine, but for the first time in ages, Pablo splashed onto the canvas bright, madder orange for her sleeve and dilutions of the color for her hand and the waves of her trussed hair.

Across the street from Frédé's place was the pink house where Germaine lived with the artist Pichot. Now and then, Pablo would run into her at the tavern and admire whatever new outfit she was wearing. He'd once found her there in a red walking dress with sleeves that extended to buttoned gloves of black suede. She was busy adjusting her ostrich-feathered coiffure when Pablo couldn't help telling her how fetching she looked.

"You should see Odette," Germaine replied, adding that their old friend had practically become nightlife royalty in Brussels, livening top cabaret stages and packing in whistling crowds. "They've got posters of her all over."

Pablo was pleased to hear this—and to spend a little time with Germaine, even if everything was different now. He did feel a twinge of jealousy when he saw her with Pichot, but he was amazed the man could keep from going crazy as Carles had, for after Germaine took up with him, she still wandered wildly, foraging for experiences, new adventure. Pablo guessed that Pichot loved Germaine in the only way one might endure—freely and without pretense of containing her. It would have been foolish to try otherwise. In return, her affection for him never wavered, and she didn't let his presence get in the way.

Together, Germaine and Pichot were remaking their Maison Rose into a boisterous inn and sanctuary for free spirits. They seemed content.

~

While strolling one afternoon by the Place des Invalides, near where the World's Fair had stood, Pablo heard a great clattering of footsteps and the blaring of a trumpet. Appearing from nowhere—tumbling, flipping, and hurtling like dancing meteoroids—was a troupe of circus acrobats.

It struck Pablo right then how every waking hour these performers were making something with their very limbs, never ceasing—just like Germaine, always up in the air, living in between trapezes.

Finally Pablo knew how it was that she'd not only mastered her body but made her very life into art. With all she did—each night out, every pose struck, one spectacular high-flying love affair after another— she wasn't pretending but creating. He had no doubt afterward that along with the ancients it was she who'd led him to understand that constant creation is the only way to keep cataclysm at bay. Forever, he would be obliged to her.

~

Pablo started rendering lovers again. A surfeit of models passed in and out of his building, and he befriended and became intimate with some of them. In his paintings, Pablo made these new subjects into flyaway angels come down to his quiet blue realm to reflect.

There was another woman, too, who sat on the bench by the fountain in the plaza, reading in the shade of the only pear tree. She was full-figured and had the most enchanting, almond-shaped emerald eyes he'd ever seen. She wore violets in her deep-amber hair and read books till dusk. He thought he caught her glancing over the pages at him sometimes, and he couldn't help but stare at her while bantering with the Catalans on a stoop nearby.

She was a model, Pablo heard, but she seemed different than the others, refined. He studied her as she came and went, tried to catch her replenishing her water cask, make conversation. But she always had a way of eluding him.

II

O pen up! I haven't any pants!"
    Pablo recognized Max's voice through the studio door and groaned. "What time is it?" he called out, hoping he might be able to roll back over, cover his ears, and wait for the disturbance to go away.

"C'mon! I know you're in there now!" Max pleaded with Pablo. He was in dire straits, he said, having dashed outside in only his knickers, possibly arousing the suspicions of the police. He might even be arrested for some dubious *crime passionnel*. "I can see the papers now: 'The perpetrator fled the scene in his checkered shorts.' I'll be referred to in the press as the Knock-Kneed Massacrer."

"You'll be famous. Please let me sleep."

"Wake up! Pablo!" Max screamed.

Then Pablo heard Paco's voice outside his door, announcing he carried with him a life-sized ceramic head he'd sculpted and was eager to show off. He must have noticed that Max was in the hallway with only the top two-thirds of a three-piece suit because he asked, "Is there a theme party tonight?"

Max explained he'd woken this morning and discovered someone had purloined all his trousers. "To think, my family in Brittany blames me for not holding a steady job. Montmartre, it's a madhouse!"

Paco said it was probably that no-count Manolo. He'd let him stay in his studio a couple days, and he came home to find his Gauguins were gone. Paco had to enter every gallery on Rue Laffitte to see if the thief had already fenced them. "There they were, hanging at Vollard's."

"Did you get them back?"

"That old buzzard said he'd bought the half dozen for one hundred francs from some scrawny Catalan, figuring he'd got the deal of a lifetime," Paco explained, adding that he confronted Manolo afterward, asking him if he'd stolen the paintings. "He looks at me, taken aback, and tells me he was practically starving, hadn't eaten anything but wine and chocolate pastries for days. Says, 'It was your Gauguins or my life.'"

"That little rat! I'll murder him!"

Seeing no chance of falling back to sleep, Pablo finally got up and opened the door. It was hot and stuffy in the studio, so they migrated outside to their earmarked spots on the stoop, to be joined by Fabián's guitar. Everyone ended up removing shirts and pants—those who had them, anyway—and tanned on their stomachs in the midday sun.

Summer had become sweltering, the air thick and tropical as a palmetto grove. There was a green zing in the way everything smelled. The sky above was dense with touches of yellow around the edges of bloated clouds, the sun every once in a while shining through and projecting warmth like an opened oven. Pablo had worked all last night without dinner and grew hungry quickly. He pulled up and noticed how the sandstone had made an impression on his skin, making it look like iguana hide, then bid goodbye to his friends.

Pablo felt the hotness gather on the back of his neck as he walked to a pleasant café with a generous owner who was happy enough to give credit to artists for a simple meal or even trade pastis for a handmade sketch. Pablo rested on a stool at a little table near the open window, dunking the corner of a croissant into coffee, craning his face to catch the breeze. A wren flew onto the ledge and beat its beak up and down, staring at Pablo while singing a rush-and-jumble melody that echoed in the air. Pablo sat, watching with his elbows on the linoleum, tearing off croissant flakes and flinging them to the bird.

Behind him, the bell dangling from a string above the door rang as someone entered. The intoxicating fragrance of lily of the Nile filled the room and mixed with burnt coffee and warm butter. He didn't turn right away, just inhaled and licked crumbs from his fingers, trying to conjure in his mind a face to match such a scent.

"Noisette," a lovely soprano whispered before asking for a scoop of ice cream on the side. The origin of the flowery aroma deposited herself at a table directly behind Pablo. A few moments later, the café owner returned with the espresso and a dish on a salver.

When the woman carefully sipped the froth from the hot liquid, the sound went straight to Pablo's ear. He was sure he could hear even the steam rise as she poured the coffee over the cold ice cream.

How perfect on this August afternoon, Pablo thought, leaning back on the stool.

Metal clinked against the dish. Pablo pictured the spoon in a delicate hand pushing deeper into the frozen mound, like a tiny plow. He heard a little smack of the lips, and a shiver ran down his spine, as if he, too, felt a cold thrill.

No longer could he resist. Pablo swiveled his neck to discover whose sounds and smell he'd been studying.

It was her. That fair artist's model whom Pablo had seen so often perched on a bench, rapt in her novel, the light filtering through the pear tree bending around her as those almond eyes peeked above the dust jacket. She was so ripe with nectar, it was almost bursting through her skin. Already, the woman's features were like an entrancing picture—the painters hardly had to work.

She acted as though she didn't notice him and carried on her way, leaving behind the ice cream dish, sugary brown and vanilla-white marbling the bottom of the glossy porcelain.

The temperature only climbed as the day moved. Heat seemed to descend from above and rise from the pavement below, compressing and cooking Montmartre's inhabitants in between. Pablo worried about his animals. His cat had given birth to a litter of calico kittens a few weeks ago. He braved the weather and walked home to make sure she had water in her bowl. Back in his studio, he found three tiny felines nursing as their mother slept, the other gamboling in the corner of the Bordeaux crate where they were born.

Pablo cupped the squeaking loner in his hands and observed the way it pawed the air. He picked up the bowl and carried them both outside to the fountain. As he leaned down to scoop up the water, there was a deafening crack that frightened the creature before the sky opened to a torrent.

Leaning forward, Pablo hugged the kitten close to his chest and ran for cover. He stood in the doorway of the stucco building and reached his arm out so the bowl filled with the water gushing from the roof. He set it down by his feet to watch the glittering streams falling from the sky. Pablo stroked the kitten, teaching him to not be afraid of a storm.

Racing footsteps clattered against the paving stones. Pablo looked up, and there was the woman from the café, her soaking wet shirtsleeve held pointlessly above her head.

She stopped in front of where Pablo was standing, her mouth gaping and her eyes batting away the drops. She laughed at the ridiculousness of it all, of being so impossibly wet.

Pablo smiled and extended his hands, opening them just enough so the woman could see the kitten playing inside.

"Where's the little darling's mother?" she asked, ducking under the narrow entrance and nudging up to watch.

"Napping," Pablo said.

"That's exactly what I should have done, isn't it? Instead, I've been all over Paris. First in the unbearable heat, now this mind-boggling rain. It's nothing I've ever seen. Like from a book."

"You read a lot."

"When I'm not modeling for twelve hours straight, you mean?"

"It's hard work," Pablo said. "The body gets tired, I know."

She told him it was nice to escape to a sunset and a novel, then apologized for not introducing herself earlier. Her name was Fernande. "And you, you're that painter everyone talks about."

"What do they say?"

"You're something of a mystery. Sleeps all day, paints like the possessed at night. But people tell me it's good, your painting—is it? Maybe I shouldn't ask. They say we're our own worst critics."

"Critics are the worst critics," Pablo said.

Fernande laughed again, and Pablo's heart fluttered like a turtledove does when a new hand reaches into its cote.

"Can I—"

"See the paintings?"

She said she'd love to, of course. "But do you have a towel?"

Pablo said he was silly, he should have offered.

"You don't seem to mind practically swimming in wet clothes," she said. "Perhaps it's nothing to you."

"I actually hate when it's chilly and damp," he said.

"I'm the same way," Fernande said.

Inside the studio, there was clutter everywhere. They had to step over spent tubes of paint and abandoned brushes, and Pablo blushed. From a whitewood table he plucked a towel and wiped away the water from her forehead before laying the cloth in her palm.

"Your hands," he said, his eyes studying them, their slenderness, the way her fingers bent far back as she received the towel, as if they were double-jointed.

"Oh, don't look," she said. "They're so hard to hide when I'm modeling. I can't bear it."

"Why?"

"My aunt says these long fingers make my hands look like spiders. Just like she says my eyes are too small."

"Is she an artist?"

"No."

"Take it from one—your hands, your eyes, they're a painter's dream."

Pablo was still holding one end of the towel. He tugged on it gently, bringing the two of them closer.

Fernande felt the touch of his wrist on her cheek, then met his lips with her own. But she paused unexpectedly, breaking away just an inch to peer around the room, noticing that it was filled with stacks of canvases in the same cold hues.

"Why," she asked, "do you paint in blue?"

"I was sad," Pablo said.

She gave another little laugh. "Not anymore?"

"What for?"

AUTHOR'S NOTE

This piece of historical fiction relates familiar and lesser-known details of Picasso's life. I drew on the labor of scholars, journalists, and scientists for source material. But what I've written over the previous pages shouldn't be jumbled with the fine works from these other disciplines. This novel was carefully researched but also just as meticulously imagined.

With that said, the following is an abridged rundown of the very many sources that I am abundantly grateful for.

In addition to Picasso's thousands of paintings, drawings, prints, and sculptures, I repeatedly turned to the books of John Richardson, who has released three excellent volumes on Picasso and has a fourth in the works.

Others biographies, such as *Picasso: Creator and Destroyer* by Arianna Huffington; *Picasso: A Biography* by Patrick O'Brian; *Picasso: The Early Years, 1881–1907* by Josep Palau i Fabre; and *Picasso: His Life and Work* by Roland Penrose, were exceptional resources that aided me broadly and in constructing specific scenes.

Picasso: An Intimate Portrait, written by the artist's friend and long-suffering secretary, Jaime Sabartés, gave helpful anecdotes from Picasso's childhood and wonderful memories of old Barcelona and Paris.

The image of Catalunya that I share, however, wouldn't have been possible without *Barcelona* by Robert Hughes. In particular, I want to recognize him for adding the context around how the era's viewers would have interpreted Ramon Casas's painting *Corpus. Sortida de la processó de l'església de Santa Maria.*

Likewise, I relied heavily on *Red City, Blue Period* by Temma Kaplan for my depictions of Barcelona's social strife and the 1902 general strike.

The description of palm-reading that I recount is derived from a real-life exchange between Picasso and Max Jacob. The resulting sketch and notes can be viewed in the Museu Picasso in Barcelona. I also am thankful for that institute's curation and display of art and artifacts from the painter's life and for producing such works as *Picasso and Els 4 Gats: The Early Years in Turn-of-the-Century Barcelona*, a series of monographs penned by various authors under the direction of María Teresa Ocaña.

The poem partially reprinted in this book's epigraph was composed by Carles Casagemas and is titled "Amor Gris." It originally appeared in *L'Eco de Sitges* and was unearthed by the art historian Eduard Vallès. I incorporated it into the thought and speech of my character Carles. Elsewhere, *The Blue Period* borrows from correspondences that Casagemas or Picasso wrote or received (many of which are also housed in the Museu Picasso).

Descriptions of the Bateau-Lavoir and the woman Pablo meets at the novel's end are shaped largely by Fernande Olivier's memoir, *Loving Picasso: The Private Journal of Fernande Olivier*, and from Gertrude Stein's *The Autobiography of Alice B. Toklas*. So, too, the dialogue here is inspired by these works.

The vision of Montmartre that I fashioned was born after reading three compelling books: *In Montmartre: Picasso, Matisse, and the Birth of Modernist Art* by Sue Roe; *Twilight of the Belle Epoque: The Paris of Picasso, Stravinsky, Proust, Renault, Marie Curie, Gertrude Stein, and Their Friends Through the Great War* by Mary McAuliffe; and *Bohemian Paris: Picasso, Modigliani, Matisse, and the Birth of Modern Art* by Dan Franck.

My picture of the Exposition Universelle was rendered primarily from *Paris 1900: The Great World's Fair* by Richard D. Mandell.

During the course of my writing, I also stumbled upon a copy of Edith Kunz's enjoyable *Fatale: How French Women Do It* and benefited from her insights.

To get a sense of the situations that the characters who are portrayed in this book may have encountered, I read Wendy Chapkis's *Live Sex Acts: Women Performing Erotic Labor*. The backstory I fashioned for the character of Odette was influenced by the semi-anonymous women Chapkis interviewed and profiled.

The chapter that deals with bullfighting draws (somewhat tongue in cheek) from Ernest Hemingway's *Death in the Afternoon* and Adrian Shubert's *Death and Money in the Afternoon: A History of the Spanish Bullfight*.

As I mentioned in the dedication at the beginning of this book, I feel an abiding affinity for Lydia Csató Gasman's exhaustive and moving analysis of Picasso's oeuvre, written texts, and life story. I want to credit her with anything in *The Blue Period* relating to cosmology or sex or good and evil or creation and destruction or the necessity of art for the endurance of humanity and the universe in spite of the powerful forces of decay constantly eating at us all—in other words, basically everything.

The account of Carles's death is shaded by translations of Josep Pla's *Vida de Manolo*, which is based on interviews with the sculptor Manuel Martínez Hugué.

I also drew on Dr. Louis Jullien's book *Libertinism and Marriage*, which is reflected in the dialogue.

My depiction of the character based on Ambroise Vollard and the galleries on Rue Laffitte were colored by his memoirs, *Recollections of a Picture Dealer*.

Moishe Black and Maria Green's translations of Max Jacob's works, as well as their study of the French writer, were most informative.

The included recipe for fudge is a variation, of course, of the one recounted in *The Alice B. Toklas Cook Book*, by Alice B. Toklas.

I learned a great deal about the craft of painting and the people dedicated to it from James Elkins's *What Painting Is*, and the idea that a young artist might initially fret that the colors get in the way of the lines I owe to a passage in this enlightening book.

Likewise, I am indebted to Victoria Finlay's *Color* for much of the material about pigments in my novel. The encounters that Pablo has with ochre were inspired by Finlay's own search for this mysterious substance. Her relating a superstition surrounding the color blue in Spain was invaluable.

In a similar vein, I paid many visits to the Brooklyn Museum's exhibit "Infinite Blue," to meditate on that which has transfixed people throughout the ages.

ACKNOWLEDGMENTS

I would not have written this book without David Blum. I thank him dearly.

I am also deeply grateful to Carmen Johnson, who inherited an unruly creature when she became Little A's editor. You were patient and thoughtful and gave me the space and support to tame this animal.

Simone Gorrindo edited this novel with such diligence and concentration that chatting with her was like conversing with a different part of myself. She helped me find ways to accomplish what I needed to do. Every writer should be so lucky.

Production editor Emma Reh's steering was nimble and steadfast. I was delighted to have her at the wheel.

Michelle Horn's talented copyediting and Michael Schuler's and Erika Avedikian's sharp-eyed proofreading were outstanding. They indulged my quirks, saved me from an inexplicable collective pronoun, and always put readers first.

I can imagine no more tangled of an assignment than to be charged with fact-checking a work of fiction. Karla Anderson took on this ironic task with precision and care.

Isaac Tobin, who designed the book cover, I'm bewildered and stirred by the image you conjured.

Thank you, also, Merideth Mulroney for the art direction and appealing presentation overall.

Kristin Lunghamer and Katie Kurtzman, I am humbled that you saw in these pages something worth sharing with more of the world. I am grateful for your labors.

To Katharine Spence, thank you for your soulful translation of Carles Casagemas's poem "Amor Gris" and for helping me render Catalan phrases into English.

I much appreciate the generous review of the book's foreign-language text elsewhere that was conducted by Aurélie, S. C., and G. M.

Juan Carlos Villars and Wesley Harris, *gracias* and *merci*, also.

Shanoor Seervai, who was kind enough to read an early version and be insightful in her critique, and Sophie Joslin-Roher, who was thorough and incisive about parsing a later one, you have my lasting appreciation.

Thank you, Mara Altman, for lending an ear when I needed someone to talk to, granting wisdom, and being my friend.

Jordan Michael-Smith, I am obliged to you for advice on several occasions.

Keach Hagey Harris, who sat in a diner and heard the entirety of this novel over a very long breakfast and then concisely summed up what was boring and what was interesting, this book became more interesting because of you.

To Scott Adkins and the Brooklyn Writers Space, thank you for providing me with a quiet place and abundant coffee.

Lastly, and most importantly, to my family—who made countless sacrifices for this to be possible—know that you mean the world to me.

ABOUT THE AUTHOR

Photo © 2017 Kristy May Photography

Luke Jerod Kummer has worked as a reporter, an editor, and a travel writer. His nonfiction pieces have appeared in the *New York Times*, the *Washington Post*, *New York* magazine, *New Republic*, the *Washingtonian*, and the *Village Voice*. This is his first novel.